THE DEVIL'S DUE

What Reviewers Say About Ali Vali's Work

Balance of Forces: Toujours Ici

"A stunning addition to the vampire legend, Balance of Forces: Toujour Ici, is one that stands apart from the rest."—*Bibliophilic Book Blog*

Carly's Sound

"Vali paints vivid pictures with her words. ...*Carly's Sound* is a great romance, with some wonderfully hot sex."—*Midwest Book Review*

"It's no surprise that passion is indeed possible a second time around."—*Q Syndicate*

The Devil Inside

"Vali's fluid writing style quickly puts the reader at ease, which makes the story and its characters equally easy to get to know and care about. When you find yourself talking out loud to the characters in a book, you know the work is polished and professional, as well as entertaining." —*Family and Friends Magazine*

"Not only is *The Devil Inside* a ripping mystery, it's also an intimate character study."—*L-Word Literature*

"*The Devil Inside* is the first of what promises to be a very exciting series. ...While telling an exciting story that grips the reader, Vali has also fully fleshed out her heroes and villains. *The Devil Inside* is that rarity: a fascinating crime novel which includes a tender love story and leaves the reader with a cliffhanger ending."—*MegaScene*

The Devil Unleashed

"Fast-paced action scenes, intriguing character revelations, and a refreshing approach to the romance thriller genre all make for an enjoyable reading experience in the Big Easy. ...*The Devil Unleashed* is an engrossing reading experience."—*Midwest Book Review*

Visit us at www.boldstrokesbooks.com

By the Author

Carly's Sound

Second Season

Calling the Dead

Blue Skies

Love Match

The Dragon Tree Legacy

The Romance Vote

Girls with Guns

Beneath the Waves

Forces Series

Balance of Forces: Toujours Ici

Battle of Forces: Sera Toujours

The Cain Casey Saga

The Devil Inside

The Devil Unleashed

Deal with the Devil

The Devil Be Damned

The Devil's Orchard

The Devil's Due

THE DEVIL'S DUE

by
Ali Vali

2017

THE DEVIL'S DUE
© 2017 By Ali Vali. All Rights Reserved.

ISBN 13: 978-1-62639-591-6

This Trade Paperback Original Is Published By
Bold Strokes Books, Inc.
P.O. Box 249
Valley Falls, NY 12185

First Edition: January 2017

CREDITS
Editor: Shelley Thrasher
Production Design: Susan Ramundo
Cover Design By Sheri (graphicartist2020@hotmail.com)

Acknowledgments

The Casey Clan has become like family after all this time, but thank you to my Bold Strokes family for the encouragement and support you give me every step of the way. Thank you, Radclyffe, for your advice, support, and for the chance to bring these characters to life all those years ago.

Thank you to Shelley Thrasher, my editor. Shelley's been my teacher and my friend, so I appreciate the patience she always shows in getting me over the finish line.

Thank you to my fellow BSB author D. Jackson Leigh for her tremendous help with this book—you're a great friend and love these characters as much as I do. Thank you to Cris Perez-Soria for volunteering to beta for this book—you knocked the job out of the park. Thank you to Connie Ward—you've been there from the beginning, and I appreciate you always answering the call. I also want to thank the BSB team that does such a great job in making every project a success. Thank you to Sheri for another great cover.

This series has been such an adventure from the beginning to this book. It's always humbling to get the emails from you, the readers, to continue the storyline, so thank you all for that. Please know that your encouragement is something I not only find humbling, but deeply appreciate. Thank you all, and as always, every word is written with you in mind.

Life is so different since the release of the first book in the series, and unfortunately the changes have revolved around so much loss. It would've been impossible to see the beauty and joy that is still around me after all that pain without the one constant in my life—my best friend. I love you, C. *Verdad*!

Dedication

For C
A lifetime will never be enough.

CHAPTER ONE

A nd?"
  "I don't know what you want me to add."
  "We'll get to that eventually." Derby Cain Casey tapped her fingers on her desk, and the random pattern seemed to unnerve the young man standing in her office. That was the main reason she did it, but it also relaxed her. When you ran a criminal empire as large and complex as hers, it was nice to have one thing that wasn't planned or structured.

She was sure her tapping was part of the extensive file the FBI had amassed on her over the years. At least she hoped it was. If they had that bit of information it'd explain the only aspect of her life she never thought about.

"Look, you called me," Angus Covington III said as he jammed his hands into his already low-slung jeans he obviously thought were appropriate for a job interview. "If you don't want me, that's cool, but I'm the best you're going to see. I got a few more places to go if we're done."

"Do you have any idea what the job is?"

"If you want me to spell it out with techno talk, I will. But why waste each other's time?"

"How many interviews like this one have you taken?" Cain swiveled her chair a little to the left so Angus wasn't in her direct line of sight. If she'd ever met anyone whose name didn't fit, it was this guy. It made her curious what Angus one and two were like. Were they as good at pretending as this poor excuse of some sort of grungy-punk wannabe was?

"A job's a job," Angus said and shrugged. "I came because it sounded more interesting than the oil-field stuff."

"My father said once that everyone should take pride in three things," she said, smiling at his confusion. He probably thought they were having two different conversations.

"Mine's only proud of his martini-making abilities," Angus said, his laugh too smug.

"I can see you're not interested in learning anything." She flattened her hand and faced him, lifting a finger to stop him from saying whatever flip drivel he planned to entertain her with next. "Don't open your mouth unless I tell you to."

Angus nodded, staring at her hand. That was the first hairline fracture in his demeanor.

"Good. You can listen when it's called for. That should count as a point in your favor." She softened her voice so he'd have to strain to hear her. "Tell me what you know about me. Give me the whole list."

"Everything?" He stopped when she twirled her finger slowly. "Okay." He recited a good list available in any newspaper or Internet search. It was well balanced enough to not sound contrived.

"Do you think I'm someone you should be afraid of?"

"No." His uncertain tone made his answer more like a question. "Look." He took his hands out of his pockets and held them up with his palms facing her. "I've got to go."

"Go ahead, but aren't you curious as to what I know about you?" She took a folder out of the top drawer and dropped it a little away from her. "This is my favorite part of the interview, but if you've got to go," she waved him toward the door, but her words had nailed his feet to the floor, "then go."

She held up a picture so he could see it. "You know, reviewing your references and finding out what they think of you." She flipped through the pictures and smiled at his tight expression. If she had to guess, Angus wouldn't be able to fit a flaxseed up his ass if she'd put a gun to his head and said go.

"How?" He took a step forward, but it was almost a stumble.

"It's what I always tell my children—homework, Angus." She flipped through the pictures and stopped at the one that'd intrigued her the most. "You have impeccable references, so you don't have a problem there." The picture she held up had been taken at his Quantico graduation. He looked so different now from the guy in the gray suit and tie, he seemed like another person in some bizarre alternate life. "It's not often we see a blue-ribbon boy like you."

"What do you mean?" Angus pulled his pants up and lost his flip attitude.

"I don't mean anything, and I'm not going to hire you. Would you do me a favor anyway though?" She folded the picture of his wife and two small boys down the middle.

"Anything you want, name it," he said, sounding like the Eagle Scout he was. Too bad there was no badge for dealing with her. That was bad luck for Angus.

"Deliver this for me," she said with a smile as she held up an envelope.

"Can I have that?" He pointed to the picture of his family.

"I like keeping resumes on file, so no. You never know when I'll need to call someone back with a question." She stood and held her hand out to him. "Good luck, and those other interviews you've got lined up—you don't mind me sharing your information with them, right? I'm guessing I know all your stops today."

"No, and I won't bother you again. Not ever."

"Good," she said as she squeezed his hand until he grimaced. "I'm not a fan of surprises."

❖

Emma Casey held on to Cain's head security man, Lou, as she came down the stairs. She was reaching the end of her pregnancy and walked like she was about to compete in a limbo throw-down. Nothing was comfortable—not her clothes, the bed, or any position that called for her to lie down or stand up.

She was grateful Cain didn't mind sleeping in an almost sitting position to provide her a backrest. "Remind me about this when I want another one in about six months," she said, making Lou laugh. "Are we headed to the club this morning?"

They'd come home after their wedding ceremony to a different New Orleans. Emma loved Cain for so many reasons, but moving their ceremony to Wisconsin because of hurricane Katrina had proved the event was as important to Cain as to her. They'd come so far since her staggering betrayal of the one person she loved above all others. That Cain had not only forgiven her for that, but then stood before their family and God to make that commitment, was a gift she at times wondered if she deserved.

They'd been luckier than most with everything else on their return, considering where Cain's businesses were located. Everything had opened quickly after some repair, but no flooding or looting had touched the house or clubs. The destruction of the city had caused some problems, but Cain also thought it provided room for expansion. That had brought its own unique problems, considering how the feds constantly scrutinized Cain's business. More business, though, meant more power, and more power meant better security.

Emma stopped when the office door opened and a grungy-looking young man walked out, Cain right behind him with her hand on his shoulder. Whoever the guy was, he appeared as terrified as Cain was amused, so she shook her head at the two extremes. The FBI was always there watching, listening, scheming, and Cain got pleasure out of making their lives miserable, if this guy was any proof.

"Hello, pretty lady," Cain said and winked at her. "Angus, don't be rude."

"Good morning, ma'am," the guy said, but his eyes were on the front door.

"Lou, walk Mr. Covington to the gate so he can join his friends outside." Cain brought up her other hand and squeezed the top of Angus's shoulders hard enough to turn her fingers white. "Remember our conversation, and learn to stand your ground when it comes to your bosses. You don't see them prancing in here, do you?" Cain tugged and brought him closer so she could talk into his ear. "I'm going to check in case you dropped anything, and if you did, I'll come by and return it. If you're one of those tattletales that reports what we discussed line for line, and someone gives me shit about it, I'll come by and discuss that too."

"Don't worry. I meant what I said. You won't see me again," Angus said, finally glancing up at Emma as if she could help him escape the prickly situation.

"Then get going on your promises, Agent," Emma said, ready for the guy to leave. She clicked her tongue when the front door closed, then accepted Cain's help for the last three steps. "Why do you waste your time on those people?"

"It helps pass the time until I'm able to hold my kid and make love to my wife," Cain said.

Emma was sure Cain's laugh that followed was meant to set her at ease. Her doctors had put the brakes on their sex life for the next few weeks or until the baby came, and the result was an overprotective but highly hyperactive partner. What Cain was doing with her time probably had those people outside watching as anxious as she was for the baby to come.

"Channeling your energies, huh?" She combed Cain's hair off her forehead and leaned back so Cain could kiss her. "I can live with that."

"How are you feeling?" Cain moved behind her so she could hold her and still run her hands over her abdomen.

"About the same since this morning. It's like having a truckload of potatoes strapped to my front, but I'm ecstatically happy about it." She rested her hands over Cain's and tilted her head to the side so Cain could kiss her neck. "Want to leave for school, then the club, before it's time for our first nap of the day?"

"Did the teacher say why she wanted to meet?"

She heard the wariness in her voice that was always present when one of the kids had a possible problem. That it was Hannah this time around had made Cain irrational after she'd read the note Hannah handed over. Their daughter, as well as their son Hayden, had inherited not only Cain's looks, but also the spirited nature of both her parents. Cain liked to call it their strain of bad grass running through them.

"Promise me you won't lose your cool no matter what it is?" she said as she turned to kiss Cain's chin. "Hannah is definitely a handful, and at times school gets in the way of that."

"So they want her to conform like all the other sheep in plaid skirts?"

"Hannah Casey will no more turn into part of the herd than you did." She put her hand on Cain's arm and held on as she did her best to balance her load. The strain on her back was starting to make her life truly miserable. "I'm sure it's nothing."

"Come, Mrs. Casey," Cain said, walking behind her and rubbing her back. "With any luck she got all your Verde calm genes when it comes to paying attention in school."

"You Xeroxed her baby, so keep practicing your fairy tales for Hannah and this one, if you believe she takes after me," she said as she quickly put her hand over the spot where the baby kicked hard. "They're all yours, mobster, and they're all like you. Live with it."

"Considering how easily you bagged me, I have every confidence you can keep our brood in line, including me." Cain helped her into the car and moved to get in the other side.

"Don't forget that in case any old girlfriends show up," she said as they pulled out, their shadows not far behind.

CHAPTER TWO

Special Agent Shelby Phillips stared at her reflection in the mirror in the ladies' room of the FBI building in New Orleans and tried to ignore the dark circles under her eyes. She was back at work after her boss Annabel Hicks had asked her to help with the agent trying to usurp her. Before that, Shelby had been on forced leave after her parents had been killed. Their deaths still seemed bizarrely surreal. Things like cancelling their summer-trip plans ripped away pieces of her soul.

In one cruel, really unnecessary moment, she'd ended up alone in the world, and no amount of contemplation gave her an easy answer as to why. She'd started something with Cain's cousin Muriel. But it'd been for her career—a fucking job. The twist of the knife had been when she fell in love with Muriel, even though she knew how they would end when Muriel found out what she was up to. It was still a mystery how Muriel had known, considering how careful she'd been, but while she was busy thinking of ways to bring Cain down, Shelby had missed the danger to her family.

"What a way to learn a lesson," she said softly. The price of stupidity was incalculably staggering. She'd lost her parents and Muriel.

Cain, in the end, had nothing to do with what had happened. She and her team had never expected their old partner, Agent Anthony Curtis, would betray them like this. Anthony had gone to work for Juan Luis, and, according to the limited information revealed, Anthony had been instrumental in planning her parents' murders to frame Cain.

How Cain had managed to find out what no law-enforcement agency in the world could was also a mystery, but her anger had momentarily disappeared when she read the paper Cain had held out to her that night in Wisconsin. If it'd been appropriate, she would've hugged her for the gift Cain had taken the time to give her right before her wedding. The small slip of paper had been burning a hole in her pocket from the moment she got it, but she still hadn't built up the courage she'd need to do anything about it.

"Shelby, you okay in there?" Joe Simmons, her partner, asked after knocking. He hadn't asked about the exchange with Cain, so she hadn't been forced to lie, because she wasn't giving up the information Cain had uncovered.

"Yeah, sorry," she said, wiping her face with a dry napkin and hoping it didn't completely screw up her makeup.

"Are you sure you don't want to take a few more days?" Joe said when he saw her. "What happened was a life-altering event, as they say. No one's going to blame you for staying home. After all, that you're back at all was a favor to the boss."

"I've been back for a while, Joe, so trust me, I'm okay. Do I miss my parents? Hell, yes, but work really does help more than sitting home alone with only the TV and my cat for company. I can't shut my brain off there."

"The cat won't help you complete any performance reviews."

"What, you're going to flunk me?" she asked as they walked to the large conference room the team had set up in. "If you're worried about your back, trust that you're safe with me."

"You can't be serious? That's the last thing on my mind." He put his hand on her arm and stopped her before she made it through the door. "I'm talking to you as a friend."

"I'm sorry." She smiled and covered his hand with hers. "I need to learn to lengthen my fuse a little."

"No worries. Just remember that you aren't alone."

Agents Lionel Jones and Claire Lansing had set up numerous boards of information throughout the room and were placing folders at the seats near their boss. Since their return from Wisconsin, where their surveillance had picked up nothing but Cain and Emma's wedding, Cain had been a total saint. The guest list had been interesting for people who protested to only being bar owners, but the most interesting drama had been on their end.

It wasn't often that the lead agent met the target of their surveillance, then literally ran away. But that's exactly what Special Agent Ronald Chapman had done. He'd run all the way to Washington, and they hadn't received any communications from him since. Then Agent Brent Cehan had been arrested on numerous charges incurred at the Piquant during Ramon Jatibon's birthday party.

Brent swore Cain had beaten him, fed him drugs, and basically set him up with a prostitute that had been found beaten with Brent's DNA on her wounds and her blood on his hands. Cain's alibi, though, was rock-solid. Considering that every federal agent in the room and their surveillance backed it up, it was hard to dispute her word in this case. So for the moment, Brent was sitting in a crappy cell in central lockup, all alone, for his protection. The local jail had been necessary since the locals were handling all his alleged crimes—none of it was federal jurisdiction. If Cain had orchestrated it, then she'd done a masterful job at revenge since they could in no way help Brent, even if they'd been so inclined.

"Have a seat, everyone," Annabel said as she flipped back to the first page of the file. "Before we begin, we need to have a conversation that can't leave this room."

Shelby sat down and gave Annabel her full attention because she was the only one who'd give them any answers. The agency always clammed up when it was convenient, especially when something potentially embarrassing came to light. When they had seen Ronald running from the field, she'd guessed Cain had struck again.

"Have you heard anything about Agent Chapman, ma'am?" she asked, figuring her team wanted to know as much as she did.

"Ronald's taken some time off, and I was told to let it go." Annabel leaned back and took a deep breath. "Do any of you know anything about what was in the envelope Cain gave him before he left? It won't go beyond this room, and we'll drop it if you all agree, but if Cain burned him and Ronald thinks it was on our behalf," Annabel looked at each of them and paused, "he'll try to bury each of us, and he'll start with me. You might not love everything about me, but I'll try to protect you all from any fallout."

"The team talked about it, ma'am, and we've got no idea," Joe said, and they all nodded. "We're all aware of Casey's largess, but this time she did something for her own reasons, and she hasn't shared that with any of us."

"I haven't mentioned this before, but she called me," Annabel said softly. "All she said was if I wanted my post back free and clear to be there that night, but that was the only clue she gave."

"Cain always does things for a reason. This time it had to do with Ronald's relationship with Brent and, to some extent, Fiona O'Brannigan," Shelby said. "Brent, I understand, but Fiona's still a mystery."

"She didn't mention it when you talked to her that night?" Annabel asked for the first time, but Shelby didn't pick up on any accusations in the question.

"Cain isn't always the monster we make her out to be, and that night all she wanted was to tell me she'd made a donation in my parents' name. They were involved in a few children's programs, and she contributed to each one." That actually wasn't all they'd talked about that night, but the donation part was true. Cain really had been incredibly generous.

"We know what to do about Casey, but what about Chapman?" Claire asked.

"If we all agree, we'll go back to our jobs but investigate Ronald on our own time until we find the truth," Annabel said, and they all nodded. "The truth, as they say, people, will not only set us free of this guy but also protect us from his inevitable retaliation."

CHAPTER THREE

"You've got to understand how disruptive it is when she does that in the middle of class," the older, pinched-looking woman said as she concluded her long list of Hannah's sins.

Emma sat with Cain's hand in her lap, a little surprised that her usually overprotective spouse had stayed quiet throughout the bitch's detailed notes of what she saw as wrong with their child. If anything, *she* was about to punch the woman in the throat, but she blamed that on her own physical discomfort. She was more than willing to take her lower back pain out on this idiot.

"Was there a reason for Hannah to hug the little girl in the middle of your riveting lecture on world history, or whatever the hell you were teaching?" Cain asked. She sounded incredibly calm, but her question still made Emma snort.

Emma glanced at Cain and immediately saw through the façade. The muscles in Cain's jaw were tight, and the hand Emma wasn't holding had curled into a fist. She could tell that her occasionally volatile partner was about to erupt, so she was glad to see the principal hovering outside the door. Sometimes it was good to have a reputation.

"Does it matter?" the woman asked, taking off her large glasses. Emma guessed she wanted to better stare Cain down. "It's not fair to the other sixteen children who were paying attention and trying to learn. Perhaps if she saw less of what I'm seeing now," the woman pointed to their joined hands with what appeared to be disapproval, "things might change."

Cain stood so abruptly that her little red plastic chair flew halfway across the room. The bigot's expression of superiority drained from her face, replaced by obvious concern as she pushed her chair slightly backward, closer to the board. "The little girl's name is Lucy," Cain said, placing her fingers on the teacher's desk and leaning in. "Lucy's parents are splitting up and it's not been pretty, so she's spent some time in our home recently because she's not coping well with her parents' fighting and the general venom they're spewing."

"I didn't know," the woman said, leaning farther back, which made Emma smile. When Cain was like this, it was like confronting a rabid dog. Your instincts were to run, but you feared the sudden movement would result in your leg being chewed off. At least, that was the woman's demeanor as she watched Cain.

"Shut up." Cain moved even closer and the woman gasped. "You've had your chance to talk."

"There's no need to be rude, Miss Casey."

"No, there's no need for some closed-minded dinosaur in the classroom either, so I hope you're prepared to defend your beliefs."

"What do you mean?"

Cain laughed, and Emma came close to joining her. The pain Cain inflicted at times when she deemed it necessary had nothing to do with guns or fists. "It means that I'm going to make you wish someone would take the time to hug you when the comfortable and secure life you know turns to dust."

"Please, Miss Casey, your threats won't work here," the woman said. She laughed but nervously rubbed her hands together.

"Emma, are you about ready?" Cain held her hand out, but her attention was on the door. "You'll be hearing from my attorney, and I'll need a cashier's check by five today for the entirety of my family's donations—all of them." The principal gripped the door at that threat. This time Emma couldn't hold back her laugh. She doubted the school had that much cash on hand, since the Caseys had been giving to the school from the time Cain had been in kindergarten.

Levi Layke, the principal, took a deep breath. "Cain, could I speak to you before you go?" he asked. His voice had a nervous quiver as if he knew Cain was talking to him about the money.

"I've wasted enough time here today, so get going. The bank will need you to take a couple of board members with you. Don't disappoint me." Cain helped Emma to her feet and put her arm around her waist. "Where's our kid?"

"In the gym," Levi said.

"What's our plan, mobster?" Emma asked as Levi trailed behind them, but not close enough to overhear them.

"Give it a minute, lass. The Catholics love the collection plate almost as much as the Lord, or so Da used to say. Levi either has to write a check or retire that bitch."

"You really think he'll do that?" They stopped at the door to the gym and glanced inside. Hannah was playing with her friend Lucy, some distance away from the other children. Hannah had been glad to share with them how the other children treated Lucy because of how much she cried. Though people often considered Cain a bully, she'd told Hannah that everyone deserved a friend. Emma was glad Hannah had taken Cain's words to heart.

"Levi knows me, and more importantly, he knows when I'm not bluffing." Cain placed her hand on the door frame and kept her gaze on Hannah. "Your mother has already put Hannah through enough. I won't allow it to happen again, especially by someone who can't see the value of our family."

"I'm—"

"We've talked about this already. You never have to apologize for something that wasn't your fault. That doesn't need to be rehashed, and the one person I do blame for that has been buried." Cain moved to her and placed her hand on the side of her neck. "Nothing or no one can bring him back or come between us again."

"Why are we talking about this?" she asked and finally realized something about herself. No matter how far she'd come and all she had—she was still waiting for the other shoe to drop. "And don't pretend that you don't think about that sometimes. You know damn well I'm mostly to blame."

"Forgive me, lass. I didn't do a very good job of explaining myself, but we've both done our penance over this. I meant to say that I want us to raise Hannah and our new baby the same way we've raised Hayden. I want her to know nothing but love and give her the confidence to know she can do anything. If taking people out of the way that don't have that in mind makes me a meddling parent, I'm okay with that."

Emma leaned against her taller and much stronger spouse and nodded. "I'm sorry to be so whiny, and I agree. The kids and I are lucky to have you."

The loud squeal that only a five-year-old could produce made them both laugh. Hannah had spotted them and was making her way across the gym with her friend in tow. "Mama," she yelled, finally releasing Lucy's hand. "Mom," she said next, leaping up when she got close to Cain, who bent and caught her. Cain was so wrong saying that Hannah didn't have a sense of herself.

"Hey, Hannah girl," Cain said, holding Hannah so she could kiss Emma. "You ready to go?"

"Can Lucy come?" Hannah asked, her hands framing Cain's face.

"Not right now, but we can call her mom later." Cain seated Hannah on her right side and took Emma's hand. "Are you going to be okay, Lucy?"

"Yes, ma'am." The small waif of a girl's glance back at the gym full of children broke Emma's heart. Lucy's unhappiness radiated from her like a lantern in a dark room.

"Cain," she said, not having the heart to leave her.

Levi hovered close by, and Emma could swear he appeared more pale and miserable than Lucy when Cain turned to him. "I'll expect you not to disappoint me," Cain said.

"Emma, come on, see reason," Levi said, his hands out, obviously hoping to appeal to the gentler parent.

"When it comes to the kids, you should know by now she's seldom reasonable about situations like this, and I don't want her to be. Kids shouldn't be made to feel bad about themselves, and I don't want someone who knows nothing about us making my kid think she has something to be ashamed of." She slipped her hand around Cain's arm. Her back hurt and she was ready to go.

"I'll have it by this afternoon," Levi said softly.

"Don't look so glum, Levi,' Cain said and laughed. "Think of this as learning the lesson I'm sure they teach here. The Lord giveth and taketh away. Now go call Lucy's mother and ask if she'd like us to take her home a little early today."

Emma laughed when Cain grimaced as Hannah squealed again, only this time much closer to Cain's ear.

Fiona O'Brannigan watched as Cain and her family descended the steps of the exclusive Catholic school in uptown New Orleans. The trio of Caseys and some other kid were surrounded by people Fiona was sure were heavily armed.

"That's gotta suck," she said above a whisper as she noticed how Cain scanned the area as if searching for a conceivable threat. She stopped when she spotted Fiona's car.

It was eerie how she seemed to know exactly where all her watchers were, but Cain did seem surprised when she spotted her. Fiona guessed the FBI van was part of the landscape Cain was used to, but not Fiona's car. She indulged her curiosity only when she wasn't on duty.

She thought about starting the engine and leaving, but that might signal fear. So she watched Cain put her partner and the children in the car and cross the street, headed directly for her. She'd have to hit Cain with her vehicle to leave now. She exhaled and thought about the consequences. One more harassment complaint from Cain to Fiona's superiors and her mother might get her wish of her coming home when the head of detectives cut her from the force.

"Get out of the car and keep your hands visible," Cain said as she stood on the sidewalk.

It irritated her how cool and sophisticated looking this butcher was. All the illegal money Cain raked in went toward putting forth this image of someone who was always in control, and the expensive suit only extenuated that fake façade.

"Shouldn't I be making that request?" she said, trying to ignore her indigestion caused by actually following Cain's order.

"Detective O'Brannigan, why are you still here?" Cain walked in the opposite direction of the FBI van and spoke softly. Was she stupid enough to think Shelby and her team didn't have equipment to hear her from space if they wanted to? "You do realize this isn't going to turn out well for you, right?"

"Your trying to threaten me is a joke. The scar on your chest should be a constant reminder that the law has some cushion when it comes to people like you."

Cain turned around and seemed to stare at the van as she nodded before continuing their walk away from it. "When you're in the bar business you learn a few things, Detective, and one of the things at the top of the list is persuasive conversations." Cain laughed and stopped again. "If you didn't understand that—it means that when it's your turn, you'll know it's your turn."

"Listen, asshole, you're a joke whose time is up, and if you didn't understand that—it means I'm the one who's going to kick you in the ass. Once that happens I'm going to come by and laugh my head off because I'll know exactly where you are."

"See you soon," Cain said and laughed when Fiona's phone rang, but Fiona ignored it. "Make sure you wear your ass-kicking shoes, but if you want my advice, you might want to invest in a more sensible pair. Give my best to your boss."

"What's that supposed to mean?" she asked and screamed the question again when Cain walked across the street and joined her family. She went back to her car and kicked the back tire a few times to bleed out the frustration. That Cain could bait her so easily pissed her off.

Her phone rang again, and she kicked her tire once more when she saw the readout. "Yes, sir. I can come in this afternoon." Sept Savoie's father, Sebastian, was the chief of detectives, and you didn't turn down an invitation from him. "Fuck, what now?"

She made it downtown quickly since the streets were nowhere near their pre-Katrina traffic. In actuality, the crime in the city had declined dramatically after the storm, but it had nothing at all to do with better policing. The city's mass evacuations had also swept away a lot of its criminals, so places like Houston and Atlanta were enjoying the company of those New Orleans could do without.

Fiona had hoped to be partnered with Sept, but she and some newbie Sebastian had set her up with were working a murder that had happened on the hallowed grounds of the best restaurant in the city. That a rookie had gotten that assignment had chapped a bit, but she still had to prove herself so she kept her mouth shut.

"Where the hell were you this morning?" Sebastian asked before she even made it into his office.

The question and tone meant Cain Casey had complained and Fiona would end up farther down the chain of command. She was curious about Cain, but that didn't mean she didn't hate her as well.

CHAPTER FOUR

Remi Jatibon stood on the balcony of her condo by the river and watched the boat traffic. The extensive flooding throughout the city had spared the new house she and Dallas Montgomery were remodeling, but her movie company's offices hadn't gotten off that easily. For now they were sharing what had quickly become a cramped space with Cain on the docks, so she missed the building where her entire staff had room to work.

"Hey, baby," Dallas said as soon as Remi answered. The sequel to Dallas's first movie had moved to South Carolina for a few months when the fucking storm had destroyed their locations around New Orleans. "It's too early for a cigar so I'd better not hear any puffing."

"I'm not smoking," she said, going back inside. "I'm enjoying the view to take my mind off the fact that our bed has become a lonely place."

"I know exactly what you mean, so don't remind me. You need to get up here and put me in a better mood before I'm accused of being hard to work with."

"Hang in there until the weekend." She sat in the study and put her feet on her desk. "Mano and I are still working on new offices since it'll be months before we're back in the building, if at all. That much flooding is hard to recover from."

"Don't say no just yet—you love that place."

"I do love it, so we'll see. If anything, we'll end up with more real estate. But I'd rather talk about how you're doing."

Dallas laughed, and the sound made Remi smile. "Oh, honey, you'd lose that rep of yours if people heard you now."

"You're complaining?"

"Are you kidding? I listen to all these people on set talking about how hot you are and how much they want you. It made me mad before, but now I know you're mine and I've got lifetime rights."

"That you do, querida." The conversation she'd had with her parents and Cain about Dallas came to mind. Dallas, she figured, knew how much she loved her, but Cain had been clear. Sometimes a girl you wanted to build a life with needed more than flowers and pretty words. The purchase of the old Casey house had been her first step in that plan. "Aside from the crew talking about me, are they treating you okay?"

"Any better and it'd be nauseating. Don't worry. I'm being well taken care of, but I'd rather it be you here coddling me. You can come, right?"

The picture on her desk of the two of them at her parents' place made her truly miss Dallas like no other woman who'd ever been part of her life. "How about I come, pick you up, and bring you home for a couple of days?"

"I'd love that, but according to the director, the weekend is going to be full of early morning shoots. My afternoons and nights will be free."

"We'll work something out then. Don't worry." If the director hadn't mentioned the change in plans, she wouldn't ruin his surprise. A man yelling on Dallas's end meant her sweet talk for the day would be cut short. "Remember to have fun and that I miss you."

"I love you," Dallas said, her voice as smooth and silky as a fifty-year-old añeho rum.

"I love you too, querida. Take care and I'll see you soon."

The line disconnected, and she swore the pain in her chest must be from some medical ailment. "Good Lord, I'm getting soft," she said and laughed.

Juno Jimenez, Remi's assistant, chuckled along with her from the door and shook her head. "You're exactly like Simon," Juno said about her partner and Remi's bodyguard. "Love makes you strong, mi vida, not soft. You need to learn to scream how you feel from that balcony you love so much."

"Don't worry. I'm not running, and Simon's not a screamer, but she gets her feelings about you front and center all the time." Remi spoke in Spanish since Juno enjoyed using their native language. "She's a hopeless romantic."

"Isn't it nice to indulge that trait when things are this quiet?"

Juno's shoulders hitched up when the words slipped out, and Remi shook her head. "You've jinxed us for sure now."

"No. I like Simon home like she's been. That's the only good that came from that damn storm."

Their clubs had been shut down for a couple of months for remodeling, repair, and security updates. The studio was for the most part being run from the California office, so their partnership with Cain was the only thing still on course. They'd been enjoying the distracted police department and had taken the opportunity to stockpile inventory. Once things in the city normalized, they'd be set.

"We need to call Cain," Simon said, walking in and going to Juno's side.

"What were you saying about not jinxing us?" she asked and smiled.

One of the guys put music on for Hannah and Lucy once they arrived at their club Cain had named after Emma. The crowds had thinned since Katrina had devastated the city, but Cain had ordered the place open every night, and everyone who'd wanted a break from renovations was appreciative.

Upstairs, though, was why they were here. The offices of Muriel Casey, Cain's cousin, were there. The adoption papers for baby number three were ready, and Emma wanted them filed. Cain didn't like how much Emma worried about every little thing, but this was easy enough to get out of the way.

"We'll file as soon as the baby's born, and since we've done this twice before, we shouldn't have any problems," Muriel said as they signed what seemed to Cain like a hundred sheets of paper. "You have time for something else?" Muriel asked when they'd finished.

"Sure. Then I'll take everyone to lunch." Cain cocked her head to the side slightly and winked at her. "Lass, do you want to go down with the kids or stay here? Might be Muriel's getting ready to bore me."

"I never find Muriel boring, and innocent questions like that seldom are, so spill it, Muriel," Emma said.

"I just got a call from Bubba."

"The idiot brother of T-Boy's, you mean?" Cain shook her head at the thought of those two. They couldn't keep a steady job to save their lives but had a streak of luck as long and wide as the Mississippi for finding information she really needed.

"The one and only. He's working the bar at the Hilton and spotted someone he thought you'd want to know about," Muriel said, glancing down at the pad where she'd obviously written the gist of the conversation down.

"Don't keep me in suspense, cousin."

"He was waiting tables last night, and he swears that Nunzio Luca was in there, talking business with the pretty blonde that was always with him." Katlin came in with a glass of juice for Emma and stayed when Cain pointed to a seat.

"The pretty blonde Kim Stegal, Nunzio's right-hand woman, who I watched get her throat slit?" She flattened her hand on the table and exhaled. Nunzio was a cockroach she'd thought she'd sent scurrying into the night. "Remind me from now on that permanent solutions to problems will make conversations like this moot," she said, looking at Katlin.

"Bubba swears it was the two of them, and they were talking to some guy Bubba thinks is moving product through that place. He doesn't have proof, but the bar owner's too flush in cash for it all to be from booze."

"You never know, cousin. Booze is a lucrative business, I've been told," Cain said, and they all laughed. "Our problem here is that Bubba is thinking, so, Katlin, send someone you trust over there and tell them to have a few drinks on us. If Nunzio has grown a pair and come back with a ghost in tow, we need to keep an eye on them."

"How about you let us handle things so you're free to take Emma to the hospital when it's time," Katlin said. She glanced over at Lou, Cain's ever-present bodyguard who stood by the door, and the big man nodded. "Lou and I'll check it out and keep you in the loop."

"I'm pretty good at multitasking, so don't forget about the loop," she said, glancing back at Muriel. "Anything else?"

"The added shipments are working, and so far, we've tripled our inventory. Nothing like hiding in plain sight."

All the supplies FEMA was sending and the massive amounts of building materials being brought in made it easier to blend in a few extra trucks. Once the city righted itself, they'd be ready to roll into the new territory they were making now.

"Good," she said, and knocked on the conference table with her knuckles. "Thanks for taking on extra stuff, but we're still not naming the baby after any of you."

"Cain," Emma said, slapping her arm. "Everyone's getting an extra dessert for that comment."

Cain nodded as she stood, but she locked her gaze on Katlin. If anyone among her family or on her payroll understood threats like Nunzio, it was Katlin. Her cousin had fallen in love with Emma's bodyguard Merrick, who was still fighting every day to get back to where she'd been physically before Juan Luis shot her in the head.

"Listen to your wife, cousin, and you don't have to worry," Katlin said, as if reading her mind. "We don't want to mess up our Christmas bonuses, so I'm not likely to miss anything."

"I'll double yours if you get me everything on my wish list." Cain had figured Nunzio wouldn't appear on her radar again, but she'd deal with him permanently if need be. She currently had her sights set on finding Anthony Curtis. The wayward FBI agent was in the wind, but he had no idea how persistent she was. When, not if, she found him, he would learn for himself exactly who she was and what she was capable of.

The phone rang and Muriel answered. Her conversation was brief. "Remi's downstairs," she said when she hung up.

"Good news travels fast," Cain said. If she was right, she'd have to talk Remi out of killing him outright. She wouldn't try too hard, though, if that's what Remi really wanted to do. After all, Nunzio had hired someone to kill Remi to make her father Ramon more agreeable to the casino deal they'd all been involved in. It was hard to forgive a shot to the chest with a high-powered rifle.

"Let's go to lunch," Emma said, holding her hand out. "Maybe a plate of good food will calm everyone down."

"Perhaps, lass," Cain said taking her hand, "but I doubt there's anything that good open in the city."

❖

Nunzio Luca looked out over the water in back of his father's old house. He'd inherited it when Junior died from a bullet to the head and his mother had decided to join his grandfather Santino, who'd retired to Florida. It'd taken him a few days to find someone with the background he needed, but the treasure trove he'd discovered in New Orleans would finally be of use to him.

He and his late mistress's sister, Tracy Stegal, had gone to New Orleans right after Katrina to beg first Emray Gillis, then Hector Delarosa for scraps to get back in the game, but things had changed once Tracy had disappeared. That betrayal he'd deal with once he found Tracy, but it was good to find out what a bitch she was before she really became an integral part of his team.

"Do you have everything in place?" Santino asked from behind him.

All the mistakes and bad luck were about to become a thing of their past. He was tired of being the screw-up and was ready for his grandfather to be proud of him. It was too late to accomplish that with his father, but Junior's death wasn't on his head.

"The meetings are set," he said. He kept his attention on the water, wanting to memorize the view. His first stop was Mexico, and depending on how that went, it was hard to know when he'd be here again. His last trip to New Orleans had lost him Tracy, but he had found something much more important.

The original supplier he was set to do business with was Emray Gillis. That asshole had never materialized so he'd wasted time with Emray's flunkies Mitch Surpass and Freddie Buhle. Mitch the ass-wipe had ended up decorating the dash of a car with his brains, but Freddie now worked for him. Freddie was responsible for the resurrection of their business and gave him the means for his revenge.

"Are you sure you want to bring Buhle with you?" Santino stood next to him and put his hand on his shoulder. His grandfather had come out of his self-imposed retirement to help him with all this. "I'm glad you found him, but he's not the brightest light I've ever met."

"Don't you mean I'm not the brightest light in the family?" His father's always condescending voice rang through his head. Even from the grave Nunzio could feel his disapproval just as easily as he could the sweat on his skin. "You can be honest about what you and Papa thought about me."

"Nunzio," Santino said as he stood in front of him. "You need to bury all that bad blood along with your father. Junior was my creation, and I loved him because he was my son, but Junior was also my mistake."

"What's that mean?" He was tired of lies and redefining their history when it was convenient.

"Junior was an asshole who seldom considered anyone but himself. He thought it's what made him a man, but it cost him the love and loyalty of his son. I don't want to repeat that mistake." Santino put his hands on the sides of his face. "No matter where you go or what you need, I'll be there for you."

The expression on Santino's face was soft and almost loving, two things not often seen on the face of any Luca male. He wanted to believe him, but like a dog whipped one time too many, he was skittish and simply nodded.

"My boy," Santino said. "You're all I've got left to carry on my father's name and take over our business. I admire you admitting to being unsure, but I'm proud of you and I'll prove it to you."

"How?" he asked, not breaking away from Santino. The last time a man had held him like this and spoken so sweetly he was five and Junior was in a sentimental mood.

"By always standing behind you no matter how many times you turn around."

"Good. I might need someone to watch my back."

CHAPTER FIVE

"If I see him in the city I'll kill him myself," Remi said, a little too loud for a whisper. From the set of her shoulders and the bunched muscles in her jaw, Cain knew the news of Nunzio's return had been a punch to the gut. "I need you to back me up on this."

"You know you're a part of my family, as is Dallas," Cain said, letting go of Emma's hand so she could cover Remi's. Seeing how angry Remi was, Cain decided to move up Katlin's visit to the Hilton for some quick information. "He'd gone home to New York, and I don't know why he's here, but I will. If you want me to drive up to Long Island and put a bullet in his head, I'll do that too. You don't have to justify why or ask twice. Our friendship is enough reason, so tell me what you want me to do."

Remi stared at her like she wanted more than air to ask for simply that—a bullet in Nunzio's head. "You aren't arguing or offering advice?" Remi leaned back and laughed, but she wasn't a woman who was in any way amused. A bullet to the chest would do that to a person so Cain couldn't blame her. "You're a lot like my father when it comes to that, so I'm suspicious when you just give in."

"You already know what I do, so you don't need to rehash or pretend we both don't know Nunzio is nothing but a snake."

"Exactly," Remi said, slapping her other hand down.

"Remi, you need to take a breath," Emma said, as if she'd figured out where Cain was going with this. "You know Cain will always be loyal to you, but the assholes three tables down will never have your back."

The storm had ravaged the selections of places to eat out, but Blanchard's hadn't missed a step; all their establishments were open for business and as good as ever. Even in this lunch crowd, though, their FBI shadows were hard to miss in the spot Emma had mentioned.

"I'm sorry, but this isn't something I'm about to ignore," Remi said softly.

"Let me tell you Cain's secret to everything when I complain," Muriel said as she gripped Remi's shoulder. "Patience, my friend. There's a time for everything, and I'm guessing our mutual problem isn't ready for a solution."

"Then when?" Remi said.

"Nunzio's a snake, Remi, but let's find out if in his time away he's become a hydra. There's too much at stake to start fighting mutual fronts if we don't do a little research first." Cain glanced at Shelby as she spoke, not worried about being overheard since the jamming equipment was in place and being controlled by Lou at the next table. "So how about tomorrow night we let Carmen fix dinner for us, and we'll talk about it?"

"There's more," Muriel said and stopped when Cain looked at her.

"Not the time, cousin," she said, wondering why Muriel would broach another subject now.

"Thank you for coming," Keegan Blanchard, the restaurant's chef and granddaughter of the owner, Della Blanchard, said when she walked over and kissed Emma's cheek. "The staff told me you were here, and I figured I might not see you for a while," Keegan said as she placed her hand over Emma's large midsection. "You do good work, Cain."

"I'll call you if the craving for garlic bread and bread-pudding soufflé keeps up," Cain said, naming the two things for which the restaurant was renowned. "Katlin mentioned a yard full of police this morning," she said, glancing out the bank of second-floor windows to the courtyard below. "If you have a problem, you know you can call me. We love this place and your family too much to let anyone hassle you."

"I promise I'll call if it comes to that, but would you mind if we didn't talk about it just yet?" Keegan's eyes filled with tears so Cain didn't push it. "Enjoy your lunch and let me know if you need anything. I'll send some treats up for the table, and especially you, Emma."

Cain's eyes followed Keegan as she returned to the kitchen. "Make some calls, Muriel, and let me know. Della Blanchard was a close friend of Da's so I don't want anyone giving them a hard time."

"I'll get something to you by this afternoon or sooner."

"So, Remi, is tomorrow night good for you and your family?" Cain asked.

"We should have something by then, so sure."

The waiters came with a multitude of appetizers and a large platter of the restaurant's famous garlic toast. The small wedges of French bread soaked in butter and garlic were one of Emma's favorite things, and pregnancy ramped up her taste for them. That Keegan had delivered some to their house on more than one occasion to satisfy Emma's craving when the restaurant was closed had made her a friend deserving of Cain's loyalty.

Keegan wasn't the only one with a problem, though, and another friend with a boulder to carry still appeared tired and miserable. Shelby seemed like a woman torn between who she was at the core and who she wanted to be. The special agent had planted her orchard but hadn't found the part of herself that would revel in harvesting her crop. Considering that Shelby was obsessed over avenging the death of her parents, Cain had a hard time understanding her hesitancy.

Cain refocused her attention to Remi's assurance that her family would be ready for a meeting tomorrow night. "Great. Then we'll move on to whatever else Muriel has. It seems it's always something."

Nicolette Blanc glanced around Hector Delarosa's office, admiring the pieces of Colombian artwork. Her father Michel had wanted her home once her lover Luce Fournier was released from the hospital after Cain's cousin had beaten her into a bloody mess, but she'd refused. He knew as well as she did that they wouldn't survive much longer without an infusion of cash and a partner that would take their business beyond wine.

She'd planned for it to be Cain Casey, and once their business partnership was established, her plan had included so much more. But Cain hadn't given a damn. The deal they'd worked on for months had died because of Luce's stupidity, so once she'd been discharged, Nic had sent her home. She didn't need anyone to fight her battles or mark her as their property, and it was time Luce learned that lesson.

"Nicolette." Marisol Delarosa made her name sound like a character in an old romance. "I must apologize for my father, but he left last night for home."

"I hope it's nothing serious, but that does allow us to perhaps get better acquainted." She stood and combed her hair back with a smile she hoped was inviting. "I believe we have much in common."

"Such as?" Marisol gave no hint as to what she was thinking. She reminded Nicolette of Hector in that he was guarded, but he'd perfected his charm much more than his daughter.

"We are daughters of powerful men, and despite everyone around them, both our fathers have chosen a woman to succeed them. That tells me that we have what it takes to not only take the reins but to remove anything that stands in our way." With Luce gone she missed having someone in her bed, but not the baggage that came from letting someone in. Marisol didn't appear to be the clingy, needy type.

"Do you have something in mind?"

"I have rooms at the Piquant, or we can stay here if the house is empty enough for some privacy."

Marisol's smile softened her face a little, but not enough to dull the confidence she radiated. "Don't worry. Your secrets will be safe within my father's walls. It's a good idea for us to get together since we will be partners, no?"

She wanted to laugh at her luck. Hector was charming, but this was the future of the Delarosa family, and her people had done plenty of research on Marisol. The main things she'd taken away from the information they'd given her was that Marisol was spoiled, had a quick temper, and was impetuous in her actions. Hector's lovely fruit probably hadn't fallen too far from the tree, but Hector had insulated himself with enough security to be as rash as he wanted with no fear of consequence. If she cultivated from the inside, though, any castle could be breached.

"Then lead the way," she said, placing her hand on Marisol's shoulder and smoothing it down her arm. "There's something I wanted to talk to you about, or really someone."

"Who?" Marisol asked, taking her hand.

"Do you know Cain Casey?"

Marisol's back stiffened ramrod straight. "I know her, but she's dead to me. I'm not talking about it, so don't bother to ask."

She wanted to let out a celebratory cheer at the reaction. The way to Cain might be easier than she thought if she'd screwed Marisol over. All she had to do now was soften Marisol up enough to get the story out of her. According to her father, one of her greatest talents was pitting adversaries against each other. With skillful maneuvering two enemies could completely destroy each other, which cleared the field for the smartest player. In this case, it would be her and her father.

"See? We already have something in common," she said, kissing Marisol's cheek. "I wouldn't mind eliminating Cain."

"I thought you were ready to do business with her."

"Until she proved unworthy of our business and loyalty. Now I'm glad it didn't work out since you seem a much better partner."

Marisol's eyes glinted at the suggestion. Oh yes, this would be really easy. Either Cain came back willingly or she'd wind Marisol up enough to take out her greatest mistake.

"A much better partner." This time her kiss found Marisol's lips.

"Sorry about earlier," Muriel said when they got back to the house. Both Casey kids as well as little Lucy were home, so plenty of noise was coming from upstairs.

"Remi will be fine once we agree to rip Nunzio's head off, but we need to postpone that for a while." She walked to the sunroom at the back of the house, not wanting to be locked away in the office just yet. Emma had gone up to try to sleep. "I'm curious as to why he'd come back here and what he's been up to."

"I'm sure it's nothing you're going to like."

"I realize it makes me look like a psychotic asshole when I clean house, but I've got to stop leaving these problems alive to fester and grow."

"Remember why Nunzio's still alive," Muriel said to her as she reached over and touched the top of Cain's hand. "Except for what happened with Emma and Merrick, Nunzio would probably be dead, but family comes first. That's a lesson neither of us has to relearn.

Your family needed you, and you answered that call, so stop blaming yourself for loose ends, as you think of them."

"How would you put it then?"

"Unfinished business, and since he's so eager to come back to town he might be making it that much easier for us." Muriel stood and headed to the windows to look out at Hannah's play equipment. "Maybe I can cheer you up a little. Finley called and needs a favor."

"Really?" she said with a smile for the cousin she rarely saw. "It must be serious if she's willing to take the chance. Did she say why?"

"She didn't go into anything, but she wants a face-to-face."

"Call her back and set something up that'll leave our friends outside in the dark. When you get her, tell her to keep her head down. The city doesn't have that many people, so our ticks and us are the only crowd around."

"Do you want me to take anything off your plate?"

"Give me another week or so, and you can have it all. I missed so much when Hannah was born, but that's my own fault, so don't repeat that since Emma would never believe me. I don't want to make the same mistakes this time around, so you and Katlin can take over for a couple of weeks until Emma's tired of having me underfoot." She moved closer and put her arm around Muriel's shoulders. "How you holding up? Just because I don't constantly ask doesn't mean I'm not interested or care. I'm trying my best not to hover."

"I'm keeping busy and getting stuff done—nothing for you to have to worry about. There's no way I'm going to crack up on you."

She squeezed Muriel's shoulder before giving her some space. "The secret to life, cousin, is to find someone to hold your hand when you have no choice but to stare into the abyss."

"Cain, I love you, but if you're talking about Shelby again I'm going to punch you in the nose," Muriel said, holding up her fist but smiling.

"I'm not talking about anyone in particular. It's a simple bit of advice."

"You're as subtle as an AK-47 with a hair trigger," Muriel said as she gently slapped Cain in the stomach. "Don't think I want to be a hermit. I really do want to find someone, but I doubt that someone's going to be Shelby."

"The romantic in me wants whoever it will be to hurry up."

Muriel moved so she could hug her. "A beautiful partner and a new baby sure bring out the mush ball in you, and I love seeing it."

"Enjoy it while it lasts. My gut says that Nunzio will never repeat those words," she said and laughed. "You want to warn Carmen about the Jatibons coming to dinner tomorrow night? I'm going up and check on my beautiful wife and baby."

CHAPTER SIX

"Can I go with you?" Kristen Montgomery asked as Remi placed a stack of folders in her briefcase. Remi was getting ready to head to the airport to fly out to meet Dallas. "I know you guys want time alone, but I miss my sister."

"It was supposed to be a surprise for both of you, but the crew's coming back next week so you'll have Dallas around again. We'll be back tonight, and she'll be here for at least a month." Remi closed her bag and grabbed her suit jacket. Everything that'd happened that day had put her on edge, and she was ready to spend the flight home alone with Dallas.

"I'll see you both tonight then, and if you had anything to do with the move back home—thank you. We've already spent so much time away from each other, I hate doing it now." Kristen was still in her early twenties, but she seemed to possess an old wisdom few ever achieved even with a pile of years behind them.

"The future's going to be different for both of you. No more living in the shadows—I promise." She dropped everything and hugged Kristen. "So do you mind me not sharing today if she's all yours tomorrow?"

"Have fun and call me if you need anything or you get delayed, if you don't mind."

The different ring on the phone meant someone downstairs was requesting the private elevator. "You expecting anyone?"

"No. I was going to grab something to eat and stay in."

"Ms. Jatibon, Muriel Casey's here for you," the doorman said. "Should I send her up?"

"Yes, please," she said, putting the phone down. "Good thing the plane has to wait for me."

Kristen laughed and followed her out to the foyer.

"I know you're trying to get out of here, but Cain wanted me to give you a heads up. Finley called and is asking for a meeting," Muriel said after shaking her hand.

"She's coming here or she wants us to come to her?" Finley wasn't a stranger to her or her family, but none of them, including Cain, ever acknowledged her in public.

"She'll be here tonight, and she asked if you could come. This is only an information-seeking thing so it shouldn't be too long." Muriel smiled, and Remi noticed Kristen smiling back.

"Considering who's asking for information, that's interesting. I should be back no later than nine, so let me know."

"Go ahead and take off. I can let myself out," Muriel said.

"Sure, but maybe you can take Kristen out for dinner so she's not out alone," she said, and Kristen moaned.

"Remi, I'm sure Muriel has better things to do than babysit me."

"So you wouldn't want to go if I asked?" Muriel said with a smile. "Come on. I know a great place."

"She's got a curfew, so break it and I'll snap you in half,' Remi said, and Kristen moaned again.

"Don't worry—you know me," Muriel said.

Kristen figured it was some part of the code Remi and her friends lived by.

Muriel gave a little wave as Remi headed out. "I'll see you later."

Kristen studied Muriel like she had on numerous occasions. All she knew for sure was that she was Cain's slightly younger cousin, an attorney, and incredibly attractive. That Muriel even knew she was alive was a pleasant surprise.

"So what are you in the mood for?" Muriel asked, slipping her hands into her pants pockets.

"You mentioned you know a place. What about that?" She found Muriel's sudden shy demeanor even more interesting. It was quite a contrast to both Remi's and Cain's alpha personalities. When she first met Remi, she was jealous. Then she'd come to realize she'd never be happy with the same things Dallas had. She had to be her own woman, and that included the type of person she needed to fit with her.

"I have a couple of places in mind, so it depends on what you're in the mood for. I'm good with anything because of the company."

She pressed her index finger to her lips—maybe Muriel wasn't as shy as she'd thought. "Is that a well-used line, Ms. Casey?"

"I haven't kept much company lately, so I might be a little rusty," Muriel said, her hands going deeper in her pockets.

"I'm sure I can find a way to oil the squeaks and knock off the rust. Do you mind giving me a few minutes," she asked, spreading her arms out and letting them drop. "I need to change so I don't look like some charity case you picked up along the way."

"Take all the time you want. I've found rushing isn't the way to go in situations like this."

Remi put the file she was working on away when the wheels hit the tarmac. She wanted to forget work until she got home, and even Finley's call for a meeting wasn't upsetting her mood. Hopefully, Kristen and Dallas would use the time it took to catch up, leaving the rest of the night for the two of them to reconnect.

"And if I get my way that'll happen with very little talking," she said under her breath, glad when they came to a stop and she saw a car waiting. "Thanks, everyone," she said when the crew opened the door for her. "Quick turnaround, so I'll see you in a few hours."

The last shoot of the day was in the middle of a cornfield, and she was amused at the crew posing someone to appear dead. Once she'd trained her and Mano's children to take over the business, she was thinking of becoming a consultant for projects like this. The quickest way to get caught was to leave someone lying around where they'd be so easily discovered.

She found the formula used by Hollywood types comical, but set that thought aside when Dallas spotted her and came running to treat her to the greeting only Dallas had ever delivered. Dallas jumped into her arms and wrapped her legs around her for a human-octopus type of hug.

"I missed you, baby," Dallas said when their first kiss ended.

"Right back at you." She kissed Dallas one more time before letting go. "Are you almost done for the day?"

"One more scene and we're good to go. The dead girl," Dallas made air quotes with a big smile, "can't stop breathing on camera."

"Tell her I'm past ready to get you alone, so get it right or I'll help her with the no-breathing part."

Dallas laughed, and Remi swore she could feel the happiness coming off her lover like raindrops in a storm. "Have a seat and you can watch me earn my keep."

The short scene took another hour, and then everyone was glad to hear they were headed back to New Orleans. That meant a week off for everyone, and Dallas was overjoyed. Their house purchase had come right after they'd started filming so she'd had to put all her remodeling plans on hold. A week would give her a head start on making it a home for them, while all Remi could do was nod.

It didn't take long for Dallas to pack so they were wheels up and headed home. "How'd you convince Kristen to stay in New Orleans?" Dallas asked from her seat on Remi's lap.

"She had a date, and I explained I was willing to share, but not yet." Remi moved in for another kiss.

Dallas grabbed the hair at the back of Remi's head and dragged her head away a little so she could see her face. "A date? With who?"

"Muriel's taking her out for dinner. Don't panic. I doubt they're picking out china for dessert." She tried to kiss Dallas again but got Dallas's index finger to the forehead. "Muriel is taking her to dinner, *querida*. That's it, and remember that I've known her practically all my life. She'd never do anything to disrespect your sister."

"Our sister," Dallas said softly, right into her ear. "Once we're married, she'll be our sister."

"I wouldn't put her in a bad situation because I love her, but right now she's fine, and I'd rather talk about something else."

"Funny," Dallas said, then ran her tongue around the curve of Remi's ear. "I'd rather not talk at all."

"When's she getting here?" Emma asked as Cain rubbed her feet. "I can't believe I haven't met her yet."

"She's a ghost who's good at what she does. Actually, she loves what she does, and I can respect that."

"Will you be long?" Emma moved around on the bed as if trying to find a comfortable spot.

"I doubt it, but I've lined up some recruits until I return to provide a backrest," she said, going to open the door for Hayden and Hannah. "And they've promised to do whatever you need until I get home."

Hannah ran to jump on the bed, and Hayden scooped her up before she could. "Just as long as some TV-watching is part of the deal," he said, Hannah agreeing by clapping her hands.

"Any requests before I get back?" She kissed Emma as Merrick came into the room with Katlin. Emma's guard was still moving a tad slower than normal, but her recovery had been miraculous so far. "You guys expand your viewing pleasure so everyone has a good time."

She kissed Emma again and waved Katlin out the door. She was trying to curtail her evening meetings, but she'd never turn down Finley Abbott. She'd also never been seen in public with Cain so as to not ruin her life by exposing any kind of connection. To assure that had cost them all something she valued above all else.

The trip to the club didn't take long, and because it was the beginning of the weekend, Emma's was packed. They went around to the back, avoiding the crowd, and found Muriel and Remi already waiting. The way they both stopped talking meant she'd interrupted their conversation.

"Problem?" She wasn't in the mood for big issues now.

"Nothing important to this," Muriel said, and Remi chuckled.

"Your cousin invited my future sister-in-law to dinner, and from her demeanor when they got home, Kristen enjoyed it," Remi said.

"I see," she said, glancing at Muriel, then to the smirking Katlin. "Trip to the woodshed is what we walked into."

"More of a friendly conversation," Remi said. "Kristen and Dallas aren't innocents in every sense, but they're special to me."

"I know who Kristen is, and I know what they've been through," Muriel said, getting close to Remi. "It's why I worked so hard to help you give them as clean a future as anyone could hope for. She isn't a conquest, and you have my word I'll be honorable." Muriel held her hand out, and Remi didn't hesitate to take it. "She probably thinks I'm boring anyway, so all this is a moot point."

"Uh-huh," Remi said but stopped her teasing when the door opened.

"Cousin," Cain said, and opened her arms to FBI Special Agent Finley Abbott, her first cousin. Finley's mother Siobhan was her da's baby sister, and Siobhan and Shawn Abbott lived a quiet life in Florida. The sacrifice of being away from family had been worth it to her aunt so that Finley could follow her dreams. "You look good."

"Thanks for seeing me," Finley said, moving to Katlin next. Her connection to the Casey family wasn't public knowledge, but her job had nothing to do with trying to bring them down either. Finley's job was prosecuting sex crimes, so Cain was interested in why she was here since she worked hard to never let the sex trade touch her businesses.

Everyone had to follow their passion. So to get what she wanted, Finley had done some pruning on the family tree and picked that particular assignment. She'd never be ashamed of who she was and where she came from, but she wanted to ensure no FBI ladder-climber could ever use her blood ties to bring her family down.

"So you ran home?" Cain asked after Finley explained a series of events that had started in New York and had followed her here. Finley had been working undercover to break up a sex-trafficking ring that used women brought in illegally from mostly South American countries.

A mass killing a block from the Plaza Hotel had dropped pediatrician Dr. Abigail Eaton and her three children into Finley's life, and she was doing her best, from what Cain could tell, to keep them alive. One of the clues Finley had pointed to New Orleans's Hell Fire Club.

"You're talking about Nicola Eaton?" Cain asked, trying to keep her tone even. She'd give Finley all the help she could and, more importantly, anything to keep her alive, but this was a cluster fuck waiting to happen. She tapped her fingers on the conference table in her usual random beat, hoping like hell Finley's answer would be no.

"Have either of you heard of the Hell Fire Club?" Finley asked, and no one minded her taking notes.

Obviously, her life wasn't going to get any less complicated any time soon. Cain gave Finley everything she had on what was basically a high-priced brothel in one of the high-rises downtown. She'd had some of her people keeping an eye on the secretive operation but had kept her distance. The Hell Fire Club, from what she knew for sure, was controlled by the Russian mob. Taking them on was like jumping naked into a well with a thousand pissed-off rattlesnakes. It wasn't impossible to survive, but very unlikely you'd walk away without a few poisonous bites.

Remi stood and pledged her help, hugging Finley before she left. Finley apparently planned to take care of this by the book her employers used, and that sounded insane to Cain.

"Finley, I can't tell you what to do, but you tip off the wrong person and you'll lose more than Abigail. Can you live with that? Be completely honest, since you'll carry that load a long time." All of her own mistakes came to mind in one heavy moment. "I speak from experience when I say it's backbreaking when you can't turn back the clock and change the things that go wrong. The load is extremely heavy on the soul."

"I'll call, I promise."

Cain nodded. All she could do now was remind Finley of her place in their family and her willingness to help before she had Lou take her back out the way they'd come. She hugged her cousin again, then dropped back into her chair when the door closed and shut her eyes.

"Nicola Eaton might be dead, but it doesn't change the fact that the Russians own the Hell Fire Club and whatever else sick shit they've got running," Katlin said. "It didn't miss a beat when the plane carrying those two pompous fucks went down."

"Katlin, they're dead, so drop that part," Cain said, rubbing her eyes. "I met Nicola here actually, but the brunette with her didn't strike me as a pediatrician. True, Nicola was a pompous fuck, but we need to keep Finley and her little troupe alive, so start digging and see what you find."

"Are you sure?" Muriel asked. "And before you get pissed at the question, remember what happened to Pandora. The Hell Fire Club is the equivalent to her box of horrors."

"I don't want to open the box if I can help it, just find the snake who owns the box. That might not be so easy, but when we do, we'll shock the operation by severing the head. The body might not wither and die, but break into smaller, more manageable little boxes." She opened her eyes and spread her hands open. "I'm open to suggestions. What alternative do you both think will keep Finley whole?"

"I'll dig and see if there's another way," Katlin said.

"Keep in mind the strongest force is always the eight-hundred-pound gorilla in the room," she said and stood.

"Are you calling us big monkeys?" Muriel said, laughing.

"We're all monkeys in the end, cousin, but if you have to be a monkey—you might as well be King Kong." She smiled and pointed to the door. "Let's try our best to keep it that way."

CHAPTER SEVEN

Nunzio glanced up from the reports on the number of kilos the bottles of tequila Freddie Buhl had led him to held. They had stolen the stash from drug lord Roth Pombo, who was currently rotting in a Mexican prison, but Roth was a genius in bringing product into the country. Liquefying the coke and reversing the procedure once it was in the country had made him a mint.

"Did you get it?" Freddie sprawled in one of the chairs in Nunzio's office, which hadn't changed at all since his father Junior occupied the space. This street rat would've gotten shot in the head had he done the same thing with the original owner of the space. Junior was a stickler for a man acting like a man and not some mindless punk.

Looking at Freddie, he could understand his father's point of view. "Sit up straight, and get one of the guys to take you to replace those clothes. If you want to stay, I don't want to see baggy pants ever again."

"Who cares what I look like as long as we get shit done?"

One of Nunzio's guards, Mike Walker, came up behind Freddie and put his pistol against his temple. The .357 magnum snub nose was a little showy with the nickel finish, but it made Freddie pale, and that's all that counted. He tried to tilt his head away, but anatomy only let him go so far.

"You picked an interesting seat in here, Freddie," Nunzio said, relaxing back in his chair. "The marble floors aren't for show or to flaunt the family money." Mike laughed at the inference. "It's easier to clean up when people didn't understand two things. First, there's respect and the understanding of our positions in life. You wanted to come back and work for me. Remember the work-for-me part, and don't talk to me like that again or I'll let Mike call the maid. You get me?"

"Yes, sir," Freddie said and stood up. He turned to face Mike when Mike holstered his gun. "You want to take me shopping?"

"Sure, kid. Pull your pants up and let's go."

"Make him look like Roth Pombo's little brother."

"What's the second thing?" Freddie asked, standing so straight he resembled a manikin.

"Respect. If you don't respect yourself, kid, ain't no one in the world who's going to give it to you. Remember that the next time you want to walk around with the desire to show everyone what kind of underwear you're wearing."

"Are we going back to New Orleans?"

"We've got a few things to take care of there, but we're set for Mexico after that. I need to get all the paperwork in place. Take the rest of the day to do whatever you have to and be ready by morning," he said, dismissing them.

He dropped his eyes to the papers on his desk, glad Mike and Freddie took the hint to leave. The bottles had yielded a hundred kilos of coke, which meant over three million dollars in street value. If Pombo was bringing in three shipments a month, he had to be clearing around eight million with really low risk. That was only one part of his operation, so it was time to put it all back in place, only with him in charge this go-round.

"In a few months, I'll own a big-enough army to crush anyone who's ever fucked me." Creating a list wouldn't be a problem.

Cain arrived to a quiet house, so she stopped and poured herself a glass of juice. Her family was important to her, but Finley's visit was something of an invitation to disaster if she let it get away from her.

"Hey, Mom," Hannah said as she walked in and fell against her legs.

She smiled, thinking about the teacher who so misunderstood this beautiful kid. Time always moved too fast when it came to her children, but she was looking forward to seeing who Hannah grew up to be. "What are you doing awake, pretty girl?" she asked as Hannah climbed her like a tree when she offered her a hand.

"I needed to ask you something." Hannah put her head on her shoulder and her arms around her neck.

She left her drink and headed upstairs with her daughter. Hannah's room was a beautiful space Emma had created for her, like she had for Hayden first, and now the baby's room. Cain sat on the bed and placed Hannah on her lap. "What do you need to ask me?" She spoke softly. Hannah was usually clingy when she was worried or scared about something.

"Are you and Mama going to fight all the time?" Hannah's voice was barely a whisper.

"Your mama's my best friend," she said as she bent uncomfortably to kiss Hannah's forehead. "I love her, so we won't fight. I bet, though, that Lucy's mom and dad fight a lot, huh?"

Hannah nodded and pressed closer to her. "It makes her sad."

"Then you have to be a good friend, and she'll have something to be happy about. You have plenty to be happy about because I love your mama, your mama loves me, and we love you and your brother more than there are stars. There's that, and Lucy can come over whenever her mother lets her." She hugged Hannah and kissed her forehead again. "Think you can go to sleep now?"

"You're staying home right now, okay," Hannah said, seeming to have forgotten her worry. "Night, Mom, love you."

"Night, and I love you more." She tucked Hannah in and stayed until she closed her eyes, arms wrapped around a teddy bear. The woman Finley was keeping safe had small children too, and they deserved to sleep without the fear of harm like her child did. She kissed Hannah's hand, her decision made.

"Mum, keep my family safe—all of them," Cain said softly as she left Hannah's room. She smiled as she entered the master bedroom and found Hayden asleep in the chair next to the bed. That explained how Hannah had got away from him and Merrick, who was sleeping on the edge of the bed.

She gently shook him awake before doing the same to Merrick. "Thank you both for staying with Emma, but get some sleep." She hugged Hayden and kissed his forehead like she had Hannah's, glad that he still welcomed that bit of affection from both his mothers. The ring that matched her own was on his finger, and she would've given anything for her father to see this next generation of their family. Both their children and all who followed would make them proud.

"Merrick, help your better half with her search. I'm sure she'll appreciate it," she said softly to her friend after Hayden left.

"It's not like Finley to ask for a meeting, so what's up?"

"Tomorrow is soon enough for all that, so get some sleep." Once the door closed she didn't bother with neatness and stripped, dropping her suit on the chair Hayden had used. Her new sleep pants and T-shirt were at the foot of the bed, so she dressed, knowing the possibility of having to run out in the middle of the night in the coming days was more than fifty-fifty. Children came in their own time and not any sooner, her mum used to say, and she was right.

Hayden had come a week early, and Hannah, according to Emma, had taken her time, arriving almost two weeks late. So far, William Cain Casey, the name Emma had fallen in love with, was predicted to arrive right on time, and she was doing everything within her power to keep it that way.

Emma moved over and used her as a backrest. "Did Hannah find you?"

"You knew she was roaming around the house?" Cain laid her hand on Emma's bulging belly.

"She wasn't roaming, mobster. Your little terror has supersonic hearing when it comes to you, and she asked if she could go since we were the only two awake. Did she tell you about whatever's bothering her?"

There was so much movement under Cain's hand that she rubbed Emma's middle softly. "She wanted to know if you and I are going to start fighting."

"What?" Emma asked. More alert, she sat up, which prompted her to get up and move into the bathroom for the first of what Cain knew would be numerous trips during the night. "Why'd she ask you that?"

"Little Lucy's made quite the impression in a short period of time," she said before she had to yawn. The nightly bathroom trips were preparing her for the baby. "I've met her mother briefly, but what do we know about these people aside from the fact they fight in front of their kid?"

"I haven't had very many conversations with Lucy's mother, Taylor, but she doesn't strike me as the devious type." Emma moved her head up so she kissed the tip of her nose. "Do you get a bad vibe off her? Sometimes pregnancy does weird things to my vibe radar."

Cain laughed, knowing it was true. Maybe that explained how Barney Kyle had been able to completely snow her years before. Emma had been pregnant with Hannah when she'd left, and while pregnancy made her more beautiful, it put her in a bit of a fog. She'd found it adorable during Hayden's pregnancy and through this one.

"I'll ask Muriel to check. Nothing extensive unless she finds something on the first go-round."

"I'd say we're being paranoid, but I'd rather you checked. If it's something to do with those idiots outside and they're trying to find a way in through Hannah, I want to know."

"You know I wouldn't keep it from you."

Emma placed her hand over hers. The baby finally seemed to calm down now that they were back in the bed. "I know you wouldn't, my love, but if I don't know, then I can't ask you for anything."

"Sleep easy, lass. Anyone who tries to clear a path through our children deserves no mercy. I think we've taught that lesson enough times to prove we'll never back down from that special kind of stupidity. It's not our fault that we're dealing with slow learners."

"Hannah and Lucy are just children."

She held Emma tighter and kissed her temple. If she was totally honest she'd admit her fear, but she didn't want to worry Emma. Only people with nothing to lose, though, had nothing to fear. Her greatest gifts were in this house, but they were also the key to her downfall if she couldn't keep them safe.

"They are, so I'll do whatever I need to make sure we're okay." She kissed Emma again and let her get more comfortable. "And I mean anything."

❖

Marisol Delarosa looked down at Nicolette, who was asleep. She was surprised at how aggressive Nicolette was in bed, but perhaps it came from all the talk about Cain Casey. It was interesting to watch Nicolette stroke the long scar on her face as she spoke about her hatred of the mob boss. She wasn't sure how it had happened, but she was sure Nicolette blamed Cain.

She was also positive that Nicolette was, in Nicolette's opinion, the smartest person in any room at any time. Her father often spoke about people like that and their obsession to show the world how brilliant they were. Intelligence was important, but brains couldn't stop a bullet from an idiot, no matter how hard you thought about it. She and Nicolette both disliked Cain, but if Nicolette thought for a minute that she'd ever control Marisol or her father, she'd have to learn a hard lesson in humility.

She needed to wait for her father to return. He hadn't shared what he knew about the Blanc family with her yet, because rumors of an uprising among some of their top lieutenants had kept them from talking before he left. So for now, she'd enjoy Nicolette like this while making no commitments or promises.

Her phone made Nicolette stir and stretch her hand out for her. Marisol answered quickly to silence the ring. "Sí," she said, irritated at the disturbance.

"Mari." She could hear the stress in the voice of Julio Rollas, her main guard. "You need to get down to the office."

"What is it?" She pushed Nicolette's hand away and got up to dress. She really needed a shower, but Julio's demeanor was a warning that she didn't have time for that triviality.

"Someone's making a move, and it's bad."

"Fuck," she said, not bothering with underwear. "Get everyone up and send someone to get Miss Blanc home." She communicated with him in Spanish but was sure Nicolette understood her. "I'll be down in a minute."

"What's wrong?" Nicolette said, standing naked before her. The woman was beautiful and hard to ignore, but she needed her out of the house.

"It's a family matter, so please get dressed and I'll have someone take you home."

"Marisol, let me help you. Not because our fathers want to work together, but because we're friends."

"I'll call you when my father gets back, but until then, get ready to leave."

She took the stairs two at a time and tried to show no emotion when she entered the office. Her father's new plaything, Tracy Stegal, and a few others were there with Julio. Unlike her father, she didn't trust Tracy with anything.

"Tell me what's happening," she said as she sat behind the desk. Julio glanced at Tracy, and she slammed her fist down. "One of you, just spit it out."

"With the storm, we took advantage of some new real-estate deals," Tracy said.

Marisol put her hand up. "I know our business better than you, Tracy, so stop disrespecting me. I'll fucking shoot you in the head, and it'll take my father less than a day to replace you in his bed. Remember that the next time you want to act like a bitch or treat me like I have no sense."

"Three of the five houses the family now owns to prepare our stuff for street sale have been cleaned out. The people in them are dead, and the product is gone."

"Which places?" The thought of facing her father with this news made her feel like she was standing in a cold draft. Hector had trusted her, and it didn't matter that she was his blood. He'd punish not only the people who'd stolen from him, but anyone who'd allowed it.

"Two in Metairie and one in New Orleans East. The two in Metairie were full, but the east wasn't going to be loaded until we could put more personnel in place," Tracy said. Her calm meant Marisol's threat hadn't rocked her that much. "Overall, it's about five hundred kilos. All of them already accounted for, and all that was left was delivery."

That meant they'd either have to give whoever had bought it their money back, or find enough to replace it. "Who the fuck was stupid enough to do this?"

"It had to be someone with enough muscle to hit all three at once so no alarm could be raised. If we look at it like that, the list isn't that long," Tracy said, crossing her shapely legs. Marisol could see what attracted her father. This woman was young, beautiful, but incredibly in control. She appeared to be a goldfish fearlessly swimming in a tank of sharks.

"Any ideas, since you're the only one brave enough to speak?"

Tracy combed her hair back and shook her head. "I've got people on the street, but no one's talking. I can't see any of the players in the area doing this. None of them seem to want to start a war, and they know Hector will destroy anyone this stupid."

"Find out something before we have to call my father." The men in the room all nodded. They understood exactly what would happen to them if Hector blamed them for this. "That goes for you too, Tracy. My father isn't the most understanding man when someone steals from him."

Tracy stared at her, then nodded. "I'd never tell you how to run your business, but I believe we need allies on this one." The suggestion made Marisol lift her fist again, but Tracy didn't flinch. "If you want to get mad at me, I can't help that. But your father left me here to assist you. As far as replacing me in his bed...I don't need to spread my legs to be heard, Ms. Delarosa. Next time you have a need to put me in my place, pick a different topic."

The woman had cojones, but being spoken to like that in front of her men was unacceptable. It was the quickest way to go from boss to *pendejo* in an instant. Marisol was no asshole, and it was time to prove it. She moved faster than Tracy could stand and punched her square in the face, sending a shower of blood from her nose all over Tracy's silk blouse.

She cocked back again and almost laughed when Tracy uncovered her face as if daring her to hit her again. Maybe the bitch got off on that kind of thing, so she obliged by hitting her in the mouth. "Get yourself cleaned up," she said, dropping her hand.

Tracy accepted Julio's handkerchief and walked with an almost dignified stride out of the room.

"You don't want to hear it, Mari, but she's right," Julio said. "We need to reach out, and we need to call your father."

"I'll take care of that, but put some people on that bitch. There's something about her I don't trust."

"Your father gave orders against that."

She cocked her fist again, smiling when he flinched. "You work for me, remember?"

"I'll take care of it."

"Good. Now get the fuck out." She collapsed into her father's chair after they left and closed her eyes until her heartbeat slowed. "Think," she said to herself as she picked up the phone. "Play this right and I can eliminate everyone keeping me out of this seat."

She took a few deep breaths as she punched in the number. "Put my father on. Tell him it's important."

CHAPTER EIGHT

L evi Lakye was waiting the next morning when Cain came downstairs, but so were Lou and Katlin. All three appeared distressed, but Levi she understood, so she had Carmen put him in the living room. She'd deal with Lou and Kaitlin first. It took plenty to make them look like they'd been sucking lemons all morning.

"I know I'm not going to like this, but let's hear it," she said, following Lou into the dining room. "Only give me a minute to have coffee." She poured a cup for each of them before sitting at the head of the long table. "Lou, call upstairs and let Emma know Levi's here. We'll deal with him together after this."

"A couple of my people on the street called and let me know Hector got hit hard last night. Whoever was stupid enough to do it is sitting on millions in street value," Katlin said as Lou nodded. "My contacts figured this would ignite a shit storm and wanted us to prepare if there's fallout."

"Did they have any idea who did it?" This wasn't what she fucking needed. She wanted and had planned for months of calm.

"The streets are quiet for the most part, so I guess someone decided to reshuffle the deck when it came to the major players," Lou said.

"And the answer to that is no," Katlin added. "But this is Hector we're talking about. You and I both know he'll blow up the entire city, then ask questions."

"Where's Jasper? Still in Houston?" She loved Jasper—the big African-American man who controlled the inner-city drug trade and was Vinny Carlotti's new partner—and his aunt Maude. Jasper and Maude had been lifelong friends, but Jasper was like any other businessman. If the opportunity was there, he'd take it. However, the consequences were a lot to chew this time if he had.

"Surprisingly, no," Lou said. "Vincent put him up while he rebuilt the compound Katrina washed away. After Jasper's arrangement with Vinny paid off big, Vincent let all the bad blood between their families run out. The main house is almost finished, from what I hear."

"Money—world's greatest healer, huh?" Katlin said with a smile as she shook her head.

"That's part of it, but I think Jasper and Vinny together are good, and it helped prove that Vinny has grown up enough to prove himself to his father. In Vincent's eyes and heart, that's way more important than a big payday." She wanted to celebrate what potentially could be the thing that drove Hector out of the city, but none of them were that lucky. "I've known Vinny a long time, so I totally got Vincent's worry."

"You don't think that hothead did this, right?" Katlin asked.

"Jasper will have his balls if he did, but I really don't see that. This isn't something Jasper or Vinny would've done without coming to us first, which either means somebody's gone nuts or we've got a new bully on the playground."

"Any clues, Boss?" Lou asked.

Cain didn't want to guess. That could be suicidal in a situation like this.

"Not a one, but this isn't our business. We do need to protect Jasper and Vinny from Hector's guaranteed blowup over this." She rose and picked up a new cup since her coffee was cold. "Be ready to go in about an hour, Lou."

"I'll take care of it, if you want," Katlin said.

"I'm not cutting you out, just giving Sept a heads-up. Try to see if you find anything else before I talk to her," she said, meaning Detective Sept Savoie, her old friend on the police department. "Have one of the guys get with Vinny and Jasper and ask if they can spare a few minutes."

"We might have a few days before it all goes to shit," Lou said. "I had Shaun check it out, and he can't be sure, but he's almost positive Hector's out of town."

The door opened, and Emma walked in with an uncomfortable-looking gait. "Good morning, lass." She smiled at Carmen, their head housekeeper, hovering close by like a hen with her pregnant chick. The sight made her wonder if Emma ever missed having a mother like Carmen. "We've got a nervous guest out there."

"Carmen and Lou mentioned him. How do you want to handle that?" Emma asked, giving Cain a quick kiss.

Carmen pulled out a chair before Cain could get to it and poured Emma a glass of juice.

"Sometimes it's better to hear the other guy out first. This conversation will be different here than at school, so let's give him a chance to rectify the situation."

"It's Saturday, mobster. Just try not to make him mess up my upholstery."

She laughed, but the little dweeb probably would piss his pants if she pushed too hard. "Carmen, could you please bring Mr. Layke in?"

Katlin and Lou left them alone, and Emma reached for her hand. "Cain...Emma." Levi looked like his legs had turned to stone as he stood close to the table. "Thanks for seeing me."

"Have a seat, Levi, before you fall over," Emma said.

"Do you have a check for me?" Cain said, holding up her free hand.

"Can we have a conversation before I hand it over?" Levi held up an envelope as if to prove he had it. "Bottom line, what do you want?"

"I want that bitch gone, and it has nothing to do with Hannah." She cocked her head slightly toward him, knowing that was a given even before he agreed. "I haven't been able to wrap my head around you having someone so intolerant in the classroom."

"The board brought her in at the end of last year at the recommendation of someone considered a friend. She was dismissed last night once the same board understood the ramifications of keeping her."

Levi stared at the envelope as if he'd written the speech on the back. Something was missing from his confession, though, and that's what he needed to spit out. She didn't care if he'd memorized it carefully or not.

Cain glanced at Emma, and she must've understood her expression because she let go of Cain's hand. Levi didn't move when Cain stood up and walked around behind him. He did take a deep breath when she gently placed her hands on his shoulders. "I'm guessing you've never had the kind of conversation we're about to have, so let's go through some ground rules."

"What about, Emma?" he asked, and she felt him tremble.

"Now, you care about my family?" She clicked her tongue and tensed her hands, squeezing his shoulders hard. "I'm going to ask you a question, and if you respond with something like 'I don't know,' it's not going to end well. At all times, remember who you're dealing with."

"The friend who recommended her is a lieutenant with NOPD," Levi said, not waiting for her question. "From what I understand he's interested in making the collar no one else had been able to, and he's been here already."

"Here?" Emma said. "As in, he's been in our house?"

"I don't have all the facts, but it was after the house got shot up."

"There were a lot of cops and FBI here until Muriel arrived and cleared everyone out, so you'll have to narrow it down," Emma said, her expression changing as if reliving that nightmarish time.

"We'll get to a name, but why now and why Hannah?" Jesus Christ, how in the hell had she missed this?

"I wasn't there for the vote, and they just now filled me in since it came back to bite them. It didn't occur to them then, I guess, that you wouldn't accept someone like this in your child's life, so they let this guy have his way. They should've asked where his way would lead them. The timing of her hire put her on a collision course with Hannah." Levi turned to face her and held out the envelope. "The woman's gone, but I made them give you the money back anyway."

"The money was the last thing on my mind, Levi, and she isn't the only one I want gone."

"Cain, you know I appreciate all you've done for me, but you can't break that much ice for Hannah. And yes, I do know who I'm talking to." He stood up and gripped the back of his chair, facing Cain. "You probably could take care of everything for her, but it doesn't mean you should. She'll never learn to fend for herself."

"Levi, don't make me hit you and don't preach to me about what's good for my kid." She pointed to the seat, and he dropped into it again. "I'll break ice, as you say, until Hannah learns from both of us to do it herself, and she will. Remember that she's in kindergarten, so I'm not going to leave her to fend for herself just yet to make you feel better about all this. It wasn't about that, so pay attention. This was about someone who doesn't know me or Emma telling Hannah that our family isn't in God's plan. She didn't exactly express those views the day we attended teacher-parent day, but I'm smart enough to get the implication."

"What's his name?" Emma asked.

"Elton Newsome," Levi said. "He's a detective, but I'm not sure which precinct."

"Take your check and go back to school," Cain said, sitting again so she could take Emma's hand.

"We've known each other since we were kids, Cain, and I do owe you for this job, but be careful. The board member I talked to said this Newsome guy is an asshole, but an asshole with a niece in our school and with some sway." Levi left the money and got up. "I don't want you to get messed up over this."

She stared at him for a long silent minute, and he squirmed under the scrutiny like he had when they were kids on the playground. Levi had always been small for his age, and he survived elementary school because of her and high school because of her brother, Billy. He was one of those people who'd needed propping up his entire life and seemed to have finally found his niche. The school was a perfect place for him to flourish, but he could never forget that her influence had paved and furnished his current position.

"Take the check, Levi. What you told me today makes us even. You know how to sell that, right?"

"Yes, and Hannah will be okay. I give you my word."

"That I'll hold you to."

❖

The table at the center of the condo on the Mississippi River might as well have been covered in gold, so Nunzio Luca rubbed his hands together as he stared at it. Five hundred and some kilos of pure Colombian white was actually worth more on the street than gold, and turning it out on the street was exactly what he was planning to do with it. No more middlemen—he was selling this himself. Once he did, and only then, would he come out of his self-imposed hiding.

"Can you fucking believe it?" Freddie held up one of the bags with the red dragon stamped on it. It was Hector Delarosa's implied guarantee that it was the best on the market. "We should do it again before they get their shit together."

"Let the dust settle and get busy repacking. Hector and his crew don't have that much inventory left, so it's time to move on to something else." Freddie and two other guys were one of the crews he'd sent to bulk up their inventory just as soon as they'd landed the night before.

Freddie slammed the bag down and glared at him. "You got people for shit like that. That's a fucking flunky job."

Nunzio took his gun from his waistband and aimed it at Freddie's head. "I thought we already had this conversation. I'm not having it again."

"I ain't complaining, man," Freddie said with his hands up. "You want me to do it, I'm on it, but I did everything you asked. All I want is some of that respect you keep talking about."

"I'll respect you as soon as I don't have to repeat myself more than once every fucking single time I ask you to do something. Get to it." He dropped his arm but didn't put the gun away. "Try to think about who we just stole from and what'll happen if he figures out exactly who was responsible. The fewer people who know about this, the better."

"You still want me to go to Mexico, right?"

"We'll get to that eventually, but I'm making the first trip alone. I'm leaving you to set up our street operation here and in New York." His best bet was to totally forget this kid or put a bullet in his head, but he was starting to like him. Freddie was a fuck-up with a bad attitude, but until recently that's how the world had seen him. "I want to be impenetrable before we crush our competition."

"You sure you want me around, right?"

"You need to learn a few things, but if you want out—get out. It won't be me putting you out."

"Then why make me do shit like this?"

"Because you need to learn patience and learn your place here. You brought me part of what we need to get back on top, but now we need the rest. To pull that off you need more experience, so prove yourself to me." Nunzio pulled out a chair for him. "You staying or what?"

"Yeah, but I get to pick my street crew, right?"

"I'll be back before we start that, so you can line them up then. I need to make sure everyone working for us is working *only* for us." The condo actually had a nice view of the river, but he'd personally closed the blinds. He needed Freddie to focus. "You got everything you need here, so stay put. You don't want the street talk to lead back to you and Hector's stuff."

"Okay, whatever."

"Freddie, I'll be gone for a few days. Take that time to decide what you want your future to be, because I'm fucking tired of you acting like a little kid who's not getting his way. The next time you shoot that mouth off like that again to disrespect me, I'm going to put a bullet through your teeth." He hit the side of his leg with his gun. Freddie wouldn't look him in the eye. "When I said this is the last time, that's exactly what it is. From now on, if I ask you to fucking wipe my ass, and you question me, you won't live to regret it."

"Don't worry about me letting you down, if that's what all this is about. You gave me a chance, so I'll do whatever it takes to earn your trust."

"Right now I need you to stay here and get this done. I want to get it ready for the street here and for transport up north. The rest that we'll need to feed the pipeline is the next step, so don't fucking leave this place. You've got everything necessary to get this done before I get back." He holstered his gun and waited to see if Freddie had any other complaints. This was a start, but not all their product could come from sheer luck and force. He was hoping Roth Pombo would help him with that part of the equation.

Freddie started working, and Nunzio left him to his penance. He'd changed his mind about taking Freddie with him because he needed someone with more finesse. This time, he decided to listen to his grandfather's constant advice of who to trust with what, so he took the service elevator all the way down to the garage. The solitude let him think about traveling without his real passport.

"You think he'll be okay?" Santino asked when Nunzio joined him in the back of the large SUV. His grandfather was hard to win over when it came to someone from the outside, so he'd waited in the car.

"Freddie just needs a strong hand," he said, flipping through the passport Santino had handed over. The picture of him with his newly colored blond hair showed it slightly longer than he usually wore it, but it did change his appearance. He hoped it would be enough to not only get into Mexico, but the maximum-security prison they would be visiting as guests.

"Good. I think the two of us can handle this." Santino put his hand behind his neck and squeezed. "My son was wrong in how he treated you, but he deserves to be avenged."

"We'll avenge him and so much more."

CHAPTER NINE

"You know, it's not like I don't have stuff to do," Detective Sept Savoie said when she met Cain the next day in front of the Casey family mausoleum. Some of the trees in the old walled graveyard had lost limbs to Katrina, but the Caseys' final resting spot seemed to be intact. Cain appeared to be alone as she sat smiling on the bench across from the mausoleum, but Sept doubted that.

Before she sat down she glanced back at the gate and to Blanchard's restaurant beyond it. The old New Orleans eatery was a beloved institution and the site of a murder she'd been tasked to solve. She'd met and gotten to know a little about Keegan, the restaurant's head chef during her investigation, so she knew they were preparing for the crowd that'd be arriving soon for Sunday brunch. But she didn't know yet whether Keegan worked Sundays.

"Maybe I want your autograph since you've been in the papers so often lately. You're so famous now, I didn't think you'd show," Cain said with a fake smile.

The known mob boss was a nightmare to law enforcement, but they'd been friends so long that Sept couldn't help but like her. "Are the kids around?" Cain shook her head, and her smile became genuine. "Good. I can tell you to fuck off without it biting me in the ass."

"Unlike the paper and our esteemed crime reports on every channel, I have every confidence you'll catch this animal." Cain stood and hugged her. "I almost hate to ask you for a favor now, but you know I will."

Cain sat down again, and Sept still hadn't seen Lou or any of the others. "You can call me to have a drink and not just for favors, you know." She reached inside her jacket when she saw movement by the gate but sat back and laughed when she realized it was a waiter from Blanchard's.

"I called you for drinks, but bars are so clichéd sometimes that I like to mix it up." The guy stopped next to the bench and delivered two whiskies, neat. "It's early, but I enjoy a drink here whenever I can. Make sure you keep that tradition if I meet our maker before you do." Cain lifted her glass and tapped it against Sept's before raising it toward the tomb. "To family and good friends."

"Definitely, and you'll cheat death like you have everything else for years to come." She took a sip and smiled. Cain had really good taste in liquor. "Are you sure you should be out here alone? You know how popular you are."

"Big Lou's right outside so we're okay."

Sept glanced at the marble with the Casey name and imagined what the world would be like one day, hopefully far into the future, when she'd visit Cain here if her friend was right. "So what's on your mind?"

"Do you know Elton Newsome?"

The name sounded familiar, and Cain's tone was so sharp and pointed she could almost touch the contempt in it.

"As in Detective Elton Newsome? That's the only one I know."

Cain glanced at her briefly, then took a sip from her drink. The story that followed seemed farfetched and impossible, but Cain wasn't much on flights into fiction land. "You know what'll happen if someone targets my children? Hypothetically, of course."

"I can poke around, but if you've found another undercover sting against you, my hands will be tied." She swallowed the rest of the drink and coughed a little. "You know I won't cross that line despite our friendship."

"I wouldn't want you to, but if he's reporting to someone who's not your father, I'd like to know." Lou stepped inside the yard when the first of the tourists showed up. "And I realize you're slammed, but there's something else."

The story of Hector's recent theft problems was equally troubling. Granted, the city was fairly empty, but they wouldn't have the manpower to stop a drug war, much less handle it well. "Can you give me a minute?" She walked a little away and made a call to her father. He promised he'd follow up, and thankfully he didn't ask where she'd gotten the information.

"You have any plans for this morning?" Cain asked when she finished her call.

"This is the first Sunday I've had in a while, so no. You have more favors to ask? I have to be at my parents' place by early this afternoon."

Cain buttoned her jacket and shook her head. "I was going to invite you to brunch, but I'm reconsidering my lapse in judgment."

The gate filled with what looked like well-armed guards, but she smiled when she saw Emma and the kids. The Caseys were a good-looking group, and if she didn't know everything she did she'd guess that they weren't any different than the rest of the bluebloods lining up to eat at Blanchard's. Cain wasn't your regular banker or accountant, though, and she was training the next generation to continue her traditions. You could see it in the way Hayden walked protectively next to his mother and little sister.

"She isn't giving you a hard time, is she?" Emma said as she handed Hannah a small bouquet of flowers and the little girl skipped over to Cain with it. Together Cain and Hannah put the flowers in the marble vase outside the tomb.

"No more than usual, so you deserve a medal, my friend, since you volunteered for a lifetime with this one." She kissed Emma's cheek and accepted a hug from Hayden. Emma's father Ross brought up the rear. He seemed to have shaken the hay from his clothes and hair, since he didn't look like a farmer anymore. "Ross, you doing okay? I don't think you ever had to survive too many hurricanes back home, huh?"

"I feel bad for everyone who suffered because of Katrina, but it'll be one of my most treasured memories."

She didn't begrudge him the happiness of Emma and Cain's ceremony, but instead of attending the event she'd been invited to, she'd been consoling her parents and family because of her sister and niece's deaths. They'd been two of the many Katrina took, but losing them had almost kneecapped her and her brothers. Her parents, while they tried to act strong, would never fully recover from the tragedy.

The mention of something that was for the Casey family a happy occasion, though, reminded her of all the joyful memories of which her family had been robbed. She tried to cage her grief, but at times like this it slithered like a snake out of a swamp and sunk its fangs into her heart that the cage sprung open. Her vision blurred with unexpected tears.

Emma put her arms around her as much as she could. "I'm so sorry for your loss. The death of a sister and niece is a wound that'll heal only with time. And while all those days pass, you know you have us to lean on. Cain has had more than her share of loss, so talk to her." Emma put her hand flat over her heart. "Don't let it fester in here."

"Thank you and sorry." Sept wiped her face and took a deep breath.

"Tears mean you've lived and loved," Cain said. "And Emma's right. Your pain will subside."

Sept nodded, but she didn't believe time would help.

"The anger, though, that'll eat you alive if you let it," Cain added.

"I think you did something about your pain, and, putting my badge aside, I never blamed you for that. Even if I'd been able to prove it, you'd still be free." She spoke softly, pausing while Emma took the children and moved away to give the two of them some privacy. "I have no one to stab in the heart to bury my anger."

"I'm not that much of a savage, old friend, but I did find a way to satisfy my sense of justice." Cain smiled and gripped the back of Sept's neck. "You can't blame a storm, so try something that calms even the beast in me." Cain turned so she could see Emma and Hayden sitting on the bench with Hannah running around in front of them.

"I doubt she's interested in me." She laughed when Cain squeezed harder.

"Perhaps your answer lies in there." Cain pointed to the restaurant and hugged her again. "I hear someone put you in your place rather nicely recently, so maybe that's what you need in your life. A woman who can actually break through that tough façade of yours and force you not to run away like you usually do."

"How'd you—"

"Easy. Whenever I want to know something about you, I call your mother. I heard you were chasing clues on two murders really close together, so I called to see if you were okay."

She laughed, forgetting her grief for a moment. "That I believe, and thank you. I'll dig into Newsome and see if I find anything. Promise me something though."

"He'll be all yours. I've got better things to do."

"You do, so try to remember that. My peers have always thought you were the devil incarnate. Well, the devil's due all the happiness this baby will bring, and you don't want anything to keep you from it."

"You have everything you need?" Remi asked Dallas as they started for the new house. Their time together had been nonexistent since Dallas had gotten home, and Remi was aggravated that she didn't have anyone to blame. When she'd returned from the meeting with Finley, Dallas and Kristen were talking and she joined in, not wanting to cut their time short. That morning had been much of the same, and now they were discussing house stuff.

"Babe, I promise tonight, no matter what, it'll be me and you, and everything we need will be in the bedroom." Dallas whispered close to her ear so Simon wouldn't overhear her. "Emma told me about this painter, though, and I want to pin him down before someone else hires him. Some of those rooms are a little bright for me, which means you'd be nuts two days after we move in."

"It's okay, querida." She chuckled at the fact that Dallas was the only person other than her parents who was willing to call her out when she was acting like a child. "I promised I wanted to help you put our house together, so forget my pouting."

Even though it was the weekend and late in the afternoon, workmen were scattered both inside and out when they pulled in. Remi quickly scanned the faces to see if anyone stood out. Emma's father, Ross, was there keeping an eye on the contractor Emma had originally hired, and she'd swear the guy had developed a nervous twitch whenever someone mentioned Cain's name. After hearing the story of how Cain had gotten rid of the bugs the FBI had placed during the remodel of the house, she couldn't blame this guy for being a little twitchy around her old friend.

"Ross," she said as she helped Dallas out of the car. "Thank you again for all the time you've put into this for us."

Ross had his phone in hand and appeared a bit off from his usual relaxed self. He reminded her of her own father in that it took something major to rile him, but obviously something had him on edge now. "No problem. You two are family."

"Are you okay?"

"Fine. Just an unexpected call."

Dallas grabbed his arm. "It's not Emma, is it?"

"No. She should be at home with Cain and the kids relaxing after brunch. I left a little early to meet the painter." He seemed to shake off whatever was bothering him and dropped his phone into his pocket. "A few more months and you should be able to move in."

"Are you really okay?" Dallas moved her hand to his shoulder and didn't seem to want to let go. "You were right in that we're family. If something's bothering you, we can help, or at least try to."

"It's my wife, Carol," he said and sighed as if the weight of the entire house was about to drop on his shoulders. "This divorce is taking forever, and I'm not sure why she's dragging it out. It's not like she wants me, much less Emma."

"How about your grandchildren? I remember Cain mentioning how close she was to Hannah." Remi stood right behind Dallas. "I'm sure you don't want to worry Cain or Emma, but I've found that Cain lives her life preparing for everything. We have that in common, so fill her in if you think there's even a chance your ex has something like that in mind."

"I'd like to think Carol isn't that stupid," he said, exhaling loudly. "And because of Cain, I was able to offer her much more than she deserved in a settlement since she wasn't entitled to the land. I hate to drop anything else on Cain or you now. Carol has been my problem for years, so I'll think of something to handle this. I'm sure you don't want to be bored with all that."

"You don't have to talk about it if it's uncomfortable for you," Dallas said.

"I've wasted too many years being silent about my soon-to-be ex-wife, so I don't mind." His smile was unconvincing. Clearly, this would only fester in his mind. "But now isn't the time for me and my problems. Let's go pick out some colors for these walls."

They let Dallas walk with the painter to look at the swatches he'd painted on the walls. "I can't tell you what to do, Ross, but you need to keep Cain in the loop."

"Yeah," he said, nodding. "Like I said, she doesn't deserve to be bothered with something this trivial, but I don't need any nasty surprises either."

"Whatever comes, you aren't alone in this. You know that."

"When I came here, I thought I'd miss the life I had for so long. But Cain gave me something I didn't imagine ever having." Ross wasn't a big man, but he seemed to have a big heart when it came to his family. Remi knew the Casey children adored him and her old friend had come to enjoy his company. Ross was nothing like Dalton Casey, but Remi knew his devotion to family was the same. "She gave me my daughter back and so much more."

Because of that loyalty, Cain would take any threat to Ross seriously. "So you've got no idea what she wants?"

"She has a hang-up, but it isn't something I can give her. I wouldn't even if I could, so I'm letting my attorney handle it before I bother Cain or anyone else."

"Do you mind if I talk to Muriel and your attorney about all this? Divorce isn't my specialty, but I might be able to help out."

"Sure. I can use all the help I can get. I simply want to put Carol in my rearview mirror permanently."

"I'm positive that's a wish we can handle," she said, and hoped he meant it. Cain's idea of permanent at times was vastly different from other people's.

❖

"Wonderful as always, Keegan," Cain said when the owner and chef of Blanchard's stopped by their table and joined them for dessert, since Ross had left to meet Remi and Dallas. They'd come back at Emma's request since this would probably be their last outing until the baby arrived, so they'd gotten in one more bread pudding. "And the next time you plan to filet Sept with that sharp wit of yours, call me.

That'd be worth driving over to see. I can vouch for her, though, so don't come down too hard." She pointed to Sept. "If you kill her, I'd miss her too much and wouldn't have anyone to deal with my parking tickets."

"The thought has crossed my mind since she thinks I'm a homicidal killer already, but I'll try to control myself," Keegan said, making them all laugh. "Let me know when the new arrival finally gets here, and dinner is on me." Keegan stood and hesitated. "Care to give me an update on what's happening with the case, Detective?"

Sept nodded, and Cain swore she saw the beginning of a spark.

"Enjoy your afternoon," Keegan said, kissing Emma's cheek before she left.

Cain smiled until she noticed Lou's expression. The only time he made that face was when a possible threat was nearby. She glanced around the room. The only possibility she could see was the guy toward the middle of the room, eating alone. His suit was a tad too tight, and his shoes were old-school cop. One cop sitting alone shouldn't have bothered her, but Lou nodded when she glanced back at him. Whoever this was, he wanted to be noticed.

"You guys ready?" she asked, prompting Hannah to jump out of her seat. "Let's take Mama home for a family movie." Cain motioned Lou over as she helped Emma to her feet. "Call Ross and make sure he's with Remi. Then send someone over for him."

"Will do, Boss. You ready to move?"

"Yeah. It's starting to get stuffy in here." She placed her hand on the small of Emma's back and started to leave, but the guy Lou had been watching got up and headed straight toward them. "Lou," Cain said in a low voice, and the big man stepped close to Emma.

"This looks like a cozy family outing," the man said as he hooked his thumbs in his belt, obviously to draw attention to his gold shield. "You gonna use some of that funny Casey humor on me?"

"I'm not the comedian you are, Detective Newsome," she said, trusting her best guess. His smile disappeared. "Shouldn't you be out intimidating small children and old people?"

"You're wrong about being a funny person." He rocked on his heels as if he were just getting started. "My plans are—"

She moved past, careful not to touch him. The only time she'd talk to this guy was when she had all the facts, and Blanchard's dining room wasn't the time to start getting them. "Take us home, Lou."

"Who was that?" Emma asked after they were in the car. She stared at Newsome standing outside, giggling like some excited schoolgirl.

"That was Detective Elton Newsome introducing himself as a part of the menagerie we've got following us around. I'm pretty sure we were supposed to cower in fear."

"Is he kidding?" Emma spoke freely since the kids were in the car behind them. "What's his game, you think?"

"I suppose it's not much different than the guys in the plumbing truck." She pointed to the large panel van following them. "Believe me, lass, if I could get rid of them forever without losing who I am, I would."

"Those guys don't bother me all that much. It's the lone wolves like this guy that make me lose sleep. They want what they assume is justice, but they're willing to burn the rule book to get it."

She nodded and kissed the top of Emma's head. "I love you, but I'm sure those plumbers are saying the same about me. Rules for some things weren't my strong suit."

"You follow the rules when it's important, my love. That should count for something."

"It counts with you, and that's all that matters to me." She let out a long hmm but couldn't dismiss the question on her mind. What had woken this guy up now? "So Newsome came to the house and Muriel threw him out, and he's been pissed about it ever since? Does that seem like the thinking of a crazy person?"

"That's what we know." Emma frowned. "I was at the hospital with you, so I never met him. Because I was, I can't give you any insight into his mental health."

"It's hard to believe he's built a grudge that went off now."

Emma glanced up, eyebrows raised. "Whether that's true or not, does it change the way we deal with this guy?"

"History is a great teacher because it gives us a map of places to avoid. Newsome doesn't strike me as a diabolical revenge planner because he got escorted out. This has to be something else."

The gates of their home closed behind them, and she helped Emma out of the car, shaking her head slightly when she saw Remi, Dallas, and Ross together. Apparently something had happened, but that they'd waited made it clear it wasn't an emergency.

"Hey," Emma said, opening her arms to Dallas. "How'd you like the painter?"

"Great, like you said. Come on. You look tired," Dallas said, but Cain didn't move away.

"How about I get you upstairs, and you two can talk swatches," she said, putting her arm around Emma's waist.

"I think you're being a bit condescending, mobster. You have until we get to the bedroom to tell me what's wrong."

"I'm sure our pal here will fill us in, since I don't have a clue. The last couple of hours must've been interesting, though, since everything was fine at lunch."

"It's nothing major," Dallas said, moving ahead of them. The children had gone up already to change for a relaxing day at home. "Your dad didn't want to worry you, but Remi convinced him otherwise, so you might want to talk to him."

"Didn't want to worry me about what?" Emma asked.

Dallas mouthed "I'm sorry" when Cain stared at her.

"Your mom's giving him a hard time, so I'm sure it's nothing much, since it sounds like she's always giving him a hard time."

"I'll talk to him again, lass."

"Dallas, would you mind looking in on Hannah for me?" Emma gave her friend an excuse to escape, then turned to her. "I know you don't like me to stress about anything," she said as she and Cain kept walking toward their bedroom, "but—"

"Your mother is an old story, lovely girl, so you're right. I'm not going to bother you with that." She let Emma go so she could fold the bed cover down and fluff up the pillows. "I loved my parents and now love my children even more. So I've never understood your mother. She had only one child to lavish her attention and affections on, and she wasted the opportunity. If she's looking for forgiveness for those sins, I hope for her sake that God has more stomach for it because she'll never find it with me."

"Thank you, my love, and thank you for helping my father through this. We're both lucky to have you." Emma sighed and sat, but she didn't let go of Cain. "I want Daddy to be happy, so hopefully these delays won't last much longer."

"If he hasn't told you, I sweetened the settlement pot for him in case she was wanting more money." She helped Emma swing her legs onto the bed as the door opened, and Dallas walked in. "She still hasn't budged, but she won't exactly say what it'll take to get this finished either. It's our bad luck that she's been able to hold it up with motions from her end. We've got plenty of friends here but a limited number in Wisconsin, so now we have to be patient."

"You have a limited talent for that," Emma said, making her laugh.

"I can do a fair impression of a bull in a china shop, but I'll never forget one thing."

Emma kissed her cheek when she leaned over her. "What?"

"Carol isn't a good parent, but I'll never forget she's your mother." She gazed at Emma for a long moment. "For that, for you, and for Ross, I'll be as patient as I need to be."

CHAPTER TEN

W ho sanctioned you?" Fiona stared at Elton Newsome with all the suspicion that was making her stomach feel like she was on a fast, jerky roller coaster. Everything he'd said was something she wanted—badly, but her pursuit of Cain Casey had left deep cuts that hadn't exactly healed. One more misstep and she'd be lucky to be walking a beat on the graveyard shift.

"All you need to know is I'm heading up the investigation, and I'm giving you an in." He rolled his glass of beer between his hands like it was an uncontrollable nervous habit. The bar he'd picked was more dive than anything else and close to City Park. "I read what happened to you, and you got a bad rap. Agent Chapman was on the right track, but he didn't have the balls to finish."

"And you do?" She waved off the waitress again, not at all interested in drinking with this guy.

"Watch your tone. I've got something Chapman didn't."

"I'm not a fan of dramatic guessing games." This was a waste of time so she stood up fast enough that Elton spilled a little of his drink. "Good luck."

"Wait." He threw a ten on the table and pointed to the door. "Give me five more minutes, and if you want, then you can go."

The walk to his car was short, and Fiona didn't recognize the woman in the passenger side, so she stopped. "You might have seniority, but you're starting to get on my nerves. Who's that, your mother?"

"Even better. She's Emma Casey's mother. Why not hear the lady out and then make your decision."

She got in the backseat and listened to what Carol Verde had to say and what she wanted. If this guy expected to get any kind of leverage on Cain with this hard, bitter woman, he was dreaming.

"Mrs. Verde, I wish you luck," she said, opening the door. "You're going to need it."

"What the fuck, O'Brannigan?" Elton screamed from the window when she got out.

She whirled on him. "No. What the fuck are you up to? You think Carol Verde testifying before a grand jury that Cain Casey is the evil spawn that ruined her daughter's soul is going to get you somewhere? Get your head out of your ass and review the case the late Barney Kyle cobbled together. He tried that shit, and not only did it not work, but he ended up spraying a transport van with his brains."

"Who the hell do you think did that?" Elton yelled.

She cursed herself silently for accepting this asshole's call.

"If you're thinking it was Casey, no one was ever able to prove it. And believe me, I read the entire file, so it wasn't for lack of trying. A case could've easily been made against the Bracato family since that's who Kyle was working for, but there was not one scintilla of proof."

"It was Casey, and you know it. No one ever proved it because every cop on the force here is like Sept Savoie—in love with that bitch."

"I know you don't think I can help, but I'll do anything to bring this monster to justice," Carol said, walking up on them and shutting Elton up. "My daughter's lost to me, but my granddaughter Hannah deserves better."

"Did Detective Newsome tell you Emma and Cain are expecting again?" She studied Carol's reaction the same as she did any suspect's. "And there's also your grandson. You didn't mention him."

"Unlike most, I know when and what battles to fight, Detective. You should learn that early and you won't be disappointed often."

Fiona turned and walked away and got into her own car before she got sucked any deeper into this black career-ending hole. Elton's screaming was easy to ignore, but Carol Verde's penetrating gaze made her pause before she started her car. Elton did have seniority over her, so she had to play this carefully.

"Fuck," she said as she pulled away. She could think of only one person to call about this. She found the contact in her phone. "Hey. Got a minute?"

❖

The sounds of the city were faint outside the thick walls, but it was hard to completely shut out Bogota's presence no matter how much insulation your money bought you. Hector Delarosa didn't want to erase the city completely, even if he could. That background noise reminded him of all that time he'd spent as a boy with an empty stomach but a head full of dreams of what could be.

He'd killed more people than he could have ever come close to fathoming back then, but he'd climbed over all those bodies to the top of the cartel. He would live with those sins since he wasn't about to give up any hard-earned ground now, but that didn't come without consequences.

One or more of the fuckers he'd killed was probably coming back to haunt him now. But whoever had dared to steal from him must realize how he'd earned his reputation. If he had to kill half of Bogota to keep what he had, he'd do it with as little remorse as before. Only this time, he wouldn't stop at just the people who'd been stupid enough to try this. No. This time he'd kill everyone in their family as insurance against any future revenge.

"You can blame me if you want, Don Hector," Ernesto Igles, his Bogota captain, said. "I've had everyone working the streets and nothing. The rumor is that it's someone from outside Colombia."

"Who told you that?" He stretched his hand out and looked at it, thinking about how his mother was fond of saying Hector had inherited his father's hands and quick temper. But he wasn't like his father, who had drunk himself blind and died in an alley with a knife in his gut. He was always so wasted he probably didn't even feel it.

"That's the excuse the man I put over the fields to the north used when he called to say someone had torched three-fourths of the plants."

Ernesto had been with him the longest, and Hector had never questioned his loyalty—not once. But he wanted to lash out at someone.

"The orders we have are going to make it a tight squeeze, but the inventory we've already sent should carry us until we're able to harvest again," Ernesto said, unaware of the entire situation. "I doubled the guard around the other six fields."

"The inventory in the US is gone," Hector said, closing his eyes in an attempt to calm himself. It'd been an eternity since he'd felt like a trapped rat. Someone was trying to squeeze him out by making every buyer a potential enemy. No one took kindly to handing over money for nothing. "You can't stretch that much to make us whole."

"Who can be that stupid?" Ernesto said as he smashed the palm of his hand with his fist.

Hector smiled, thinking of his old friend and growing up with him as they were both earning their street creds. Ernesto wasn't a big man, but he always jumped into any fight no matter the size of his opponent. Eventually everyone had steered clear after he'd developed a reputation for the type of ruthlessness that came from a bit of insanity.

"I'll fucking cut his balls off," Ernesto said, and Hector believed him.

"Once I find who did this, that'll be merciful, considering what I intend to do to them. Whoever it is must have the kind of resources that can stretch from here to the US. That should narrow the field for you and the others."

"You have my word, amigo, that I'll find them. Once I do, they'll curse that their parents even met when I'm done with them."

"Once you do that, call me and let me know before you move in. This had to be the action of more than one person, so I want to make sure we find them all before we go killing anyone. Go tell the others I'm not going to put up with not knowing for long."

He embraced Ernesto before he left to trawl the streets again for information, and he hoped on his father's grave it wasn't someone like Ernesto making this move. Not that he'd hesitate to kill him, but he didn't have many friends left from those old days of eating out of the trash to live another day—always with the hope things would get better. People like Ernesto not only were loyal but understood where they'd come from and what it'd taken to get here.

"It's time to show yourself, *hijo de puta*," he said. He needed to get out of there, so he called his guard. "Tomas, bring the Jeep around. I want to see the field that got torched." Maybe the best way to find answers was at the very beginning. The fields were the life blood of all he had, so he wanted them replanted and producing again as soon as possible. "Just bring a few. No need to give whoever these fuckers are a chance to take a free shot."

❖

"You don't know anything about what Carol wants?" Cain asked Muriel once the house was quiet again. The night and dinner with friends had made both Emma and Ross forget their trouble, and she wanted to keep it that way. But until she'd driven a stake through the bitch's heart—and even then she wasn't sure Carol would truly disappear—she wouldn't be done with this.

"She wants plenty of things that aren't within her right to ask." Muriel threw the comment out and flinched as if it'd caused her physical pain to say it. "You didn't want me to handle it personally, so I gave it to my associate Sanders Riggoli. He's doing a good job, but you know how the court works."

"Give her what she wants and get it done." She tried to unclench her teeth as she spoke, but this subject always blew her temper the hell up.

"She wants visitation rights in Wisconsin as often as possible with only Hannah. Are you sure about giving her what she wants?"

It took a moment to work through the rage to remember Muriel wasn't the enemy, but she was close to panting when the fog cleared. "She'll get her hands on our daughter only if I'm dead, and then she's got Emma to worry about. Why the fuck didn't you tell me?" Vulgarity wasn't her norm, but she had a tenuous hold on her control.

"Because no court, no matter how friendly toward Carol, is going to give her that, so I wanted to spare you this aggravation." Muriel came closer and placed her hand over her heart. "Sanders tried the easy and fast route, and he fell for Carol's game and her country-bumpkin-acting lawyer, so I'm keeping him on the case but providing him a list of instructions. Tomorrow he's going to dismiss the divorce petition in Wisconsin."

"And start this over again?" Another year or six months of waiting wasn't in her plan, and she doubted Ross would agree.

"I've already spoken to Judge Mary Buchanan. We're going to refile in Louisiana, and it'll go smoother and faster. Once I argue Ross's mental distress, he'll be the city's most eligible bachelor." Muriel patted her chest before resting her hands on her shoulders. "I was only trying to keep you from thinking this to death. Don't be pissed—I'll take care of it."

"I appreciate it, but I want this done. Carol has been nothing but a cinderblock around the ankles of my family, and it's time to cut them free." The addition of one more thing to her loose ends wasn't what she wanted to think about, but she'd do whatever was necessary to enjoy their new baby.

"No matter how long it takes, though, remember Carol is Emma's mother. That's the one good thing she's done. For that she deserves more than she has a right to."

She stood up and faced Muriel. "I mentioned that to Emma, and Carol has nothing to worry about when it comes to any of my problem-solving skills. I trust you to take care of it."

"One more thing."

Muriel shrugged when she cocked her eyebrow up.

"Pretty soon I'm going to ban you from the house."

"It's about Finley and her problems."

She didn't think Muriel and Merrick had found anything so far, but from Muriel's expression this had the potential for real implications regarding their future. "Tell me."

Muriel started talking, and she was almost sorry she'd asked. "I'm not sure where Finley found this woman, but it's going to be a problem to get clear of the baggage she comes with."

"Let's hope that Finley understands the option here."

Muriel followed her toward the stairs. "Don't you mean options?"

She smiled and shook her head. "Life isn't always multiple choice, cousin. Go home and we'll talk about it tomorrow."

The van outside now had cable-company decals, and Muriel hoped that meant Shelby was off for the day. Any love she had for her family's somewhat enemy had died away because of Shelby's betrayal, but she couldn't help but care for her. If Shelby was in as much pain as she was because of the loss of her father, Jarvis, she deserved some compassion.

The thought of her empty house was enough to make Muriel head toward Cain's Irish pub in the French Quarter. A beer and the promise of old Irish tunes would fill the silence that had dominated her life since her da had died. The only good thing that had come from the days after his death was the easing of the guilt that was choking her faster than if someone had wrapped a rope around her chest and thrown her off a building. What Cain had repeated often finally made sense. A life wasn't judged by a few weeks, but in its entirety.

"Da, I hope you and the family have forgiven me my stupidity," she said as she turned onto St. Charles Avenue, glancing down when her phone rang. "Hello," she said, not recognizing the number.

"I wasn't that boring, was I?"

She laughed at Kristen's way of starting a conversation. "Boring isn't how I'd describe you, so I'm sorry for not calling sooner. Work is my only excuse, but I'm sure that's not what you want to hear."

"Actually, what I want is to see you again. Are you free?"

She smiled at the forwardness but appreciated Kristen's bravado. "I was on my way to the Erin Go Braugh. Would you like to join me?"

"Drinking alone, or do you feel sorry enough to make me a third wheel?"

"A beer alone is good for the soul, but one with a beautiful woman is even better." She headed to the river and Remi's condo.

"It's good to hear that you don't think I'm a kid."

She laughed as she glanced in her rearview mirror. "No, not in the kid category." A vehicle was behind her, but it was only Cain's overprotectiveness. "Want to join me?"

"I'll meet you downstairs."

"I'll come up and get you in about five minutes."

Kristen laughed, and she suddenly couldn't wait to see her. "Anyone ever tell you that you're a bit old-fashioned?"

"The old ways are at times the best, Ms. Montgomery." She stopped in the front of Remi's building and handed the keys along with a twenty to the valet. "I'll be right down, so can you pull it to the side?"

"You got it," the guy said and pointed to a spot near the garage exit. The car coming down didn't have tinted windows, and she could've sworn the old guy in the back looked incredibly familiar. "Or I could be paranoid," she said as she headed inside where the elevator and Kristen were waiting.

This time Kristen wore tailored slacks and a vest that looked like there was nothing between it and her skin. It was like a sexy executive outfit that made it hard to look away. "Ready?" Kristen asked as she looped their arms together.

They were quiet on the way down, and Kristen smiled when she opened her door for her. Kristen reached for her hand before she moved away and tugged her closer. "You look beautiful."

Kristen nodded and let her hand go so she could put it behind Muriel's neck. "Thank you, and thank you for seeing me again."

"You'll never have to thank me for that." She decided to go against her natural caution and kissed Kristen. The touch of her lips ignited something in her that fractured her pain. It didn't completely die away, but it eased considerably.

"And thank you for finally doing that," Kristen said as she placed her fingers against her mouth. "It was as good as I thought it would be."

"Are you sure? You're starting out, and you probably would do better with—" She stopped talking when Kristen pinched her lips together hard.

"Sometimes life should be spontaneous, so let go of all that stuff in your head and concentrate on right now. Don't go much beyond that." Kristen let her go and kissed her again. "Think you can manage that?"

"I can muddle through with a few reminders." She smiled as she walked along the front of her car, ready to leave. The image of the old man came to her again as she placed her hand on the door latch. There was a reason he caught her attention—the older man resembled Junior Luca so much she couldn't believe it hadn't come to her sooner. "Damn," she said, figuring her unplanned night was about to become more complicated. "How about one quick drink upstairs?"

It took an hour, but Remi was able to get a complete list of the tenants in her building. None of them jumped out as overly suspicious, but after Muriel's visit she wasn't taking any chances, especially since they were still living in the penthouse. Cain couldn't blame her old friend for that since the only person Junior Luca had ever looked like was his father Santino.

If Santino was in New Orleans, he was there to prop his grandson up, so it was imperative to find them before they started their business again. Cain sat at her desk and went down the list again on the chance something would pop out after another viewing. Eventually it would take a door-to-door search to make absolutely sure, but she hoped the two people she'd put on surveillance duty would take care of an exact location.

"What do you want to do?" Muriel asked.

"It's late, so nothing now. Tomorrow we'll start actively searching. Before you leave, though, I do want to hear about you and Kristen." She glanced up and smiled at Muriel's somewhat joyful expression.

"You were right about that too. Every so often something falls in your lap and you simply have to enjoy it and not question it." Muriel's smile widened and she laughed. "She's probably too young for me, but she pinches the hell out of me whenever I mention it."

"I'm going to like her," she said as the phone rang.

"Sorry to disturb you," Carmen said, "but someone named Yury Antakov wants to talk to you."

"Thank you." She looked at the blinking line, thinking of everything both Muriel and Finley had said.

"Who is it?"

"Finley's answer, if I had to guess, but why call here? There's no way he found out this quick we were asking questions about him." She shrugged and cracked the bones in her neck before punching the button to pick up. "Cain Casey," she said and waited.

"Ms. Casey, you don't know me, but I have a problem I need help with." There was only a hint of an accent, but it almost sounded as if he was trying to accentuate his language with it. "My name is Yury Antakov."

"What can I do for you, Mr. Antakov?" She tried to keep her voice light, but it was a challenge considering what his business was built on.

"My associates tell me New Orleans is your town, so I wanted to thank you for allowing us to start our business, the Hell Fire Club, without problems. It's time for us, though, to sit and discuss terms and mutual respect, but I have to ask for your help as well."

The little speech cleared up who owned the Hell Fire Club, but not who Nicola Eaton was to him. "What can I do for you?"

"I'm looking for a woman, and if you can help me, I'll owe you a favor in return. We don't know each other, but believe me, having me in your debt will be advantageous."

"If I can help, whatever you need is yours." She smiled at his chuckle. Men like Yury achieved the power they did from their need to control everyone around them. His debt to her was as much a figment of pure fantasy as Hannah's cartoon collection. If she showed any inclination to help him, he'd convince himself eventually that she was weak.

"I'll see you tomorrow night then," he said and promised to have one of his people call to make the arrangements. "I need to find this woman fast."

"Tell big Lou to prepare for a visit. Let's have it at the wine cellar," she said to Muriel as she searched for Finley's number. "I got an interesting call from someone you're looking for."

"That was fast," Finley said, and Cain momentarily heard small children in the background. "Did you make some calls?"

"I didn't get a chance. My new friend Yury needs my help finding a woman. He didn't give me a name, but I'm guessing it's your new friend. He'll be here for a meeting tomorrow night."

"What did you tell him?"

"That I'd give him whatever he wants, but I need you there to prove who this guy is or isn't. Only don't come unless you're prepared to acknowledge you might have to make choices that aren't in your employee manual. I've exposed the family now so I can't take any chances."

"If I can, I'll follow my training, but I'm not gambling with Abigail or the children either."

"Our blood is the same, Finley, but our lives aren't. Once you have your proof, if you want, I'll take care of this."

"Maybe this time we can both get what we want."

CHAPTER ELEVEN

"A re you sure this is a good idea?" Emma asked as they showered together the next night after Remi, Dallas, and Remi's family had gone home following dinner. "I've read about some of these Russian mobs, and they're vicious."

"If my info is right, they're here already, and they don't play well with others. I think it'll be dangerous to leave these people unchecked, and this particular snake doesn't crawl out from under his rock often." She wanted to make Emma comfortable before she left, because her night was far from over. "And it's for Finley too. I'd sit this one out, but I always consider if I was in her situation and no one was around to help."

"I'm glad you can help her, my love, but promise you'll be careful."

Cain kissed Emma's temple and placed a hand over Emma's abdomen. "I have a bottle of Irish whiskey ready to welcome this Casey home. I'll be careful, lass. There's too much at stake not to be."

"Good, because we don't have much time." Emma covered Cain's hand with both of hers and pressed back against her. "Are you ready for this?"

"We might not be perfect in any other way except in how we parent, my love. But we are good at that, so if this was our tenth and you were asking me that question, my answer would still be yes. I'll never tire of bringing children into this world with you, especially since they're all perfect and gorgeous like their mother."

"Let's hope they all inherit your healthy sense of self-esteem, mobster. Now help me get my pjs on so you can get going."

She'd dressed, after she'd given Emma what she wanted, and left for her office to get something they'd perhaps need later. Merrick and Katlin had found what she'd been looking for and, more importantly, what Finley needed, so it was time to act. Even though it was Sunday, this was too important to ignore. So she got into the backseat with Lou and let one of the guys drive them to the riverfront.

A dozen Surburbans—all matching the ones she and everyone else in the family used—were parked inside the warehouse where her office was located. She'd had them moved in a few at a time after they'd met with Finley. She figured they'd eventually need them for something like this. The only thing not in her plan so far was the quick turnaround on what they'd found.

When the doors came down, obscuring the view from the FBI across the street, she headed to the back of the warehouse where the mechanics room that housed all the electrical and air-conditioner units was located. She, like her father before her, knew it'd be the first place the feds would look if they ever got a warrant, but sometimes there was value in anticipating how people thought. Since she always tried to avoid the obvious, she came up with this spot for one of her father's favorite things.

She pressed down on a board with her foot and pushed on one of the air handlers at the same time. The board slid back, revealing cash packed carefully to thwart the humidity and a gun. Tonight, the gun had to come out of mothballs because no amount of money would fix this problem.

Once she was ready, the doors opened and she sent out a few of the vehicles to the Quarter before the warehouse was locked again. A few minutes later, the next set of SUVs was released to head for Emma's, and they, too, picked up a tail.

"Keep up, guys, and make sure everyone follows the timeline Katlin set out," she said as she left for her meeting. "I wouldn't want our friends to miss anything."

"I know she thinks we're totally stupid, but this is ridiculous," Joe said as the fourth set of black SUVs left the building. "There are more people in the bureau than just us. She does realize that, right?"

The door opened again and a few more cars emerged, turning to go uptown. Joe dispatched another team to follow.

"It's a game she likes to play because she's good at it. One set of cars is hers, but the first stop isn't her intended destination. If I had to guess, I'd say we need to keep tabs on the car that makes the most stops." Shelby didn't look away from the warehouse and smiled when the doors opened again. This seemed excessive even for Cain.

"Don't worry. I'm not explaining another screw-up to the boss."

"Any ramblings I haven't heard about?" If this was something important, she estimated Cain would send out at least two more decoys. "We'll spend a lifetime obsessing about Cain, but I'm sure other things are happening around town. If we knew what else was going on, we might be able to narrow this down a little."

"I had all these guys ready to go because we did get some intel from the NOPD." He threw his hands up when she turned around and stared at him. "Wait…before you decapitate me, I just got it like two hours ago."

"What is it?" She spoke to accentuate every word. The door across from them opened again, and she almost snorted.

Joe recapped the report about someone who'd become a ghost around town. When Nunzio had run home to New York months before as if his life literally depended on it, she'd thought he'd be one less problem because he'd be too busy helping his father salvage their empire. Whatever Nunzio had to do with Cain when he'd been living in Biloxi hadn't materialized into much.

But Ross Verde did now own the Luca family's casino, so perhaps that wasn't completely true.

Also, before Nunzio could land in New York, his father Junior was killed by a bullet to his forehead. They needed to check with the New York office to see if there'd been any developments in uncovering who was behind that hit, in case Nunzio in any way blamed Cain. If he didn't, they could leave him to the DEA agents she assumed were still following him. If he did blame Cain, they'd have problems on this end.

She really didn't know very much about Nunzio Luca, but her limited knowledge left her with a sense that the man had very little or no finesse. That could never be said of Cain, though, so the old saying about a fly being in someone's ointment came to mind.

Nunzio, who was no strategist, had probably learned the meaning of that saying if he'd tangled with Cain and lost. If he had tried something back then, which had blown up in spectacular fashion and he was back for revenge, he'd find that in this case the fly was more the size of a dragon with an Irish temper that would burn you from head to toe without hesitation.

Then again, Nunzio could be back because of what had happened with Remi. That shot to the chest had been big news around town for a while, but nothing ever came of it. No leads or information materialized, even with the news footage. And surprisingly, none of the Jatibons had complained too much to them or the NOPD. That probably meant that the problem had been taken care of in-house, which translated into it not being a problem anymore. In her opinion, Junior's demise could be a result of the failed attempt on Remi and have nothing to do with Cain.

"That's it?" Shelby asked.

"There's plenty going on, but the rumor about Nunzio was the only one I could connect to Casey. From the feelers I put out, Nunzio's not in town now, but I alerted every agency in the city that might be interested. We've already looked at that crap with the safe houses around town, and I use that term loosely. But so far no one's claiming ownership, and according to the narcotics division, they couldn't have been anything but drug-storage facilities. Whoever hit those places didn't mind killing everyone inside. That might be a Nunzio kind of move, but we can't rule out Casey."

"I can't believe I'm going to say this, but that doesn't sound like Cain. No matter her disregard for the law, she isn't into drugs. Not that we've found anyway." The door opened and a few more big black, boxy vehicles came out. Six sets was a good number for a wild-goose chase through the city. "Well, let's get going. Something big is going on and no one invited us. Let's make sure all your teams know it's imperative not to lose any vehicle. If they stop and can go in, tell them to stick close."

"If you had to guess, which one is she in?" Joe joined her at the window, and it seemed the warehouse was empty.

"I'd narrow it down to the first or the third, but that's only a hunch. Once we know some destinations I might change my mind."

"The first vehicles pulled into the private drive at Emma's, so that's a good guess."

"Where's the third set?"

"They went back to the house and into the garage."

She put her jacket back on and nodded. Her heart wasn't in this tonight, so she touched the small slip of paper in her pocket and made up her mind. She didn't have any more excuses to get rid of the burning ball of rage in her stomach, so it was time to do something about it. Whatever tonight was about, for once she prayed Cain was as good as usual. She didn't have time to deal with the end of the chase now.

"Let's head over to the club and see if she'll talk to us before she adds to whatever all this crap is."

"I'm not in the mood to be that forgiving. Let's wait it out and see what the play is. The string of different cars to different locations isn't fooling anyone." Joe pointed to the door and their team got ready to go. "It's time to prove we're not so simple-minded."

"Uh-huh."

❖

"We're good to go, Boss," Lou said after speaking to his nephew Dino, who'd moved up in their ranks after the Juan Luis situation had been resolved. Cain trusted the kid, who'd often visited his uncle at the house when he was working.

"No one's left in the rat hole across the street?" The fall weather was windy but in no way cool, so she took her jacket off and sat in the small kitchen of the tugboat. While the feds chased the SUVs around New Orleans, they'd used the small catwalk under the docks to board a boat for a trip up the river to the grain silos in St. Charles parish right outside New Orleans. It wasn't far to the industrial park on River Road from there, one of their new investments buried by Muriel's talent of legal layering. The paper trail ended with the name of a corporation in the Cayman Islands, but Muriel had structured the deal so that it took about twenty jumps and a lot of know-how to follow the maze back to her.

A federal agency would notice the property only because of suspicious activity, so they'd leased about seventy percent of the park to various small and average-sized businesses doing the mundane things usually found in an industrial complex. She'd only been interested in the warehouse space fronted by a plastics company with its own set of legitimate papers.

"Seems they must think something big is going down, so they called in the cavalry," Lou said. "They've got every vehicle buttoned down."

She laughed and handed the captain an envelope before stepping off. "Thanks, Tucker," she said, shaking hands with the son of an old friend who had a gambling jones but no luck to go along with it. Favors like this meant his debts were paid until the next time and his legs would stay intact for now. "If need be, we'll meet you later with something a little faster than this, right?"

"I'll be waiting. Don't worry."

The car Lou had driven out the day before was parked inside one of the warehouses along the bank, registered to yet another shell company. She wanted to be as careful as possible, for Finley's sake. Lou shook his head when she got in the front seat, but she simply smiled.

"Just try to not get pulled over and we'll be fine." The office was still dark, but she saw the SUV parked out front and figured Remi had beaten her there. "Anything on Santino or his idiot grandson?" With Junior gone, Cain figured Nunzio's strings were now being pulled by the only man left in his life with any influence over him.

"If they're in town, we haven't found them. Our contacts at the Hilton did say Nunzio was there but stayed under a different name. What doesn't make sense is that the front desk guy talked about the pretty blonde with him." Lou parked and looked at her. "If he had someone with him, it might or might not be important. But I've got my guys looking anyway. The woman might be an easier way to find out what he's up to."

"This teaches me that, no matter what, don't leave bastards like this around if you can help it. But we don't have time to think about that tonight."

"You sure about this, Boss?" Lou wasn't usually so chatty, but she understood the reason. "The Russians might be a big mouthful to swallow."

"Emma asked me the same thing right before we left. It's true that I'm doing this for my family, but we'd eventually be doing it anyway. Think of it as trimming the oaks in your yard before a storm. These guys won't leave us in peace forever if we ignore them, so we're going to do a little trimming before any major damage occurs." She patted him on the shoulder before she opened her door. "It should make you feel better to know what I'm planning after it's done. While a lot of braggadocios would pat themselves on the back and recount their momentary blaze of glory, I'm not taking any credit for my landscaping skills. Once we do this, we'll put the remains through a wood chipper that in no way will leave a trail to our door."

❖

"What does that mean?" Carol said, gripping the phone so hard her hand hurt.

"The court date for later this month has been cancelled. I wasn't in court when Ross's attorney filed the paperwork, but he withdrew the divorce petition and the judge later agreed." Dennis Parpan was one of five attorneys in Haywood and the only one Carol had found who hadn't done any work for Cain and her extensive new investments up North. "Since we've fought this from the beginning I couldn't object. I know you're angry to learn about it days later, but I couldn't find you. I've been calling every number you provided, and you never got back to me, so I had to go forward without your advice."

"You think Ross and I are going to live happily after this, like in some movie? He's crawled into that demon's house so I'm sure he's up to something. You need to find out what that is because I don't plan to lose again."

Carol hung up and closed her eyes to recite a string of prayers begging God for patience. When the day came for her to be judged, she wanted God to know she'd done everything she could to save Hannah's soul. The rest of them would burn, but it was by their own choice... even the boy. That someone so young could already be so corrupt was beyond her comprehension, but he'd been made in Cain's image and seemed to revel in that truth.

"What's wrong?" Elton Newsome asked when she answered the door.

"I just got some bad news from home, but I prepared myself for this kind of thing when Ross filed to divorce me. I always knew it'd be a fight, but I'm not going to bend or break no matter what they throw at me." She recounted what her attorney had said as she moved around the room, too restless to sit.

"He dismissed the case?" Her newfound friend sat at the edge of the bed and hit his knees with his fists. "That can't happen. You need to get those visitation rights so we can get a reaction out of Casey that'll get us both what we want."

"I know that. But as much as I'd like to, I don't control Ross. Not anymore." She had to think, and she needed to be alone for that. "He's here, so I'm sure he's getting advice from that woman. Ross was always a simple man who can be easily led."

"I've got some ideas so we won't have to wait." He stood up and rocked from foot to foot as if anxious to leave. She should be offended, but he always seemed ready to run off somewhere. "If you hear anything, let me know."

"What about your promise of seeing my granddaughter? I've been here for days and you've never mentioned it." No matter what men like this promised, they were all the same. All of it was pretty words meant to pacify while they got what they wanted. "I'm running out of patience."

"Look, don't do anything stupid that'll mess everything up for both of us. You've been through this before, so you know it takes time." He moved closer as if to intimidate her, but she'd shed her fear long before now. "The last time it failed because the guy in charge was on the take, so you have to trust me."

"Barney Kyle might've been working for the wrong side last time, but at least he had a team backing him up. You can't even get that woman to work with you, so trust isn't a given here."

Elton bent to put his face close to hers. "Listen to me and stay in this room until I say otherwise. I want this as badly as you do, but all we've got going for us is the element of surprise so don't screw that up."

"Get out, and don't come back until you can be more civil." He didn't move so she pushed him hard enough to move him a step back. "I said get out." She didn't breathe again until he gave in and left.

It took some time to stop shaking, but she decided Elton Newsome could no more help her than Barney Kyle could. She needed to make her own plan to get all the things she wanted. The phone her brother had insisted she take was in the room's safe, and she hoped it was still charged.

She waited for the ringing to stop, crossing her fingers that her sister-in-law wouldn't be the one to answer. "Hello." Morris Upton's gruff voice made the salutation sound almost like a curse.

"Morris, it's me." In her opinion, her brother was the only other person on the planet, aside from her and Hannah, who had any decency left. They'd both had the bad luck to marry weak-minded individuals with no idea of what it took to raise the next generation of Uptons like their father had. The senior Upton had beaten their love of the Lord into them from the moment they could put their hands together in prayer, and their education hadn't ended until they'd buried him. She'd tried that same way with Emma at first. But Ross hadn't allowed it. It was one more reason to hate him. The man was not only weak, but weak-minded when he couldn't understand the danger that came from sparing the rod. "Has anyone come by the house?"

"That attorney fella was looking for you, but I didn't tell him anything. It made him mad, but your business is your business." She could hear Morris's wife in the background yelling something. "Shut it. I'm on the phone," he yelled back.

"No one else came by?" She figured what Ross had done was only the beginning of what was coming, so she needed a hint of what that could be. "Ross cancelled everything in court, but I doubt he wants me back."

"Man's a fool, so you're better off with us. Are you sure he wants to cancel the divorce?"

"For now, but you know that's not going to stick. I'm coming back, but not before I see my angel."

"What about the policeman who wanted to help you?"

"He's a fool not even smart enough to realize Casey will gut him when she finds out what he's up to."

"You stay safe, and call me more often. You know I worry."

"I will, I promise. But I have to make sure Hannah's okay. After all this time, I'm willing to almost kill to make that happen."

"Just get back here, and we'll find an answer together."

"The answer is to beat the devil at her own game."

CHAPTER TWELVE

After greeting Finley, Cain got everything in position for their guests. For the moment, Finley would stand among her and Remi's guards so she could observe. Cain had no idea who the players were, but Finley had at least half the equation. At least, she hoped she had half the information, because if someone other than who they anticipated showed up, this charade would have to continue.

"No matter what, you stay over there and don't say a word," she said to Finley as a car approached the building.

"Boss, we're ready," Lou said after finishing a call. There were some tense moments as Lou and the others disarmed the muscle their guests had brought with them.

"I thought you offered your friendship?" Yury—at least that's who she guessed he was—scowled at her.

"I start most friendships with as little weaponry as possible. If you object, then you can leave." She pointed to the door with a smile. "In my house, we follow my rules."

Yury nodded, then, as if he owned the place, waved her over to the chairs that had been set out. The woman with him sat like a trained seal.

"I'm Cain Casey," she held her hand out, "and this is my friend Remi Jatibon. Remi's my business associate as well, and she's here to help."

"Yury Antakov," he said, accepting her handshake. "This is my wife, Valerie."

"I'm sure you've got plenty on your mind, so what can I do for you?" Cain asked as they all sat.

"I am sure the most important thing in your life is your children," Yury said, his head slightly tilted, giving him an air of sincerity. "Am I right?"

"My children, my wife, my entire family. Yes. I'd think anyone with an ounce of honor would feel the same way. Does this have something to do with your family?" She wanted to get to the point before the night was done.

"My daughter Nicola, like you, married a woman she loved. They had three children. At Nicola's passing, this woman cut us from their lives." Valerie only nodded as Yury spoke.

"Do you mean Nicola Eaton? I met her a few times but never had the pleasure of getting to know her well."

"I thought it best to change the name once our business was established, but the Antakov name still demands respect on the street. I am sure you understand that as well. My daughter-in-law, Abigail, does not. My wife cries for wanting these children in our lives, and this woman spits in her face."

Cain nodded, glancing briefly at Finley. Her cousin appeared ready to strangle Yury and Valerie simultaneously, since her shoulders seemed tight, her fists were clenched, and her mouth was set in a thin, grim line. "What reason does she give?"

"I don't like talking about it," Valerie said, her impatient tone belying her role as the wounded grandmother.

Yury lifted his hands, palm up, and gave her another altar-boy head tilt. "My daughter's children have a right to grow up with the knowledge of who they are."

"This woman, Abigail, doesn't want that?" Remi asked.

The viper in Valerie broke its restraints. "Abigail was Nicola's mistake, and she's too weak to raise Antakov heirs. We need them back, and my husband's giving you an opportunity for easy money if you help us," Valerie said, her eyes only on Cain.

"I'll help, but I'll do it from friendship. You won't owe me anything," Cain said. Yury was cold-blooded, but nowhere close to his wife's league. If their relationship was supposed to be a balance, the scale of cruelty tipped more toward Valerie. Cain took down their contact information and escorted them out.

"You'll help them for friendship? Are you fucking kidding me?" Finley vented because she'd let them leave, and Cain thought it was a hell of a time for her Casey genes or nature to come out of hibernation. "Those animals want Abigail dead and want to raise her children to become pimps. They make a lot of goddamn money doing what they do, but that's all they are. No expensive suit or impeccable manners are going to cover up the smell of shit on them."

"Stick with what you know," Cain said, holding her hand up to forestall Finley's anger. "You understand what has to happen. I couldn't let that take place here. They need to be seen somewhere else so this doesn't come back to us. Think about the ramifications. These kinds of people don't work in a vacuum."

The reality of who these people were dawned in Finley's eyes as she stared at Cain. This was real and very scary. Finley couldn't hide behind the computer screen Cain knew was her normal job. "They'll never stop coming after Abigail, will they?" Finley's fire seemed to dampen in the cold reality of what she faced.

"No. Not even if you have enough to put them away for life." Cain couldn't sugarcoat the truth or take a lot of time to decide the logical next step. That pained her because that type of decision changed your life and, in Finley's case, would perhaps prevent her from going back to the job she loved.

Forty minutes later, Finley seemed at peace with the only real choice that would keep her new family safe.

"Are you sure?" Cain asked one last time, since Finley had been quiet for the entire ride into the city. Finley nodded, so she reached in the backseat for what she'd brought with her.

"Yes, and that's why you don't have to stay," Finley said as she accepted the tommy gun that had belonged to Cain's father. They were parked not far from the building that housed the Hell Fire Club, waiting for Yury and Valarie.

"It was Da's. It's unregistered, and when you're done, it'll go back into mothballs. I just thought if you wanted to be sure, this'll guarantee it."

She saw the car with Remi and her people pull away, getting in front of the Antakovs' vehicle, so she followed and lowered the passenger-side window. Yury and Valerie turned toward them as every member of their protection went down from the hail of bullets from Remi's vehicle. If Finley froze, Lou and Katlin were right behind them, but that didn't happen. Finley opened fire, hitting both her targets repeatedly.

Cain drove calmly away, leaving their targets where they landed, and kept going until they reached the spot Lou had scoped out for this. Once they were out of their vehicles, Lou and the others scrubbed them down before they torched them. Finley seemed okay, but it'd take a few days for the shock to set in. Maybe by then she'd be ready for the new life that awaited her back with Abigail and her family.

"I owe you, Cain," Finley said as she embraced her.

"You're my family, so we'll never have debts between us—never."

❖

The quality of the gate kept the numerous agents Joe had brought outside until he threatened to blow the hell out of it. He shoved the warrant through the wrought iron, almost slapping the guy on the other side in the face with it. "Open it now, or I'm cuffing you as soon as I open this gate with a grenade. Then I'm going to bulldoze the front door so you can explain it to your boss."

Of all the things that bothered Joe the most about this job, it was the smug smiles all these wise guys wore. The guy still stared at him, moving only after his phone rang. He listened for a moment, then pressed a button and the gate unlocked. Joe needed to get inside before Cain could make it home in time to establish an alibi.

The goose chase had ended in a gunfight downtown that had left eight people dead in front of some building that mostly held oil-field companies. Joe and the others concluded that Cain had somehow shaken her surveillance, then killed a bunch of people for whatever reason. He'd moved fast as soon as the call came in, wanting to be in place when she came slinking back with some flip response as to where she'd been.

"Joe, I've got your back but go easy. If she feels cornered, this might end badly," Shelby said, glancing at her phone every so often. "Let's see who exactly this hit took out."

"Cain isn't going to rush out guns blazing with her family in there. I came prepared this time and got a warrant ahead of time." He gestured for the other agents to circle the house. "Get out back and cover all the doors."

He unholstered his weapon and moved to the house but stopped short when the door opened. The older woman who appeared in the doorway wrung her hands in distress, so he slowed, his gun pointed at the ground.

"Can I help you?" the woman asked.

He flashed his credentials, hoping the large letters of FBI would get her out of the doorway. "Please step aside, ma'am. We have a warrant to search this house."

The woman hesitated but stepped back to let him pass.

"Try the office first," Shelby said, pointing to the hall at the other end of the foyer.

"Can I ask what you're looking for, or is it a secret?" The voice at the top of the stairs made Joe spin around, and he had to fight his instinct to lift his gun. "You've got a warrant, but I still have a right to know what you're here for."

"We're searching for evidence from an altercation tonight," Shelby said, moving in front of Joe.

"I don't know if it was you two, but someone followed me when I came home." Cain came down in a robe and bare feet. "Did someone get in a fight in my yard?"

"This dumb act on your part is getting old," he said, holstering his weapon. He'd never seen Cain dressed so casually, and he was irritated that it made him uncomfortable. "You'll need to come in and answer some questions about tonight. This can go easy, or it can go otherwise."

"I'm familiar with the otherwise." Cain spoke softly, her expression giving away nothing. She seemed to be looking behind him so he couldn't help but glance back. The young agent appeared almost fearful, judging by his pained expression, and he remembered this was the kid who'd delivered the envelope from Cain to Annabel. "You got me out of bed, and my attorney will be here shortly so I'm not going anywhere. My wife's expecting, and since you waste your days watching me, you should know that."

"If I want you to come in, you're coming in," he said. For once, this was in his power to do. "I'm not sure how you beat me back here, but we both know you're responsible."

"I don't need to put special in front of any title I might have, *Special Agent* Joe, to know that if you have or have ever had proof, you wouldn't need to ask questions. Questions are like worms. They're bait that you cast out and wiggle to make themselves enticing. But I'm not your ordinary stupid fish." She moved away from them to the closest room at the front of the house. At the living room's center was a small table with two dolls sitting around it. Judging from the china tea set, Hannah liked to play here. Cain sat on the sofa. "What did I do now?"

"Any bait-wiggling will happen downtown." Joe ignored her gesture inviting them to also sit.

"Actually, my client has been home all night," Muriel said as she entered and sat next to Cain. "After a meeting earlier tonight, Cain returned here, and the others went their separate ways. Those associates are still out celebrating a few things talked about at that meeting, so unless a quiet night at home and a few beers with friends have become a crime, my client's not going anywhere."

"We've got a lot of people dead on the street, Counselor. As you should've learned on the first day of law school, that's a crime."

"Joe," Shelby said, "give me a minute outside."

He pointed at Cain. "Don't move."

"I wouldn't dream of it," Cain said.

Her smile infuriated him, and he jabbed his finger in the air to punctuate his words. "These people who were killed are the type that won't be forgotten. Local and federal law enforcement will be under pressure to solve this case, so it won't go easy for you. Think about that."

"Listen—" Shelby said once they were in the yard.

"We need to start looking for a connection between the Eatons and Casey." He talked over her, but Shelby kept her tone even.

"We need to get back to the office, so take a breath and calm down. The Eatons aren't what they seem, and our office is raiding a place called the Hell Fire Club right now. Agent Hicks said a group from the New York bureau is here with information about all this. Tonight might be a gang war, but it's got nothing to do with Cain."

"What do you mean, the Eatons aren't what they seem?" He rubbed his forehead even though his neck hurt. If he'd jumped the gun, Cain would throw his attitude back at him a hundredfold.

"The agent from New York has some extensive files for us to go through. I doubt we'll be the ones to investigate the case, but Hicks wants us to be sure." She stared at the house and cleared her throat.

Joe turned and exhaled when he saw Cain walking toward them.

"Are we done? I love when you guys visit as much as a root canal, but I need to get back upstairs."

"We're done for now." Joe hated admitting that. "But don't leave town."

"I guess I'll have to cancel my trip to Transylvania for my fang-sharpening visit," Cain said. Her smile held no humor and her eyes turned cold. "Next time you feel like fishing, Special Agent Joe, pick another pond. Not all bad roads lead to my door." The yard filled with a lot of big guys as Cain returned to the house. They obviously were to be their escort out.

Joe knew he'd blown any future opportunity to get back inside the Casey gates. Muriel would make it much harder to get another warrant. "You really think she wasn't involved?"

"I can't read her mind, but Cain doesn't exploit women, and that's what this is about," Shelby said. "Cain concentrates more on exploiting the government and guys like us."

"Her luck can't last forever," he said, waving all their people out.

"I wouldn't take that bet," Shelby said. She looked up and found Cain staring at them from the upstairs windows. "Whatever we may think of her, she seems to be blessed with an abundance of luck."

"Maybe we should ask her to share."

CHAPTER THIRTEEN

Another week went by, and the Hell Fire Club story died away since the media seemed more interested in the bizarre deaths being investigated by Detective Sept Savoie. It was good for business since the police seemed obsessed with trying to calm the serial-killer hysteria spreading through the city. Hector was back from Colombia but still no closer to finding an answer to who had hit him both here and at home.

Pressure was building to solve this mystery, since failing to fulfill orders would start a war, and wars took money to survive. He'd been through a number of them, using the chaos to climb higher up the cartel. But he'd known every player during those fights. Fighting blind was the fastest way to lose.

"You didn't find any clues in the fields?" Tracy spoke in Spanish.

"The damn place was burnt to the ground. My farmers said a plane came by and sprayed something, and then a number of explosions took care of the rest. Whatever they sprayed has ruined the ground, so it'll be months before I can start planting again."

The condo in the French Quarter he'd leased for Tracy was quiet, but the light from the street illuminated her skin as he observed from the window before joining her in bed. Tracy had been an even better asset than he'd first imagined, though Marisol didn't want to accept that fact yet. He ran his hand from her thigh up to her breast, but he couldn't stop looking at her face.

"I've got everyone on the street offering a reward, but so far nothing." She didn't move when he gently touched the side of her nose that was bruised and still a bit swollen. "Marisol didn't care for my idea of reaching out to see if anyone else is having this kind of problem."

"Why didn't you call me when this happened?"

"That would've been like admitting I couldn't handle it. I understand that Marisol doesn't like me, but I don't want this to become an everyday kind of thing." She reached down and wrapped her hand around his penis. "Maybe you can set some ground rules."

"Worry about this right now." He moved to lie on his back. "I'll take care of the rest." She straddled him without letting go. He'd been with so many women, but not many truly loved to fuck more than Tracy did.

He came hard and way too fast but didn't have time to enjoy anything else before his phone rang. "I said no calls," he said when he answered it.

"Señor Hector." Gilberto Medio was his new guard. "I know you didn't want to be disturbed, but someone just arrived at the house, and Marisol wanted to warn you."

"Tell me already." He felt another twinge of desire as Tracy took him in her mouth.

"Señora Raquel is here to see you."

"My wife's in New Orleans? Why?" He ran his fingers through Tracy's hair. "Never mind. She's going to have to wait."

When they were done, Tracy was skeptical, but she dressed and accompanied him to his house. Raquel Delarosa was a beautiful woman, but she didn't get up and greet Hector when they arrived. She glanced between Hector and Tracy. Marisol obviously had spent some time filling her mother in on some things.

"Hector, if you want I'll wait in the office," Tracy offered. She twitched her fingers when Marisol smiled.

"Sit down," Hector said as he moved closer to Marisol. The smirk disappeared from his daughter's face when his fist landed perfectly against her nose. Tracy grimaced at the spray of blood and slightly shook her head, knowing a relationship with Marisol would be impossible now.

"Hector," Raquel screamed when he drew his hand back again.

"Shut up." He turned so fast that Raquel sat back down with an expression of fear that Tracy interpreted as someone expecting to be hit, and hit hard. "It's time everyone in this house remembers who gives the orders."

"Papa," Marisol said, her voice muffled by her hands pressed to her face. "I did what you asked, but that bitch disrespected me."

"She disrespected you by trying to make you think?"

Marisol screamed as Hector hit her again, landing a blow to her mouth. She covered her head to protect herself.

"You wouldn't have let anyone speak to you like that," Marisol said from her knees.

"Stop talking before I send you home to replant my fields all alone." Hector stretched his hands as if the two brutal blows had stung. "I talked to Julio as well and threatened to blow his balls off if he lied to me, but he was smart enough to know who he worked for."

"Hector, por favor." Raquel pleaded with him but didn't move from where she sat. "She made a mistake, just like you did coming up. It's not worth losing teeth over."

"Everybody out." Hector grabbed Marisol by the hair before she could get up. "Let me warn you about something. I don't give a shit about your ego or how humiliated you feel. If something happens to Tracy, I'll blame only you, so you better start praying she has a long and happy life."

"I'm your heir. No one's going to care about you more than me." Marisol held onto his pants leg. Her tears had mixed with the blood and mucus from her nose, so Tracy glanced away to not embarrass her any more than Hector had already.

"Do you understand me? Do both of you understand me?" His words squeezed through his clenched teeth, and Marisol simply nodded.

Tracy made eye contact with Raquel and almost laughed at the way the woman was glaring at her. One more Delarosa woman that hated her wasn't the end of the world unless they somehow got to Hector. If he turned against her, she'd pray that what he'd done to Marisol would be the extent of her punishment.

"Both of you get out of my sight," Hector said, walking away from Marisol. "And next time, Mari, try not to act like a weak bitch. Julio told me Tracy took it without a tear, so try to learn a lesson from that. Never show your weakness."

Tracy guessed the insult was too much, since Marisol ran from the room sobbing. "She'll try to kill me after that," she said as Hector caressed her cheek. "Her mother certainly appears ready to."

"I don't think you'll kill that easy." He moved his fingers to lift her chin. "And Raquel isn't Marisol's mother. My daughter had a much more colorful start than that." He laughed as he led her to the leather couch in his office. "No, her mother died in a whorehouse since she couldn't control herself around men. The only good thing the bitch ever did while she was with me was give me Marisol. Even my sons don't remind me so much of myself, but I can't let her run wild. Whatever business I leave her will be gone in a month if she doesn't start thinking."

"I'll try never to disappoint you."

"Then it's been a successful day so far."

The next morning Special Agent Russell Welsh gathered all his files from the office Annabel Hicks had lent him and shoved them into the boxes the New Orleans office would be sharing with Miami. That was his next stop after the Hell Fire Club had been dismantled here and closed in Florida. The Miami bureau wanted to go in, but he wanted his own people in there. They deserved it after the months of investigations they'd put in.

The only thing left to do was meet with Finley and get her back on the case. Abigail and her family should be okay going forward, and Annabel also had promised to keep an eye on them. Finley had been sifting through all the information they'd found at the club but hadn't joined him here. All of her intel had been spot-on though, so he hadn't forced the issue.

"You all set?" Annabel asked as a crew came in to collect his stuff.

"Miami's waiting, but I'll swing back around if you find anything else." He shouldered his bag and signed the papers on the clipboard one of the guys handed him. "We're still searching the ledgers we found in a warehouse this Eaton guy owned in New York, so there might be more to investigate here."

"I have to thank you," Annabel led him to her office. "The Hell Fire Club was on no one's radar, so you helped us maybe stop another mob family from taking root in the city. We've got enough to keep up with."

"If we find anything helpful—you'll be my first call." He held out his hand, ready to go. "I have a meeting before my flight. We'll talk soon."

The place Finley picked wasn't far from the bureau office so he walked, amazed how empty the streets were in a city the size of New Orleans. He found the restaurant and smiled when he saw his best agent. The place wasn't crowded, which would keep their conversation private.

"Did the president put you in charge of the bureau yet?" Finley asked when he sat.

"You know it, since you refuse to take any credit," he said and laughed. "Are you ready and packed? I need you on this."

Finley looked at him and shook her head. "My gut says to turn in my resignation, but I know you wouldn't take it, so I put in for a leave of absence."

"Why the hell are you doing that?"

Russell's volume caused the people closest to them to glance their way.

"I've been about the job all this time because there was nothing else, but now I want to explore something outside the chase."

"The lady got to you that bad?" He smiled. "You can date and work, Finley. They're not a one-at-a-time kind of thing."

"I know, but Abigail's family and life are here. I'm not ready to leave, and I gave you everything you need to finish this." She handed over another external hard drive with all the information she'd found on her own and with Cain's help. "Give me a month or so and we'll talk again."

"Nothing I can say will change your mind?"

"Thanks for everything, Russell. You've been a great teacher, but this case cut deep. Yury and his family destroyed so many people, and I'm tired of thinking about it. I want the chance to help the most innocent of his victims heal."

"Take care of yourself, kid, and in a month I'll be happy to welcome you back. I figure you'll get restless soon enough."

They ate, and Finley drove her boss to the airport by the lake where the FBI plane was waiting. "What are you wearing?" she asked into the phone as she waved to Russell one last time.

"Could be earrings and a smile, and you're nowhere to be found," Dr. Abigail Eaton said, and laughed when children's screams erupted behind her. "But as you can tell, you're not that lucky. Will you be back soon?"

"One more meeting, and then we'll take the three wild things out for some fun. They deserve it after being cooped up for so long." She smiled in anticipation of time with her new ready-made family. Still, she carefully studied every aspect of the parking lot as she went back outside while still holding the phone to her ear. No one in Yury's organization probably knew she was alive or existed, but this wasn't the time to get sloppy.

"This meeting—" Abigail hesitated as though she didn't know exactly what to ask.

"If it works out, it'll keep us here close to family."

"Mine and yours?"

"Yes, but we'll talk about mine later, if that's okay?" The place was fairly busy, but three cars pulled out with her. Maybe someone was interested. She looked around for the quickest way to figure out if that was true. "I won't be long, so keep the sofa warm for me."

The gas station coming up meant crossing traffic, but that was a good start. She took the left and only one car followed, so once he'd committed to a pump she backed up and photographed the license plate. The other cars had kept going in the direction she'd been headed. She took the opportunity to slip into a neighborhood close by and hoped, at least for now, she'd lost anybody tailing her.

She headed back to the city after taking a circuitous route, at Cain's request. She knew it had nothing to do with Cain, but Cain trying to protect her. The gesture helped soothe the acid that had built in her stomach since she'd gunned down Abigail's in-laws. It wasn't exactly guilt since she'd do it again, given the threat both Yury and Valerie posed to Abigail and her family, but taking life like that did change you.

The parking lot of the Canal Place Shopping Center was more crowded than she anticipated, so she had to go all the way to the roof. Katlin was waiting not too far away, and Finley climbed into the backseat of the vehicle Katlin pointed out. She'd never been to the house Cain had purchased after the death of her Uncle Dalton that followed losing both her parents and two siblings. She thanked God that Cain had found happiness after that stack of tragedies.

"You doing okay, Fin?" Katlin asked. She started out of the lot, taking her time. The windows were so tinted nobody would see her.

"A few antacids should fix what ails me." She glanced back when they were on Canal Street but saw only regular traffic. "Thanks for finding all you did on those bastards so fast."

"You can thank my secret weapon later." Katlin laughed and turned to go uptown. "Merrick is as good at uncovering stuff as she is beautiful."

"There's a woman alive that tamed you?"

Katlin laughed again. "From what I hear, we've all been snared, so no ribbing me."

Not much later the gates opened and Katlin pulled into the large garage out back. The entrance into the house was through the kitchen, and she stopped to admire the two children sitting at the table in front of the large bay window. They couldn't deny their lineage. They were Caseys, judging from their dark hair and brilliantly beautiful blue eyes that held an intensity not often seen in children.

"Hey, guys," Katlin said. "This is your cousin Finley."

Hayden stood and hugged her, followed quickly by Hannah. "Your mom was right when she said you're a good-looking lot."

"The word of a Casey's always good," Cain said. When Finley turned toward her, Cain embraced her in a bear hug.

The room cleared out when Finley began to cry.

Cain held her tighter. "You're okay now, Finley. I promise you."

"I'm sorry," she said, finally catching her breath.

"What happened is nothing to be sorry about," Cain said as she held her. "But I am sorry if it's too heavy a burden to bear. I'm here for you no matter what, but maybe it's time to take a break and go see your parents. They'll help you put those sore spots to rest because they love you."

"I am planning to take a break, and I'm pretty sure it's going to be permanent. I thought maybe I'll stay home for now and keep Abigail and the kids with me. If it works out, I'll have to look for a bigger place, but there's worse problems to have."

Cain walked to a large sunroom and offered her a seat. "You talked about that lot and house for months when you bought it, so I know how much you love it and the location."

She nodded as she peered out the windows. "I didn't think I'd have all this so I built it to be comfortable for me, and maybe weekend guests like my parents. If I take your advice, the house will be the least of it."

"Can you do me a favor?" Cain leaned forward and placed her hand on Finley's knee.

"Sure. I owe you quite a few after all this."

"We have no debts between us, Finley. My favor has more to do with your time off."

Finley glanced over Cain's shoulder and smiled at the very pregnant blonde holding onto Lou's arm and headed toward them. "Let me take care of you while you take some time to reorder your life."

"I'd like that, and it might be a good time to reconnect with my family—all of my family. You knew all the choices I've made had nothing to do with the family business, right?"

Cain stood and helped her wife to the sofa, putting pillows behind her back. "Finley, I love you. Your job choices never have or will change that. I was proud of the work you were doing and the results you got."

"Thanks, but I'd like an introduction now."

"Emma, this is the black sheep of our clan, Finley Abbott," she said, making Finley laugh. "Finley, my wife Emma."

"Welcome, Finley," Emma said, leaning heavily against Cain. "Cain has told me about you, but also about Abigail and her children. I was hoping to meet them as well. It's short notice, but I thought you all could join us for dinner tonight."

"They'd probably love it after all the confinement I've subjected them to."

"That's a good idea," Cain said. "I want you to start getting used to being here. I've missed you, and you did mention the family business."

"Can we talk about that? I want to stay here, and I need to untangle myself from my current job."

"You'll have a place with us, but my friends outside don't have to know. Call your girl and tell her to pack and we'll have someone pick her up. The particulars about everything else can wait."

"Are you sure? I don't want you to believe it's something I'm not really interested in." She hoped Abigail would be okay with all this.

"I see you need to learn the same lessons Muriel did. Patience, cousin. You'll be fine because you're our family."

CHAPTER FOURTEEN

Emma led Abigail into the kitchen an hour after she arrived with her children and tried to ignore the nagging backache that was giving her a headache as well. She was happy that Abigail had lost her shyness when Hannah stole the hearts of her youngest children, Victoria and Liam, since it seemed like they'd forged a friendship Emma was sure would last a lifetime.

Emma pointed to the counter where Carmen, with the help of her father, had set out dinner. She pressed her fingers to her temple, hoping the pain would subside. "Carmen, would you please call up and have all the kids come down? Maybe between Hayden and Sadie they can take control of the hyped-up trio I hear running around up there," she said. The request was barely out of her mouth when a spear of pain hit her. Abigail and Carmen came to her side and placed their arms around her waist as she grimaced and held onto the counter.

"How about you sit for me first," Abigail said, glancing at Carmen since Ross had glued himself to Emma's side. "Could you go get Cain, please?"

"I'm okay, really. It's just this load is giving me fits. The end can't come soon enough, but I'm still a few weeks out." Sitting was making her nauseous, and all she wanted to do was lie down.

"I could be wrong, but I think you're about to get your wish. The date shouldn't worry you. If the baby's ready, it's ready." Abigail placed her hands on Emma's abdomen and pressed in a few spots. "Then we'll have something in common."

"Stretch marks?" she said, and they both laughed.

"There's that, yes. But we'll also have three kids each." Abigail turned as they both heard someone running toward them.

"What's wrong?" Cain, out of breath, knelt next to Emma.

"Nothing, but Abigail thinks we might have a ride to the hospital in our future." She ran her fingers through Cain's hair to comb it off her forehead. "Let's call Ellie and Sam to see if they want us around."

"Let me take care of that," Abigail said. "Those two are good for my business, so you go somewhere and try to get comfortable."

"Thanks, Abigail, and sorry if this ruins our dinner plans."

"As if you need to worry about that." Abigail helped Cain get Emma on her feet. "You concentrate on not having any complications, and Finley and I'll take care of everyone else. She needs the training."

Cain and Ross led Emma to the sunroom and made her comfortable on the sofa, but her nagging back pain wasn't easing up. Cain looked worried, and her father was in the same state. "Relax, mobster. It's going to be a while yet," she said as she gripped Cain's hand.

"All that matters now is that you listen to what Abigail said about no complications." Cain lowered her head and kissed her, then her midsection. "So take your time, both of you."

The gesture made her bite her lip to hold back the sob wanting to escape. She didn't have enough words to describe how much she'd missed Cain at Hannah's birth. All those hours of misery, followed by years of isolation and abuse from her mother for every bit of her Carol found lacking, had left scars on her soul that still ached. She was grateful when Ross left them alone for the moment.

"Lass," Cain said softly.

When Emma looked up, her tears started to fall.

"You need to bury all of that," she said as she wiped Emma's face with her thumbs.

"How'd you know?"

Cain smiled, and Emma was shocked to see Cain's face wet with her own tears. "Because you're mine, lassie. You're mine so I know your heart like you know my own. Those memories we wish we could change are only as important as we make them. Our little girl will only remember how loved she is now, not where she started, so give this one a happy beginning."

"You are my life," she said, crying harder when Cain held her tight against her.

"The luck of my ancestors is still with me then," Cain said as she kissed her temple. "I've lost my heart to only one woman, but it's a good thing since you've taken such good care of it."

"If you two are done with the mush, it's time to go," Finley said from the door. "Abigail and I are going to stay here with the kids, so don't worry about anything."

"Thanks, Finley, but if you have to leave, they'll be in good hands," she said, not wanting to let Cain go.

"If I tell Victoria and Liam we have to leave their new buddy Hannah, I'd fear for my life. Lou's waiting, so get going. Once you're out the door I can start drinking your whiskey and raiding your refrigerator."

"Thanks, cousin," Cain said, kissing Emma again.

"It's nice to do for family again, so maybe I should thank you. Do you want Abigail to go with you two?"

"Stay and have dinner. Remembering our childhood, it might be good to have a doctor in the family. If she has to put stitches in anyone, don't tell me until I come back," Cain said with a laugh.

Emma laughed as well, and despite her discomfort, she was happy. "I'm glad you're here, Finley, and even gladder you're staying in town."

"Thank you for being so welcoming of Abigail and her kids. They've been through so much."

"They're not alone any more, and it makes me happy that they'll have cousins around to make memories with. We just met, but Cain's told me about growing up with all of you so close. We're lucky to watch that happen in the next generation."

"You're a lucky woman, Cain," Finley said, placing her hand on Cain's back.

"You know it. Could you get Ross back in here? I'm sure he's going to want to come with us," Cain said as she gazed at Emma. "You ready, my love?"

"For this and whatever comes next."

"You do realize you threw me out, right?" Nicolette asked as she sat at the desk in her new French Quarter apartment. She'd barely glanced at Marisol since she'd walked in, her face bruised and swollen. Something had happened, but her curiosity wasn't strong enough that she'd demean herself to ask. "I haven't heard from you since some guy that works for you escorted me to the door."

"If your father had called, you'd have ignored him?" Marisol dropped into the only other chair beside her. "All that talk was just crap, wasn't it?"

"I came to you and offered my friendship and so much more." She put her pen down and stared at the deep cut across Marisol's lips. The wound looked like it would reopen if Marisol smiled too widely, and her off-center nose was hard to ignore. Whoever had hit her had definitely broken and pushed it to the left. "You repaid that by throwing me out like some whore who'd finished serving you."

"My father's business was in trouble. Try to understand that. We were attacked and I needed to get answers. It had nothing to do with what we talked about." Marisol's voice rose, anger flaring across her abused face.

The bruises didn't make sense, but she could guess now who'd put them there. If she was right, she and her father could exploit this opening. It was time to show a little mercy. "I'm sorry." Nicolette stood and walked to the kitchen for a wet towel. "You're right. I would've done the same thing." She pressed the towel gently to Marisol's top lip where it had started to bleed. "Are you going to tell me what happened?"

Marisol appeared reluctant at first, then started talking. She surprisingly included all the details of her family's dispute that ended with Hector beating his heir apparent bloody. "That bitch is going to pay, and my father will just have to accept it."

Whoever this Tracy Stegal was, the woman had replaced Cain Casey on Marisol's list of people who needed killing. That Hector had forbidden her from any type of retaliation was obviously making Marisol crazy, so it was important not to push too hard right now. "He hit you for defending your honor? I would think a man like your father raised you to not take abuse or disrespect from anyone."

"He did, and he would've never allowed anyone to speak to him like that. This is all because that bitch is spreading her legs for him, and she complained the minute he got back. He's my father and I love him, but the man can't function when some fucking idiot is sucking his dick." Marisol flinched when she finished her rant, and the bleeding got worse.

"Come on." Nicolette held her hand out to Marisol and waved her people away for the night. "You need to stop talking and rest."

They moved to the partially furnished master bedroom. The decorators were filling in as her things arrived from France, but the king-sized bed she'd bought here was all she needed. She handed Marisol the towel and slowly undressed her, making sure to caress every part of the unblemished body she uncovered.

"Let me fuck you," she said when Marisol stood with her legs spread open. She was wet and hard. Perhaps Marisol had more in common with Hector than she might want to own up to. "Sit." Marisol grabbed her by the hair when she knelt between her legs, but Nicolette persisted. "Let me take care of you."

Marisol gave in, and Nicolette did her best to make her feel good. Once Marisol was satisfied, she lay back in the bed, and Nicolette took the opportunity to start closing her trap. "Are you going to trust me to help you?"

After a pause Marisol opened her eyes. "Help me how?"

"I keep telling you that you and I will be great partners. We have the same interests, the same enemies, and the same ambitions. If you let me take care of a few things for you, we'll be free to take control of this city."

Marisol sat up a little on her elbows and stared at her. "What ideas do you have in that pretty head?"

She smiled and ran her hands up Marisol's legs. "Nothing that anyone involved will ever see coming, so leave it to me."

❖

"Do you want or need anything?" Cain asked.

Emma took a deep breath. The pain had grown progressively worse, and she felt rather idiotic for not realizing sooner that she was beginning labor. Cain was about to crawl out of her skin with restlessness, and it was making Emma nuts. She'd already sent her father to the waiting area to try to relax since the two of them together were too much.

"Baby, I love you, but you've got to calm down." She held her hand out and laughed at how quickly Cain took it. "Do you know something?"

"That I'm about the happiest person alive right now?" Cain leaned over the bed, thankfully not shaking it, and kissed her.

"There's that, but that's not what I was thinking about. You are the love of my life, and I'm glad you've been the only one in it. I'll try for many lifetimes to repay you for all the happiness you've given me, but I think I'll fall short." She picked Cain's hand up and placed it on her abdomen. "This baby, our family, and you are my greatest gifts." She finished as the first strong contraction began. "Shit," she said loudly once it was done.

"That's a good way to punctuate all that, my love," Cain said with a smile. "And in case you're curious, I feel the same way."

"Are you in the mood to change diapers?" Dr. Sam Casey said as she let her partner come in first. "Because I think your slacking time is up."

"Who are you calling a slacker?" Cain pointed her finger at Sam and tried to appear menacing, but Emma saw through her façade. Sam and Ellie had been good friends as well as her OB/GYNs for years. Cain had always told Sam she put up with her because of her blessed last name.

"Now that the children are finished poking at each other, how are you feeling, Emma?" Ellie Eschete asked. Ellie and Sam were more than partners in business and had a baby together.

"The contractions are starting but my water hasn't—" The sensation was like the first two times, unpleasant and wet. She grimaced as she soaked the bed. "Just once I'd like to be somewhere near a bathroom when that happens."

"Sam's right," Ellie said as she pushed the nurse call button. "I hope you two are ready and don't have plans for tonight. You either ignored the signs all day or this one is in a hurry to get here, so try to relax. Do you want an epidural?"

"Let's wait. If he's in a hurry, I'm not going to slow him down."

"I'm not confirming that you're right, but did you peek during one of those ultrasounds?" Sam asked.

"Just a hunch so don't ruin the surprise for me if all my scientific guessing is wrong."

"Can you guys unhook all this stuff for a minute and I'll clean her up," Cain said.

"It's okay, love. The nurses will do it."

Cain kissed the top of her head and then her lips. "I could do it or pace, so I'd rather take care of you. I don't mind."

It didn't take long to change her and the bed. Emma grabbed the railing when her contraction hit since Cain had gone to change into the scrubs they'd brought her. She was breathing deeply, on the downside of the contraction, when the phone rang. She answered it, glad for the distraction. "Hello."

"Hey, Mama." Hayden sounded so cheerful, she could imagine the size of his smile. "You doing okay?"

"I'm doing great." She massaged the side of her abdomen as the pain briefly subsided. "Are you ready to be a big brother again?"

"You think it'll be today?"

"The doctors are fairly sure either today or early tomorrow. Depends on how stubborn this one is. If they're anything like you and your sister, we might need a crowbar to get them out."

"Really? I don't think you or Mom ever told me that story."

"Do you want to hear it now?" she said and clicked her teeth together as another contraction started. She was caught off-guard by how close together they suddenly were. "Just…give me…goddamn."

"Are you sure you're okay? You sound like you're in a lot of pain." He sounded anxious now, like Cain when she was worried about her. His concern made her smile through the pain. Receiving her son's forgiveness and regaining his love had been one of the greatest accomplishment of her life so far.

"Hey, son." Cain returned, taking the phone from her. "Your mama's fine. The cursing is simply a side effect of pregnancy, so how about we call you in a little while?"

"Can I come? I promise not to be in the way."

The phone was close enough that Emma could hear, and she nodded.

"Sure. Have Mook bring you over, and maybe you can take my place holding your mama's hand for a while. I'll tell you that story about your birth while she's busy insulting me," she said and laughed. Cain took Emma's hand after ending the call. "Thanks for agreeing to that, lass. I think he gets more like me every day, especially when it comes to worrying about you, so being stuck at home would've driven him crazy."

"Baby, could you get the nurse for me, please? These contractions are coming way too fast." The one that started while she'd been talking to Hayden had finally eased up, so she took some more deep breaths, lay back, and tried not to freak out.

Ellie reappeared after Cain pressed the call button and examined her. "The first one is murder because it takes so freaking long," Ellie said when she glanced up at them. "At least in my experience it seemed like days, but the second one is easier, even if not everyone agrees. The third one, though, seems to fly by in comparison, my patients tell me, so you'll have to confirm it for me when we're done, Emma. We'll be ready to push soon, so do you mind me hanging out with you for a bit?"

Hayden arrived not long after and led Ross back into the room. Their son stared at her with wide eyes as the contractions came and subsided for another hour. She smiled at him as he wiped her forehead with a wet cloth and said a silent prayer the new baby would have as good a heart as both Hayden and Hannah.

When Ellie checked again, she confirmed that it was time.

"Hayden and Ross, how about you go wait for a few minutes with your mom's guys. I promise we'll come get you as soon as we're done," Ellie said.

"I love you, Mama," he said and kissed the back of her hand. "Please be all right, okay?"

"I'll be fine, and I love you too." Emma was sorry to see him go, but she didn't want to traumatize him.

Ellie lifted Emma's feet into the stirrups as soon as the door closed and looked to her, then Cain. "You guys ready? It's time to push." The door opened again, and Sam came in with another stool so she could sit close to Ellie.

"I'm ready," she said, her eyes on Cain. "Thank you for this," she said as Cain kissed her. "I thought I should mention it before the pain takes over and I say something that might make you think otherwise."

"You let those curses fly, lass. I'm dying to meet this little one so I'll develop a thick skin."

She started pushing when Ellie commanded her to do so, and she gripped Cain's hands so hard she expected to hear bones breaking, but Cain never complained. She had taken over Hayden's job and mopped Emma's forehead as the exertion made her sweat.

"Come on, Emma," Sam said after another hour. "Give me another one and bear down hard."

She clenched her teeth and pushed as hard as she could, but she was getting tired. A little movement from the baby made her scream and she pushed again, not caring if Sam or Ellie weren't ready. "Shit," she said when she lay back down.

"I can see the head, so once you're ready, let's go again," Ellie said, making Cain glance down.

"You move and I'll break all your fingers," Emma threatened, wanting Cain with her.

"I'm not going anywhere, my love. Whenever you're ready, go ahead. Let's both meet this bruiser." Cain wiped her face and kissed her forehead. "You're the bravest woman I know because I think I'd rather take a bullet than do this."

The comment made her want to laugh and cry all at once, but she tried to focus on Cain's face and sat up a little to push. She put the last of her energy into the motion, and in a rush, it was over. It was a strange sensation, but she gave in to her tears when she heard a cry a moment later.

"You were right. It's a boy," Sam said as she let Cain cut the cord. "And from the look of him, he's definitely yours," she said to Cain, laying him across Emma's chest.

The sight of him made Emma cry more. If her life ended in that one second, she'd go with a happy, full heart. William Cain Casey was red-faced and loud, with a full head of coal-black hair that gave her a flash of memory from both Hayden and Hannah's births. He was beautiful, and she forced herself to glance away from him and look at Cain, who was crying as hard as she was.

"I told you it was a boy," she said as she touched Cain's cheek.

"That you did, lass. I was hoping for a blond one this time around, but this particular model is so beautiful he makes me want to dance a jig. Maybe four will be the charm."

"Let her recover from this one, Cain, before you go ordering any more," Sam said as she stood holding Ellie's hand.

"I don't mind those special orders, Doc." Emma looked at the baby again and fell in love with him like she had the first two.

"He's beautiful, lass, and he's ours," Cain said with so much pride that Emma beamed.

CHAPTER FIFTEEN

"Go tell Hayden and Daddy, then call the house," Emma said as the staff started cleaning the room up. The hospital had remodeled since their first pregnancy and made the birthing room look like a bedroom at home.

"I'll be right back so keep an eye on the kid."

Emma laughed at Cain's joke but accepted her kiss before she left. The waiting room contained a mix of big burly guys in suits and anxious-appearing family there for other patients, and the sight made Cain laugh. Their life was different, but no one could ever accuse them of being boring. The men and women to whom she entrusted her family's safety were part of an extended family she'd come to love and respect. So she was happy they were there to share their happiness.

Hayden jumped up when he spotted her and came running, his bodyguard Mook not far behind.

"You're a big brother again, and you have a little boy to look after now."

"Really? I was hoping for another girl, but a little brother might be fun." He hugged her and glanced down the hall as if that's where he needed to be.

"I had one of each, and they were both special in their own way."

"Emma's okay?" Ross asked, glancing toward her room as well.

"She's as okay as your new grandson is."

"So what'll we call him?" Hayden asked, his arms still loosely wrapped around her waist. How different the last year had been for him, going from just the two of them to a house full of family. But he seemed happier. He was more of a kid, and for that she had Emma to thank. Hayden wanted to step into her shoes eventually, but there was so much more to life before he got to that, and she was happy to see him so involved at school and at home with Hannah.

"Your mama wanted William Cain Casey, but he's a little small for that big string of names, so how about we go with what my da called my brother."

"Billy?" Hayden smiled. "Can I see him before we pin something on him that'll stick for life?"

"Sure, but let's give your mama a few minutes to get cleaned up." She shared the news with their people and sent Lou out to the car for the cigars she'd ordered.

The call to the house was next, and she smiled at Carmen's tears of joy. Their housekeeper had loved Emma from the moment she'd moved in with Cain and had taken special care to make Emma feel at home. Carmen had very limited family, so she treated Emma like the daughter she never had, and the children were, by extension, her grandchildren. She spoiled them accordingly.

"I bring the little one by in the morning, Miss Cain, but you tell Emma I bring my special soup to make her feel better too."

"Will do. And can you let Finley and Abigail know the news? If they want, they can take off for the night."

Hayden sat next to her, drumming his heels into the ground until she was done with her calls to Katlin, Muriel, and Remi and Dallas. Ross had gone to get them some coffee from the shop downstairs.

"Something wrong?" She recognized the drumming as one of his nervous tics.

"Can I ask you something I never really thought about until now?" He looked away as he spoke, his voice barely a whisper.

"You can ask me anything you like. You know that."

"Why didn't you give me a first name that reflected our family?" His head bowed lower. Finally, he was showing a little of the jealousy every kid went through when one more came along to grab the family's attention.

"Hayden," she said, putting her fingers under his chin to lift his head. She wanted to see his eyes. "Your mama started telling you this story, but do you mind me finishing it?"

"About when I was born, you mean?"

"Let's start a little before that. When your mama first agreed to come live with me, it was a little bit of an adjustment for both of us. She'd been on her own for a few years and I wasn't exactly the nest-building type, but we loved each other. Every day was a kind of learning experience, well, for me at least, and through all of it, your mama simply made me smile no matter what. My family loved me, just like I love you, but when you find the person who owns your heart it's a wondrous experience."

"You mean finding your safe haven, like you told me before?" He leaned closer to her and rested his head on her shoulder. She wondered if he realized he'd inherited his need to be close from Emma.

"Emma is so much more than that to me. We might've hurt each other, and you and Hannah by default, but I'm glad it brought us to a place where we're more equal. Remember that before you get married."

"That'll be years off. I've heard some of those stories about you, and I'm hoping I'm that lucky before I get married, but don't tell Mama," he said and laughed. "Sorry if that weirds you out some."

"Not exactly, and eventually you'll have to let me know who in the hell told you that, but back to what we were talking about." She ruffled his hair and laughed along with him. "We were in love, but one day we knew we had so much more to give each other, and we decided to expand our family."

New Orleans Two Months Before Hayden Casey's Birth

Cain took the steps two at a time, careful to keep the sunflowers in her hand from hitting the stair railing on the way up. The day had been a drag, and she'd been ready to get back here hours ago but didn't have the heart to tell Vincent to shut the hell up. Their bedroom was empty, so she picked the next logical place to find Emma.

She smiled when she saw her folding a pile of tiny all-in-one pajamas, and she was pretty sure it was the same pile she'd found her folding the day before. Nesting, the young doctors Sam and Ellie had explained, was very real, so she should just smile and go with whatever flow Emma decided to follow. At the moment, Emma was rearranging their baby's nest to make it right. Cain watched as Emma picked up the last garment and pressed it to her face.

"Do you need to sit down?" she asked when she saw Emma massage her back. Her petite partner resembled a woman with a beach ball glued to her front, but in her eyes Emma had never been more beautiful.

"Hey, I was just thinking about you." Emma dropped the baby clothes and walked over to hug her.

"Anything good?" she said and smiled when the baby came between them. "Come take a nap with me."

"I got up like five minutes ago, but if you insist," Emma said and winked at her. Once they were comfortable and the flowers were in water, Emma closed her eyes as Cain ran her hands along her abdomen to spread the lotion Sam had recommended. "Know what I was thinking about today?"

"If it's that we need more baby clothes, I think we got that covered, lass. We could change this kid fifty times a day and still wouldn't have to do laundry for like a month."

"Review what you just said, and that's what I was thinking about."

"You know you can get whatever you want. I was just kidding."

"No. You're right about the clothes, but we can't keep calling the baby this kid or our kid. It won't look too good on his birth certificate."

She moved a little so she could see Emma's face and still hold her. "Any ideas?" She didn't want it to appear she was imposing her will, so she wanted to know what Emma had come up with.

"I never met your father, but maybe this would be good time to recycle his name," Emma said and gazed at her as if gauging her reaction. "He was so special to you, and you're so special to me that I thought you might like that."

"Pretend my father and I weren't close. What would be your second choice?" she asked, figuring it was the only way to get to the truth of what Emma wanted.

"If it's a boy I'd like to name him after you, but you shot me down on that idea a few weeks ago so I thought this might be a good choice."

"What's your father's name?" she asked, hoping it wasn't Ross. Not that there was anything wrong with it per se, but Ross Casey didn't exactly have the right ring to it. "I was close to my father, but your father's a good man who loves you."

"I know that. But this is our baby, so we should find something we both can be proud of."

"I'm going to be proud no matter what, baby, but I want people to know this is our child. This kid is a Casey, but he's also a Verde, and I want everyone, especially the baby, to know where he comes from. He'll be part of both of us, so his name should maybe reflect that."

"My dad's name is Hayden Ross Verde VI. His parents for some reason never called him by his first name, I guess because it was also his father's name, so Ross is all he's ever gone by. As you can tell by the number, it's an old family name."

"What about Hayden Dalton Casey if it's a boy, and 'this kid' if it's a girl?" she said, and Emma slapped her arm. "Tomorrow when I come home and find you folding clothes we'll talk about girl names that aren't 'Carol,' but how about we say we've got the boy name hammered out?"

"I love you, and my father will be thrilled."

"I love you too, and I think my da will be happy to be included as well. We're beginning our family, but there's nothing wrong with paying homage to our history."

"Hayden," Emma said as she placed their hands over the spot where the baby was kicking. "You're going to be some lucky kid, and we can't wait to meet you."

❖

"Grandpa Ross's name is Hayden?" Hayden asked when she was done.

"It sure is. So you carry not only one, but two names that reflect who you are and where you came from. I can't believe I've never told you that," she said, seeing Ross come toward them. "I wanted exactly what we talked about that day. You are our son, and we gave you a name that would tell the world exactly what your history is and, more importantly, who you belong to."

"Hey, Grandpa, I'm named after you," he said, going to hug Ross. "Why didn't you tell me?"

"I'm sorry you didn't know, but I'm sure there's been a long line of dairy farmers milking in heaven with a big smile on their face since the day you were born." He hugged Hayden to him before slapping him on the back. "How's my new grandbaby?"

"Let me go check if the coast is clear, and I'll come back and get you. Hope you both ate to keep up your strength. Your mama gives birth to some big babies."

"I'm sure that's all got to do with her," Hayden said, and they laughed.

When Cain returned to the waiting room, the whole family was there, including an excited Hannah, who was glued to her big brother. Cain smiled when she saw Muriel holding an old bottle of Irish whiskey and accepted a hug from her and the others before they all headed for Emma's room. The nurse glanced up but seemed to understand it would be a bad idea to mention that visiting hours were over or the visitor limit per room.

Hayden and Hannah had taken turns holding their new brother. Then Muriel opened the bottle and poured a little into the glasses Katlin and Merrick had brought with them. Cain took the baby and sat on the bed as Emma held her glass.

"In a few weeks we'll stand with Father Andrew and baptize this little one into the church, which will make my mum smile down on us from heaven. But first we'll welcome this Casey home."

Cain cradled her boy and remembered the words they'd all been told at their births by proud parents who'd survived on their traditions for centuries. "William Cain Casey." She said the boy's name with all the pride she felt for him already. "The Catholics, they'll get ahold of you soon enough, but the whiskey—that's a Casey baptism. This spirited drink's in your blood, Billy, and no oil and water a priest pours or rubs on you is going to wash that away. The whiskey's not only our business. It's our heritage, our history, and soon you'll help your brother Hayden and sister Hannah keep that tradition alive."

She barely dipped her finger in the liquid and placed it in his mouth. "Let this be a bit of a reminder of who you are and what you come from. You're a Casey, and you're ours, but only for a time. When we set you out in the world, you'll go with that rich history not only in your head, but more importantly in your heart."

Muriel raised her glass and the others followed. "To William Cain Casey and his family. May those who came before us watch over him, may God bless him, and may he always know how loved he is."

"Clan," everyone else, including Cain and Emma, said before they drained their glasses. Cain dipped her finger again and put it in

Hannah's mouth, then Hayden's. "You both are mine, but only for a time. Remember always that your mother and I love you more than life."

Right then, Billy opened his eyes, and Cain let out a delighted laugh. Perhaps someone upstairs had been listening when she wished to see something she loved so much about her wife. The boy had the Casey coloring, but his eyes were the same bright-green shade as his mother's. It would certainly distinguish him among the Casey children.

CHAPTER SIXTEEN

The next morning, Nunzio and Santino sat in their hotel's restaurant having coffee, trying their best to not attract attention. After a few bribes, they'd gotten the lay of the land and the information they needed to visit the maximum-security prison this pathetic little village was famous for.

Roth Pombo had lived the good life for years, and for the poor bastard to be rotting away in that hellhole was justice to some, but Nunzio thought he'd prefer death to that if he was ever caught. He didn't want to endure a cage simply to keep breathing. Maybe he'd change his mind if it came to choosing that or death, but he doubted it.

"This guy, are you sure we need him?" Santino asked softly as the waitress dropped off a huge amount of food on two large plates.

"Hell of a time to ask, Nino," he said, using the nickname he'd given his grandfather as a toddler. "We could probably set it all up without him, but why reinvent the wheel if we don't have to?"

"What are you planning to give him for this shortcut?"

He cut one of the fried eggs and stuffed it into his mouth, cursing when a drip of yolk landed on his tie. "Fuck." He dipped his napkin in the water and scrubbed. "Think about how grateful someone like Pombo will be if we can give him what he wants more than a woman right about now."

"You're not talking about his freedom because that's something we can't deliver, and he's going to know that."

"That's exactly what I'm talking about. You're going to have to trust me, but I did a little research on this guy before we got here."

"What kind of research?" Santino pushed his plate away and lost his smile. "Remember that while you're snooping, it's easy for someone to watch you."

"Like I said, trust me. How I did it and what I found out isn't going to come back and bite us in the ass." He shoved more food in his mouth to keep from saying something that would end in a fight. Although Freddie was an ass, he regretted not bringing him now. Freddie wouldn't be chewing his butt or questioning his every move.

"Do you mind if I join you?" The older but handsome man spoke with a Spanish accent that sounded like it was perfected in some exclusive US college.

"We're talking here," Santino said, and he put his hand up to cut the man off.

"Mr. Hernandez?" Nunzio said and held out his hand as he stood. "Thank you for coming."

"I hate to be rude but I can't stay long. My employers are expecting me in less than an hour, so I must ask you to get to the point."

"I'm sure the Masurdo brothers won't mind you being a few minutes late," he said as he sat and picked up his fork again. "How do you like working for them?"

"I like them well enough, and I understand more than you what they mind or don't mind. At least they don't play games like this. What do you want?"

This guy wouldn't dare say a wrong word against his bosses Muñoz and Ernesto Masurdo, the two butchers who'd filled the void Roth Pombo had left. Roth's old attorney, though, had more class than that, and it was Nunzio's way inside. "I want to give you an old friend back. Someone I believe valued you more than your current two bosses do."

"Mr. Smith, if that is indeed your name, I'd like to give you some free advice. No one comes here and talks with disrespect toward the Masurdo brothers and their family. In your country that might be accepted, but here such things are suicidal." Hernandez spoke in a normal tone, Nunzio noticed, so this guy wasn't exactly scared, but he was keeping his head down. He obviously didn't want to advertise his presence.

"I came a long way to see your old boss, and I think I have something he would find enticing." He brushed his hair back, not used to the new length, and almost snorted when Antonio glanced up at him with what appeared to be contempt. "I'm sure your job is lucrative, but think about working for Roth again. I'm sure he had much more respect for you than you find in your current situation."

"I cared deeply for Mr. Pombo, but he's beyond our reach. Whatever you have in mind, leave him alone. It would be cruel to instill any hope in him because of where he is. That place will crush it before it has time to root."

"All I need is what guard to ask for to get in. I need to talk to him and ask him a few things. Then once I'm done, if he calls you, please don't ignore him."

"There's a guard on the three o'clock shift, which is the last visiting hour of the day. Ask for Rico and take a hundred bucks. That should give you thirty minutes without the cameras. If you see Roth, please let him know he's still in my prayers." Antonio stood and left as soon as he was done talking, but Nunzio was sure they'd see each other again.

They waited until the three o'clock visiting hour and stood in line with what seemed like family members ready to see their loved ones. For two hundred dollars they got a private room with the customary two-way mirror, but Rico promised no one would be on the other side. Roth was done with all his court appearances so he was no longer the big fish who had to be monitored constantly. From what Rico had said, the man had gone a bit mental from all the solitary confinement.

"Who the fuck are you?" Roth asked when he dropped into the aluminum chair bolted to the floor. His hair was wild, and he'd gained weight since the one picture Nunzio had found of him.

"I'm an old friend, remember?" He held his hand out, and when Roth took it he pulled him forward so he could talk directly into his ear. "Your old friend Antonio gives his regards and wants you to know he's still praying for you."

"What do you want? Antonio isn't coming back, because I told him not to. The idiot brothers, I hope, are taking good care of him." Roth rocked a little as he spoke and twirled a lock of greasy hair around his finger as if he constantly needed something to do with his hands.

"What I want is a piece of what you had," Nunzio said, glancing back at his grandfather. "I came a long way to talk to you, so I'd appreciate your attention. If you help me set up the old supply chain of tequila, I'll give you something in return."

Roth laughed and rocked harder. "What? A blow job while wearing a blond wig? I fucking loved blond women before they threw me in here, but those days are over. You see these gray walls?" He waved his hands around before he started pulling his hair again. "I'm going to die here, and that's the fucking last thing I'll ever see."

"All you need to say is you'll help me, and I'll return the favor. Give me the first of your contacts."

"Help me how?"

"How about a vastly different view? Think about that, but don't think too long. My two hundred bucks will only get me so far."

"You have to head to the coast. The guy you need to see is Cesar Kalina. He's not the first contact. He's *the* contact." He stood up and put his hands behind his back. "One warning about Cesar. Fuck him over or give him even an inkling that you're going to, and he'll kill you before you can scratch your ass."

"Thanks. You'll hear from me again."

"I doubt that, fucker, but thanks for blowing smoke up my ass."

"If you think that, why help us?" Santino asked.

"Because in all the time I've been sitting in here, no one's ever asked me anything remotely like this, so why the hell not?"

It was too easy. That Roth would give up his contacts so fast was making Nunzio twitchy. "So you'd give it up to the first person that asked?"

"Nothing in life is that easy, Mr. Smith. Talk to Cesar, and I guarantee I'll see you again."

They waited until they were back in their shitty hotel to talk again, and Santino shook his head. "I don't like it, but we've come too far not to take the chance. The only thing is the Mexican coastline is not only long, but there's two of them. He didn't make it easy for us, did he?"

The knock made them both jump, and it only occurred to Nunzio then how exposed both of them were here. Airport customs meant they didn't have any guns to fight back with if death was waiting outside the door. He opened it when the knocking got louder and found Antonio Hernandez. This guy wasn't as out of Pombo's life as he professed to be.

"You'll need this, and make sure you tell him Roth gave you the number. When you talk to him, it'll only proceed if you have something to offer, and not just promises of something. Remember that, Mr. Smith."

"What do you mean exactly?"

"Cesar trusted Roth, and Roth took the fall for him. So Cesar's still incredibly loyal to a man everyone else has written off as dead. You try to make a deal with Cesar and cut Mr. Pombo out, you'll never leave Mexico."

"I'm not planning to cut him out. I want to make Roth my partner. Those kinds of partnerships, though, take trust and time, so stop threatening me."

"Good luck to you then. You're going to need it."

"I make my own luck so here." He handed over his contact information. "It's time for both of us to do better than we have so far."

❖

The crying woke Cain instantly, and she smiled when Emma moaned a little. This was the fifth time she'd been summoned to the basinet by a robust little voice that seemed not to care how much sleep his parents were getting. "I see he's inherited your patience, my love," Emma said and laughed when Cain stuck her tongue out at her. "Can you believe it? I kept pinching you last night to make sure I wasn't dreaming."

"Here I thought you agreed with Sam on my slacking," Cain said as she unwrapped him from the blanket the nurses had swaddled him in to check his diaper. He was still a little red from all the crying, and she imagined from the birth, but he resembled Hayden so much it stunned her. "He's not wet yet, so I guess this is a boy in need of his mama."

Emma untied the unflattering hospital gown and accepted the nursing pillow they'd brought from home and made him comfortable. She smiled through her intake of breath when he started nursing and finally laughed when she looked at Cain.

"What?" Cain asked and winked. It was silly of her to be this proud so soon, since all Billy could do was nurse and cry, but she was puffed up so much about being a parent for the third time, her chest almost hurt.

"This is another one for you to spoil, but he's a beauty for sure. It's like a dream, isn't it? You can go from rock-bottom to elated so fast you can get whiplash." Emma laughed a little and wiped the corner of her eye. "I remember that day under my tree, and it's like a fairy tale."

"Lass, you have and always will have my heart, and there's no other woman I would've wanted to share this miracle with but you. My mother would've had a statue of you made for the yard by now for all these beautiful grandchildren."

"For their sake, I wish they'd gotten to meet both your parents. They'd be unbearable from being so spoiled, but think of the joy your parents would have brought to their lives."

"Between Ross and Carmen at home they'll get more than enough attention. According to Merrick, Carmen's been cooking for you since I called last night to make sure you keep up your strength."

The baby took a break but went right back to nursing when Emma tickled his cheek. "Speaking of the other side of that spectrum, have you heard anything else about my mother? I haven't forgotten about her, and my father never talks about her because he doesn't want to worry me. But not knowing is worse."

"Muriel's got Sanders Riggole from her office working on it. Muriel had him drop the petition in Wisconsin and refile here. This will guarantee we'll be working with a much more favorable court. Refiling might set him back, but only a little, Muriel assured me."

"Can he give her whatever it is she wants?"

"If it was money I'd have written the check myself and gladly handed it over naked, but he can't give her what she wants."

"I thought you didn't know what it was."

"When we last talked about this I had no clue, so don't get mad at me. It might've pissed you off, but I would've told you then if I'd known."

"What does she want, mobster?" Emma asked as she handed the baby over for her to burp him.

"Maybe you should finish this before we get into all that." She patted him gently on the back and smiled when the tiny infant let out a rather large belch. When she handed him over for Emma to let him nurse on the other side, she almost laughed at the glare.

"I promise not to curdle his milk, so tell me already."

"Your mother's under some delusion that we'll grant visitation with Hannah, and she'll in turn give your father his freedom. Muriel told me and I talked to him about it. He hadn't mentioned it because he thought I'd be pissed, and he was right." She sat on the bed and put her hand on Emma's shoulder. "Your dad told Carol he couldn't give her something that wasn't in his power to grant, so she came back with more objections to the divorce. I guess that's her strategy for getting what she wants."

"She thought for one second I'd let her anywhere near Hannah?" Emma said with such menace that the baby stopped suckling. Cain lifted him and tried to burp him again and sighed when he spit up on her. It was a good sign as to how this conversation was going.

"You don't need to spend any time worrying about your mother. In a few months she'll be counting her pennies in that frozen tundra, wishing she'd just accepted the first offer Ross made. You have my word on that, and so does Ross."

"Can we get out of here today? I'd feel better if we were all together at home."

"I know the two people who can help you with that, and they promised they'd be by," Cain glanced at her watch, "in five minutes. I already asked that question and they didn't seem too opposed to it, so we should start packing."

"Trying to leave without paying the bill?" Sam asked as she entered with a chart. "How about you show me your credit card, and I'll get you a ride out of here?"

"Thanks for everything, Sam." Cain walked over with the baby and let their friend hold him. "You and Ellie are in my debt for taking such good care of these two."

"The best part of this job is seeing the beginnings of families and when folks want to add to that. You have a beautiful family, so you'll never owe me anything. Well, maybe let me cut the line at Emma's when I can talk my wife into a date night."

"That's an easy request, so put your dancing shoes on."

It took another two hours, but they headed out with Lou and Katlin and arrived at a quiet house. The kids were still in school, but they would be wired when they got home, so Cain took Emma up for a nap. She left the baby with Carmen, who was getting a raise for all the cooing she was doing over Billy as she carried him to the kitchen to show him off to the other staff.

"When he sleep, Miss Cain, I bring him in, so don't worry."

"Thank you for everything, Carmen, and thanks too for being so good to my kids and Emma. I'm glad you've been here through all this."

"You and Emma are my family, so I glad too. I work for you, but you and Miss Emma, you make pretty babies easy to fall in love with."

When Cain got back to the bedroom, Emma asked, "Think we can sleep for about an hour?"

"Carmen and the others are babysitting, so we should be good until the kids get home. Once they're here and see that baby, all bets are off. Especially since they were up way past their bedtime last night." She lay down and let Emma find a comfortable spot. It was strange after so long to not feel the baby bump between them, but the joy of them getting back to somewhat normal was a good feeling before falling asleep.

"Sweet dreams, lass."

"You're here, so that's all I need."

"May it always be so."

CHAPTER SEVENTEEN

Is she in the bathroom?" Sabana Greco, the guard Cain had placed with Hannah for the moment, glanced at her watch. The kids had been up so late the night before that she'd come by a little before the bell with Cain's blessing to take Hannah home before the traffic around the school became gridlocked. Very few children that attended Hannah's school rode any type of bus or public transport. Either soccer moms or people like her picked them up.

"Let me check again. I'm not sure what's taking so long." The school secretary looked up at the wall clock to check the time, as if agreeing Hannah should've been escorted to the office by now.

She'd been standing in the office for fifteen minutes, and no one had produced Hannah or told her what the hell was going on. "Do we have some sort of problem here? You need to let me know now, if that's the case." Sabana was familiar with Cain's temper and coughed when the taste of bile filled the back of her mouth. She didn't want to call her boss and tell her something had happened to her kid.

"What are you talking about? What kind of problem?" Levi emerged from his office and the secretary shook her head, but it appeared like the move was more out of confusion than disagreement.

"I'm here for Hannah Casey." Sabana handed over the papers that allowed her to remove Hannah from school. She was beginning to hope that was the reason for the delay. "I've been waiting, and it seems like you can't find her. If that's true, then you need to say so."

"I'm sure she's just packing her stuff or something like that, but let's go check." Levi pointed to the door, and Sabana followed him to a classroom close to the front office. She cursed softly when Levi visibly paled as he glanced inside. "What are you doing here?" he asked the older woman in the classroom. "The board wanted you out immediately."

"According to the rules the school put in place, I can appeal their decision. So they had no choice but to give me my job back until that process is complete. I've done good work, and the board had no grounds for firing me."

"Where's Hannah Casey?" Levi asked, his voice loud enough to make the children stop playing and sit quietly.

"Right at this moment I have no idea," the woman said and smirked.

"Mr. Levi," Lucy said, holding her hand up like the children had been taught in order to be recognized. "She let Hannah go at recess with this lady that came. I don't think Hannah wanted to go, but she made her."

"Fuck me, I'm dead." Sabana struggled to get her phone out of her jacket pocket, her fingers almost numb from fear. "Lou, we need to get people to Hannah's school. She's gone."

"Gone? What the fuck does that mean?" Lou screamed, and she knew her life would never be the same. The only luck she'd have left would be to have a life at all when Cain found out, even though she had nothing to do with this.

"Hannah's friend Lucy said the teacher made her go at recess with some woman. The school is under strict orders on who can take her off these grounds, so I'm not sure who that could have been."

"Find out when, so we'll know what kind of head start whoever this was has on us." Lou was breathing hard. It sounded like he was running to the school, but she sensed the same fear that was making her want to puke. Cain forgave many things, but anyone who would harm Emma or her children had very little wiggle room. "Sabana, it's really important you gather as much information as you can before we get there."

"Lou, she'll be okay, right?" She hadn't wanted this assignment at first, but you couldn't spend time with Hannah and not fall in love with the little girl so full of joy. She wanted her relationship with Hannah to be like the one Mook had with Hayden. Her involvement with the next generation would eventually help her be close to the top of the family's power structure.

Even if she hadn't fallen in love with Hannah, she owed Cain a lifetime of loyalty. She would never forget Cain taking her to the cemetery one afternoon. The two of them had stood in front of a grave with the name Juan Nadie carved into the stone. The name translated to John Nobody or John Doe, but it was in fact Juan Luis, the man who'd ordered her brother to be killed. Under that name, "Not soon enough" was carved in Spanish.

She'd begged to work for Cain to have the opportunity to kill him, but his death was enough, even though she hadn't pulled the trigger. Cain had given her that gift, so she'd do whatever it took to find her daughter and bring her home.

"Whoever took her won't be okay, but we'll find Hannah." Lou paused. "Don't worry. This isn't on you, and I'll make sure the boss realizes that. You'll be okay too."

Sabana put her phone away and took a deep breath. "Who did you let her leave with?" she asked the teacher.

"I'm not at liberty to say," the woman said and laughed. "Stop worrying. She's safer now than with you or her family."

Sabana's phone rang again, and she answered it immediately when she saw it was the house. "We're on our way, but tell me what happened." Recognizing Cain's voice, she walked into the hallway and explained all she knew and what the woman had said. When she described the teacher for Cain, she could've sworn that her boss growled into the phone. "Make sure that old fucker doesn't go anywhere, and when the police get there, tell them I intend to press charges."

"Do you want me to call the cops?"

"I've already taken care of it, so make sure no one leaves. I'll be there in five minutes."

Sabana stepped back into the classroom. "If you want to help yourself out, tell me who she left with," she said to the teacher. "Cain's on her way, so why not make this easy for everyone involved?"

"I told your boss when she was here that threats don't work with me. More importantly, I didn't do anything wrong. I followed the rules this school loves to enforce."

"We'll see about that," Sebastian Savoie said as he entered with Sept and another young man with a gold shield clipped to his belt. "Let's go to the office and have a chat."

"If I'm not under arrest, I'm not talking to you. I know my rights," the woman said.

Sabana wanted to punch her hard enough in the face that she'd lose teeth.

"Detective Blackman, please read the legal genius her rights as you escort her to the office, and make sure you don't skip any words. We wouldn't want it to be said later that we didn't cross every T and dot every I." The young man left with the teacher, and Sept followed him out.

They both stopped by Cain, who appeared a little undone with her mussed hair and a wrinkled shirt.

Sebastian gestured with his chin for the two detectives to keep going. "Cain, let it go for now."

"Levi," Cain said, her voice so low Sabana barely recognized it. Cain's anger seemed to consume her and make her appear larger since her shirt was tight in the shoulders and her breathing was heavy. "You gave me your word you'd look out for her," she said, pointing her finger at him.

Radiating fear, Levi backed up and put his hands out to his sides as if that would explain everything. And he should be afraid, Cain thought, because if something happened to Hannah, killing Levi would only be the beginning of her rampage to find everyone responsible.

"Cain, Hannah's friend said the teacher made her leave with a woman at recess," Sabana said.

"How long ago?" Cain said, and Levi took another step back, getting closer to the door. "Levi, you're never going to run fast or far enough away, so how the hell long ago was that?"

"Okay, kids. Let's all go next door except for Lucy," Levi said. The kids practically ran out of the room to escape the agitated adults. He turned to Cain. "The last recess was about an hour ago, and no one came to the office to check Hannah out, so we had no way to know our protocol wasn't followed. I didn't walk the halls today, so I had no idea Hannah's teacher was back. The board doesn't always share its decisions with me right away."

"Lucy," Cain said, sitting in the tiny chair and taking the little girl's hand. "Did Hannah tell you the woman's name?"

"Are you mad I didn't say nothing?"

"I'm not mad at you at all, but I need to find Hannah. If she told you the woman's name, please tell me what it is." Cain could feel her phone buzzing in her pocket. She didn't have to look to know it was Emma calling. Her wife had no choice but to stay home with the baby, and that was driving Emma mad. Still, Cain kept her eyes on Lucy.

"Mom," Hayden said as he ran in with Mook, his tone making it obvious he knew what was going on.

"Just a second, son," she said, putting her free hand up. She smiled at Lucy. "Did she tell you who the woman was? Was it someone you'd ever seen before? Someone at our house or at the club when you two get to dance there."

"I wanted to go with her because I thought they were going to your house, but Hannah didn't want to leave." Though Lucy spoke in a rush of words, Cain wanted to shake her to get them out even faster. But she'd come to truly like the little waif who Hannah loved, so she listened intently. "Our teacher took her hand and made her go. Hannah was crying and saying no."

"Did you see the woman?" Cain lifted Lucy up to her lap.

"We saw her at the front fence. Hannah said her name was Grandmother Carol and she wasn't nice. Not like you and Miss Emma and Hayden."

Cain's vision seemed to dim, and she thought her heart would hammer out of her chest with anger, but she stayed perfectly still for Lucy's sake. "Are you sure it was an hour ago?" she asked no one in particular.

"We can go to the office and check," Sebastian said. "In the meantime, where would this woman take her, if that's who we're talking about?"

"Carol Verde is Emma's mother. We didn't know she was in town, but if she plans to leave with Hannah, we need to flag any flight heading north. This might have simply been a whim today, or she might've been planning it for months." Cain kissed Lucy's forehead and set her down. "Thanks, Lucy. You were a real big help."

"Mom, you can't let Hannah leave with her," Hayden said as he combed his hair back a few times, trying to keep it completely off his forehead. "She's our grandmother, but she's totally crazy."

"Cain, there's someone here to see you," Levi said.

Cain hadn't noticed he'd come back into the classroom after moving the children. She turned on him, frowning. "Later on, I'm going to have a talk with you and with the board. Pray that we find her and she's fine when we do."

"Can you tell me what's going on?" Shelby stepped around him, and Levi took the opportunity to leave with Lucy.

"I don't have time for your bullshit, Agent. You spend all that time watching me, and you completely fail when it comes to someone harming one of my children."

"Sir," Shelby said to Sebastian. "I recently had a conversation with one of your detectives because she wanted my advice on something. Someone by the name of Elton Newsome had approached her and asked her to join a task force he was putting together. It had something to do with Cain and her business. Out of curiosity, she went to the meeting and found out then that Detective Newsome alone was the task force. But he told her he had what he thought would be a secret weapon."

"Let me guess. Carol Verde?" Cain squeezed her hands together to keep from punching someone. "That bitch tried this once before, so you'd think she would have learned something, because Detective O'Brannigan sure as hell didn't."

"You don't know that," Sebastian said, but his words lacked conviction.

"That's who came to talk to me," Shelby said.

"I want Carol Verde found and arrested for kidnapping. She in no way had permission to remove my kid from this school, and if you let her play the grandmother card and weasel out of this, I'm going to have every one of you bastards in court."

"Cain, calm down a minute, okay?" Sept said. "The kindergarten teacher from hell said Verde had some kind of court papers from a Wisconsin court, so she gladly turned Hannah over. It seems you've met with this teacher before, because I get the impression she didn't look real close since this was her chance to put one over on you."

"Where is she, Sept?" Cain didn't care what papers Carol showed the teacher. No one should have handed her daughter over unless she'd gone through the school office, and someone there would have called her and Emma. Hayden felt like a lifeline in rough seas when he stood next to her so he could put his arm around her waist.

"Let's all go to the station, and I'll call Newsome and O'Brannigan in. If they met and he introduced her to Verde, then he must know where she is," Sebastian said. "Go ahead and tell Blackman to cuff this teacher, and we'll sort it out at the precinct."

"Sebastian, as a favor to me, please have Newsome waiting when we get there." The invisible band around Cain's chest loosened slightly since, no matter what, she didn't think Carol would hurt Hannah. Carol wasn't exactly a friend, but she was infinitely safer than someone like Nunzio or another enemy.

"We'll find her and have her home in no time," Sept said.

"Let's hope, because there'll be hell to pay if she's got a scratch on her."

"It's not wise to threaten physical violence in a room full of law-enforcement personnel," Sebastian said, but his smile contradicted his warning.

"I seldom make threats that I don't intend to carry out, but in this case the one you should be worried about is the pissed-off woman I left at home. Emma's hormones haven't leveled out yet, and in the mood she's in right now, she'd skin and filet you without a thought."

❖

"Won't it be fun to be back on the farm with all the animals again?" Carol said as she and Hannah sat in the first ice cream parlor she found. Looking at Hannah through that fence, holding that little girl's hand, had been the first warning she might already be too late, so she had no choice but to act. "All the cows and chickens missed you. They told me so," she said, trying to ease the tension between them.

She'd been talking since they'd left the school, but Hannah hadn't lifted her head once or said a word. It was too late to get a flight home, so she'd have to stay out of sight for one more day. Then they'd be free to go. She had to win Hannah over before then, though, so she wouldn't be a problem when they went through the security line or on the flight back. "You know it'll be for the best since your parents don't want you anymore. Your mama just wanted that boy back, and now she has a new baby too, so there's no room for you anymore. I'm the only one left who loves you."

"That's not true. Take it back." Hannah screamed the words, and everyone around them stared. "I want to go home...now."

"Hannah Marie," she said in a scolding whisper. "You keep your voice down or you know what'll happen." She held her hand up, and Hannah cringed back into her chair. At least the child remembered something of their time together. A smack with the hand was a good learning tool for a precocious child like Hannah, who seemed to have a free will that always led her in the wrong directions.

"Is there a problem?" The teenaged girl who'd scooped their ice cream came over as soon as Hannah started crying. "Are you okay?" She crouched down next to Hannah.

"I want my mama and she won't take me home," Hannah said between hiccups and sobs. "I don't want to go with her. I want to go home."

"Excuse me. Get away from her. This is nothing to do with you." Carol gathered her things and stood so they could go.

"Ma'am, I'm going to take her behind the counter and clean her face. Please wait here."

"You can't do that." Carol reached for Hannah, but she'd wrapped herself around the girl. Prying her off would make a scene. "She's my granddaughter. You have no right."

"Please don't make me go," Hannah screamed through the worsening tears.

"I'm calling 911," the woman at the next table said, and Carol turned quickly toward her, cursing herself for not just locking them away in her hotel room. Hannah could have cried herself to sleep then and after a few days would come to realize this was the way it had to be.

"Give me my granddaughter," she said, pulling on Hannah's arm, and the motion made Hannah howl as if in excruciating pain. "Hannah, come on. We have to leave now."

"Look," the girl said, glancing at the woman on the phone. "If you really are her grandmother and this is just a tantrum, I'll apologize, but I can't let you take her."

Carol was through being nice. Her whole life she'd been nice, and all it had gotten her was a weak husband and a perverted daughter. She pulled her arm back and slapped the young woman as hard as she could muster to force her to release Hannah. She also caught the side of Hannah's face with the force of her blow.

That move spurred the young man behind the counter to come running toward them, so she had no choice but to leave and find Elton. He owed her so he'd have to smooth this over. Outside she heard the sirens, so she hurried out of the shop and turned at the first corner she came to. She glanced back. The woman who'd called the police was standing on the sidewalk, watching her as if noting every step she took.

She ran as best she could out of sight, down the side street, mumbling angrily. "You'll have to accept that I'm what's best for you, Hannah. I'm the only one who cares. When you're a young woman with a strong connection to God, you'll thank me."

CHAPTER EIGHTEEN

"Cain, you have to find her, and promise me you won't do anything to my mother…yet," Emma said as Cain sped to the police station with Hayden. "I swear if she told her anything that causes Hannah nightmares or hurts her, I'll ask to borrow a gun and kill her myself."

"I'll keep you updated, but we're here so I have to go now, lass. Make sure your father or someone stays with you." Before she could get out of the car, Sept came running over. "What?" She really hadn't meant to scream, but if something had happened to Hannah, she'd never be able to face Emma again.

"I think we found her. Do you mind if I ride with you?"

Lou got them to the ice cream shop in record time, and Cain jumped out first. She slowed when she saw Hannah sitting on the lap of a young woman wearing a striped red outfit. Her daughter was crying and the girl was trying to comfort her, so Cain took a deep breath before going in. She didn't want to add to Hannah's trauma.

"Hey, Hannah girl," she said as she squatted down close to them. She wanted to join Hannah in her tears when the little girl ran to her and hugged her neck so hard she could barely breathe. "It's okay, sweetheart, it's okay. Hayden and I came to get you. Let's go home to your mama and little brother." Cain had to bite her lip when she saw the red mark with a mean-looking scratch on Hannah's face. "Do you want to tell Hayden hello? He's been worried about you."

Hayden took her and kissed the scratch on her face, and Hannah began to calm.

"Thank you." She held her hand out to the girl. "If it was you who called the police, I owe you whatever you want. You have no idea what you prevented."

"Your daughter didn't act right from the moment she got here, and that woman with her seemed a bit off. I tried to help, but that lady was the one who called the police." She pointed to a woman standing nearby.

"What happened to your face?" Cain saw the red mark that matched Hannah's.

"That bitch slapped me," the girl said, then shook her head. "Sorry about the language."

"Trust me, she is a bitch, so no worries."

"Do you mind coming with us and giving the police a statement? You too," Sept said to the woman after introducing herself.

To make things easier on everyone, Sept took them all back to the Caseys' house so Emma could see her daughter. There was more crying when mother and daughter were reunited, so they went upstairs while Sept interviewed the two witnesses who'd gotten Hannah away from Carol. Before they left the house, Muriel handed each woman an envelope that held a token of Cain's appreciation for taking a chance and getting involved. The checks for ten thousand dollars each would give them good reason to continue as Good Samaritans for the rest of their lives.

"We'll find her, I promise," Sept said, hugging Cain before leaving the Caseys to recover from the traumatic experience. "I might not work the case, but I promise my dad will get it done."

"If you want to arrest me, go ahead, but I hope for Carol's sake that he finds her before I do."

Sept didn't say anything as she nodded, though their years of friendship were enough for Cain's old friend to know she wasn't kidding. But right now her focus was her family. Hannah was still crying a little when she stepped into the master bedroom, and Cain was glad to see Hayden still there as well. Emma was sitting on the bed holding and rocking her daughter and wiping her own face, so Cain picked Hannah up and held her.

"She said you didn't want me no more since you had Hayden and the new baby, so I'd have to go live with her." The tears picked up again, and Cain stared up at the ceiling to hold back the devil clamoring to go after the twisted bitch. "I don't want to go. Please don't make me."

Her child needed reassurance. The devil could get her due later.

"Hannah," she said, sitting with her daughter in her lap so she could see Hannah's face. "You know what the three happiest days of my life were?"

"No." Hannah sniffed. The strange question stopped her hysterical crying.

"They were the day Hayden was born, the day you were born, and yesterday when Billy was born. All of you are our children, and we love you all the same. There's no way, no how, that I'd let you go, any of you. Your grandmother Carol lied to you."

"But she's an adult."

"That's true, but not all adults are good. From now on, I don't care who tells you something like 'come with me,' even if they're an adult. If you know it's not what you want to do, then I want you to call me or your mama."

"Even if it's because I don't want to eat something?"

She laughed and was relieved when Hannah joined in. "If it's your mama, then that deal won't work, but if it's someone like Grandmother Carol, then it's okay to say no." She kissed Hannah's forehead, holding back her own tears as she cuddled her daughter. "You owe your friend Lucy a new toy for telling me who'd taken you. She really likes you."

"Really?" Hannah brightened at the idea.

"Come on, Hannah. Let's go get some cake downstairs." Hayden turned to offer his sister a ride, and Hannah gladly climbed on his back. "I think that'll make us both feel better."

When the door closed, Emma reached for Cain's hand and brought it to her mouth. "I'm sorry, baby," Emma said.

"For what? It's me who should be apologizing. I want to wrap them in cotton to keep them safe, and then shit like this happens."

"This wasn't your fault. My mother is deranged, but now at least she'll be out of our lives. It's the only good thing I can come up with to be happy about in this whole mess."

Cain stretched out on the bed next to Emma, feeling as if she'd run a marathon. She'd gone from a nap to finding out Hannah had been kidnapped. If she'd needed a heart checkup this year, she could cancel it. She figured surviving this afternoon without a major heart problem was a good sign she was healthy.

"Carol told Hannah we didn't want her?"

"It should shock me, but it doesn't. My mother has a strange sense of the world and how things should be, but I guess because she's my mother, I can't ask you to kill her." Cain knew Emma was dead serious. "I can ask that Muriel do anything she can to legally keep her away from us and the children. I never want to see her again."

"There's death, and then there's pain. Your mother will soon find out the difference and wish I'd picked one over the other."

Fiona had a hard time picking her feet up as she walked into NOPD's main offices after Sebastian had once again summoned her. She'd called her mother, Judice, and told her what had happened. They hadn't had much contact after Judice had gone back home to California, and until Fiona found herself in trouble again, she hadn't realized how much she'd missed her mother's counsel. She'd been so focused on Cain she'd severely neglected the one person in her life who would always be on her side.

If whatever this was meant the end of her career in New Orleans, she was looking forward to finding out the rest of what her mother had yet to tell her. There was still a huge secret between them, and nothing she'd threatened—not even her putting distance between them—had made her mom break. Up to now all she could guess was it had to do with the two mob leaders her mother worked for but never acknowledged in any conversation. Colin Meade and Salvatore Maggio were both killers very much in the vein of Cain Casey, and both men ran a criminal enterprise in California no police investigation had been able to crack. That her mother had served them well through the years was something that plagued her, but no amount of coaxing had ever made her mother say why she'd chosen that life.

"Do you want your union rep here?" Sebastian asked when she sat where he'd directed.

"Do I need my rep? I did what you asked and stayed clear of Casey and everyone you mentioned." No matter what he said, she concentrated on keeping her hands and body loose. She wouldn't let her body language hang her.

"Did you meet with Elton Newsome and Carol Verde to discuss any action against Cain Casey or her family?" Sebastian wasn't being overly aggressive, but he was trying to set her up for something. His line of questioning was like a bat to the knees in the clue department that she'd be blamed for something.

She should've checked to see if anything was going on or if something had happened before coming in to face him. The way she'd left things with Elton probably meant the asshole was the one trying to set her up. "I met with him about a taskforce he was putting together, but when I got there, he'd exaggerated what he'd said on the phone. So I left. As I was leaving, he did introduce me to Carol Verde. He was under the impression she'd help him bring Cain down."

"And you waited to inform any of your superiors about this until now because why?"

"Detective Newsome has much more seniority than I do, so I figured he'd cleared everything he was doing, but I wanted no part of it. I talked to Shelby Phillips from the FBI, and she agreed I shouldn't get involved." She had to straighten her fingers when her hands had, without her attention on them, curled into fists. "Did he say something to you, or did something happen?"

"Carol Verde kidnapped Hannah Casey today and vanished."

She leaned forward, her body suddenly heating as if she were sitting under an oven. No matter how she felt about Cain because of what had happened to Shelby's parents, she'd never wanted her family harmed. "Do you have any leads?"

"The little girl was found, but now I'm having a hard time locating Newsome and this Verde woman. Get on the phone and find out if any court in Wisconsin granted her visitation rights." Sebastian put his hand up when she jumped to her feet. "I don't need to mention what course of action you should take if Newsome contacts you, right?"

"No, sir. I'll call you directly if he does. Are you sure you don't want someone else on this, considering everything we've talked about before?"

"You can think whatever you want about me and Sept, but we've known Cain and her family for years. She's far from perfect, but her children and family are off limits in my book, and you should learn not to believe absolutely everything you hear about her. My contacts at the federal building tell me she had nothing to do with the death of your rabbi on the force. You need to let that go, so think of this as your way of redeeming yourself."

Fiona wanted to go and do whatever was necessary to help with this situation. Her mother might've worked for dangerous men, but Sebastian was right. Even their code of honor prevented them from going after children. "I'm sorry I didn't come to you with this, sir, but I really thought he'd cleared it with whoever needed to give him the go-ahead."

"Get moving and report back to me anything you find on those court papers. I'm holding that teacher for now, but I don't want any ready-made mistake on our part to turn into a get-out-of-jail-free card for some defense attorney later on."

Fiona drove to her office and found Sept there. The first murder Sept and Nathan had started investigating had turned into quite a few, but a whole team was working those cases to get a lead on a suspect. Still, Sept seemed to be waiting on her. She'd blamed Sept from the time she got here of being suspiciously close to Cain. Now it all seemed like one misstep too many, and she'd lost the opportunity to get to know Sept well.

"How'd it go?" Sept asked, sitting in the chair crammed up against Fiona's desk.

"He wasn't happy, but I didn't have anything to do with Newsome or Verde. I got a reprieve, I guess, since he has me running down some information for him." She touched the mouse on her computer, and Sept seemed to take it as a sign to leave.

"Look," Fiona said, stopping her. Sept sat down again. "I fucked up when I got here, and I've done nothing to improve on that."

"Fiona, you need to learn one thing if you want to stay and succeed here. Cain Casey isn't some evil bitch, but she isn't white as the driven snow either. We grew up together, and despite our families and what we stand for, we became friends. I respect Cain because she's my friend, but if I find out something that proves she's broken the law, I'll take her in. Despite your experience here and with the feds, people like Cain don't buy and sell all of us."

"I know. Your dad said the same thing. I need some help with what your father needs, though. Any suggestions?"

"I'll put someone with you, but don't blow the opportunity to mend some fences. You keep treating everyone here like they're suspects, and you'll be alone on the street. In a place like New Orleans, that's a dangerous proposition at times."

"Thanks, and if it matters any, I don't think what happened today was right. Hannah seems like a sweet kid, so I won't drop the ball on this."

"Let's hope that's true. Teddie," Sept said loudly, getting the brunette by the copy machine to whip her head up. "Can you come here a minute, please?"

"What's up?" Detective Teddie Anderbrock walked toward them with a pronounced limp.

"You heard about the Casey thing today?"

"Yeah. They found that woman yet?" Teddie glanced at Fiona.

"Fiona's working on it. Would you mind giving her a hand?" Sept asked. "She's running down leads for the old man."

"Yeah, sure, if you don't mind I'm not one hundred percent?" Teddie watched Fiona as if to gauge her reaction. "Got an infection in my leg from debris in the storm, and it's not healing right."

"Sure, if you don't mind working with the new fuckup?" Her comeback drew a laugh from both Sept and Teddie. "Let's see if I can make any contact in Wisconsin, and then we'll take a ride to look for Newsome."

"Does Casey know about him?" Teddie asked.

Sept nodded. "Since she does, I imagine it'll make it that much harder to find him. If he's got any brains left, he should stay nice and quiet in whatever hole he's found to hide in," she said. "While you're poking around, see if there's any old or recent skeletons in his closet."

"Will do, and thanks, Sept."

"Hey, even fuckups deserve a second chance every so often. Don't make me sorry."

"I'm thinking the only two sorry people here are going to be Newsome and Carol," Fiona said.

"Especially if Cain finds them first," Teddie added.

They all nodded. True that.

CHAPTER NINETEEN

S o she's okay?" Remi asked Cain as they finished their meeting in Cain's home office.

"Emma's mother did a number on her, but for the most part she's fine. Sept did me the favor of coming by and photographing the scratch on her face and taking Hannah's statement, so we shouldn't have a problem once they find Carol." Cain had spent most of the afternoon upstairs with Emma and the kids to give Hannah back the sense of safety Carol had stripped away. She doubted it was over, but nightmares only faded with the passage of time and with her and Emma being there to make them go away.

"Do you want me to send out some people to look?"

"If we were trying to find anyone else, I'd say yes. But it's Emma's mother. In my opinion, she needs killing. But she's Emma's mother. I won't have that on my head, and I wouldn't do that to Emma." She sighed and tried hard not to yawn. After the last couple of days and all that had happened, she was tired. "She might want that kind of closure, but eventually Emma would come to regret that decision."

"We're here to help, you know that. My father is in love with Hannah, so he'll probably call you tomorrow to say the same thing."

"I appreciate both of you, but I'm leaving this one to Sept and Sebastian. Once all this settles, we'll have to take a trip out to Biloxi and get the casino up and running again, but I hope it's okay that's it's not a priority right now. Moving the structure inland saved us from a total loss, and the little damage we did have should be repaired by then."

"Ross knows we'll need him to come along, and he's as eager to help as ever, considering what happened today. I saw him at the house earlier and he seemed afraid to come home, so you might want to talk to him."

Cain smiled and shook her head. "I'm not that scary, am I?" They both laughed, which lightened the gloom that had brought her down all day. "You know how much I miss my father because I realize how close you are to yours. It's not just about the advice he was always happy to share when I asked, but simply the talks we had about so many subjects. Da was a big reader, so we'd sit outside and share a drink on most afternoons, and he'd tell me about whatever he'd found interesting that day."

"Papi's the same way. Considering how close we are and how you and your father were, I'm not sure how well I'm going to handle losing him."

"To tell you the truth, you don't. Not really anyway. It's the number of days that come after that loss that dull that pain, but it's always there." She got up and poured two drinks. She handed one to Remi and sat next to her. "My relationship with Ross has made me in a way miss Da more, but on the other hand helped me feel better. He's a world different from Dalton Casey, but they have one thing in common. Both of them love their children, and in our case, that means he loves my children like he does Emma."

"Then when he gets back, you need to remind him that you feel that way. He's a good man, and I'm enjoying working with him."

"Will do. Now get out of here since he mentioned he was cooking something up for you that has nothing to do with business." Cain slapped Remi on the back and got up. They went up and found Dallas holding and cooing over the baby while Emma watched.

"Ready to go, querida?" The smile on Remi's face telegraphed how she felt about Dallas.

"As soon as we can I'd like to babysit, so don't forget," Dallas said as she handed Billy to Cain. "And call me if you need anything at any time."

Remi held Dallas's hand on the way down the stairs and helped her into the car, eager to start their night. "Where do you want to go?" Dallas asked.

"How about dinner someplace romantic, and we'll go from there?"

They kissed as Simon turned out of the gate, and Dallas broke away from her when they stopped a few minutes later. "Do we have to go in? I was looking forward to a night off with just you." The house was so close that once they had children, they wouldn't have to go far to play with the Casey kids.

"One thing upstairs, and then I'm all yours." They got out and she winked at Simon, knowing she'd go as soon as they were inside. Her overprotective guard and friend insisted on a small group on the grounds, but they'd be alone otherwise. "Ross said something about some samples he left in the master-bedroom bathroom that you need to decide on, since they're ready to get started on that in the morning."

They climbed the stairs, and Dallas turned to her after she glanced down the hallway to the large master suite. The door was open, and it was easy to see the glow of candlelight, so Dallas grabbed both Remi's hands and walked backward for a few feet until Remi swept her up and carried her the rest of the way.

A few dozen candles illuminated the mattress at its center, along with a food basket and a champagne bucket.

"What's all this?" Dallas held her hands up to her face in a clear expression of delight.

"I've told you before that I loved this house because it holds a lot of good memories for me from when I was a kid. Our family spent time here running around with Cain and her siblings, so I saw that as a good omen," she said as Dallas gravitated to the windows that overlooked the large yard and guesthouse, as if imagining what Remi was saying.

When Dallas turned from the windows, she gasped. Remi was on one knee.

"A good omen that one day our children would play here with the friends and cousins that'll always be a part of their lives and help them build our business," Remi said.

"I want that more than anything."

"Dallas, you might not have started in the best of places, but I love you for the strong woman you are, who overcame all those obstacles. In my eyes, you aren't simply beautiful but perfect in the way you care for and protect those you love." She reached into her pocket and retrieved the box that held the symbol of the commitment she sought. "There will be no other woman for me for the rest of my days because I've found the one who is the other half of my soul. Dallas Montgomery, will you marry me?" Remi opened the box and took out the ring.

"Yes," Dallas said, running and throwing herself at Remi so hard that she almost knocked her on her back.

"Are you sure? Because once you put that ring on, I'm never letting you go."

"I've never been so sure of anything, and I've got a bucket list a mile long when it comes to the life I want with you."

She slid the ring onto Dallas's finger and closed her eyes as she kissed her knuckles. It wasn't something she'd ever thought she'd be truly ready for, but if Dallas had said no, it wouldn't have been easy to recover. Dallas's laughter made her forget any thoughts of sadness, and she opened her eyes to Dallas with her hands on her, taking her shirt off.

"I'd live my life over again a million times if I always end up here with you." Dallas looked at her hand and smiled when she studied the ring.

Remi had obsessed over it for months. With her mother Marianna's help she'd finally picked the square-cut diamond set on a platinum band.

"I love you, and I can't wait to start planning, but I need you to touch me," Dallas said.

Remi stood and unzipped Dallas's skirt, letting it drop to the floor. The white-lace underwear made her want to rush. It seemed like it had been so long, but tonight she wanted everything to be perfect. Dallas pouted a little until she began to strip, finishing what Dallas had started, and helped Dallas with the rest of her clothes. No way in hell was she letting this much time go by again without the sensation of Dallas's skin pressed against hers.

Dallas spread her legs as soon as they landed on the bed together, with Remi on top. The sensation of Dallas raking her fingernails up her back snapped her resolve to go slow. Without moving too much, she reached down and slid her hand between Dallas's legs, finding her wet and her clit as hard as the stone in her ring. When she pinched Dallas's clit between her fingers, Dallas dug her nails in hard and moaned.

"God, I've missed you," Dallas said, lifting her head and biting her neck gently. "But tonight isn't going to be just about you driving me insane before I touch you."

She moved her fingers up and down, and Dallas bit her harder. "You can do whatever you want, but I have to touch you."

"And you will," Dallas said as she pushed her off and rolled with her so she was now on top. "But first I want something from you."

"Whatever you want is yours."

"Are you sure, because I have something in mind." Dallas sucked on her earlobe as soon as she'd whispered that in her ear.

"Whatever you want, querida, but remember that I have to live out the night if you want me to walk down the aisle," she said and laughed.

"Then surrender," Dallas said as she moved down her body and knelt on the bed, looking at her in a way that Remi felt devoured.

"I'm yours," she said the second Dallas put her mouth on her. It took all her control to not come as soon as Dallas moved her tongue up her clit and then sucked her in. With one hand in Dallas's hair and the other strangling the sheets, she gritted her teeth. It was easy to hold on since Dallas had stopped.

"I don't want you to keep anything back from me," Dallas said before returning to what she'd been doing. She couldn't deny the request, so she let her legs fall open and allowed the rush of the orgasm to flood through her as she pressed her heels into the mattress. It was way too fast but gave her the opportunity to touch Dallas while she caught her breath.

She wanted to taste Dallas, but Dallas held her in place. "Right now, I need you to love me while I can look at you. I want you to see how much I love you and that I'm yours. It doesn't matter to me what the rest of the world thinks or wonders about us. I just want you to see that's the truth every time you look in my eyes."

Remi held her gaze and moved her hand between Dallas's legs. Dallas didn't last much longer than she had, and she laughed as she held her afterward.

"What's so funny?"

"If being engaged makes loving you a race, we may have to rush the wedding."

"Oh no," Dallas said, and pinched her side. "You've given me a fairy tale up to now, and I want the rest of it."

"I seldom skimp on anything, much less what makes you happy."

❖

"Where is he then?" Cain asked as Katlin and Muriel explained that Nunzio and Santino had disappeared from both New York and New Orleans. "Think about what can happen if we ignore this."

Muriel nodded and glanced at Katlin. "We've got someone reliable keeping an eye out in both locations. I agree that we can't let it go this time, because Nunzio's planning something. We'll keep searching until we've got all the pieces."

"Any luck finding where Santino was in Remi's condo building the night you saw him?"

"None of the names on the leases raised red flags after we checked them out, but I'm not taking any chances. We got the maintenance guy, who requested a favor afterward, to start checking every apartment. Tomorrow, we'll finish with the last five."

"What about Hector?"

Muriel smiled, wondering if Cain's brain ever truly slept. The strategizing that constantly went on in Cain's mind seemed almost second nature and was impressive to see on a daily basis. Carol Verde should've been the single thing on her cousin's mind, but she wasn't wired to ignore other potential problems. In Muriel's opinion, the only thing that would cheat Cain would be death, but not until she was done with everything necessary to keep her family safe for the next generation and Hayden was truly ready for that mantel.

"He's back, and from what we hear, he's got trouble in his ranks at the very top. Marisol's been getting cozy with Nicolette, and Hector has supply problems," Katlin said. "The safe houses that were hit had plenty of his supply, and he's going to have to start a war to get his toehold back."

"It's late, so get going. Tomorrow we'll have to meet with Ramon and Remi as well as the others to make sure Hector's war doesn't take any shots in our direction." Cain smiled and pointed to the door. "Go home. All this overtime is costing me a fortune."

They laughed. For all that went on in Cain's head, Emma and the kids really were the most important now and always.

Muriel thought about that as she headed home to her quiet house. At night, when the place creaked and settled around her without her father for company, she sensed the loneliness of her life the most.

She left her car in the front drive and went in to find her housekeeper in the foyer. "Anything wrong?"

"You have a visitor so I thought it wasn't a good idea to leave them alone." The woman pointed to the den. "If you're hungry, I left dinner in the oven."

"Any hints?" she asked, curious when the woman hesitated, then shook her head.

"It's better to discover some things on your own," the housekeeper said and winked. "Have a good night."

Muriel stood there until the back door closed. Whoever was waiting obviously didn't pose a threat. She opened the doors to the den and found Kristen at the small desk with a few books open. Homework, she guessed, which made her pause. Schoolbooks made their age difference feel like a slap in the face. This might be a bad idea for this beautiful young woman.

"Such gloomy thoughts already?" Kristen said without lifting her head. "The way I see it, you have a choice, Counselor."

"What's that?" She took a seat on the leather couch not too far away.

"You can eat alone or you can take me out to dinner. And depending on how good the meal is, your night might hold promise." Kristen got up and straddled her lap as she slid her fingers into Muriel's hair. She hardened instantly at the touch. It'd been so long since she'd even thought of having sex with anyone. "And I peeked in the oven. You're better off taking me to dinner."

Muriel cocked her head back and put her hands on Kristen's hips, which was the only encouragement she seemed to need. The passion in their kiss made the objections in her head disappear, and she moved her hands up to the undersides of Kristen's breasts. "Are you sure you want to go out?"

"There she is," Kristen said as she put a little separation between them. "I knew you weren't made of stone, but the ten years between us seem to be worming through here whenever you first see me," she said, tapping on the side of Muriel's head as if she could read Muriel's thoughts with the touch. "Now you know, like I do, though, time is relative when we want what we want."

Muriel watched Kristen as she dipped her hand under her skirt and between her legs, but only briefly. "You want to be honorable, but I just want you." Kristen brought her hand back up to paint Muriel's lips with her wet fingers before sliding them into her mouth. The little taste made Muriel want more.

But wanting more wasn't exactly the right way to describe her feelings. She needed more and now. "Are you sure?"

"That I want to go out to dinner with you? Yes, I'm starved." Kristen stood up and held her hand out. "Ready?"

"You want to go out now?" She was so hard and ready that walking out of the house would be a problem.

"Baby," Kristen said, leaning over and running her hand from Muriel's knee to her crotch, "we're going out, so come on."

"We can order in."

"I want you to sit in a crowded place and think about two things and forget two things." Muriel took a deep breath when Kristen took her hand.

"What?" she said, and her voice sounded two octaves higher.

"Tonight I want you to consider that I've been sitting here imagining us together, which made me crave your touch and forget about all those objections of how this might be a bad idea. I know what I want and what I'm doing."

"That's one thing to think about and one thing to forget."

"Then I want you to think about the fact that nothing is standing in the way of what you want." Kristen guided her hand under the short skirt to show her that nothing was keeping her from touching her. "I also want you to forget who we are as individuals."

Kristen was so wet Muriel was having trouble understanding what she meant. "The first part I get, but not the forget part."

"You're Muriel Casey, Cain Casey's cousin and advisor. I'm Kristen Montgomery, future sister-in-law of Remi Jatibon. Individually we're that, but together it'll be something else, and it'll be ours."

An hour later they were sitting in Vincent's restaurant with Kristen's scent on her fingers and her foot halfway up her pants leg. It was an exercise in patience, but she knew Kristen's game. By the time they got home she'd be lucky to make it to the door before she gave in and eased the profound pain she was experiencing. For that she had to smile. There were worse tests in the world and worse positions to be in.

"Muriel." The person who'd uttered her name dampened her desire considerably.

"Agent Phillips," she said, looking to her right to acknowledge her old lover. "Thank you for any help you gave in finding Hannah."

"How are you?" Shelby appeared haggard and exhausted.

"I'm fine, thanks for asking, but if that's all, we were in the middle of something."

"I'm sorry to do this here, Muriel, but you won't take my calls. What I did was wrong and I know there's no going back, but please know that I'm sorry for hurting you. Nothing was worth losing you, and I didn't realize that until it was out of my reach."

Shelby's betrayal hadn't completely killed any feelings they'd once had for each other, because even now a small part of her cared for this woman. Then again, Emma was a stunning example of seeing how the heart could forgive. But Shelby was no Emma Casey, so it was time to let go for good.

"Thanks for saying that, but as I said, we're in the middle of something."

Shelby nodded, and Muriel watched Kristen stare at the door for a long moment after Shelby exited.

"Is she why you're holding back?" Kristen asked.

Muriel shook her head.

"Then go after her and ease her into that frame of mind. I promise I'll be here waiting."

Shelby was right outside, her head tilted back as if studying the cloudy night sky.

"If it helps, I understand what you did and why, but you also had to realize there was no going back once I found out."

"I thought I was careful, but I forgot who your greatest champion is. In the end, I was an idiot."

"So this is about getting caught?" She owed Cain so much more than just for getting her out of this situation.

"No, Muriel, it's about thinking that my job was more important than my heart. You're never going to believe me, but I love you. In you I found what I didn't think existed, and by my own choice or fear I gave it away."

"If you need me to say it, I forgive you. We can't go against our nature no matter how hard we try or how enticing the prize. You're good at your job because you pour yourself into it, and I'm a good Casey because I'm loyal to my own. Neither of those things can survive and thrive with the other."

"Maybe you've found your answer then, and she's waiting inside."

"Don't…I'd wish you luck, Shelby, though that wouldn't be smart for my family. But I do hope you find something or someone who'll hold you while your heart heals. I barely remember my mother, but my father's loss helps me understand your pain. If I can do something for that, please call me. I also believe that losing your parents the way you did played a part in your actions. You betrayed me for what you believed my family did, and you believed it because one of your own set it up that way. Perhaps you don't owe the job absolutely everything. For once think of yourself and what'll make you feel better."

"Thanks," Shelby said softly, her eyes shiny with unshed tears. "And I really am sorry. After the chance you took, you didn't deserve that betrayal." Shelby's car arrived, and she waved before tipping the valet and leaving.

"I had them wrap it to go," Kristen said when she got back inside.

"I'm sorry." And she really was since her body at the moment didn't understand or care about her heart or her head.

"The night's not over, baby, but maybe the next part should be Vincent's chicken on the sofa and an old movie."

"How'd you get to be so smart?" she said as the waiter came back with a bag and instructions to leave without worrying about the bill.

"My sister's taught me many things, but the most important is that nothing you want for your future can be built on the wreckage of the past. You've got to sweep it away so you can lay a new foundation. That woman was your past, and in the light of day, maybe tomorrow or the next day, you'll see a glimpse of the future." Kristen reached for her hand and smiled. "This time, though, you don't have to worry about the soundness of what you want to build."

"I'm beginning to see that even in the darkness."

CHAPTER TWENTY

"I'm not telling you what to do, but keep your mouth shut and listen to this guy carefully," Santino said as they sat outside on the veranda of their suite. The resort they'd picked was full of tourists trying to escape the cold of the northern United States, but the crowd would also prevent a surprise attack if Roth tried to double-cross them.

"I know what I'm doing," Nunzio said, already aggravated.

"How the hell do you think I've lived this long and your father didn't?"

The question was as effective as a slap, and Nunzio peered at him, remembering who his grandfather was and how important he was to his future. Santino was older, but he'd built an empire out of what his father had left him, and he'd done it one vicious act at a time.

"I didn't spend all my time trying to prove something to everyone around me except to the most important person."

"In my case I guess that'd be you, right?"

"Where in the fuck did I go wrong with your father, because as sure as hell whatever he taught you, like him you're always the victim no matter the situation?"

Nunzio cocked his fists and moved back, ready to hit Santino and send him packing to Florida to rot. "You're just like him. When things are out of your control, you lash out at me because you think I'm stupid."

"Keep acting like this and you'll prove me right. The person you have to prove yourself to isn't me or any other man you know. Look in the mirror and try to gain some respect for yourself." Santino got up and buttoned his jacket. "Until then you're like a little kid going around trying to be the loudest, as if that'll prove you're the smartest and the strongest. That'll get you killed before you leave here, and I refuse to sit around and watch that. I've already buried my son, so one of your goons can take care of that for you."

The old man started walking, and if he called him back he'd be right back where he started when he was under Junior's thumb and disapproval. "Wait," he said, not having the guts to chance it.

"Before you say anything else," Santino said, not turning around, "I'm not here to put you in your place. I'm here to teach you what Junior refused to learn. That's it. Agree to that, and you'll live to see your grandson take over what you've built. Don't, and you'll be keeping your father company in that marble box."

"All right, but you should know my father thought you lived this long because you're a coward not capable of taking chances." He couldn't help but throw out the one shot he knew would inflict the most pain.

"We have in common our feelings for my son, Nunzio, but stop wasting your time trying to find ways to hurt me. If you think I didn't know exactly who Junior was and what he thought, then you're as stupid as he told me you were, and I've given you too much credit," Santino said, skillfully twisting the knife he'd unsheathed himself. "That you said it at all means I'm wasting my time with you, so good luck."

"Wait," he yelled, but this time it was from fear of being alone. "I'm sorry, Nino. I know I've got to control myself better, but I can't get my father out of my head." Santino had stopped but hadn't turned around. "I need you here and with me. Please…I'm sorry."

The knock came before Santino could answer, and Nunzio fully expected his grandfather to open the door and keep walking, but Santino welcomed whoever it was. "Thank you for coming, Mr. Kalina. My grandson is right out here." Santino walked back with him and smiled at him as if to say they were fine.

They all shook hands, and Kalina's men waited outside the door, so he poured the sangria he'd ordered and put his sunglasses back on. "Considering Roth Pombo set this up, I want to thank you for coming. I realize it's not something you had to do," Nunzio said.

Cesar glanced between him and Santino but said nothing as he took a few sips of his drink. "Santino Luca, you I recognize, but you I don't know," Cesar said finally. "I seldom talk, much less do business with someone I don't know."

"Have we met?" Santino asked, and Nunzio decided to follow his advice and stay quiet.

"I was at one of Junior's infamous parties, and you were sitting in the corner looking down your nose at everyone there." Cesar drained his glass and laughed. "I'm sure it's because there was a time people like me bowed and scraped at your feet and were happy with the scraps you gave us. To treat us as equals that night seemed to be too much to bear."

"A healthy ego is necessary in this business, but I was fair with everyone I dealt with."

Cesar laughed again as he poured himself another drink. "I'm shitting with you. I'm here because you did business with my uncle years ago. Roth can't touch me now, so I'm not here because of him. My uncle, though, he vouch for you, so what you have in mind?"

"Roth and his representatives are under the impression he took the fall for you, or something like that," Santino said, and brought his glass up, but Nunzio doubted he tasted the sweet wine. "Are you done with him?"

"Roth Pombo's a smart man and a loyal man, so I'm not done with him at all. He make me a lot of money when things were good and stayed quiet when he could help himself by talking." An uproar came from the direction of the pool, but it was only a group of kids having fun so they all relaxed. "Roth want out, I know this, but not to restart the business he had. If he out he can still be valuable."

"What's he interested in then, revenge?" Nunzio asked, and Cesar shook his head.

"It happens to all of us some time, but you have to learn to control it, or you land in a place where the lights never go out and it make you crazy." Cesar twirled his finger next to his ear. "He went loco before the federales stuck him in that fucking cement box, but it was because of the woman he meet, so he fell in love and he surrender to protect her more than me. I never thought it was because he owe me too much. Many look, but we all know she end up with the money. A lot of it."

"What do you want with him?" Nunzio asked, and his grandfather cleared his throat.

"The same thing you want. Roth make the route, and the product always get there safe. No problem through customs or anywhere."

"How do we get him out?"

"It take a little time and plenty pesos, but I have a business deal for you," Cesar said and held up his glass for a toast. "We must all show a little faith in the other to make it work though, so think about it."

"Give us something to think about," Santino said as he tapped his glass to Cesar's.

"I'll give you that and a shipment. You don't need no money."

"What's the catch?" Nunzio said, knowing no one in this business gave you anything except a bullet to the brain if you let your guard down.

"The shipment will be your responsibility from here to the street. Once you see how much you make, you buy Roth's freedom. You see from this how hard it'll be, so you understand how important it is to get him out." Cesar got up and shook their hands again. "You have a few days to decide. If your answer no, don't stay here too long. Mexico is not safe for tourists who go looking for trouble."

Freddie dipped his finger in a pile of coke and ran it along his gums. For the last few days it was the only way to keep the boredom away, but he'd had enough. Nunzio and the old man had left him here like some fucking flunky, no matter what Nunzio said about it being an important job. At least Santino had been more honest about it when he'd come by to see him before they left on the trip he was supposed to go on. The old man had promised to kill him if he didn't start learning to take orders, and until he did, he'd be doing this kind of shit.

Proving himself worthy of the great Lucas, though, was about to make him go fucking mad staring at the empty apartment except for the mounds of drugs they'd stolen from Hector.

"Fuck this," he said, heading to the bathroom and turning on the shower. His buzz was driving his need to be around people, even if it was in a bar. When he was clean, he dressed and headed out with the keys and pass Nunzio had left by the door.

It was late, and all he could find open was the bar at the Piquant, but all that mattered was it was full of people having fun and getting drunk. He smiled when he saw all the women sitting alone. Maybe fucking someone would be motivation enough to finish packing all that shit waiting on him back in the condo. He hadn't let go of the notion that Nunzio would actually share it with him since the mountain of white powder was there because of him, and him alone. The fucker would eventually show a little gratitude and respect.

"Beer and a shot of vodka," he said to the bartender when the woman got close enough.

He glanced around the room, and none of the women he stared at seemed too interested since they gave that usual disgusted expression when he looked them up and down, so he concentrated on the beauty sitting close to him. "Can I get you something?" he asked, and the woman turned her barstool toward him. Fuck, he thought as he saw the scar that ran up the otherwise pretty face.

"Does this bother you?" she said, outlining the entire thing with her index finger.

"Nah," he lied, figuring he could always fuck with his eyes closed. "I just want to buy you a drink. Give her another of what she's having," he said when the woman put his order down. "You new to town or just visiting?"

"I'm a new resident, but I needed a drink before I went to bed. You use all your FEMA money on that suit?"

The dig broke through his high, but he didn't say anything rude. "How'd you know it's a new suit?"

"You forgot to uncover one of the expensive buttons," she said reaching over and taking the tissue paper off the bottom one, and her accent intrigued him. "Off the rack but nice." She ran her fingers along the lapel and went back to her drink.

"I work for Nunzio Luca, so money's not my problem." He threw the shot back and coughed a little when it burned the back of his throat.

Nicolette was about to leave to get away from this loser, but the name he mentioned sounded familiar. "Give my friend another shot and I'll be right back." She stood and placed her hand on his chest. "Promise you won't run off."

"I'll be right here, beautiful."

In the bathroom, after checking to see if she was alone, she called home and smiled when she got Luce. "Remind me again who Nunzio Luca is."

"He's a dealer trying to rebuild what his father had before he got killed, from what I understand," Luce said, not bothering with small talk since she hadn't either. "Compared to Hector, he's small and not worth wasting time on."

"What about—" She started to ask another question, but the line had gone dead. "You were always a child, weren't you?"

She came back, glad to see this idiot had followed directions, so she smiled at him and chose to sit next to him. "So you really work for Luca?" she asked as she put her hand on his leg. "I hear he's a bad man, but that sounds so exciting."

"He's not too bad, but like every boss, he can be an asshole. I'm like his right hand, so pretty soon I'm going to be a big man here. At least a guy with a load of cash who can buy you nice shit."

From the look of him and his eyes, he was high, and probably not from beer and vodka. "Really? Does he really sell drugs?" she whispered in his ear as her hand went higher. "I always wanted to fuck someone like that." It would've been too fast had it been any other guy, but she figured this little man full of himself was as easy to break as straw. If he had what she guessed he did, she could cut Marisol and her father loose. She wouldn't need either of them going forward.

"Fuck me instead then," he said and laughed, putting his hand over hers as if to make sure it didn't disappear. "I sell the drugs for him, and we're about to make a killing."

Hell, this was so easy she thought it might be a setup. "Are you sure you should be talking about this?"

"Who you going to tell?" Freddie said and laughed as he downed his second shot. "I'm glad I got out of that fucking room for a little while, because you were right here waiting for me."

It amazed her that someone this stupid could function on a daily basis. What was Nunzio Luca thinking having someone like this on his payroll? "What room?"

"That I can't tell you." He shook his finger in her face, his pupils so dilated she wondered if he was seeing her clearly. "Nunzio would kill me for that. What's your name, anyway?"

"I'm Nic, and I'm good at keeping secrets," she said, moving her hand again until it covered his crotch. "If we go back to your place I'll show you just how badly I want to fuck someone who's no nice guy."

"We can go to your place. Can't take you to mine." He held her hand and rubbed it over his hardening dick, closing his eyes.

"Not unless you want to meet my husband." She broke his hold and stood up. "Maybe some other time."

"Wait." He ran his hands over his head, messing up his hair to the point it was standing straight up on his head. "Fuck me." He kept at it as if trying to make a decision in his inebriated state. "Okay, but if you tell anyone I'll kill you. Understand?"

"Perfectly. Hell, I don't even know your name," she said, shaking her head slightly when her people began to follow them out. "So you scored big, huh?" she said as they walked in a weaving pattern down the street, the guy practically hanging on her, trying to reach over her neck to her breasts. She figured she was on her way to finding Hector's stolen stash.

"Real big, and twice too. It was all me, and I brought it to Mr. Luca, so that's how I got up that ladder so quick. A year ago I was selling dime bags on the corner, and now I'm sitting on a big pile of shit waiting to make my fortune."

"Then you need to tell me your name, so I'll get wet thinking about tonight when I hear them mention you on the news."

"It's Freddie, baby, and you'll get plenty wet tonight when I take care of you." The building behind the Hilton by the river wasn't where she thought they'd be going, but Freddie came to a sudden stop when he saw the front of the place swarming with cops. "Fuck, no," he said holding on to her for what now felt like real support. "I'm a fucking dead man."

CHAPTER TWENTY-ONE

Katlin stood in the shadows of Harrah's casino across from Remi's building and watched the cops respond to the call she'd placed earlier. After an extensive search, it would've had to be the third-to-last apartment they looked in, but it'd been worth it. The condo two floors under Simon and Juno's place was full of drugs, and a lot of it had Hector's markings on the bags. That answered the question of who'd stolen from Hector, and it also meant their call to the police effectively kept it out of Hector's reach. A double win as far as Katlin was concerned.

"So Sept got the cavalry there in time?" Cain asked over the phone.

"The cavalry and the marines, from the looks of it. Place is swarming with cops, so hopefully Remi's home to keep them from getting creative."

"I called her so that's not a problem." Katlin heard someone come in and say something. "Hang on," Cain said as she obviously listened. "When?"

"What is it?"

"Merrick said the alarm on the warehouse in Destrehan just went off. Someone broke in."

"You want me to go?" she asked, starting her two-block walk back to her car.

"I want you back here, but call and pick up Finley before you get here. We need to have a talk."

"Cain, are you sure?" She quickened her steps but didn't run with so many cops around. Running in situations like this was like screaming you were guilty of something. "That place is full of inventory, so we need to get someone over there unless you want to see what's happening here play out over there as well."

"We'll talk about it when you get back, but be careful with Finley for now. Eventually she'll be free to come and go as she pleases, but I'd like for the Antakov thing to die down a bit." Cain hung up and glanced at Merrick. "This'll be the shortest vacation ever."

"Not necessarily, but we knew this might happen. You can plan for everything, but someone's still going to blame you for something." Merrick sat down and rubbed the side of her head.

"You feeling okay?" she asked, coming around the desk to join her. "I don't want you pushing yourself to the point of pain."

"My head hurts sometimes, but I'm getting used to it so it doesn't bother me as much as it used to because the headaches aren't as bad. Hopefully the doctor's right and eventually they'll disappear altogether."

Merrick did seem to be regaining the appearance of health she'd had before all this happened. The physical therapist still came three days a week to work with her, so her movements looked smoother and not as stiffly concentrated as they were when she finally started walking again. Overall, from both the doctor's opinion and the physical therapist, Merrick's recovery had been miraculous up to then.

"Whenever it's too much, don't be afraid to say something."

"I will, so drop it, Boss." Merrick patted her hand like she would've done for a small child in need of reassurance. "I fought too hard to get back here to slow down now. So you want me to go out to the warehouse and see what's going on?"

"Tonight isn't the time," Cain said, not having the patience for this. "Like I told Katlin, let me talk to Finley and we'll take it from there."

"If I know Katlin, she's freaking about all that booze the police might be carting off if we wait and don't control the situation."

"Let me worry about that while you worry about something else for me." She'd been thinking about something since before Emma had gone into labor and just hadn't had time to do anything about it. "I need you to find what you can about the parents of Hannah's friend Lucy. Something's strange about this whole thing, and it's making my head buzz a little. I'd rather be sure it's simply a bad divorce and nothing else."

"You got some names for me?"

"From what Emma tells me, it's Drew and Taylor Kennison. He's in the oil industry, and I'm not sure about her."

"You want to share what's making you curious?" Merrick asked, but not in a joking way.

"I'm not sure. Something just feels off." The sound of Katlin and Finley's conversation made her stand and open the door. "I might be getting paranoid from the lack of sleep lately, but check it out."

Finley hugged her as she came in and then went to shake hands and introduce herself to Merrick. Once the niceties were out of the way, Katlin asked for a few minutes before she sat with Finley.

"You want me to set anything up with Delarosa?" Katlin asked. "You know he's got to have someone on the payroll at NOPD by now with the kind of cash he's putting on the street."

"Did *our* payroll contacts tell you if they found any idea of who was inside, aside from Santino? If he was coming out the day Muriel saw him, you know it's got to be from there, but I doubt even Santino's that into his work."

"Not yet, and I doubt we'll know who it is now if he sees all those cops crawling over every inch of the place." Katlin opened the door and let the others back in. "I'll keep checking and make some calls tomorrow."

Katlin and Merrick headed out, and Finley got right to the point. "Did you think about what we talked about before?"

"Are you sure? The love of what you do doesn't change overnight, no matter what happened." What Finley wanted would be the equivalent of her leaving her family's business and becoming an FBI agent. Not impossible but highly improbable. "If you come to work for me and the feds find out, it's going to put you in a tight spot and lock a lot of doors for you. The kind of doors you worked damn hard to open. No matter what, I don't want you to be sorry for something because you didn't think it through."

"I caught perverts, Cain, and that'll continue with or without me. This case with Abigail and the family she married into changed something in me, but it's not what my old workmates are going to think if they find out about you."

"I'm listening." This would have to be the toughest job interview she'd ever conduct because of the long-lasting ramifications.

"From a young age I wanted to pursue something that went against that Casey stream that runs strong through both of us, but you and the rest of the family never tried to change my mind. I only thought about one thing in all those years, and that's what *I* wanted." Finley sat with her hands pressed together between her legs. "I never thought about anything else until I was the only thing between men with guns in a hotel room in New York and a group of innocent people. The choices Nicola Eaton made cost Abigail and her children everything. I'm tired of doing that to my family. You can deny it to make me feel better, but we both know that's the cold truth."

"Did you talk to your parents about all this? Working for me won't be what you think, and I want you to apply what you just said about Nicola. Don't go from a job that stripped away family relationships from necessity, to another job that could put Abigail and those kids in the same place for a slew of other reasons."

Finley's hands were becoming whiter from the strain of how hard she was holding them together.

"I can't go back, and I don't want to transfer here, so you'd turn me down?" Finley asked tightly. "And yes, I talked to my parents. My father worked for yours, and my mother's the best person in the world to talk to about this because, like you, she grew up here. She knew precisely what I was asking and, more important, why I was asking it."

"I already knew that because I talked to Aunt Siobhan," she said and smiled to loosen Finley up. "You need to stop thinking your family sacrificed everything. Sometimes everything in your life is about making your children smile, and you're getting ready to find out what you're willing to do for your family's happiness."

"So I have a job?"

"I lost a kid special to me for a stupid reason, and I've never replaced him. Now fate has told me why. Bryce was my IT specialist, and he died at the hands of someone trying to prove to me only that he could be killed even with my protection." She thought about Bryce and his enthusiasm for a job that would've driven her nuts because it required sitting in a room all day. She'd taken care of his family but still was furious with herself for not taking better care of him. "Not the best endorsement for a job, but I think that's the best place for you to start."

"I can do more than that. Come on. I'm a trained agent."

"Let's start with you setting up a business, legit and away from me. Feel free to take on other work like Muriel does, but working for me means that you have to change sides. I've got my own little team out there that wants nothing more than to find the one conversation, move, or screw-up that they can use to lock me up."

"Don't worry, cousin. I'll have to work hard to keep up with all the new technology they'll be using once I resign, but I've got an idea of what they've got set up to keep eyes and ears on you."

"Then equip that office, and I'll have the bank call you about an account for it. We'll agree that you're going to be our intel and security specialist. That'll bring you back into the fold and will make me feel better that you have my back."

"Anything important you want me to start on, aside from the guys outside?"

"The place we met with the Antakovs was broken into, so I want you to check it out and see what you find. Don't go alone. In fact, take your brother with you, and I'll get a few more guys to tag along. If it's anything at all to do with that meeting, call me immediately so I can put a wall between your new family and the idiots that might be looking for payback."

"You got it, but the cops didn't show up?"

"Not exactly, and whoever was stupid enough to break in didn't exactly find what they were looking for either, but I'd like to know who it is."

"Can I take a bottle of wine?"

"If you can find one, then go ahead," she said, and laughed.

❖

The sky outside was violet, and Cain noticed the van under the streetlamp. She was walking the floor with the baby even though the little boy was sleeping, as was Emma. "What do you think they're doing in there, huh?" she asked the baby softly and smiled when he opened his eyes. The shade of green was a perfect match to Emma's. "I guess they think I must sneak out at night and suck people's blood around town, but all I'm doing is keeping you company."

Billy blinked a few times and grasped her finger when she touched his hand. "Are you looking at this kid from heaven, Billy?" she said to the brother she still missed. Billy had always been there to get into trouble with and to watch her back, and she'd loved seeing him live life like he knew his days were limited.

"If this one is anything like you, I'll be gray way before I'm fifty." The baby yawned, and she sat with him to see if he'd go back to sleep.

"If you hold him like that all night, he's going to think that bassinet has ants in it," Emma said, not lifting her head.

"How is he ever going to learn the family history if he's cooped up in there?" she asked, and sighed from total contentment as he yawned again. "It'll be a much more riveting tale than anything they'll teach him in school."

"True, but we've got a lifetime for him to get all the facts. For tonight, put him down and come over here and tell me some tales."

She held Emma as soon as she knew he wasn't going to fuss and caught her up on everything that was going on. "They haven't found her yet?" Emma asked about her mother. "She's a housewife from Wisconsin, not exactly the clandestine type, so I'm shocked she's eluded you and the police."

"She probably ran to Newsome and he's got her stashed somewhere. He'll keep her under wraps until he finds a way to get out of the shit hole he landed himself in." She kissed the top of Emma's head and tried not to think about how long it would be before they got back to being intimate. She missed that part of their relationship. "We'll find her, don't worry, and for once I'm going to enjoy calling the cops."

"What about the rest?"

"I'm not at all a friend of Hector's, but I'm going to give him a call tomorrow and invite him to the office for coffee. What the cops confiscated tonight was his, and I'm positive Nunzio stole it from him."

"What does that have to do with having coffee with him?" Emma asked and, like the baby, yawned in her arms.

"When you have too many fronts to fight on, it's best to take out what you can using someone else. Nunzio could be a problem for us, so I'm going to tell Hector exactly who stole his drugs." She could feel Emma's steady breathing against her shoulder so she closed her eyes and concentrated on the sound. "I figure if Nunzio ends up dead, it's a win-win situation. I don't care who does it."

CHAPTER TWENTY-TWO

Muriel grabbed for the phone, not coordinated enough to not knock it to the floor, waking Kristen. They'd come back to her house the night before and watched an old Audrey Hepburn movie Kristen had found, then gone up to bed. The playfulness they'd shared before they went out and ran into Shelby had vanished, but Kristen had gone into the bathroom and come out wearing her shirt with no intention of going home. They'd spent the rest of the night talking and finally falling asleep holding each other like in some romance novel, which made her roll her eyes, knowing how crushing it was to her reputation.

"Hello," she said, squinting to see the time.

"Muriel, did I wake you?" The man's voice was loud, and she had to think a minute before she figured out who it was. "I thought Cain said you never slept."

"Colin, if it's five thirty here it's damn early where you are. Can't get to sleep?"

"I'm in town, and I need to see you and Cain."

She sat up and rubbed her face, knowing if he couldn't wait until a decent hour, whatever he needed wasn't good. "You don't mean now, do you?"

"No. I got some stuff to do until like two, but then you gotta get me in to see her, okay? After the shit before her wedding, I didn't want to do anything before I talk to her."

His explanation was as foggy as her head at the moment. "Give me your number, and I'll call you as soon as I get to Cain's." She wrote down the information and sighed. "You sure you're okay?"

"I got some shit going on, but really, it's fixable. Sorry I woke you," he said, and the line went dead.

"What the hell was that?" she said as she lay back and could've cared less what the problem was when Kristen put her head on her shoulder and pinned her down with her leg.

"Tonight let's try this again, without the phone and clothes, okay?"

"I'm sorry about all that last night. We should've stayed home and ordered pizza."

Kristen put her hand on her abdomen and rubbed it in small circles. "There's things you should be worried about, and all that crap isn't one of them. Maybe, though, I should be worried that she's still got the hots for you."

"Shelby knows as well as I do that there's no going back." She smiled when Kristen moved on top of her. "So when do you graduate?" The question should've made her cringe, but that was hard to do when Kristen bit her chin.

"Two more semesters, and then I'm done. Why?"

"Seeing how much time I have to shop for a gift. How about breakfast?" She rolled them over and put her hands on Kristen's hips. She kissed her, and getting up really dropped down the stack of her priorities.

"I guess the phone call means you can't take the day off," Kristen said, tracing the outside of her ears with her fingertips. "Tonight, though, don't make any plans." Kristen kissed her again and slapped her on the ass. "Come on. I'll cook for you."

"You know, this can wait," she said, pointing to the bed when they got up. "I'm not going anywhere if we do."

"If you ask my sister, she still believes I'm like twelve, so don't ask her, all right," Kristen said, and laughed. "But I'm okay with this and who I'm with. I'm not sure if you know what happened to us, well, mostly to Dallas, but I've waited a long time to find someone I feel this comfortable with. I'm sure I have, so I'm not interested in waiting any more. Does that make sense?"

"Perfect sense, but I'm patient, so don't be afraid that I'm only here because I expect something like that."

"You're here because you live here, but I get you."

She dropped Kristen at her door and drove to Cain's, seeing Fiona O'Brannigan outside in her car talking on her phone. That someone

Cain really didn't care for that much was camped outside the gate made her want to go out and see what she wanted.

"The world's gone a little nuts, hasn't it?" Cain asked from the garden Ross had planted. She was dressed and had a coffee cup in her hand, but Muriel doubted she was trying her hand at farming.

"Did you see who's out there?" Muriel left her briefcase on the hood of her car and joined Cain, holding her cup when she stopped at the last crop of sunflowers Ross had planted and pointed out to her a few days before. Cain cut a bouquet of them and headed back inside. "Are you ever going to tell me what bothers you so much about her, aside from what happened? I know there's got to be more to the story than her ganging up with that FBI asshole over something you didn't do."

"Eventually, but can you give me some more time? I'm still working through it." Cain stopped at the stairs and put her hand against Muriel's neck. "If I forgot we had something this morning, forgive me, but I'll just be a minute."

"We didn't, but I got a call earlier this morning you need to know about. Take your time."

The sound of Hannah running around and Hayden getting ready for school made her say a quick prayer of thanks since whatever had happened with Hannah hadn't left any permanent scars. Muriel was surprised Cain was letting her go back so soon, but then both their fathers had been firm believers in getting back in the saddle before you developed a fear of the horse.

She rode with them to school at Cain's invitation and waited in the car as Cain walked Hannah to the door and the teacher waiting there. No one seemed to have a problem that Sabana was going in with her, so Hannah hugged Cain good-bye and ran inside like she had nothing in the world to fear.

"Who called?" Cain asked as they headed back.

"Colin, and he's in town. I'd tell you what he wants, but he wasn't in a talkative mood for once."

Cain nodded and drummed her fingers on her knee for a few minutes. "If he gave you a number, let him know that this afternoon will be good whenever he's ready, and if you're not swamped this morning, can you stop by and see Merrick? I have her working on something, and my gut tells me the answer is more important than I give it credit for."

"Sure, but do you need anything else?"

"To see a man about a revenge plot, but that should be easy."

"Yes, sir, it happened last night," Mike Walker, one of Nunzio's men, said over the phone from the house in New York.

"What did the little fucker say exactly?" Nunzio asked, punching a hole in the wall of his bedroom at the resort.

"He just said he'd needed a breather and left for like thirty minutes, and when he got back, the place was crawling with cops. He doesn't know if they were in your place, but he didn't want to go in and find out."

"Get on a plane and meet me in New Orleans. Do whatever you have to to find him and what the hell happened to my shit, or if anything happened to it at all." He punched the wall again, even though his hand hurt like hell. "And Mike, don't fuck this up."

"Don't worry, I'll take care of it. What about Freddie? You want me to take care of that too?"

"When you find him, drop him in the river. He'll be more useful to the fish than to us. I gave that fucker the last chance he's ever going to get." He hung up and screamed one more time.

"What now?" Santino said as he rushed in.

The last thing he needed was a lecture on how'd he screwed up trusting Freddie, but they had to get it out of the way so they could plan their next step. He told Santino what Mike had reported and was surprised when he didn't immediately light into him.

"If the cops were there because of that apartment, every bit of our extra stash is gone. That's what I was going to use to start buying from Cesar and Roth." God, he should've killed Freddie the second he took him to that hotel room full of bottles of liquid coke. But he didn't have time to worry about shit he couldn't do anything about, much less change.

"The only move we have left is to call Cesar and tell him we'll take the shipment and do what he asked. If we can pull off getting Pombo out of that hellhole, then we won't have to worry about inventory—we'll be swimming in it."

"You don't think Cesar or Pombo won't double-cross us if they get the chance?"

"The secret here is to divide and conquer."

He wanted to punch something again and didn't care if it turned out to be his grandfather if he didn't speak clearer. "What the fuck is that supposed to mean?"

"That the first step is to get Pombo out and on more familiar ground. Our ground."

CHAPTER TWENTY-THREE

The club always appeared so different in the light of day, but the cleaning crew made sure it never smelled like old booze. Cain always insisted on that since it set them apart from so many places. She sat at a table and stared at Emma's name etched into the mirror behind the bar. Once the city became busier and people returned, she planned to open a few more places, but this would always be the jewel in the city.

"Tell me you did not get me up early to gloat," Hector said when he entered with a few people and Marisol. His daughter resembled a prizefighter after a night in the ring, with no gold belt to go along with the ass kicking someone had given her. "I'd think that wasn't your style, but I'm glad you called. I have a few questions that your past rudeness makes me have to ask you."

"I called not as your friend, but to prove I'm not your enemy either." She waved to the chair across from her and waited.

"For someone who claims not to want to do business with me, you call quite often." Hector sat, and Cain wanted to give him her full attention, but the blonde close to Marisol was hard to look away from. It was like seeing a ghost from Nunzio's past get up from having her throat cut to walk into her club.

Her face, though, was younger and the gaze not quite as calculating as Kim Stegal's. This girl had to be her sister, and from the way she was glaring, Cain knew exactly who she blamed for her sister's bad luck.

"You could go into politics with lies like that, Hector," she said, not wanting to waste too much time with this fool, but it was important to load him like a cannon and aim him in the right direction. "You've evidently been having a bit of bad luck lately and don't know where to point your gun to make it stop."

"And you do?" Hector laughed, but he was the only one in his party who did. Whoever the blonde was, she was pissed, and Marisol seemed to be in the same mood, but her eyes never left the back of Hector's head. It was a big clue as to who was to blame for her appearance.

"Not long ago I heard someone got hit and lost some people in what the rumor mill said were safe houses for large amounts of coke. After they got taken out, the owner couldn't exactly call the cops to file a report, so I imagined what I'd do if that happened to me."

One of her crew put down two espressos and went back to sit at the bar. "Are you going to tell me something important or talk me to death?" Hector asked.

"I could just leave you here to your coffee and curiosity," she said, taking a sip of the strong brew. They'd have to set up a machine at home so she'd be functional until the baby slept through the night. Hector held his hands up and bowed his head a little. It was as much a sign of surrender as she'd ever get out of him. "I'm not sure how many friends you've made within the police department, but a little bluebird told my people something important to whoever lost all that coke happened last night."

"That's a lie. Nothing was reported to us," the blonde said, and Hector turned around so fast, Cain thought he would get up and slap her. The move made the woman click her mouth shut and cock her head back.

"Then I guess you truly don't have many friends in the police department. Last night the cops raided an apartment downtown and recovered a large amount of coke. About three-fourths of it had a dragon stamped on the bags." She took another sip as Hector continued to glare at the woman. "Any idea who those might belong to?"

"This place that got hit by the cops, where was it?" he asked, looking at Marisol now.

"Surprisingly it was in Remi's building, but neither of us had a clue until the cops showed up. If any of it was yours, it's all sitting in an evidence locker now."

He turned around and faced her. "I'm sorry for my rudeness before. I've had a long string of days trying to put out fires. Do you know who the apartment belonged to?" He took a breath and emptied his cup in one swallow. "I believe you when you say you didn't know. I've asked too many times for you to suddenly change your mind about my business one way or another, as you Americans say."

"The bags were being repacked for street sale," she said. She'd gotten that nugget from Katlin that morning when one of the guys who'd been inside called her with the information. "The tables were full of small bags with a bull's head with horns." She waited a beat to get the reaction she wanted. "Does that sound familiar?" She'd lined the shot up perfectly and maybe hit the bull's eye dead center.

"*Hijo de puta*," he screamed, and for the first time Marisol's expression changed to one of almost glee as she glanced at the blonde. "You sure about this?"

"I didn't see them, but that's what my contact said."

"Why call us with this?" the blonde asked, and Hector put his hand up as if for silence.

"No, it's a good question. Hector, we'll never be business partners, but we're neighbors. This has nothing to do with me, but I heard this and thought you'd want to know. I don't want you to think I'm moving against you in any way, despite what my refusals might seem like." She held her hand out and he readily took it. "Maybe one day you might be in a position to return the favor."

"You have my word, and I won't forget this. Thank you."

"No problem, and if I hear anything else I'll give you another call."

She almost wished to be a fly on the wall of the car as they headed wherever Hector was going, since everyone appeared tight and wound up as they walked out. Nunzio was now on Hector's list of people to kill with as much pain as possible, and he had the network to get it done, so for the moment she'd bought them some room to maneuver until Nunzio resurfaced.

"Where to now, Boss?" Lou asked.

"Let's go see what Colin has gotten himself into. Knowing my cousin like I do, it's either his mouth or a woman."

"Which are you betting on?" Lou said and laughed.

"I'd lay even odds on both. He's like a hyperactive horny teenager."

"Hey. I was one of those once upon a time." Lou laughed harder.

"The horny part disengages your brain, which makes you lose control of your mouth, and the hyperactive part doesn't help, so I'm glad you've outgrown that part. I love him though, and since we're related it prevents me from shooting his balls off," she said and laughed along with him.

❖

Freddie stared at the ceiling in the bedroom Nic had put him in before she left and tried to think about what his next step should be. It seemed strange that this woman, whoever she was, would be doing all this for him, but he didn't care why at the moment. For the next few hours he was safe in a small apartment at the cusp of the French Quarter, and he promised not to move until she got back.

He didn't plan to leave, but he had a strong urge to go see if all that shit from the night before had to do with Nunzio's place. If it did, the mound Nunzio was stoked about was gone, and his punishment would be a bullet to the brain. His only redemption this time would be to find another shipment of shit before Nunzio got back, but no one was that lucky twice.

The door opening made him freeze on the bed, and he held his breath, wanting to become as invisible as possible. "Freddie." When he heard his name in that sexy French accent, he almost wet himself in relief.

"Yeah," he said, his voice hoarse and raspy. "In here." He walked out and joined her at the small table in the tiny kitchen.

"I tried to find out what happened, but the police are keeping everyone away. They are carrying many bags out, so I think it's what you feared."

"Thanks for checking." That was the end of his rope with Nunzio, so his only hope now was to run. "And thanks for hiding me, but I gotta get out of here."

"First I want to ask you a few things," she said, opening the bag she'd brought and pulling out an assortment of stuff to eat. "But promise me you won't run when I'm honest with you."

"Sure," he said, trying to be casual, but the ball of ice in his stomach was growing.

"My father and I have business with Hector and Marisol Delarosa," she said, and he jumped to his feet.

He needed to run but was paralyzed. Hell, Hector's goons were probably waiting outside to skin him for stealing his shit. "What kind of business?" His voice rose along with his panic. He felt the sweat on his hands and his ass clench.

"Sit down, please," she said, but her commanding tone didn't make her request sound as polite as the words did.

"What do you want from me?"

"I want to know how you knew where to go to steal from Hector, and I want to know Nunzio's plans for the future of his business." She bit into a croissant and made a downward motion with her finger for him to sit. "Let us be honest with each other, Freddie. You left Nunzio's place, and the cops show up a few minutes later."

"I didn't do anything wrong."

"In the end it's the best thing you could've done to avoid a lot of jail time, but do you think Nunzio will see it like that?" She shook her head and took another bite. "I don't think so, and if you have even a little intelligence, neither do you."

"I'm smart enough to have found him plenty of product and those places Hector owned."

She smiled at his outburst, and he knew right then that she'd played him. "Going forward you have one chance to survive this, and that's with me, because where I come from, people with your luck are seen as snitches. You try to double back to get in either Hector's or Nunzio's good graces, and I'll gut you and watch you trip over your entrails."

"And if I say no?"

She pushed the plate of pastries closer to him. "No man should have this as their last meal. They are good, but there are so many more better last suppers than muffins and croissants."

"What do you want?"

"So many things, but let's start small."

Colin Meade stared out at the big houses going by as the Town Car the hotel had provided traveled to the address he'd given. New Orleans was one of his favorite places, but this time around his visit didn't have anything to do with fun. The driver said the house was coming up, and he told him to give his name at the gate so the guy could drive in.

As the driver dealt with Cain's gatekeepers, Colin glanced around and saw Fiona sitting in a car close by. The memories of her as a child running around the front yard when he'd come to visit her mother came to him, but they didn't bring any fondness. Fiona had always been too holier-than-thou for his tastes even back then.

When the car stopped, he turned his head back toward the house and smiled when he saw Cain standing outside holding a blue-wrapped bundle. If there was a way to go back to those days in his own life, he'd take the chance, if only to undo some of his decisions that had led to some bad mistakes.

"You look like a proud papa," he said when he got out, not waiting for the driver.

"Something like that," Cain said, tapping on the window with a twenty. "You can take off. We'll get him back."

"Thanks for seeing me," Colin said, placing his hand on the baby's back. "What's his name?"

"William Cain, but he'll grow up to be another Billy, I'm guessing, so that's going to be his nickname. The kids voted, so I think the little guy's stuck with it."

"Your brother was one of the finest men I have ever known, so may this little one live up to the name and may it bring him good fortune."

"Thanks." Cain led him to the kitchen, and he went and hugged Emma, glad to see her again. His cousin had done well for herself, and that only made him feel more a fool. "Congratulations, Emma," he said as he hugged her. "You did good with this one too. He's beautiful."

"Thank you, and I hate to run off on you, but it's snack time for our boy." She took the baby from Cain and slowly made her way toward the back of the house with an older woman.

"Come on. Let's get comfortable," Cain said, going to the table in the corner, and the only other woman in the room walked out. "I'm happy to see you, but you don't look too happy. What's wrong?"

"I have to do something, but I wanted to talk to you before I do, so I've come asking for permission, if that's what you want to call it. I didn't want to act without your blessing."

Cain nodded. "Colin, I know we don't exactly conduct business the same way, but I'd never shoot you down if you *have* to do something."

"I have to kill Judice O'Brannigan, and if I don't, I don't think Salvatore will let her live out the week," he said of Salvatore Maggio, the other mob boss Colin did a lot of business with. "You remember that Judice works for both of us."

Cain stood up and patted him on the shoulder before going to the counter and picking up the pitcher of iced tea and two glasses. She tried not to show too much emotion, but what he'd said made her react completely opposite to what she would have ever guessed.

The memory of Judice in her office that night as she'd rocked Cain down to the very solid foundation Dalton had forged came to her, and she thought what Colin was asking should've brought the kind of closure death almost guaranteed. Only it didn't bring her one iota of relief.

"This is the same woman you were interested in keeping, as it were?" she asked, trying to buy herself some time.

"You obviously know her, since you called about her and that bitch of a kid of hers, so yeah, she's someone I'm willing to spend time breaking my marital vows over. But she's fucking me over instead of fucking me."

"Colorful and cute," she said, shaking her head at his words. Colin Meade was the closest thing she had to seeing what Billy her brother might've been like with a few years on him. Colin liked to have a good time, was fun to be around, but didn't always think things completely through. "What's the problem?"

"A lot of money is missing from both Salvatore and me, and there's only one logical explanation. Salvatore has already made up his mind, so I have to go along with him."

"Go along with him how?"

"I need to have a conversation with Judice to get the money back, and I don't think after that she's going to be happy about just letting it go once we're done talking. So you realize what has to happen." He slapped his fist into his palm and looked at her as if begging her to give him the right answer. "You know like I do she'll go running to Fiona, and that kid will end up right where she is now outside your door. She's there now plotting on how to get in here and fuck you over."

"Colin, I don't really have the right to tell you how to run your business or how not to run it, but I am going to ask you for a favor for the very reason you just gave me. Fiona's been like a pit bull since she got here, so I don't need that situation getting worse." She wanted to keep Judice's secret right now as fiercely as Judice had done all her life, so she'd have to bargain for her life. A conversation with Colin meant that to get answers out of Judice might have more consequences than she was willing to gamble on.

"I'm more than willing to let you handle it, but I'm not the only one out here. Salvatore isn't as nice and forgiving as we are."

"How about you hang out here for a few days, and if I can't fix it or get your money back you can call him and you both try your best to get what was stolen from you?" She placed her hand on his shoulder and waited, glad it didn't take him too much time to nod. "Good. You comfortable where you are, or do you want to stay with us?"

"The Piquant's good, and I don't want to be underfoot with that new baby around, but I wouldn't mind spending some time catching up. The reception at your wedding wasn't a good time for that."

"I'll have one of the guys be your driver for the days you're here, and they'll bring you back tonight for dinner. We'll get all the cousins together and talk about good times and all the ones yet to come. How about that?"

"You're blowing smoke up my ass, but you're so nice about it, how can I say no?"

"You can't, so go get a massage or something and let me take care of this for you."

She walked him out and waited until he was out of the gate before making the call she never thought she would. "Before you hang up, listen to what I have to say."

"I didn't think there was anything left to say between us," Judice said but did as directed and stayed on the line. "We should both let rabid dogs lie."

"You can question my motives later, but what I'm going to do isn't for you or your daughter. It's for my father. What happened and what you did was wrong, but something about you must've softened his heart, so I won't leave you out in the cold."

"You're more like him than you know, and by that I mean you're both full of shit. You could care less about me or Fiona."

"You're absolutely right." Cain took a deep breath to keep from hanging up and leaving this bitch to the two men that wanted her dead. "But your daughter's blood is precious to me, even if I'll never acknowledge her. That alone is why I picked up the phone."

"I'm listening."

"Good. Start packing."

CHAPTER TWENTY-FOUR

Finley and her brother Neil sat in the SUV Cain had temporarily provided her with and watched the warehouse during business hours to see if anything was off aside from the fact the front door had a hole cut out in the glass close to where the lock was. They'd sent Lou's nephew Dino to the places close by to let them know they'd taken care of it so they didn't need to call the cops.

"You want to go in or what?" Neil asked.

"You guys wait here and let me go in first," Finley said after a few more minutes of looking around the parking lot.

"No way," Neil said, and Dino agreed. "Cain will have my ass if something happens to you the first day out. We're coming with you, so live with it."

The front office was just like she remembered it but did appear drabber in the light of day. Whoever had broken in had gone through the door to the back space, and that's what she was interested in seeing. If it was something to do with the Antakovs, then they'd have done something to sabotage the crates she'd walked around when she'd come in through the back door.

She found only a few sheets of some kind of plastic material that seemed in keeping with what the business was supposed to be. From the time Cain had found out about the break-in to now, no one could've moved all the stuff in there unless they'd brought major help. Maybe this had nothing to do with her situation at all but just someone looking to make a big score with stolen booze.

"You might want to take a look at this," Dino said as the security-closet door appeared to be pried open. The system Cain had in place seemed to be top-notch, but the essential parts they'd need to see who had come in were gone. Whoever had pulled it off knew their stuff.

"We're dead in the water without the three missing components," she said.

"Sis, if you're going to work for Cain, you should know a little about her anal-retentive side. Dino, what do you have?" Neil asked him, since Dino was flipping through a set of keys.

"She said if this place had stuff missing to go to the backup site." He found the keys and walked out the back. "Neil's right about Cain's overlapping security measures. The other thing, though, is her sense of humor." The small building not too far away had a shed that seemed to hold all the maintenance and lawn-care stuff and a bathroom for those workers to use. Inside the bathroom was another door with a simple deadbolt.

"That doesn't exactly scream secure," she said, figuring she'd pick that in nothing flat with or without her FBI training.

When Neil opened the door, the one right on the other side wasn't so easy to get through, since it appeared to be some sort of almost vault-like door. "Two keys and a pass code with a fifteen-digit pin would take considerably longer than the first door, true," Neil said, punching the code in. "But by the time you tried breaking the code you'd have company." He pointed to the camera right above their heads.

She took her laptop out and downloaded the security-tape footage of two people walking through the space slowly, as if searching for something that had nothing to do with liquor. They took the recording devices of the security system, and one seemed to leave something else out of sight. She had a feeling they'd just tripped it.

"Okay, lock us in and close the other door," she said, realizing whoever had gone in didn't have to sit around watching for who showed up. They'd left the best lookout ever. "Can we get a call out?"

"Why?" Neil said and laughed. "You've been watching too many movies lately. Our life is never that exciting." Right as he said it they heard the loud explosion from close by. "What the fuck was that?"

"Give me the number to the house," she said to Dino, and to save time he dialed it. "Don't send anyone to the warehouse, and we'll find a way home. Whoever broke in left a motion tracker, and if we'd lingered we'd be toast."

"Where was it?" Cain asked.

"In the security closet, so whoever cleaned the place up should be glad they decided to stay out of it."

"I trust you implicitly, but the Antakovs not at all, so I couldn't take the chance with what was in there if someone decided to come looking for where Yuri and Victoria went wrong."

"Cain, I'm so sorry," she said, and meant it. Her problems weren't going to die with Yury and his wife.

"For what? You fell for a woman with a few problems, and you have family that'll help you solve them. Nothing to get in a twist about, and certainly not anything I didn't expect. If you didn't, review the file you compiled on these people. You should've seen it coming a mile away."

"So now what?"

"Tell Dino to give Beaver Jones a call, and he'll get you all back."

"Do I want to know who Beaver Jones is?" she said and guessed no when Neil and Dino laughed.

"He cuts the grass over there, but he's not the best driver in the world, so hang on to your ass. You'll never look at River Road quite the same way ever again."

"I'm going to be saying thanks until I'm old and deaf, huh?" she said and needed to get back to Abigail to make sure she was okay.

"Only if I was an asshole," Cain said and chuckled. "But I'm more the good-looking, pragmatic type."

"We all know Neil is the prettiest one in the group, so we'll wait for Beaver and talk about it later."

"Check on Abigail and the kids first, and then worry about all that. If they're watching, they're watching everybody. But if they've got their eye to the scope they're going to learn a valuable one-time lesson."

"What?" she said as Dino spoke quietly into his phone.

"Seeing the bullet up close isn't going to change the outcome of surviving it. You destroy something of mine, and I'll make you pay. This time it's personal because of who they're aiming at, so I'll show no mercy."

❖

Carol was too worked up to fold anything so she simply shoved everything into her suitcase and tried to not make any noise, afraid it might attract attention to her room. After what she'd done, sleep had been impossible, and Newsome wasn't answering any of her calls. Her brother had told her to come home, but to not take a plane. He'd left the night before since he knew the authorities would have her in custody in minutes after she showed her ID at the airport or train station.

She wanted to go back home and pray about what to do next. The door opening made her scream, and Elton was on her quickly before she could make another sound. "You stupid old bitch," he said, so close she could smell the alcohol on his breath. "I told you to stay put and I'd handle everything, but you had to go and fuck everything up."

"Don't talk to me like that, and you had no intention of giving me what I wanted most."

"With time and with Casey in jail, you would've gotten all those brats, but no. You couldn't wait that long. Now Casey's going to bury you so deep under all the police and judges she knows, you'll be lucky to get a slice of bread a day. I could give a shit about that, but you had to drag me down with you." She cried out again when he threw her on the bed. "So now what? You're running back to that crazy son of a bitch you live with?" He picked up the blouse at the top of the suitcase, wadded it up, and threw it at her.

"Morris will be here to get me so you'll never have to look at me again. Get out of here. I'll fight for Hannah on my own. You're drunk, and you're no gentleman."

"That's rich," he said and laughed as he grabbed her by the chin and squeezed. "I fucking hate Casey, but now I could give a shit about that. What I need to do is find a way to untangle myself from you."

"Fine." She tried to pull back, but he only increased the pressure. "Get out and do whatever you want. I want no more to do with you."

He didn't let go of her and reached behind him for something. "You think it's going to be that easy? You can't be that stupid, can you?"

"What do you mean by that?" she said and started really struggling when she saw the cuffs in his hand. "You get out of here, or I'll gladly call the police no matter what happens."

"I am the police, Carol," he said, and acted as if he'd told the best joke ever when he laughed hysterically. "And you have the right to remain silent." He cuffed her to the sink in the bathroom and turned on the television to muffle her cries.

"You can't leave me here," she yelled as she heard him talking to someone, so she stopped to listen through the door.

"Yeah, my wife's not feeling well, so tell the maid to skip us until I call back. No sense in all of us coming down with whatever this is."

"Don't do this," she said when he opened the door again.

"If you know what's good for you, keep your mouth shut until I get back. I need time to think."

He left and she started crying, hoping someone would hear her or check eventually. If not, maybe Morris would be here in the morning and they could leave. All she wanted now was to not have Elton come back until then.

"My Lord, I may not understand all these trials you set upon me, but give me the strength to get through them. I'll gladly do it if you punish my enemies." She'd lived a righteous life, so she deserved for the wrath of God to be aimed at those she hated.

Elton stood outside and listened to see how loud Carol could get and felt like an idiot for falling for what this woman was selling him when she got to town. The only way Carol Verde was bringing Casey down was if she shot her square in the chest.

He made sure the Do Not Disturb sign was in place and headed out. This had gotten way out of hand, and he had to think of a way to come out with his pension intact. The elevator bell made an idea germinate in his head, and it was the only real way to not sink with Carol tied around his ankles. "If I couldn't get you to make a mistake if Carol got custody, there's one sure way to pay you back, Casey."

He had the perfect way to rid the world of Cain Casey, and she was cuffed in the bathroom. "Who'll give a damn if the one thing you're convicted for is the one thing you're innocent of?"

The front drive was full of cars, so Remi let Simon drop them off for dinner. "Did you tell them the surprise?" Dallas asked as they walked to the front door.

"No. Everyone's here for a family dinner for Colin, one of Cain's cousins. He was the loud, funny guy at the wedding."

"He was certainly memorable." Dallas said, tugging on Remi's fingers.

"Yeah. You seldom forget anyone who can drink that much and still walk out. He's a good guy, though, and Cain is like his godmother even though they're close in age." She handed their coats over and headed to the den, since that's where all the noise was coming from.

"Welcome, you two," Emma said and screamed when Dallas held up her hand. Remi's mother, Marianna, and her sister-in-law, Sylvia, ran over.

"Quick announcement, Colin, so please forgive me for stealing your spotlight," Remi said. "I asked this beautiful woman to marry me, and she said yes."

"What'd we miss?" Muriel asked as she came in with Kristen.

"Nothing except that my sister's getting married," Kristen said, joining the others who were admiring Dallas's ring.

Carmen came in with some of the others on staff not long after with bottles of their best champagne, so Cain could make the first toast. "To my friends, Remi and Dallas. If you're even half as happy as I am, you'll have a long and joyful life. But since I've known Remi from the time we were five, I realize what an overachiever she is, so I hope you're ready for one hell of a ride, Dallas, because she'll move mountains to make you happy."

"Truer words, my friend." Remi lifted her glass but kissed Dallas before taking a drink.

They enjoyed the company and relaxing atmosphere and told old stories the kids had probably never heard, but the night was for celebrating, not business. The large dining-room table Cain had inherited from her mother was just big enough to fit everyone, so if for once the feds could hear every word, they would've had to turn the volume down.

"No cigars for you," Emma told Cain as they were about to head back to the den and the others to the sunroom, since so many people were there that Cain's office was out.

"You know," Cain said, and smiled at the way Hayden walked around carrying his little brother. "That tone of voice gives me ideas I have no business having right now."

Emma kissed her and moved her hand down over the curve of her ass. "Too early for me but way late for you, so don't take all night."

"At this rate, she might be pregnant again already," Colin said, and Cain smiled at Emma's blush. "Sorry," he said, but Cain could tell that was about as far from the truth as Colin could manage.

"Come on before you encourage him anymore," Cain said, kissing her again. In the sunroom they all grabbed a drink and lifted it toward Remi. "I really am thrilled you're joining the best club in town, marriage. Congratulations, and I hope you don't mind they're in there planning your future."

"Complete with nose ring, I'm sure," Ramon said, and they all laughed. "I keep mine in my wallet, so I can't say anything. I get out of line, and Marianna pulls it until I'm on my knees."

"We need to get a few things out of the way before we give you a hard time again." Cain sat and accepted another small whiskey from Katlin. "I met with Hector about the condo we found in Remi's building. He caught a clue as to who stole from him, so I put him on the hunt."

"Do you think we need to meet with Jasper and Vinny and give them the information?" Ramon asked, glancing between Raul and Remi. "I'm not sure what that does to his business, but if it's anything like ours, it's going to take time to come back. If that's the case he might go looking for filler where he has no business looking."

"I think we have another year of rebuilding before you see things level off. That we're taking that time to rebuild will eventually pay off big," Remi said. "But you're right about Vinny and Jasper."

"If we can do anything from our area, you know I'm a phone call away," Colin said.

"My boy says the supply chain has a kink in it somewhere and no one's talking," Vincent said.

"With careful planning, Jasper and Vinny can only get a better hold on their business, but let's set up that meeting and make sure they don't need any muscle to keep things together," Cain said, and the others nodded. "The kink is coming from Hector's end, but I haven't figured out what happened in Colombia."

"From what Jasper and Vinny tell me, someone burned his fields to the ground. That they won't be back as soon as they thought has put the market in flux," Vincent said.

"Maybe here, but in California the Mexican cartels are filling the void. Hector and his problems have caused the price to go up, and the cartels are using that excuse to control the supply and keep it right under demand," Colin said. "We tried to get into that action and were doing pretty well until we hit a snag."

"What?" Vincent asked, and Cain shook her head a little where only Colin would notice.

"It's an internal thing. If you want I can hook your guys up for now until things level out."

"I appreciate the offer, but let's hold off on bringing in any more players than we can handle," Cain said. "Right now I'm worried about keeping Vinny and Jasper whole until all this stuff is over because, if I know Hector, he'll start killing and won't stop until even a perceived threat is dead."

"He does that, and I have the word of both of you that we'll hit back, right?" Vincent said.

"With everything we have. Together is the only way to survive," Ramon said.

"Not only survive but succeed," Cain said, and everyone lifted their glass to that.

Cain and Emma stood at the door and bid Remi and Dallas good night. The others had left earlier, giving the friends a chance to sit and talk about the upcoming ceremony Dallas and Remi wanted. "The day I first saw you together I knew this is where we'd end up," Emma said, and Dallas hugged her.

"I'm so glad I listened to your first lecture about this one." Dallas pointed her thumb over her shoulder at Remi. "As thrilled as I am to tie my life and future to her, though, your friendship, both of you, has been one of the best things that's ever happened to me."

"We love you both so that goes both ways. In all these years I never thought Remi was capable of smiling this much," Cain said. "Once you're through with all your announcements, we'd love to throw you guys a party to celebrate that ring."

"I'll call you as soon as the new filming schedule comes out, but thanks for inviting us tonight." Dallas hugged them both again and took Remi's hand.

"Colin's being here, everything okay with that?" Remi asked.

"He needed advice on something, but I think we can reach some agreement that'll give him what he wants. If not, I'll call you."

They went upstairs and checked on the baby before heading to the bathroom for a shower. "What advice does Colin need?" Emma asked, slapping her hands away so she could unbutton her shirt. "He didn't seem like his usual over-the-top self, so for a minute I thought he was sick."

"He thinks Judice is stealing from him and Salvatore, so he wants to take care of the problem but remembered my call before our wedding. He's here for my blessing."

"He wants to kill Judice? Seriously?"

She stood as Emma took her belt out of the loops of her pants next and threw it on the growing pile. "After a conversation about Hector's problem I now know where he's making all that money, but I don't know who's skimming, so I bought Judice perhaps a few days. Colin will be easy to hold off, but from what I remember of Salvatore Maggio, her luck might not last."

"You know Fiona will come knocking on our door first if that happens." Emma dropped the simple, shapeless dress she'd chosen for the night. "Are you ready for that?"

"Lass, I think my father would be mighty disappointed in me if I let someone kill the mother of one of his children. I may not agree with what Judice did, what she stole from my da, and how she handled this whole situation, but I'm not going to leave her for the wolves to finish off." She dropped her pants and wrapped her arms around Emma. "I'm not a fan of Fiona, but her mother is all she has."

"Eventually she might have you as well."

She hadn't even thought about that, but like Marie and Billy, Fiona was her blood—her sister. "If I were inclined to accept that kind of relationship with her, I doubt Fiona would. Finding her true family tree would only drive up her hate for me."

"Never say never, lover." Emma let her step under the spray first and stood behind her. "But don't say it right this minute."

She smiled when Emma brought her hands forward and down so they landed between her legs. "I've missed this," Emma said when she ran her index finger the length of her sex. "Have you?"

A certain insecurity always came with being pregnant with Emma, and then even more insecurity once the baby was born, leaving her body, in her words, in shambles. "I've missed your touch, starting about an hour after we had to take a break or risk sending you into labor. I love you, and you're the most beautiful woman I've ever been lucky enough to lay eyes on."

"You're a charmer, you are. A charmer capable of lying when need be, but I love you for it." Emma stepped in front of her and put her hand back between her legs, stroking her clit until it was stone hard and she was really wet. "You're mine, aren't you?"

"All yours, love," she said, having a hard time thinking because she needed to come so bad. "And everything I have is yours."

"I'm just interested in this." Emma stroked harder and faster, and she had to put her hands on the wall to stay on her feet. The orgasm was intense, and she had to keep her hands on the tile to keep from taking Emma the same way. That would have to wait awhile.

"I think that pudding tonight was stiffer than my legs feel right now," she said, and Emma laughed. "Even though I feel a bit selfish, thanks for that. You do know how to get your ownership rights across and understood."

"As soon as Sam and Ellie give me the green light, make sure you're ready."

"My mother didn't make them tall and sturdy for nothing."

Emma slapped her on the butt and smiled. "True, and with any luck I'll do as well as your mum did."

CHAPTER TWENTY-FIVE

A re you sure?" Cain asked as she dressed the next morning. "I can take them." Emma had just informed her she was taking the kids to school.

"I know you can, but I have to get out of the house for a little while or risk driving you mad, and if I'm gone my father will have no choice but to finally talk to you."

"Be careful and don't strain yourself."

"I'm dropping them off, mobster, not carrying them both in. Don't worry. I'll be careful, and I'm sure Merrick will make sure I follow orders. The baby's fed, and I really do want you to put Daddy out of his misery today."

"You have anything else today?"

"I'm having lunch with Dallas, but she's coming here, so put that vein in your forehead away."

She smiled and helped Emma down the stairs to meet the children out front. Her good mood quickly disappeared when she saw the healing scratch on Hannah's face, but it didn't seem to bother her daughter as she skipped around the car.

"Have a good day, you two, and watch out for your mama. Don't let her get out of the car."

"Yes, ma'am," Hayden said before he hugged her, followed by Hannah.

Inside, Ross sat at the table rolling scrambled eggs around his plate in what seemed to be a daze. She loaded her own and went to sit by him. "You know something?" she said to break through the iceberg in the room.

"That you regret bringing me here?" he said, quickly making eye contact before dropping his head forward.

"No. I was telling Remi recently that I miss my father, but your being here has made that part of my heart not ache as much." She put her arm around his shoulders and shook him gently. "Hannah's a bright little girl who'll forget what happened much sooner than any of us give her credit for. In her heart she knows no one will ever take her from here, and I'm doing what I can to find Carol."

"I still can't believe she did that."

"She did, and it had nothing to do with you." She turned in her seat a little so they could face each other. "From the beginning of all this divorce business, the only thing I haven't understood was her reluctance to give you what you wanted, even with all the money we put on the table. I guessed spite first, then settled on getting back at you for loving Emma."

"It eats at me how I let that woman treat Emma. From the day she was born she was nothing but a joy and wanted nothing more than to be loved."

"My mum used to say some people were broken inside for whatever reason and sometimes no matter how much we give, we love, and accept, they can't be fixed. You need to put all that behind you and think about what comes next."

"What do you mean?"

"Hannah went through that with Carol and we found her, but our little darling girl has delivered us once and for all from the wicked witch of Wisconsin." She pushed his plate toward him and handed him his fork. "Eat up. We have an appointment today."

Ross insisted on changing clothes before they left and stayed quiet as they entered the temporary courthouse that had been set up after the city's historic flooding. Muriel had filed with Judge Mary Buchanan on Ross's behalf, and they were adding some requests that morning. Usually Cain tried to avoid any kind of legal proceedings, but she wanted to have a chat with her old friend.

Mary had graduated a few years before her, but when it was time to do something about her political ambitions, Cain had cleared the path by sweeping away some potential concerns on the campaign trail. That had been a while ago, and Mary had gone on to a successful career on the bench.

"Come on in, Cain," Mary said from the door. She shook hands with her, Muriel, Sanders, and Ross. "What can I do for you all?"

"You can give me what I want most."

"They don't actually have any free passes out of prison, no matter what people have told you," Mary said and accepted the file Sanders handed over.

"I'm still working on that, but today I want to make my father-in-law a free man. He's ready to date and needs to cut the old ball and bitch off his ankle."

"That's funny, and I got the paperwork, so it's in the system. It's just a matter of months now."

"There's more," she said, tapping the file.

"With you there always is." Mary opened it and put on her glasses.

"No need to get cute. I helped you out but didn't destroy the files your first opponent was dying to find."

"Come on. I was joking. What happened here?" She held up the picture of Hannah's face.

Sanders gave her a long and overly detailed explanation of what had happened and the fact that Carol was still missing, followed by Muriel and her reasoning for a protective order. "It's simple. I want her nowhere near Ross, Emma, or my children. Nothing illegal, just the facts, and I don't want anything holding it up."

"My clerk will file all this tomorrow, giving Mrs. Verde plenty of time to appear if she so chooses. If she doesn't, considering the seriousness of the charges and your proof, I'll grant your requests whether she's here or not."

"Thanks for that, but you still owe me that pass when it's available. Can you do me one more favor?"

"Sure. It's early yet and I'm feeling generous."

"If some little dweeb attorney from Wisconsin contacts you about this, can you give Sanders a call? I don't want anything delaying the final outcome. Ross and my family deserve peace."

"Just remember that if she resurfaces, any move against her will only slow the process down." Mary closed the file and put her hand flat over it. "Leave this one to me."

"That's why I'm here, Mary. I trust you to understand what those pictures of Hannah are doing to me. I'll never feel comfortable with Carol being around any of us, but I have no other fight with her. I just want her out of the city and back where she belongs."

"Consider it done, and I'll call if I hear from anyone in regard to this."

"Easiest campaign contribution you ever earned for the next election."

❖

Cain had Lou drive her to the office to make the next few calls, not wanting them tied to the house in any way. She'd looked around, trying to see if Fiona was still sitting and following them, waiting for something to happen. All that was out there was her usual tagalongs, so she had Katlin change the song for their enjoyment.

"Any requests?" Katlin asked from the front with Lou.

"How about that purple-dinosaur song. That would drive me to retirement if I had to listen to it more than once." She got out inside, not needing to poke the bears across the street today. "If you two have anything to catch up on, I'll be about an hour."

"Merrick gave us some homework, so let us know when you're ready. We'll be in the conference room."

Cain sat at her desk and picked up the phone, pressing it to her chin so she could go over what she had to say. It rang only once before someone answered it with total silence on the other end. "I need you to come here and not let Fiona know you're doing so."

"Tell me what this is about first, or I'll take a pass on that."

"I know that Colin and Salvatore have been dabbling in a new business that's been really lucrative. Colin told me."

Judice sighed, but she wasn't complaining or trying to get off the line, so that was progress. "Not my thing, but that's not my job with them. All I do is try my best to launder as much money as I can, and I'm only admitting that because I know Colin told you that too."

"He didn't give me any kind of percentage to go by, but enough money's missing from that new deal that they noticed. He's not an accountant by a long shot, so it had to be significant for Colin to realize it. Only one person has their ass in a vise over this, and it's not me." This wasn't going to be easy since she had no idea who all the players were.

"Did you help convince him it was me? It's the easiest way to get rid of your father's mistake."

Cain flipped through the mail as she talked to Judice, who gave stubborn a new meaning. "If you want to figure this out all on your own, then go ahead. I did my part by calling you, but I can pretty much guarantee that you won't leave the meeting they're going to drag you into alive. Love makes people do strange things, but money makes them focus on finding answers. The people we're talking about will be very creative."

"So you're going to protect me?"

"I'm going to give you a chance to discover whatever the truth is."

Judice sounded tired and resigned, all of a sudden, since she was just breathing into the receiver. "I didn't steal from Colin or Salvatore. I know better than that."

"For once I believe you, Judice, but do you want to leave Fiona here alone? You know they're not going to stop with you, especially Salvatore."

"I'll be there as soon as I can."

"I already took care of the reservation. Your flight leaves at nine tonight, so you'll be here in the morning. Drive to the grocery as if you're shopping, and leave your bag right inside your unlocked door. Someone will meet you there and take you to the airport. Once you get here, someone will pick you up."

"You were so sure I'd say yes?"

"I bought the ticket and made the arrangements. That's as far as I was willing to go."

"For once I'm ready to believe you."

Cain laughed at her change in attitude.

"When I said you were a lot like Dalton, I was right. He didn't leave much to chance, and he was as good a guardian angel as there was."

"Try to keep your head down, and I'll do my best to keep it in one piece."

❖

"Will you be home soon?" Emma asked as Cain and Katlin finished all the business paperwork that had piled up.

"One more stop, but I need the sun to go down first. I'm sorry I've been gone so long. How's the baby doing?"

"He started reciting poetry so don't dawdle. You'll miss his next reading."

"Funny girl. Remind me to spank you when I get home." Cain packed away the files in the safe in the wall and locked it. "Everyone else doing okay?"

"Hannah wants us to let Lucy move in with us, so I'll leave that one to you."

"I'll talk to her." That added one more stop to her day before she called it quits. Katlin hadn't mentioned it, but she wondered if Merrick had found anything.

"What aren't you saying?" Emma asked, just as the baby began to cry.

"You'll know as soon as I find out, but I had Merrick look into who these people are. I'm not completely sure about this, so it's me being me." She sat and massaged the back of her neck. "Do you think I'm crazy?"

"More like I'm crazy about you, and I think you're right. While you were out today, Lucy's mom called and asked to meet me."

"Did you arrange something?" The information made her sit up straight and pay close attention.

"I'd rather you at least be in the house when that happens, so I told her I'd get back with her." Emma spoke in a sing-songy tone to get Billy to calm down. "Don't take too long, okay?"

"I promise."

She sent Lou and Katlin out and waited to see what happened across the street. Like clockwork the van pulled in behind them, so she waited another thirty minutes and walked along the river for about four blocks. From the bar not too far away, after going two blocks in from the river, she took a cab to a block from where she was going. She went through the back door and sat in the darkness, hoping she could keep her word to Emma.

The front door opened less than an hour later, but the cat on her lap didn't move. "Shelby, don't turn the light on," she said softly and hoped she wasn't about to get shot.

"Are you crazy?" Shelby said in a hiss but sat down across from her.

"No. I'm being a good friend and seeing how you're doing. Muriel mentioned you saw her so I wanted to check on you, but I can't just stop by, you know. All your other good friends would get the wrong idea about us."

Shelby lifted her legs and sat on her feet. "How'd you do it? Live through this goddamn pain, I mean."

"When my father got killed I tried to do everything he would've wanted and expected me to do, so being strong for my mother and family made it easy to bury the ache. But when my mother got killed, followed by my brother, I almost lost my mind." She took Shelby's hand. "In the end it wasn't the revenge or anything like it that gave me something to live for."

"The thought of killing the bastards didn't drive you?" Shelby said, and hung on to her like Cain would keep her head above water.

"My sister did, believe it or not. Marie couldn't take care of herself, so I had no choice but to swallow what had happened and help her through it. And then there was Emma. Love does heal a multitude of pain and forgives as many sins."

"Do you want to volunteer her to come over here and sit with me?" Shelby said and laughed. "Most nights I think I'm losing my mind, and the only person who understands me is the woman I spend my days watching. There isn't much more for me to do but to take your gift and do something about it."

"I'm never going to make your job easy for you, but wait on that for a little while longer." The cat jumped from her to Shelby's chair, and she saw the gift of a lap full of cat hair on her dark pants. "You won't live to get what you want doing that alone."

"Who's going to help me?" Shelby asked, and Cain could hear the tears in her voice. "You?"

"I'm not going to answer that, but give it more time and the answer will come just like the names did."

"How long do I have to sit on this?" Shelby held on tight when she went to stand up. "You wouldn't wait. I know that much about you."

"Everything we want comes when we least expect it. However it comes and from wherever it comes, that shouldn't be important as long as it does."

"Don't steal this from me, okay? That's all I ask."

"I wouldn't dream of that. When it comes, it'll be you in control, and the knowledge it's done might ease that load some." She patted Shelby's knee and stood up. "All I'm asking is that you live to see that day."

CHAPTER TWENTY-SIX

Nunzio and Santino landed in Lafayette, Louisiana, not wanting to take the chance they'd run into anyone who would cause a problem. The stress of going through customs in Houston with a passport that wasn't Nunzio's had exhausted him, so he wasn't thrilled when Mike told him they'd checked into another hotel, leaving all their stuff behind, when they noticed a suspicious group of men in the lobby. They'd had the same suite for a few months with no problems.

"How long have they been there?" he asked, putting his head back to try to get rid of the headache starting to take hold in the base of his skull.

"Phil noticed them yesterday, but they're still there now. It could be coincidence, but I didn't think you should count on that, so we moved you to a place down the street. I'll start getting all our bags slowly so I don't attract attention."

"Have you had any luck spotting Tracy?" That he'd completely lost touch with the sister of the one woman who he'd ever admitted to being his equal was making him a little crazy. He still thought of Kim every day and missed her soothing touch no matter what was going on.

"Our guys working the streets say she's Hector's new bitch." Mike could've stated it differently, but he guessed it was his way of ripping the Band-Aid off with as little lasting pain as he could. "She's been keeping company with him, but Marisol, Hector's daughter, supposedly doesn't like her."

"That means she'll be lucky to live out the year. I mean, if Marisol kills her, what's Hector going to do, retaliate? He won't come down with a life-ending punishment since she's the next in line for him."

"We have to find Freddie. All those cops took in our entire inventory. It won't take long for word to get back to Hector that a lot of that stack had his mark on them."

That made him lift his head, and he cringed when the pain shot forward. "Does anything in there lead back to us?"

"Yeah," Mike said, glancing in the rearview mirror with an expression of confusion. "The other bags had our mark on them, sir."

"How long before we get back to the city?" Santino asked.

"A couple of hours, depending on traffic."

"Then give Phil a call and tell him to start putting money on the street for information on anyone who can give us the names of anyone who stole from us."

Nunzio rubbed the back of his neck and smiled. "Good idea, Nino. Then tell him to find someone willing to swear on his mother that the theft leads back to Casey. It'll make sense to Hector that if she stole from me, she's responsible for those houses of his that got hit too."

"Tell him we'll need like three people willing to tell that story. Once you get them lined up, then we'll have to make sure Delarosa's people find them as well." Santino reached over and massaged the back of his neck. "Get some sleep," he said as Nunzio closed his eyes. "We need to redirect Hector for now so we can work the deal we made."

"I don't think Hector will figure it out that fast. He doesn't have the network in town that Casey or the others have, so I doubt any of the cops are letting him know what's going on," Nunzio said as he tried to fight through the wave of nausea threatening to make him order Mike to pull over. He took a bunch of deep breaths, but his headache got worse and he started sweating.

"Hector might not be liked, but he's got the cash that will grease cooperation."

"Then let's hope that we're done with Cesar by then," he said before he couldn't hold it anymore and was suddenly sick. He opened his mouth and a wave of vomit came out, covering his shoes and bottom of his pants with what they'd eaten on the plane earlier.

Santino shied away at first but yelled at Mike to stop when Nunzio slumped into his lap. "Nunzio," he screamed over and over, but there was no response.

"Find the closest hospital," Santino said, forgetting about the mess in the back of the car. "Don't you dare quit on me now," he said as he held Nunzio as best he could, relieved that he was still breathing. "We have too much to do for you to give up."

❖

It was late by the time Cain finished with Shelby, so she felt bad having to get Katlin out of bed to come back and pick her up, but she didn't want to lose the freedom that going out the back way gave her. That the feds hadn't covered that part of her office with their surveillance surprised her, but it was either a logistics problem, money, or they considered her a creature of habit.

If it's the last reason, she thought, they should've caught on by now. In her opinion, her only habit was to not adhere too much to habits.

She glanced down at her phone as she got back inside the warehouse and smiled when she saw the picture of Father Andrew with Hannah that Hayden had taken the last time he'd come to dinner. "I'd have thought all good shepherds would've been asleep by now."

"Every so often we stay up nights worrying about the black sheep in our flock," he shot back, and she laughed. Her father's old friend had been good to her through the years, and she truly enjoyed his somewhat cutting humor. "I'm calling, though, because I heard there's a new Casey for the Lord to watch over."

"William Cain got here just fine and took it easy on his mom," she said, still basking in that happy moment despite the rest of the shit going on.

"Could I come by tomorrow and take a look at the boy and his beautiful mother?"

"I'm sure she'd like that. You two can discuss when we take that fancy dress out of mothballs and baptize him."

"There's another reason I called, Derby."

"You need another drop in that collection plate?" she said and stood back as the doors opened and Katlin pulled in.

"You're more than kind in that regard, so no. I had a dream about your father and woke up thinking about you all day, so I thought I'd check in and see how you're doing as well." Andrew had an almost trance-inducing voice, and she sat for a moment and relaxed as he spoke. "You've always got a million things going, but I want to be sure you're not forgetting all the things most important."

"Before this baby came, I tried my best to find ways to make peace and be able to go about my business without a lot of problems."

"But," he said, and she nodded.

"But the past isn't always my friend, Father," she said, and Katlin shut the engine off. "I can confess, though, that the fight this time came looking for me, not the other way around."

"If you're like your father, and you are, down to that lock of hair constantly in your eyes, all the fights come looking for you."

"I'd worry if they were battles I thought I'd lose, but I've got you in my corner, so I sleep better at night knowing that."

He laughed and said a quick blessing over her. "While you do have me praying for you, still take care to not step in front of any bullets. The Lord will protect you only to a point."

"Will do and I'll see you tomorrow."

"Things okay?" Katlin asked.

She wanted to sit up front to make it easier to talk, but tonight it had to be the backseat.

"Between me and you, I have a feeling that all this stuff is like a thousand tea kettles on hot fires. They're rolling and boiling, but they haven't whistled yet." She was surprised to see some people already had their Christmas decorations up, since Thanksgiving was still a week away. "It's all going to stay that way unless I can start to find some of these people and put myself out of my misery."

"What do you think about the warehouse in Destrehan? And who the hell did you have empty that place out?" Katlin took the most direct route and went a tick over the speed limit, seemingly anxious to get them home.

"Merrick had some guys take care of it, since I figured Yury and Victoria wouldn't necessarily die on the street. Someone somewhere has to be pissed about that, and they met with me last. I'm the first logical person to hit."

"By blowing up an empty building?" Katlin honked the horn for a second halfway down their street so the gate would be open when they got there. "That doesn't make sense."

"It's like the birth announcements Emma's mailing out as soon as they're done. A big boom says here I am. It also says I think I know what you did, but I'm not sure."

"So it's one of their lieutenants or something?"

"It's like Nunzio and Santino's whereabouts. I don't know." She got out and glanced toward the pool house and saw the lights still on. "And in our world, those are the most dreaded three words I can think of. 'I don't know' can get people killed."

"Want to come over for a drink or something?"

"Tomorrow's soon enough. Get some sleep, and let Merrick know I'll expect you both for breakfast."

"Will do, and kiss the baby for us. He's a cutie."

Before she headed to bed she stopped and checked on Hannah and Hayden, finding her son still awake with a book in his hand. "It's late, buddy." She sat on the edge of his bed and put it on his nightstand when he handed it over.

"Anything going on, Mom?" he asked, moving to lie down.

"Plenty, but I'm working on clearing my load so we can go have some fun when your mama feels better." She combed his hair, remembering what Andrew had said about that stubborn lock. From the look of it, the damn thing skipped no generation.

"I think you should take Mama out on a date," he said, and the order made her chuckle.

"Oh yeah?" She moved her hand and laid it flat on his chest. "Anything else I should do?"

"I was thinking the other day about what it was like with just the two of us."

"I'm not neglecting you, am I?" That was one thing both she and Emma tried not to do to either him or Hannah, but she'd have to try to do better now.

"No. I was thinking about how we were happy, but it's so much better now. I don't want anything to happen that would change it, so you have to find Grandmother Carol and do something." He twisted his blanket in his fists, and his voice had grown softer but fiercer. "I was so mad when I saw Hannah's face that I would've hit her if she'd been there. My sister's a sweet little kid who doesn't hurt anyone."

"You'd have had to stand in line, but this one time we both would've been wrong. Carol deserves to be punished for what happened, but we're going to let the police handle it." She bent and kissed his forehead. "I love you for how well you take care of Hannah. Later on, when she's older and it's some boy that gets out of line, then you can do whatever you think is right," she said and winked.

She opened the door to their bedroom after that and found Emma sitting up and feeding the baby. Emma had shed her nightgown, and the sight of the two of them made her think she'd done something right in this world no matter her sins. She quickly got undressed and slipped in behind Emma and let her lean against her.

"How'd it go?" Emma asked, holding the baby's hand and kissing it a few times.

"Work's done for the night, so let's enjoy this while we can. Pretty soon he'll be in the next room reading books about zombies way past his bedtime." She ran her fingers gently over Billy's head, and he let Emma go and seemed to stare up at her with a bit of a milk mustache.

"I think he knows the sound of your voice, love," Emma said, trying to get him to keep going. "So zip it until he's done or we'll be up in an hour."

"He doesn't like to sleep because he thinks he's missing something. Remember Hayden?" The nights of walking around with him had made her think the dark circles under her eyes would never go away, but they'd learned to nap when he was finally so tired he had no choice but to sleep.

"Hannah wasn't any different, so you're in for it." Emma moved the baby up so she could burp him, then rested him against her upturned knees. "You know we haven't had a chance to do this."

Cain watched as she took his pajamas off, and he instinctively held his arms out when he was down to his diapers. She watched in wonder as Emma counted all his fingers and toes, kissing each one as she went. Billy was long, and his hair would eventually thin but then come back thick and dark. It amazed her how much you could love someone so new to your life.

"He's perfect," Emma said, finally handing him over so she could change him and redress him. She sang him the lullaby her mother had sung until they were in their twenties, and he was asleep when she put him down.

"He's yours and mine, so of course he is," she said as she came up behind Emma and wrapped her arm around her waist. "Do you have any regrets having another one?"

"What kind of question is that?" Emma's head shot up so she could look back at her.

"A stupid one, I guess, because even though he's so new I couldn't imagine us not having him now, but I also imagine what one more would be like."

"You're going to have to share this one, you know. Hayden was the center of your world, but I think this kid will think that of his siblings too."

"I know, and I felt that way about my siblings, but you're wrong." She moved so she could look down on Emma. "Hayden was the beginning of the family I've always wanted, but my wife was and is the center of my world."

"And you ask why I love you?" Emma caressed her cheek and welcomed her kiss. "I'll always remember spilling that tray on you and seeing those eyes for the first time. In that one moment I knew for certain I'd be lost forever, so my wish was you'd notice me even a little."

"Ah, my little hayseed," she said and dragged her hand down Emma's body. "To this day I always thought it was my da's hand on that tray. It was his version of a slap to the back of the head to say, 'Pay attention to this one, Derby.' I love you with all I am, lassie."

"I need you to touch me," Emma said, kissing her again.

"Not as much as I need to touch you." She put her hand between Emma's legs and placed one finger on her clit. No matter how much Emma begged, she wouldn't move it from that spot and she'd be gentle. "Seeing you with Billy makes me believe there is good in this world, my love. But being with you makes me know for certain that you are mine and I'll love you until I have no more days left."

Emma got hard under the pad of her finger, and she dipped it down just to get it wet. This too had happened after Hayden's birth, and Emma had convinced her it was okay despite what Sam and Ellie warned about, so she listened, knowing Emma knew what she wanted.

"I've missed you so much," Emma said as her legs came farther apart, so she sped up but didn't apply any more pressure.

Emma's hips came off the bed, and she pulled hard on the hair at the back of her head, so Cain glanced down, knowing if her nipples were as hard as her clit she'd come. Like in the shower with her, Emma didn't take long, but she grabbed her by the wrist when she started to move her hand. "It's been a long while, so what's your hurry?"

"If I get in trouble with Sam, I'm blaming you," she said, pinching Emma's clit between her fingers. "Want to try again? I'm pretty sure I can do better."

"Always the overachiever," Emma said as she pushed on the top of her head.

"There's that, and then there's this," she said right before she put her flat tongue where her finger had been and just as fast took it away. "Stop me if I hurt you."

"Stopping isn't really what I have in mind right now, mobster," Emma said, moving her head back by her hair. "As a matter of fact, stopping isn't coming up again tonight."

CHAPTER TWENTY-SEVEN

Cain went down first the next morning and carried the baby with her so Emma could sleep a little while longer. "Hey, Mom," Hannah said when she sat at the table in the kitchen and held her arms out for her brother. She smiled as Carmen hovered close by.

"How about you, Hayden, and me go ride the carousel this weekend?" Carmen took Billy when Hannah took her hands off him to clap. "We'll give your mama a break and go have some fun."

"Can Lucy come too?"

"If her mom doesn't mind, sure." She'd mentioned the fun to see if Hannah would tell her anymore about Lucy or her parents. "I bet her mom misses her when she's over here though, huh?"

Hannah shook her head, and her smile disappeared, so perhaps there was more that she wasn't saying. "She likes it here better."

"You're a good friend, princess, but you know if anything bothers you, that's what Mama and I are here for." She reached over and picked Hannah up and put her down on her lap. "You're getting big."

"Mama told me that too, but I got nothing to say," Hannah said, and Cain still wasn't convinced.

"Then we'll have fun, and if you need to say something I'll be happy to listen, and no matter what, I won't be mad."

"Thanks, Mom. I love you." Hannah gave her a hug, then went with Sabana when she walked in. "See you later."

"Miss Cain," Carmen said, bouncing Billy as she walked around with him. "That little girl's mother call for Miss Emma today and say she coming here. I say okay, so I hope you don't mind."

"Actually, that's a good thing. I'm dying to meet her," she said as she made a plate to take up to Emma. "Do you mind watching him a minute?"

"You take all day if you want." Carmen kissed the top of Billy's head and smiled. "I could do this all the time, he so sweet."

"You're better than a massage at the spa, mobster," Emma said when she delivered breakfast. "Did I leave you in a horrible state when I finally fell asleep?"

"Nothing that'll kill me, so eat up. You'll need it."

"If you have time this morning I'm raring to go again." Emma winked as she took a big bite of a biscuit.

"You'll have to go all right, but unfortunately for me, it's downstairs to meet Lucy's mom." She accepted a bite from Emma and watched as she walked naked to the bathroom. "Carmen said she called earlier so she should be here soon."

"Want to take bets on what these people are like?" Emma said, sounding muffled through the wall, so Cain went in and joined her.

"We'll soon find out, but let me go and see if Merrick and Katlin have arrived yet with a hint." She kissed Emma before she shoved the toothbrush into her mouth and waved over her shoulder. "Take your time."

"Don't scare anyone until I get down there."

"I'll try my best," she said and laughed all the way to the first floor, finding Hayden and Hannah ready for school. "You two have a good day and call if you need anything."

"They'll be okay, Boss," Sabana said and herded the two out the door.

"For the sake of my sanity, let's hope so. Thank you for calling and getting us organized so fast when that happened to Hannah," she said softly. "I haven't had a chance to say that."

"I was glad to help."

She entered the kitchen, and Merrick was holding the baby and making faces, which, considering who she was, made it all the more humorous. Everyone had a soft side when it came to babies and small children. "Taylor Kennison's paying us a visit today."

"Why?" Merrick said, not stopping her attempt to entertain the baby.

"To see how well Lucy has laid the groundwork for her to waltz in here would be my guess."

"Or she could simply be a woman going through a bad divorce and needing a shoulder to cry on," Emma said when she entered in jeans and a loose-fitting shirt.

"I might have to side with Cain on this one, Boss," Merrick said and frowned a bit when Carmen took the baby back, but it looked like she was leaving to change him. "I've looked everywhere to find a Taylor Kennison with a child and bad husband that fits this criteria. Muriel followed that up with a search of her own."

"I found a couple in north Louisiana, but the number and names of their children are wrong," Katlin said. "Today, if you can try to fit in some questions people usually ask when trying to get to know someone, we might have more to go on. I also asked Finley to check it out as well to see if she had any better luck."

"Miss Emma, there's a lady here to see you," one of the maids said.

"Thanks. Can you show her to the den for me?" Emma held her hand out to Cain and glanced over her shoulder to Carmen coming back in. "We might need to borrow him for a minute, *abuela*." Emma used the Spanish word for grandmother, and Carmen's eyes grew glassy with tears. "I kept trying to think of something the kids could call you that holds more meaning than Miss Carmen, so I hope you don't mind."

"Oh, Miss Emma, I love it."

Emma kissed her cheek as Cain took the baby from her and headed to meet their mystery woman. "Is it just us, or does this weird stuff happen to everyone?" Emma asked as they walked to the back of the house.

"Unless everyone has a reward for information leading to my arrest, then I'd go with no."

"Oh," the woman said, standing up when they arrived. "I didn't think you'd both be here."

"The baby was fussy this morning, so I can't get rid of her when that happens." Emma walked up and held her hand out. "Hi. We met briefly at school, but I'm Emma Casey, and this is my wife Cain."

"I feel like I know you already because Lucy talks about you so much. Since she spends a lot of time with Hannah, I thought I should come and introduce myself and thank you for all the kindness you've shown her. I'm sure you know things haven't been rosy at home."

"Lucy's a pleasure to have around and Hannah loves her, so we're glad to help," Cain said, keeping her distance to put the woman at ease. "I'm hoping things are getting better for you."

"Once Drew, my husband I mean, realizes it's over, I'm sure things will be fine."

It surprised Emma that this total stranger would be so forthcoming, but it could also make this easier. "I'm sure he'll see reason once he realizes you're serious about whatever you want."

"I don't want to bore you, but this had been long in coming," Taylor said, sighing for added emphasis.

When she lowered her head, Emma glanced at Cain, cocked her own head toward the door, and smiled. "I think this one needs a new diaper, so it was nice meeting you."

"Likewise," Taylor said in a tone that sounded like she had recovered from the emotional outbreak. "She seems devoted," Taylor said as Cain walked out with the baby cradled in her arms.

Emma watched Cain go and nodded. "She's a definite keeper." She plastered on a smile, and her impression so far was that this woman was full of shit. "Can I get you anything?"

"No, I'm fine but not fine, you know."

"I do, and if you want I'll be happy to talk to you about it. Drew, right?"

"Yeah, that bastard." Taylor certainly sounded like a woman scorned. "He cheats on me with his secretary and then doesn't want me to leave him. Can you believe that?"

"Maybe he's come to see his mistake," Emma said, lifting her hands momentarily. "Where does he work?"

"Why?" Taylor went from mad wife to suspicious in a flash.

"If it's one of the big companies, it'd be hard to fire this woman without letting him go too. Getting fired might put you all in a tight spot if he's still seeing her on a daily basis."

"He works for Shell, so it's like the old boys club. He's probably getting an award for what he did, but I'm not going to forgive that since I'm sure he'll do it again."

"Do you work?"

"My, you're full of questions, aren't you?" Taylor stood up and walked to the fireplace to study the pictures along the mantel.

Taylor stopped at the family portrait they'd taken at the wedding and took it down to look at it. Cain and the kids looked so happy, Emma smiled just thinking about it. Of all the ones they'd taken it was her favorite.

"I'm sorry. I didn't realize I was being nosy, Taylor. I'm glad you came so we could discuss Lucy. She and Hannah do like spending time together, and we don't mind having her, but I wanted to make sure you didn't have any problems with that."

"Sorry. I guess I'm on edge from everything. I work for an attorney downtown, but only part time, and I simply want Lucy to be happy and away from both of us right now. You and Cain have been really nice to have her over so much."

"Like Cain said, she's a beautiful child and our Hannah loves her, so it's no problem."

"Great. I have to go. Work and all, you know." Taylor laughed nervously and ran out of the house like Emma had threatened her with a loaded shotgun.

"That was damn bizarre," she said, going back to the picture and picking it up. She turned it around and studied the back. If you weren't looking for it, the extremely small device would've blended perfectly with the black backing. "Wasn't that nice for her to come over," Emma said when Cain came back in and opened her mouth to say something. "She's having a rough time." She pointed to what she'd found.

"I hope you let her know we'll be happy to help out however we can. Let's go finish breakfast, though. Carmen's sending someone in here to clean."

"The place is spotless so they can skip it." She followed Cain to her office and slammed the door. "I didn't want to believe you were right about them using Hannah."

"I'm not sure it's who you think it is, but let's make sure."

"What's your idea?"

Cain put her arms around her and rocked her gently, as if to calm her. "You're going to continue to be the devoted friend she obviously wants, we're going to let them listen to Hannah sing at the top of her lungs in there, all while we double back and sneak up on them."

"Can you explain that so that I understand?"

"We need to know exactly who they are before we do anything, but I truly think our bozos outside have nothing to do with this. That means someone else is pulling the strings, and I'm interested in the puppet master. Once I know that, it'll be easier to whittle them a new head."

❖

Carol stared at the faucet on the sink and couldn't believe it was so close, she was so thirsty, yet she couldn't get anything to drink. She had no idea how long she'd been in here, but her whole body hurt from the awkward position Elton had left her in. "Please, someone help me," she said, but she was hoarse from screaming.

The only way she was getting out of here was to break the pipe Elton had chained her to so she started pulling, but the cuffs cut deep into her wrists. The pain prevented her from doing it for very long, and she figured she'd pass out before she could rip the plumbing apart.

She tried one more time and was grunting through the pain to try to maintain the pressure longer when the door opened. The possibility that Elton had come back to kill her made her panic and tug harder. When they'd first met she'd figured him for a man of principle who understood her plight, but she guessed he couldn't let her tell anyone what he'd done. Killing her was his only option.

"Hello," a woman said with what sounded like a Spanish accent. "Housekeeping."

"In here, hurry, please," she screamed, hoping the woman understood her. "Please help me."

"You okay in there?" The woman sounded as if she'd come closer. "You want me leave."

"No, please help me," she yelled, and finally the door opened and it wasn't Elton. "Call the police."

"*Dios mío*," the woman said and took her radio out. She said a lot of things in Spanish and took one of the cups on the counter and helped her drink something. "People coming."

"Don't leave me," she said, starting to cry. The relief of all this being over was overwhelming her. It was time for her to give up for now and go home. "Please don't go," she said as the woman cleaned her face with a warm face towel.

"You okay, lady, you okay," the maid said and only moved when more people arrived.

"What happened?" a middle-aged man asked when he arrived and introduced himself as the manager.

Carol gazed up at him and could only come up with one name. "Cain Casey did this. She tried to kill me."

The police behind him had arrived in time to hear her say it, and she tried hard not to smile. Elton Newsome could go straight to hell. If you wanted something, you had to do it yourself.

"Please don't let her kill me," she said, slumping forward as if she were too weak to sit up. "Cain Casey did this."

CHAPTER TWENTY-EIGHT

Judice came down the concourse at the airport and halfway expected to see Fiona waiting on her like she had the first time she'd come after such a long absence from the place she'd been born and raised. This time, though, she thought she recognized the tall man usually with Cain standing on the other side of the security stand. If Cain planned to get rid of her, she'd made it plenty easy by leaving home with no word to anyone as to where she was going.

"Welcome, ma'am," he said, taking her bag and pointing to his left. "I've got the car waiting right outside unless you checked something."

"That's it. I wasn't really planning to stay long." She walked away, glancing over at him every few steps. "I'm sorry I don't recall your name."

"Lou Romano, ma'am."

He was tall, solid, and very good-looking in a dark, rugged kind of way. "Do you think I'll get to see Cain this morning?"

"She has someone at the house, but I'm sure as soon as she's free she'll come by and talk to you." He got in the front, leaving her the backseat as if to emphasize how truly alone she was in all this.

It took less than twenty minutes to drive into the Piquant's grand entrance, and the bellman took care of her bag as Lou gave her a set of keys. "He'll take you up, but if you need anything, please don't hesitate to call me directly. Cain wanted this to be as easy and stress-free as possible for you." He handed over a card with his name and number on it.

"Thanks, Mr. Romano. I appreciate you getting me here."

"Please, ma'am, call me Lou." He smiled and then was gone.

Upstairs, a breakfast tray arrived right after the bellman placed her bag on the stand, and only then did she realize it'd been a while since she'd eaten. Whoever had taken care of the food had ordered plenty, and on the side lay a handwritten note.

Thank you for coming and for agreeing to meet with me. I'd imagine that trust isn't something you blindly give any more than I do, so I'll try not to disappoint you.

I shouldn't be too long, but please enjoy the breakfast and try to spend some time thinking of who might be responsible for your current predicament. Perhaps together we can figure it out so Fiona will be safe from what could happen.

Cain

That was the problem. She accounted for the money Colin and Salvatore made, then provided instructions as to what to do with it, but had no authority to move, touch, or withdraw any herself. It wasn't a trust issue on Colin or Salvatore's part, but because she'd never wanted to face anything like this. This system she'd put in place was as foolproof as she could make it to protect her from false accusations. Colin especially couldn't have forgotten that.

Her ringing phone stopped her train of thought, and she took a deep breath to calm her nervousness when she saw it was Fiona. "Hello, sweetheart."

"Hey, where are you? I tried calling you all last night and this morning. I was getting worried."

"I was dead tired so I must've not heard your call last night, and I've been running errands all morning and forgot my phone. Is something wrong?"

"No. I just wanted to tell you about the assignment I got. You'll never guess who the head of detectives has me investigating."

She smiled at Fiona's enthusiasm for a job no one in her family would've thought to have. "Not Cain Casey, right?"

"Actually it's her mother-in-law. The crazy woman tried to kidnap Cain's little girl and hurt her in the process. Not in a bad way but slapped her hard enough to scratch her face. I'm on my way to some hotel in the French Quarter where the maid found her handcuffed to the bathroom sink." A horn blew in the background and Judice grimaced.

"Try to get there in one piece and call me when you're done. For once that job of yours sounds like the makings of a good book."

"Thanks, Mama, and you're sure you're okay?"

"I am now that I got to hear your voice. Be careful and I love you." She hung up and thought about what her daughter had reported. "Hell, I should check out the plumbing in the bathroom and see how easy it would be to escape from if that's what she has in mind for me."

❖

"Where have you been?" Marisol pushed her way into Nicolette's apartment.

"Working," Nicolette said in as stern a tone as she could muster, since Marisol had awoken her from a dead sleep. "I'm here, but we still own a winery, remember?"

"When I call I expect you to answer. It's been more than a day."

"Look, you don't own me and I don't work for you, so cut the crap." She tied her robe tighter, got her Italian coffeepot down, and filled it with water and espresso. "That may be what you're used to, but I'm not your whore or groupie."

"It could be that I was worried about you." Marisol sat on one of the stools and watched her every move.

She snorted and lit the stove. "The way you came in is the way you show concern? If it is, your technique needs lots of work." No way she had time for this today. Freddie had spent the night before explaining how some dead woman who owned the bar at the Hilton had brought in drugs, and it was genius.

Pouring wine out of their bottles and filling them with liquefied cocaine would allow them to buy all the land her father wanted for planting. With enough money they could get back to simply making wine, and she could leave animals like this behind.

"My father met with Casey, and she told him who stole his drugs. It was great that Tracy interrupted while Cain was talking and basically called her a liar. One more stunt like that, and Tracy will be fertilizing some field somewhere." Marisol picked a stem of grapes from the bunch in the bowl close to her and started eating. "The one thing my father hates is someone who can't keep their mouth shut in front of someone like Casey."

"Who ripped your father off?"

"Some lowlife who thinks he's a big shot."

"What's his name?" The thought of spending a lifetime with this woman made her contemplate taking her own life, if it came to that.

"Nunzio Luca. The dumbass didn't even bother to throw my father's marked bags away."

"How'd Cain find out?"

"The cops were all over the place, and some friend of hers called and told her. She called my father so he wouldn't think it was her and kill her ass."

Talking with your mouth full of grapes was disgusting, but Nicolette wanted to hear more. "So you can't get it back?"

"Not unless you know of a way to break into the police station."

"So what now? What does this do to our deal?" She had to play the part of the wounded business partner. "My father has invested plenty of our money and time because your father said he could deliver."

"Are you seriously questioning what we can do for you and your father? If we said we could do it, we're going to do it, so don't mention that again." Marisol slammed her hand down and smashed a few grapes on her marble counter. "We have enough problems, and I don't need you telling anyone we can't keep our word."

"I'm not asking because I'm trying to bring you down. I need to know our money is safe. You'd be doing the same thing if it was you and your family's business at stake." She poured coffee into two small cups and added plenty of sugar to hers. "Do you think I need to meet with Hector?"

"Are you crazy?" Marisol slammed her hand down again. "You talk to him, and he'll know I told you shit I wasn't supposed to. I did, though, because I trust you."

"Okay, but you have to promise that you'll let me know if I have anything to worry about. I'm not familiar with all this since wine really is our business."

"Don't worry. I'll take care of you, and you won't lose anything."

"I have no choice but to trust you now," she said, and Marisol got up and left without another word. "Luce is looking better these days," she said when the front door slammed closed.

❖

Finley cued the footage to the beginning again and played the clip in slow motion in her office at home. The explosion had rocked her since she'd been in the building a few minutes before it went off, so it was important to find out who had done it. If it had been a cleaning crew or one of Cain's people, no one deserved to die like that.

The two people who'd come in had cut through the glass and walked slowly through the office out front and rifled through the two desks. Once they found nothing, they moved to the almost-empty warehouse space and headed to the security closet. The shorter of the two ripped out the recording devices and the feed ended. Watching it again, she saw the other person squatting by the door.

"That has to be them setting the bomb," she said softly to herself.

"What are you doing?" Abigail said as she put her arms around her from behind. Abigail hadn't been thrilled to hear what had happened the day before but had agreed to wait to talk about it.

"The system Cain put in had a backup, so this is who broke in. It's a shame they wore a mask, and since the place is totally destroyed, there's no way to find prints or DNA." She stopped the frame as one person took out the equipment and concentrated on the one by the door. "See how they're doing something here?" She pointed to the screen.

"Is that the bomb?" Abigail asked, coming around to sit next to her.

"It was a little more than that. It's a bomb as well as an electronic trigger. If someone came looking for them, the closet would've been the first place to look, so they basically booby-trapped it."

"Can I talk to you about that?" Abigail reached for her hand and sandwiched it between her own. "I have children to worry about," she said, and Finley nodded.

"That's something I never forget, no matter what I'm doing. Whatever future I want with you means I'll share it with the kids as well." She didn't want to lose Abigail, but she wanted to stay close to Cain as well, if only to keep them safe. "You have to admit that our meeting wasn't your typical coffee date followed by a family dinner."

"Yes, I realize that. It's just that…don't take this the wrong way," Abigail said and stopped to fidget with her fingers. "I've already gone through a relationship with someone who had no regard for the laws or rules of society. I don't think I could survive one like that again."

"So it's my working for Cain that bothers you?"

"That's part of it, yes. You might've grown up considering someone like Cain normal, but that's not who I am, and I don't want my children exposed to that way of life."

"You do remember that we found Yury and what Nicola was doing because of Cain?" She wasn't upset by the conversation, but she wasn't giving up the chance to stay here and get closer to her family. "How about you and me meet with her, and if you're still dead-set against me working for her, I'll try to find a job with the Geek Squad or something?"

"I don't think I'd be comfortable going over there and calling Cain out on who she is."

"She's got thicker skin than that, and I really want you to talk to her before you make up your mind. It'll be okay."

"All right," Abigail said, but sounded extremely hesitant. "Mom and Dad are here to take care of the kids, so can we go now?"

"I've got to tell her about this anyway, so let's go." She called and told Katlin they were coming, so Katlin told her to wait for a ride. "They'll be here in thirty minutes or so."

Abigail walked toward her slowly and pressed herself tightly to her. "You're not going to hate me, are you?"

"I really don't think that'll ever happen, but I need you to keep an open mind. There's no chance of history repeating itself because I'm no Nicola, and more importantly, neither is my cousin."

When Katlin dropped them off, the maid showed them to the sunroom, and they found Cain on the floor talking to the baby while Emma watched, laughing at the faces and noises her wife was making. Emma stood and hugged them both and accepted the baby when Cain got up.

"Do you mind if I hold him?" Abigail asked, remembering those first days with her three.

"Sure. I can't tell for sure, but I'm sure he loves the attention."

Abigail took him and gave him a bit of a checkup. "He's beautiful," she said and looked over at Finley. Would a baby they had look something like this?

"I'm going to catch Cain up, so will you be okay?"

She nodded and went back to admiring the baby.

Emma sat close to her and called for some coffee. "I hope you don't mind decaffeinated."

"No problem. I already gassed up this morning, so any more and I might regret it." She moved her attention to this petite woman who seemed to revel in the partnership she had with the reputed mob boss Finley had walked out with. "You seem really happy."

"Life isn't always peach cobbler, but lately it's been as perfect as it gets," Emma said and reached over to squeeze her shoulder. "I wanted to let you know how sorry I am that you've had to go through what you did. Cain told me a little about it, and I'd have been terrified."

"Has anything like that happened to you? I hate to ask, and I mean no disrespect, but when you live this life, it's like inviting it in, isn't it?"

"When I met Cain, she was the most exciting and fascinating person I'd ever come across. She was this womanizing, charming, bad girl that was like a beautiful flower and I was a helpless bee. I not only couldn't stay away, but I didn't want to." Emma smiled when the baby stretched and made a small sound. "Once I got to know her, though, I found out she's loyal, charming, and a bit rough around the edges but basically good. Cain is someone the world sees a certain way, but who she is truly is the woman you just saw who lives to sit on the floor and idolize her children."

"I thought I had that before, but it was such a lie. Finley wants to be with us, that I'm sure about, but she also wants to change her spots and go to work for Cain. Like I said, I don't want to insult you, but I have my children to think about."

"Abigail," Finley said, and she glanced up at the ceiling, hoping like hell that Cain wasn't with her, but when she turned her head that way her luck ran out.

"Finley, she's got a right to question. It makes her a good parent," Cain said. "Would you mind taking a walk with me outside? You can help me cut some flowers for my wife."

They walked out, and she noticed the similarities between Cain and Finley that went beyond physical attributes. Both of them seemed to have an inherent self-confidence that came out in their movements, and it was attractive, like Emma had said. "I'm sure Finley's having a fit inside," she said to break the silence.

"Fin's a special person that I happen to love. Believe it or not, but I'm so proud of her for the job she's done. Exploitation of people weaker and more desperate than you deserves what agents like my cousin can mete out." Cain did in fact take some clippers from a small box next to the rose garden and start cutting.

"Doesn't that slice into your business?"

"No one in my family in this generation, past or future, will ever make their living off unfortunate people submitting to unimaginable things." She handed over a bouquet of pink roses and kept cutting. "I told your father-in-law the night we got together on the pretense of finding you that I'd met Nicola Eaton at my club. The woman with her, from what I remember, wasn't you."

"Yep. I was an idiot."

"I'm not telling you that to rub it in. When Finley talked about you when she came to see me, I thought what an idiot Nicola was."

"You didn't know me, so how could you think that? I could be a bitch she couldn't wait to get away from, which, after this, is probably what you think," she said, and Cain laughed.

"I knew because I thought even then that my cousin had fallen in love with you. That'll be a first for her so you had to be special. What you should take away from this morning, though, is that I also love her, and I'll do whatever I have to within my power to keep her whole and her family safe."

"She didn't exactly tell me what happened, but I'm free of the Eatons, and I know you had a lot to do with that, so thank you. Even before I learned the whole truth about these people, I didn't want my children to spend much time with them. It was a gut-reaction kind of thing."

"The Antakovs won't be a problem for you any longer, so that's not the issue this morning."

"This morning? Should I be afraid?"

"No, not from me, and I know Finley wants you more than she does anything else, so I'll watch over you no matter what you think is right for your future. Hopefully you'll eventually see that we want the same things for Finley."

"Can I ask you one more thing?"

"I'll answer anything you like," Cain said as she put her clippers away.

"That explosion in the warehouse—it had to do with me, didn't it?"

"It's more of a message to whoever these people blame for what happened," Cain said, sounding sincere. "I guess the best answer is, from what Finley found combined with what I knew, killing the head of the snake hasn't killed the body yet. What comes next isn't exactly a surprise, so try not to let it worry you too much."

"That's a tall order," she said and could find nothing in this to blame Cain for.

Cain stopped walking and took her free hand. "Family, in my experience, comes in so many forms and from so many places. You picked someone you love to make a life with and gave her children like Emma did for me. What she did had nothing to do with you and everything to do with her upbringing."

"So what's your advice, Dr. Casey?" she asked, and Cain smiled in a way that made her think of Finley.

"That you started a family with Nicola, but Finley's the better fit. She'll be loyal to you and your children, and she'll instill in them the lessons we all got growing up. Emma is my wife and, more importantly, my partner, so give Finley the opportunity to provide you with that. I swear you'll never have reason to regret that decision, and you'll never have any reason to question my place in Finley's life, just like you'll never question her loyalty to you."

"She was right about you."

"About me being the better-looking one? I'm glad she's big enough to admit it."

Abigail smiled and thought about fighting the upcoming battle alone, but it held no appeal for her. "I'll hold you to the rest."

"My word means everything to me, so welcome to the family."

"Thanks for understanding, and I haven't admitted it to her yet, but you have to know I feel the same way about her. If I didn't, none of this would've mattered to me."

"There's no time like the present, Abigail. Love isn't something you should put off."

CHAPTER TWENTY-NINE

The hallway on the floor where Carol's room was located was crowded with police, and Fiona and Teddie walked under the crime-scene tape to talk to Sebastian. "What's all this?" Fiona asked as the CSI unit worked the room collecting evidence.

"Mrs. Verde made a statement before she was taken to the hospital to be checked out."

"About what, the kidnapping?"

"Sort of. She claims Cain kidnapped her, handcuffed her in the bathroom, and was planning to kill her. I doubt that's true, but we're going to have to investigate her claim so she can't try to get out of anything involved with Hannah. This doesn't seem like something Cain would do. Also, the handcuffs she was held with were police issue."

"So Newsome, you think?" Fiona asked, and he nodded. "Do you mind if I interview her and then consult with Shelby? Casey might not be my favorite person, but I agree with you that she didn't do it. And in this case she has the perfect alibi, the kind that comes with video and FBI reports." They followed him into the room and looked in the bathroom where Carol had been kept. "Anything as far as fingerprints?" Fiona asked when she noticed the black powder on every surface.

"Plenty. We'll sort through them as soon as the room is cleared. Anything on the paperwork she showed the teacher to take Hannah Casey?"

"The attorney representing her said he had no idea where she got that, so we asked the judge overseeing the divorce case. Turns out one of the clerks for the other judge in their courthouse is related to Verde somehow so she drew them up and stamped them. They're as legal as toilet paper and worth about that much." Teddie opened some of the drawers in the room and went through Carol's bag with the tip of her pen. "The sheriff in Haywood has taken her into custody."

"Let's head over to the hospital and have a talk with Verde. We'll report back," Fiona said.

The uniformed officer at Carol's door nodded when they showed their badges before going in. "Mrs. Verde," Fiona said to get Carol to open her eyes and acknowledge her. "I don't know if you remember me, but I'm Detective Fiona O'Brannigan. This is my partner Detective Anderbrock. We have some questions for you."

"Did you arrest her?" Carol asked, sounding extremely feeble.

"Who's that, ma'am?" Teddie looked at her and winked.

"Cain Casey. I'm lucky to be alive after what that monster had planned."

"So you're saying Cain Casey handcuffed you in your room and left you to die?" Fiona said as she wrote in her notebook.

"It was her. I know who she is, and she hates me because I know the truth about her." Carol seemed to regain her strength as she dumped on Casey.

"Are you sure this has nothing to do with what happened with Hannah Casey? You did take her without permission from her school and, according to the little girl, held her against her will." She delivered the accusation in a nonthreatening way but was interested in Carol's response. "Wasn't Elton Newsome helping you with that?"

"I have a right to see her. I don't care what Cain says."

Not a denial, but this woman obviously would fight until the end thinking she had right on her side, even if the court system didn't. "We're looking through your room now for evidence of what happened, but for now I'm going to read you your rights and take you into custody for parental interference. You have the right to remain silent," she said, and Carol glared at her through the rest. "You'll stay here until you're discharged, but then you'll be moved to the women's section of central lockup."

"You have no right to do that. I haven't done anything wrong." Carol pointed her finger at them, and her back came up as if she wanted to hit her. "You came that night because you know like I do what Casey is."

"I suggest you try to retain an attorney," she said and followed Teddie out. They had to stop to let in a man with the same pinched expression as Carol. "I'm sorry. You're going to have to wait until Mrs. Verde is moved to visit."

"She's my sister," the man said, putting his hand on Fiona and pushing her backward. "I have a right to see her."

Teddie removed her cuffs and slapped one side on the hand the man had put on Fiona. He screamed, echoed by Carol when Teddie then shoved him against the wall and yanked his arm up to make him stop fighting. "Keep it up and I'll rip it out of the socket," Teddie said, and he stopped moving. "Let anyone in here and I'll have your badge," she told the guy outside as they led the guy out.

"And make sure the ray of sunshine in there doesn't go anywhere."

"Where's the wee babe?" Father Andrew Goodman said as he stepped through the door, handing the maid his hat and coat. Cain waited until he was done to place Billy in his arms. The only other man aside from her da that loved children and babies this much was Andy. He'd have been a great father had he chosen a life outside the church.

"Give him to me and no one gets hurt," he said, but stopped to kiss Emma. "You are a saint for putting up with this one, but the Lord loves you for all these beautiful children."

"You think you might have room for us after Thanksgiving?" Emma asked, smiling when Andy wrapped her in a bear hug. "That'll give me time to plan a little family get-together following the baptism."

"You know you're my family, so I'll make time whenever you're ready, sweetheart." He accepted the baby from Cain and walked to the den to sit down. It was the room he usually sat in to entertain the children, and Cain was glad he was that familiar with their home. "Look at this little boy," he said, holding the baby so he could see his face. "He's another one for your clan, Derby."

"Not quite." She tickled Billy's cheek so he would open his eyes. "This one will be the first in a while with green eyes like his mama."

"Look at that," he said as he placed his hand over his chest and closed his eyes as his lips moved in prayer. "May God bless you, William, and keep you in His heart," he said before finishing with an amen.

"Thank you, Father, and if you don't mind sitting with Emma for a little while, I have to go out for a meeting."

"You're behaving, aren't you?" he asked.

"If I told you where I was going you wouldn't believe me," she said and placed her finger to her lips as Emma showed him the bugged picture on the mantel. "Just be happy that I'm doing God's work."

He laughed and went back to looking at the baby. "And Emma says you can't learn."

Cain headed to the Piquant and walked up to the lobby with Lou. They followed their usual route of two floors past where they needed to be and took the stairs down. Lou knocked on the door, and the woman who answered seemed smaller than the last time Cain had seen her. But then she wasn't really paying attention to much except what was coming out of Judice's mouth that night. Everything that had happened since that visit must've taken a heavy toll.

"Thank you for seeing me, Judice," she said, shaking the woman's hand.

"I think it's me who should be thanking you." Judice let them in so they could sit in the suite's small living room. "And no matter what you may think of me, I had nothing to do with the theft. I've worked for Colin and Salvatore for years, and I've done my best and been grateful for making more than a decent living."

"I'm not here to accuse you of anything, just to understand what happened." She leaned forward and read the titles on the ledgers on the coffee table. They seemed to be the financials for both men. "Whatever we talk about today will never leave this room."

"What do you want to know?"

"From my understanding, Colin and Salvatore became involved with the Mexican cartel and started accepting and selling shipments of drugs to take advantage of the shortage coming from other areas. They were successful and used your services the same way they always did." She touched the outside of the book but didn't open it. "Is all that right?"

"Yes, but it was way too much money for me to use the usual methods I'd developed. I mean, it's not always the same, but I have to come up with different ways to report the money that won't ever raise red flags."

She nodded and studied Judice's face. "What kind of money are we talking about?"

"The operation started small, but in the last couple of months, they're bringing in a little over ten million a month. All we can do is stockpile the money, because there's no way to deposit that or invest it without some sort of authority coming down on us hard."

She whistled, impressed with Colin's setup. "So where did they stockpile all this cash?"

"That I don't know, but I was working on bringing it into our system slowly. The actual movement and investment part wasn't my responsibility. I never wanted anyone to accuse me of stealing a cent from these guys. Someone told me a long time ago that to play the game, you had to understand the rules and, more importantly, what could happen if you didn't."

"Da," she said, having gotten that lecture herself. "He had good advice, but I want to know who did touch the money?"

Judice laid out the whole thing and who she dealt with every step of the way. They compared who from that list actually had the power to lay hands on the money. An hour later, Cain punched a number into her cell phone.

"Colin, are you in the hotel? Good. Come to the tenth floor," she said, giving him the room number.

"Are you sure about this?" Judice sat so upright, her tension practically vibrated in the air. "If he really wants to kill me, here I am."

"Colin has a soft spot for you, but he's not going to forgive being stolen from. Since I know it's not you, I don't think it'll be a problem."

Ten minutes later, Lou let Colin into the room. He stopped when he saw Judice sitting there. "What the hell is this?"

"How much money is missing?" she asked, patting the seat next to her.

"Over a million." Colin sat, his hands that rested on his thighs curled into fists, and glared at Judice. "I know, considering how much money we've made, that doesn't sound like a lot, but I would've given it to you if you'd asked. Why fuck me, Judice?"

"Cousin, calm down and listen to what I have to say," Cain said, wrapping her hand around his bicep. "You've got a thief, but it's not her. How would she have done it?"

"Who then?" Colin said, staring at Judice as if daring her to pick a name so he could knock her teeth out. If she'd known all this time and hadn't told him, that's where he'd start and work his way to killing her. "Salvatore said it had to be her."

"Of course he did, but I can't know for sure. It has to be someone who not only has access to the money but knows where it physically is. From what she said, only five people have that information, and she's not one of them."

Colin squeezed his hands hard, and Cain thought any more of that and he'd cut through the skin. "You really didn't do it?" he asked Judice.

"After everything you've done for me, you would think I would?" She surprised Cain by standing up, going to him, and placing her hands on his shoulders. "I love you, Colin, and I've never given you everything you wanted because you're married. Those vows you took mean something to me, but it doesn't mean I love you any less." She rested her cheek on top of his head. "I'll never be able to repay you for taking me in and giving me a chance all those years ago."

"Then who?" he said, reaching up for her hand.

"I had no idea anything was missing, so I can't answer that," Judice said.

"The way I look at it, the five people who would have enough access to steal would be you, Salvatore, your wife, Salvatore's son-in-law, and his daughter. Unless your wife's finally had enough of your affairs and is starting a nest egg, it has to be one of the other three, so which of them has had a change in circumstances?" Cain logically counted them off. "And since Salvatore has done nothing but point his finger at Judice, that might be who's dipping his hand deeper into the well."

"There's no way to tell that now since so much money is involved. I might not be able to figure it out, much less accuse Salvatore or someone in his family of stealing from me. You know how he is."

"You're going to have to, and you're going to have to make peace between the two of you." She stood, expecting Colin would stay to speak to Judice privately. "Just give me your word you'll offer Judice your protection." Cain was working toward peace these days—throughout the Casey clan. "I suggest you change how you do business when it comes to the payout. Once you do, whoever complains the most is where your problem lies and you'll know for sure."

"Thank you," Judice said and took her hands. "I don't think I deserved your help, but I'm grateful for it."

"I'm just a bull in a china shop," Cain said, recalling that Judice had once said that about Dalton. "But I try not to spend every day smashing things."

"I'm sorry for that," Judice said.

"Let's both agree to forget. Feel free to stay as long as you'd like until Colin clears the way for you to go back." She let Judice go and decided to throw her another bone. "I'm sure Fiona would love to see you."

CHAPTER THIRTY

"That was a nice thing, Boss," Lou said as they climbed the stairs to the floor where they'd gotten off the elevator. "It was your good deed for the day."

"Actually my good deed for the day will be to go home early so you can take off and maybe go on a date with whoever you're seeing these days." Cain slapped him on the back and laughed at his expression of a small boy getting caught with a fistful of cookies.

"Are you admitting you don't know who it is?"

"If I admit that I do, you'll think my wife's a snitch. So I'll just tell you that if you're seeing someone, I'm happy for you."

They continued to tease each other until the elevator stopped at the third floor, the lobby. Lou called to have the car brought around as they walked across the lobby to board another elevator to exit onto the street. He immediately reached into his jacket when they stepped outside the hotel, but Cain grabbed his arm.

"Don't give them an excuse," she said, then put her hands slightly up in front of her.

"Keep your hands where we can see them," the uniformed policeman said as he aimed his weapon at her.

"What's this about?" she asked, glancing at Lou to make sure he kept his cool.

"We're taking you in," the guy said as his partner came forward and roughly jerked her hands behind her back. To treat her like this for what seemed no reason made her want to kick the guy between the legs hard enough that his future children would feel it.

"I can see that, but why are you arresting me?" The hold he had on her made her want to grimace, but she refused to give him the satisfaction of showing any sign that he was hurting her.

"Because you finally couldn't help but go for the most obvious victim."

"Lou, call Emma and let her know what's happening. Then get Muriel to meet me," she said as he read her her rights, then shoved her into the backseat of the cruiser.

Lou ran to the car and called the house, hoping Muriel was there already. "Carmen, is Muriel there?" he yelled into the phone when she answered.

"No. You want to talk to Miss Emma?"

Actually, that was the last thing he wanted to do since he didn't want to stress her, but he had no choice when Emma came on the line. "What's going on?"

"I'm not sure, but the cops just took Cain in. She wanted you to know and to have Muriel meet her at the station."

"Carmen, please find Muriel for me and have her call Lou. Tell her it's an emergency." He heard Carmen's quick "Yes, Miss Emma" as he tried to keep up with the cruiser.

"Why did they pick her up?" Emma was speaking to him again.

"The asshole wouldn't tell her, and nothing comes to mind that would've made them do this."

"Tell me which precinct and I'll meet you."

"She'd probably want you to stay home, Emma. I promise I'll call and keep you updated, but I want to make sure this isn't something that's setting up something else you could get caught in." They stopped at the station downtown, and he turned off toward the visitor parking. "They're at the downtown headquarters, but please, stay home for now. She'll kill me if something happens to you."

"I'll give you one hour, and then I'm coming," Emma said, and he heard the baby start crying. "Make sure you remember to call me."

"I promise. This is nothing but bull, so I really think we'll be home soon after Muriel gets here." His phone buzzed, identifying Muriel as the caller. "That's her on the other line, so I'll let you know what's happening." He disconnected and answered the waiting call.

"Lou, where are you?"

"I'm downtown. Some uniformed cops picked Cain up and took her in, so you need to get down here."

"Anything going on she didn't tell me about?"

"You know everything I do, so this makes no fucking sense."

"Hang tight and keep your cool. I'm like ten minutes away."

"Make it faster than that. Just remember last time."

❖

On the way to the station Cain thought about what the guy had said. It made absolutely no sense, but going through a check list of her recent actions took her mind off her numb hands. She'd taken a break from her unique style of persuasion. It hadn't been necessary, as she planned for a future that would put her in a position to expand safely and grow her power as well as territory.

She planned to cover from New Orleans to Biloxi and everywhere between for now. That would double her current business. Eventually they'd expand those borders to Florida and Texas, but that could wait.

She was taken to an interrogation room, and the guy who'd brought her in cuffed her to the table, taking the pressure off her shoulders. The games were just beginning, and she guessed the next part would involve a long wait to drive up her apprehension. "You'd think after a few times of this exercise, we'd just get on with it. The only way to intimidate me is to tell me either my mother or my wife is behind that glass."

"Ms. Casey." A young man wearing a bad suit came in with one of the uniformed officers that had been at the Piquant. "My name's Raymond Johnson. I'm with the district attorney's office." He took out a folder and slapped it on the table as if to accentuate all the offenses she'd committed. "Do you know why you're here?"

"Do you know why you're here?" She figured he'd been out of law school maybe two weeks. "And do you have permission from your teacher to be out of class?"

"These guys told me about you," Raymond said, opening the file. He lost his smile when she didn't glance down. And he swiveled around quickly when the door opened and Muriel strode in.

"Did they tell you about me too?" Muriel sat next to Cain and pointed to the cuffs. "Do you think my client's going to attack someone?"

"It's standard procedure," the cop said, and Raymond nodded.

Muriel glanced at her watch, making a note of how long they'd keep Cain cuffed. "Ms. Casey will not be making a statement today, but since you're here and the clown show outside said you're with the DA's office, let's hear the grounds for my lawsuit."

"We found Carol Verde this morning," Raymond said, fidgeting when both Cain and Muriel stared at him as if he were completely insane.

"So you found my mother-in-law, and I'm in custody? Have you completely lost it, or did your boss need some press to help his re-election campaign?" Cain asked.

Raymond shook his head.

"She claims you're responsible for her condition when she was found and that you planned to kill her." Raymond seemed much less sure of himself. "I have her statement here."

"So on the word of a kidnapper, you arrested me?" Cain had to laugh. "Is this some kind of joke? If it is, you have a very strange sense of humor I don't find funny in the least. But I'll get that last laugh everyone talks about."

"I'm not sure what you mean, but Mrs. Verde was in a very weakened condition when she was found, according to the initial report. So, my boss didn't want to waste any time picking you up. We didn't want to allow you time to destroy evidence."

"And your boss is?" Muriel asked.

"Come on. Don't keep us in suspense." Cain didn't take her eyes off him until the door opened yet again and Fiona entered with some other woman. "Then again, everything is becoming clearer."

For once, Cain was wrong.

"Why in the hell did you pick up Ms. Casey?" Fiona glared at the policeman, who crossed his arms over his chest as if to protect himself from what was coming. "Answer the question," she yelled.

"Raymond called. He said he had a warrant and did I want to have a little fun, so I said why the hell not."

She narrowed her eyes at the officer. "You have an appointment with the police chief." Then she turned to Raymond. "And you have one with the DA, so I suggest you don't keep them waiting." Fiona took her cuff key from her pocket and released Cain. "I'm sorry for what happened, and I thought you'd want to know that Carol Verde will be taken into custody as soon as she's out of the hospital."

"What's she in the hospital for?" Cain asked, rubbing her wrist. Fiona told her in as much detail as possible what had happened to Carol and how she'd been found. "Did the cuffs belong to this Newsome guy?"

"You would've made a good detective, Ms. Casey, but I can't comment on that. I'm sure you'll hear from someone in the department when we have it sorted out. Again, I'm sorry for what happened. My initial report didn't recommend that anyone take action, but just to take Mrs. Verde's statement and begin verifying the facts."

"I'm sure you're disappointed then." Cain felt like an idiot now, after the good she'd done for this woman that morning.

"I saw the pictures of Hannah's face. So no, you got that part wrong. My partner and I hadn't finished the report because I was checking in with Shelby to verify your whereabouts."

"And you said paying my taxes wouldn't pay off for me, Muriel." Fiona actually cracked a smile at Cain's remark.

"Am I free to go?"

"Yes. We'll even offer you a ride."

"No. All I'm interested in is Raymond's contact information and the name of his overzealous boss."

"Why?" Raymond said, sounding incredibly whiny.

"You went to law school, Raymond, so my cousin here is going to file a whole lot of papers on my behalf. Then you'll get to take your degree out for a spin and see how good you are." She stood and leaned over him. "My advice is to take really good care of this suit. It'll be with you for years to come."

❖

Nunzio opened his eyes, then regretted it when the bright room made the pain in his head pound like someone was hitting him with a hammer. He closed his eyes, then tried again when he realized the room and bed weren't at all familiar. "Where am I?" His voice was raspy and his throat dry.

"Thank God." Santino was suddenly next to him, holding his hand. "You've been out all night, but you're going to be okay."

"What happened?" All he could remember was sitting in the car. Now, his entire body hurt and he couldn't breathe.

"The doctor thinks it's a bad case of Montezuma's Revenge, but they need to keep you a few days to be sure. Usually people get sick, but not so violently that it knocks them out. You've been sleeping the last day or so because of something they gave you to calm your stomach."

"I can't stay here for a couple of days, Nino. We got shit to do."

"It's going to get done, but you're not leaving until the doctor okays it. I'm going to leave Phil here with you and get back to the city so I can start the process. Early this morning, Cesar called and said the shipment has left and should be on the Louisiana Coast soon." Santino let go of his hand and went back to his chair. "I've got Mike working on having some of our guys in position to pick it up and get it to the guy who'll change it for street consumption."

"Are you sure you'll be okay?" He closed his eyes to the glare and concentrated on his breathing. "I want to go with you and help."

"You got us this far, Nunzio, and once this is in place I'll go back to my house and play golf so I'll be out of your hair. The only reason I came was to help you get back what was yours. Not to be a meddlesome old man."

The little speech made him squint to look at his grandfather, who in a short time had treated him much better than his father ever had. "I don't want you to go back. When we get this rolling, I want you with me so we can work together."

"That means the world to me." Santino smiled, and Nunzio felt as if he'd finally found his place in the world. "The other good news is that Mike brought a couple of guys by last night to talk to me about Hector's safe houses and who ripped them off."

"You got some guys to finger Cain?"

"Two, and they promised no matter what, they're going to stick to their story. Once they finally get that meeting with Hector or his daughter, they'll wait a day or so to call us."

"Mike's sure we can trust these guys?" He was able to open his eyes more after Santino closed the blinds. "Cain has a way of sniffing out this kind of shit like no one I've ever seen."

"She's not going to be a problem when Hector goes at her with everything he has. Then we can go after Remi and her goddamn family."

"You sure you'll be okay?"

Santino came to the bed and leaned over so he could kiss Nunzio's forehead. "All you have to worry about is getting better. I will take care of this. Once Cesar sees we're reliable, we'll be kings."

"Okay, and as soon as I'm out of here, I'll meet you in the city."

"Just remember that I'm proud of you," Santino said, kissing his forehead again. This time, though, a chill ran through Nunzio. It felt like a bad omen, and he wanted to beg him to wait until they could both go. But he was afraid Santino would laugh at his overactive imagination.

The door clicked closed and his heart raced. He struggled to breathe as panic started to make his body seize up. He had to go after his grandfather, but when he swung his legs over the side of the bed, he fell to the floor. He was too weak, and his head pounded so bad he grabbed the sides of his head and grunted at the pain.

"Nino, please," was the last thing he said before it all went black.

CHAPTER THIRTY-ONE

Lou, get some of our best guys on the street and find this Newsome guy. If he's willing to set me up for this kind of shit, then I'm going to give him a reason to hate me. The only thing is, he's not going to live very long to be able to do anything about it." Cain had followed Muriel out of the police station and had to walk the gauntlet of news media outside. Before they even made it to the car, the DA was calling Muriel's phone, but Cain told her to ignore it.

"At the risk of pissing you off more, you need to calm down before you make any major decisions," Muriel said.

"Waiting gets you into trouble, cousin. I waited with Juan, and look where that got me. Then there was Anthony Curtis, Nunzio, and every other idiot who thinks it's okay to take a potshot at me because I'll turn the other cheek." Cain wanted to rip someone's head off but tried to regain control since Muriel and Lou weren't to blame. "Did you call Emma?"

"I called her, and she said no matter what, I had to bring you home," Lou said, finally making a dent in Cain's anger. "I hate to mention it, but Colin called, and he's got another problem."

"What the hell? I wasn't in there that long, was I?"

"Once you told him to change the way things were done, he, in typical Colin fashion, called Salvatore."

"And Salvatore blew his world to shit?" She shook her head. As much as she loved him, Colin was a three-year-old when it came to business. Truthfully, she was amazed he was still breathing.

"He accused Salvatore's son-in-law of stealing and trying to pin it on someone else. Colin questioned Salvatore's manhood for allowing a woman to take the fall."

"And?" She wasn't at all interested in getting involved in Colin's business.

"Salvatore told him to watch his back and hung up. The next phone call Colin got was from the crew at his pub. The place is on fire right now."

"Where is he?" This could only mean she'd have to back him in California or support him in New Orleans. The second option would be the worst choice for her own business, so she'd have to fix the California problem, no matter what.

"I told him it'd be best for him to wait it out at the hotel, and you'd call him."

"Give me his number," she said, and Lou handed over his phone. "I need you to listen, okay?" she said when Colin picked up. "You should've waited until you could change how you do business to see who complained. I believe that's what I said, so do me a favor and hold on before you retaliate."

"You'd fucking hold on?" Colin screamed so loud that she had to pull the phone away from her ear. "The rat bastard's such a good friend that he hit me the second he hung up."

"Salvatore Maggio's been an asshole all his life. You were the one who went into business with him even after Da and I told you not to, so hold on. It's not going to be forever. We'll deal with this guy when we're ready to deal with him, and not any sooner."

"Come on. I'm ready now."

"Colin, something like this has to be over and done in one night. All of it." She said the words slowly. "Do you understand what all that means?"

"I don't have that kind of manpower."

"No, you don't, so we're going to have to wait. Give me a few days and pack your stuff. I don't exactly trust you when left alone to pout. Lou will be there to get you in a little while."

"Thanks, Cain. I know I'm a fuck-up at times, but I appreciate you helping me with this."

"You're just you, Colin, and we love you for it, but there's got to be some changes going forward. Lucky for you, though, big sweeping changes sometimes leave you on the top of the mound."

"As long as it's not shit, cousin, I'm okay with it."

"Shit's not my business or my style, so you've got nothing to worry about."

❖

"So who are these two lowlifes?" Hector asked Tracy as she stood in front of his desk.

"They met with Marisol, and she said it was important for you to talk to them." She knew this would be the test of her future. "They claim they can tell you for sure who hit your places."

"I already know that."

"They said it was Casey who stole from you and tried to drag you off the scent by pointing the finger at someone else. Marisol thinks it makes perfect sense, because of where the stuff was found. That and the fact that the cops got to it first proved she wanted you to know she stole from you and found a way to keep it out of your reach."

"What's Marisol's theory then?" He leaned back and laced his fingers together over his stomach.

"She said Casey stole the drugs and put them in her partner's building. Since Remi was three floors up from where it was, it means they're guilty."

"What do you think?" he asked.

There it was. She had to either agree with Marisol or tell him the truth.

"Maybe this time, you should talk to Marisol about it. I'll work the angle I've been trying to prove. If I do, we'll know for sure."

He stood and came up behind her, pressing himself tightly to her. "You are young and beautiful," he said, kissing the side of her neck as his hands came up to cup her breasts. "But you are so much more than that, aren't you?"

"The most important thing you should remember is that I'm loyal to you."

"I know that. I only meant you're brilliant for one so young, so tell me what you think. If you're afraid of Marisol's shadow, then you'll be of no use to me." He pinched her nipples hard enough to get her attention.

"You know if she wants to kill me, she's going to do it because she's sure the punishment won't be as bad as keeping me around."

"Come here." He led her to the sofa behind them. "When I started I had nothing. Some days I ate trash from the streets to stay alive. So when I got here, I knew it was me and no one else that made that happen. Today—because of all the men I've killed, all the drugs I've moved, and all the things I was willing to do—I owe no one anything."

"I didn't start where you did, but all I had was Kim. And because of Nunzio, Casey, and Jatibon, I lost her. The money and power aren't important to me, but I simply want to live long enough to see them pay for what they did."

"I can give you all that, but you have to promise me one thing. No matter how hard the answer to any question I give you, always tell me the truth. You're here and with me because I value your opinion."

"Nunzio has asked you for months through your old business manager Miguel to supply him, but you strung him along. Then he stopped asking."

He nodded but twirled his finger in the air as if to get her moving in the story. "I know that part. Roth Pombo was moving his shit with someone named Emray Gillis, but I think everyone with that crew is dead, as is Miguel. That's old news."

"It is, but if you remember, Roth's last shipment, or maybe two, was never found, so we figured Nunzio found it and cashed in. That can only mean that someone in Roth's or Emray's crew lived and decided Nunzio was the smartest move. I was with the pig for months and know how greedy he is. If he found it, he probably decided it wasn't enough and hit your places."

"We were careful, so how'd he find that out?" Hector stood up and paced in a circle. "There was no way anyone with us betrayed me, knowing I'd kill them."

"I think Nunzio already took care of that for you when he hit the locations and killed everyone in them. Whoever double-crossed you will never have the opportunity to do it again or to confess who stole your merchandise."

"Remind me to never play chess with you," he said, kneeling before her so he could hold her hands. "So Nunzio stole from me and is trying to blame Casey for what reason?"

"That I don't know, and while I want her dead too, she didn't do this. It seems reasonable to me because it was too contrived, right down to where he picked as his safe house."

"So these fools waiting to see me are working for the Luca family?"

"There's one way to find out without getting your hands dirty."

"Let me hear it," he said, kissing both her palms.

"Pay them for what they bring you, but tell them you need to draw Cain out of that fortress of hers. If they can do that, there'll be another payday."

❖

"Look, I did what you asked and now I'm in a world of shit. You have to vouch for me so I can go in and not be in handcuffs," Elton Newsome said from his brother's house in Baton Rouge. The money he'd gotten as an advance to get Casey to fuck up had run out a week before, and because of Carol there'd be no more. "Either help me or I'm going to Sebastian with what I have."

"That'd be the worst thing you can do, Detective Newsome. You knew the risks, and you decided to do it anyway. At the time, I didn't really care that your willingness wasn't career motived, but more for the ten grand than for the glory of bringing her down."

"No. That's not how you sold it. You said low, if any, risks because all I had to do was wind Carol up and let her loose." He combed his hair back and separated the curtains to peer out when he heard a car door. "Well, that crazy bitch got wound up all right, and she fucking blew up. I'm not going down in that blast. You understand that?"

"Let me see what I can do, and I'll get back to you." The man hung up before he had to listen to Newsome really get going about how everyone was shitting on him and how his boss owed him the world for his brave service.

It helped that he knew where Newsome was in case he needed to make a call and turn him in, but he'd wait for the cop to do something stupid that would make it easy on him and his boss. The decision wasn't his, but it was time to cut Newsome loose and leave him to finish himself off. He selected the contact he had on speed dial.

"Sir," he said when the call connected but no one spoke.

"Angus." The voice of the man he'd never met but talked to often was soft, as usual. "Is it important?"

"I just talked to Newsome, and he's starting to fray along the edges. The situation will become a problem sooner than later." Angus watched the map on his computer to see if the signal would stop bouncing all over the United States and give him more of a solid location. "Mrs. Verde was arrested this morning."

"I'll take care of it. Unless we've got a problem with the others, try not to call me again. The only way this operation will work is through the absence of contact."

"Yes, sir, and thank you for taking care of Newsome." The bouncing died again without a location, so Angus Covington had to trust that the instructions he'd been getting would lead to the promotion the man promised. He was still wary of the secrecy of the limited contact, but, so far, he'd been trusted with the Carol Verde and Elton Newsome part of Operation Octopus.

The lead agent he dealt with was heading up a multipronged approach to snag Casey and squeeze her to death. Any question he had about their methods had died the day he stood in her office and she showed him a picture of his wife and kids. Casey had to be destroyed, but he wouldn't underestimate her. The fact that she'd found out anything about him was a professional move that proved she wasn't your average thug.

"When the lead agent makes his move, I pray he kills her. Her death is the only way I'll live the rest of my life not looking over my shoulder."

CHAPTER THIRTY-TWO

S hould we have everyone over for Thanksgiving next week?"
Emma asked as they dressed for the day. Once Cain had
returned home after her arrest the day before, they'd stayed in, and
everyone in the house had tried to take her mind off what had happened.
At least now it'd be easy to keep track of Emma's mother.

"If you can talk Carmen into it, then sure. I'm here only as your sex
slave and to provide witty remarks. Cooking isn't one of my talents."
Cain came out of the closet in khakis and a sweater, since she was
planning to take the kids to the park later.

"I do love your sexual services, but I also like to cook so I'll be
happy to help out. This year will be rough for Remi and Dallas, since
they're in the middle of construction, and Colin might still be here, so I
thought a big family celebration might be the ticket."

Cain kissed her and nodded. "I'm sure they'll love you for putting
all that together. It'll be fun, and we've got plenty to be thankful for."

The knock made Emma groan. Too bad for her it wasn't because
of the kiss Cain had just initiated. Whoever was on the other side of the
door had stopped something promising. "Come in," Cain said as she sat
on the bed to put her shoes on. "Good morning, Merrick."

"Depends on who you asked, I guess," Merrick said as she stood
by the door. "We might have a problem."

"Story of my life lately. What now?" she asked as Emma handed
over her watch.

"One of the store owners on Magazine Street just called and said
there's 'a guy outside flapping his gums.'" Merrick made air quotes.
"He thought you'd be interested."

"What's the gum-flapping about?" she said, smiling.

"He just scored big by telling Hector it was you who ripped him off."

"Am I the last person that hasn't lost their mind left in the city?" Cain rubbed her jaw. "Where's this guy?"

"I'd think he's in the car with Katlin. She flashed a grand out the window to hear the story up close."

"I'll be back as soon as I can, lass. Tell the kids not to worry. We'll do something even if it can't be the carousel."

"Are you sure this isn't some kind of setup? I'm never going to trust Hector or Marisol." Emma said both names like she was trying to spit something nasty out of her mouth.

"I'll have the overprotective squad with me, so don't worry about anything. Since we both know I didn't steal anything from Hector, this shouldn't take long. I mean, why would I steal from the man when he's more than willing to give it away?"

"Call me when you're done," Emma said, then kissed her before she stood up.

"Which way do you want to go, Boss?" Lou asked as they waited for the gate to open.

"Take your time and head to the office." She glanced in the side-view mirror and confirmed the usual tail, so she closed her eyes and enjoyed the quiet. When they arrived, she had Lou park outside and went across the street for coffee to wait for Katlin's arrival.

"Think the weather will be decent next week?" Lou asked.

"Emma wants the entire crew so bring a date, and I'm not taking any chances so I'll have Vincent's catering crew come by with a tent." They both laughed since she'd turned off the jamming equipment for the moment so the feds could enjoy the more mundane aspects of her life.

"Let's go over the details with Katlin," Lou said, pointing his thumb at the warehouse. "She's here."

They walked slowly and waved to a few of the locals who were outside in the cool weather, and she wondered if the feds still took pictures of these little walks or if they had a whole gallery of them. It didn't matter and it was time to go to work, so she put it out of her mind. "Remind me about ordering fresh turkeys," she said as they walked in and headed to the conference room where the rug was rolled up slightly at one end, exposing the trapdoor.

They headed down the stairs, and Lou helped Katlin get the guy into the chair at the center of a large patch of plastic sheeting. It was obvious he hadn't wanted to come willingly, so Katlin had knocked him out and dragged him down there. He seemed young but also street-hardened.

"Any trouble?" she asked as she went through his wallet.

"He's a greedy little bastard," Katlin said as she finished duct-taping him to the chair.

Cain had taken a total of six thousand dollars in two big rolls out of his pockets, so she gave Katlin her thousand back. "If he was telling the truth about the payoff from Hector, he sold cheap." She fanned out the five thousand and thought about how best to return it to its owner. "Wake him up. I've got stuff to do."

Katlin snapped a tube of smelling salts under his nose, and the guy came to so quickly, he almost knocked the chair back. "It's been a while since we've had one of these heartfelt talks," Katlin said as she slapped the guy a few times to get his attention.

"For a guy in ripped jeans," Cain said, tapping on the stack of bills, "you've got a load of cash. You'd think you would've picked something better to go around in."

"That's mine," he said and strained against his bindings to the point he was grunting.

"I know, and I'm going to let you walk out of here with it, but I have a few questions first. Let's start with the story you told Hector Delarosa. People who go around telling lies about me upset me." She crossed her legs and stared at him. "And if you told my pal Hector I stole from him and killed some of his people, that would upset me even more."

"I didn't say anything like that. Who told you that?"

Cain pointed at Katlin. "She did, right after she paid you a grand to hear the story you were spouting outside that convenience store." She stood up and walked closer to him. "Before you start telling more lies, you should ask yourself: 'Will she believe my story?' A few before you in this same position learned about the lie penalty the hard way. I'd like to avoid that because it makes a mess, and no one wants that."

"Hector gave me that money for selling some shit for him," the guy said, straining again. "It didn't have nothing to do with you. I don't even know who you are."

"I'm sorry. I'm Cain Casey." She put her index finger on his forehead and tilted his head back so she could look him in the eye. "And I don't believe you, so you've earned one of those penalty shots. The operative word here is shots."

Katlin came forward and pressed her gun to the top of his knee. He started, screaming, "Wait. Just wait, okay?"

"You said you didn't know, so I find that first bullet does wonders to jog the memory."

"Look, I did tell Hector that story, but he's not who gave me a chunk of that money." He tried to move his bound body away from Katlin. "Some guy that works for Santino Luca did."

"Did you talk to Santino or just the guy?"

"If he's some old guy, then probably yeah. He really wanted me to keep at it until I got to Hector or his kid. I talked to the daughter, and she got me right in."

"Where did you meet with Santino?"

"The bar at the W Hotel. He wanted me to tell the story for him beforehand to make sure it sounded believable, I guess. He gave me four grand when I was done."

"Hector would've never believed only you, so who went with you?" Cain asked as Katlin put her gun back. "Think very carefully before you lie. I let you off that first time, but it won't happen again."

"My friend, Little Ink, was with me, and Hector believed us because we told him you sent us, like we were part of your crew."

"I'll have to remember to shoot Hector if he believed that," she said, and Lou chuckled. "Hang tight and let's see if that's true." She picked up the phone and went through the steps to make sure the call was secure. "Mr. Delarosa, please. Tell him it's a good neighbor calling."

"Cain," Hector said, sounding like he was in a good mood. "Did you get my gift?"

"How much did it cost to get it where I would pick it up?"

"Not as much as you would think. It was a bargain. I had to get you something to repay you for your gift, but I think we're shopping for the same thing." She understood that he didn't believe these guys. "After I thought about it, the story didn't make sense, but I understand why they're trying to sell it."

"So do I, but I'll take care of it. Thanks." She hung up and stared at the guy, not really caring what his name was. This asshole had tried to set her up. "So the W Hotel is where you met Santino?"

"I just saw him there. That guy, Mike, was with him, and they seemed like they were working something big."

"I'm sure he shared that with you, but it's Nunzio's family we're talking about, so maybe he did." She stood up and the guy smiled. "Katlin, try to find out what room Santino's in, and make sure we find both of them. I'm tired of thinking about these idiots."

"You got it," Katlin said. "Head on out and I'll take care of this. I'll get Dino to come help me."

"What about me?" the guy said as she started up the stairs.

Cain stopped on the stairs and smiled to set the guy at ease. "Did you ever hear my name before Santino and his sidekick Mike asked you to lie about me?" She pointed at him in warning. "Remember, it's time to tell the truth."

He had a hard time maintaining eye contact, but he started talking. "Yeah, but I figured it wouldn't hurt nothing since you don't deal. Who would've believed me, so it was an easy score." He whipped his head up when she came down the stairs and Katlin handed her a gun.

"No one believed you, so I'll make this quick," she said, aiming the gun at him. When he opened his mouth to say something, she shot him squarely in the middle of his forehead.

"Send Shaun over to the W and make sure he knows who he's looking for."

"I'll make sure he blends in," Katlin said as she cut the guy's bindings and pushed him onto the tarp. "What's your plan once we find him?"

"Let's get creative. But no matter what, we're going for a happy ending. For us anyway."

❖

When Cain returned from the park with the kids, Sebastian and the police chief were waiting for her, wanting to smooth things over about her arrest.

"It was simply an overzealous assistant in the DA's office, and he promised to take care of it so it's not repeated. We understand what happened isn't easily forgotten, but we believe neither you nor anyone in your extended family had anything to do with what happened to Mrs. Verde," the police chief said. "Aside from the maid, the only other fingerprints we found belonged to Mrs. Verde and Elton Newsome."

"What's this guy's story?" There had to be something, because him getting thrown out of her house couldn't have caused this kind of animosity. "Going out with my family while people like him are waiting outside that gate is starting to make me nervous."

"As soon as we find him, I'll ask, but no one in the department has green-lighted a taskforce. You've got a right to be angry, but I'm asking as a favor to let it go," Sebastian said. "The only way to know if he's dirty is to interrogate him, and if that's the case, then he'll pay the worst punishment in prison."

"All I ask is that someone like that idiot Raymond doesn't let him slip through a loop made from his own stupidity."

"You have my word, as long as I have yours, and you know I'll hold you to that."

"Believe me, Cain, we want this guy as much as you do," the chief said and offered his hand.

"What happens to my mother now?" Emma asked. Cain felt her tighten the grip she had on her hand.

"She was moved to the women's section of central lockup this morning, and since her brother showed up intending to take her back to Wisconsin with him, she's been denied bond," Sebastian said. "After what happened to Cain, the district attorney himself went to court for her arraignment and asked the judge for no bond, and that was granted. Mrs. Verde won't be going anywhere because she doesn't think she did anything wrong. I blame Elton Newsome for convincing her that she had the right."

"You must not know Carol very well then," Cain said, and Emma snorted. "She did it because she thought she had the right, no matter what that guy told her. In that thick skull of hers she had a God-given right."

"It's not important now. She's locked away, and the only way to get out of it is for you not to press charges," the police chief said.

"I want to see her before anything else happens," Emma said, and Cain understood her request. Carol was finally in a position to listen; she'd have no choice.

"I want to come with you." Ross had been quiet, his face tight with what Cain could only decipher as rage.

"No time like the present, if that's what you want. I'm sure Sebastian and the boss here can set that up," Cain said, and Sebastian nodded. "Let's go then."

Sebastian told them where to go and to wait for him in the main lobby so he could arrange a private room away from the regular visiting venue. She and Emma sat alone in the back while Ross rode with Lou in the front to give them some privacy. His reason to see Carol probably had something in common with Emma's, but she guessed Ross felt so much more for this woman he'd married.

"You okay?" she asked Emma, who was pressed against her.

"Not really." Emma put her head on her shoulder and sighed. "My mother and I have never seen the world the same way, and if you meet my Uncle Morris you'll see why. Their father must've done a number on them. They both drank the Kool-Aid and mixed it up for the next generation. Only I refused to take a sip."

"A religious zealot you are not. That I agree with," she said, and kissed Emma's head.

"My cousin, Morrie, ran as soon as he was able, just like me, and it was one more thing my mother blamed me for. I'm not really sure what happened to him."

"Hopefully he's got as good a life as you do. After meeting your mother, I think the guy deserves it," she said, drawing a laugh from Emma.

"Do you want to see her alone? I don't mind waiting outside since Carol already knows how I feel about her." The car stopped and Lou waited to open the door. "Whatever you decide, though, I'll be okay with it. She's your mother and you're my wife, so I'll understand no matter what."

"You think I'd let her walk?"

"I love you, but I don't think this is my decision. You and your father have to do that because it's the only way to find satisfaction with the future."

"It was Hannah, baby. I can't let that go."

"Lass, you know what I would do without hesitation, but she's not my mother. I'm not questioning your judgment. I'm telling you that

I'm here and whatever you want won't change anything between us. Hannah's going to be fine, so put all this to rest."

"Let's go. She'll just have to deal with you being there, because I want you with me."

When Sebastian led them to a room, Carol was already wearing an orange jumpsuit that made her appear pale and gaunt. "Come to gloat?" Carol said, keeping her head up as if in some sort of defiant stance.

"More like I've come to ask why," Emma said, taking one of the two other chairs. Cain pointed Ross into the other one. She'd stay because Emma wanted her to, but she didn't want to get too close because of her urge to choke the shit out of this woman.

"I wanted another chance to make things right for Hannah. You're lost to me and I accept that, but I refuse to let my granddaughter go down with you. You know I'm right, so the best thing you can do is let me go and give me Hannah and the baby." Carol glanced down and smiled. "I see the little bastard has arrived."

"Carol," Ross said, making Carol jump when he barked her name. "I tried giving you the life you wanted by sending you to live with Morris, but you couldn't or wouldn't let go. If you'd simply stayed in Wisconsin, you and that brother of yours could've read scripture to yourselves until even God got tired of listening to you." He combed his hair back and slammed his hand on the table. "You weren't like this in the beginning, so I'm not sure where or what changed that brought back that son-of-a-bitch father of yours, but no one cares anymore. I sure as hell don't."

"You take that back. My father was a good man."

"Your father was an abusive bastard, and the only two people in the world who never saw it were you and Morris. Why else do you think your mother killed herself instead of living with him one more day?"

"She was weak," Carol said, screaming so loud someone rapped on the two-way mirror.

"You'll have plenty of time to think about it, Mother," Emma said softly as if to calm Carol down. "I had thought maybe there was something to salvage in you, and Cain encouraged me to at least look before I made up my mind." Carol glared at her and Cain simply smiled. Maybe letting the police handle more of her problems might be more gratifying than actually pulling the trigger herself. Well, maybe in this case.

"You're a stupid little fool, Emma. You fell for the first devil to come along to steer you toward the flames, and instead of seeing her for what she was, you ran to her."

"I chose happiness with someone who didn't see every fault in me. Cain loved me enough to give me the things I valued most, and she did it because we wanted the same things." Emma stood and held her hand out to her, and Cain gladly took it. "We have a family and a home to raise our children where neither one of us spends our days tearing them down. I know why you did it to me, but I refuse to repeat that atrocity with my children."

"You don't know anything. I tried to build you into a decent woman who would do her duty to the Lord by bringing forth other good Christians."

"I gave birth to three kids who'll be strong and loving. They'll know who they are and that we love them. What they won't ever know is you. With time, you'll fade from their memories as fast as I'll forget you when I walk through that door."

"You'll never forget what I taught you because you'll always know that what you're doing is wrong."

"Cain and I plan to press charges and give the district attorney permission to cut a deal with Elton Newsome and the teacher at the school. I'm willing to sacrifice their punishment and lay all this at your feet. Your only hope will be to live long enough to go back to your brother's family. You have no place in mine."

"Good-bye, Carol," Ross said, and followed them out.

When they got back in the car Emma let her tears flow, and Cain knew it wasn't from satisfaction. Her wife loved and felt too much to ever get pleasure from tearing someone down, but she wouldn't allow anyone to harm their family. Cain simply held her and let her mourn the relationship that had never materialized between her and Carol.

"You left kind of fast, so did y'all make any type of decision?" Sebastian said when she answered her phone. "I was on the other side of that glass, and I'm not sure I've ever run across someone like Carol Verde before."

"We'd like to press charges," she said, and Emma peered up at her with a swollen face and eyes. "But see if she'll make a deal," she said, giving Emma and Ross what they wanted but also an outlet for any guilt that would come later. "Make sure that part of that deal is not only jail time, but that she leave here and stay away from us once she does her time. If there's such a thing as a permanent order of protection, we'll take it."

"I'll get the DA's office on it, but you're sure about the deal? She could get some real time for what she did, and it'd guarantee that you know where the hell she is at all times."

"I'm giving her the benefit of the doubt that she'll learn from her mistakes once she realizes orange isn't her color. If she's a slow learner, we'll talk again."

"Remember this conversation if it comes to that."

"Sebastian, if there's one thing about me that you should realize to be true, it's that I seldom forget anything. My memory's just fine, especially when it comes to my family. So remind Carol of that if she needs convincing."

CHAPTER THIRTY-THREE

I'm fine, really," Emma said a few hours later. "I'm not going to crack up. I just needed closure. My mother never did disappoint when it came to that."

"If I could stay home I would, you know that, but I can't skip this," Cain said after getting a call from Remi.

"Cain, can I talk to you both before you go?" Ross said, coming into the sunroom without knocking. "Emma, I'm sorry for being such a lousy father and not getting you away from her long before you left. Of the two of us, you had way more courage than I ever possessed, but in a way, you set us both free." Emma stood up and hugged him so they could cry together.

"Right now all I care about is that you're here with us and you're staying. No matter what, Daddy, I knew you loved me, and believe me, it was enough," Emma said, causing Ross to wipe more tears from his eyes.

"You two are going to be okay. And Emma's right. You've got a place with us until we're all old and gray." Cain put an arm around both of them. "The best revenge, my da always said, was to live well so you could rub it in the other guy's face. Carol was a necessity so I'm glad you married her so Emma could be possible, but now it's time to get on with the living well."

"There's one more thing," Ross said, laughing and slapping his hands together as if just remembering something.

"As long as you don't tell me Carol's pregnant so you can't leave her," Cain said and Emma groaned, "I'll be okay with whatever you've got to say."

"I love you both for giving me a place and never making me feel like I'm a burden, but being here helping take care of the kids has—"

"Please don't tell me you're leaving," Emma said, gripping his biceps.

"No, lass, I think he's going to tell you he's dating Carmen." Cain laughed when Ross's ears turned scarlet, followed by the rest of his face.

"How'd you know?" Emma said, a delighted smile lighting her face.

"I thought you'd figured it out yourself when you started calling her *abuela*. But to answer your question, I thought it had to either be that or Ross had developed a serious coffee addiction since he's in the kitchen so much. No matter how I figured it out, I'm happy for both of you."

"So you're not upset?"

"Carmen's been part of our household for years, and somewhere along the way she became family because of how well she takes care of Emma and the kids. That she might eventually be family makes me happy."

Emma nodded and hugged him again. "See, I told you she was something all those years ago when you met her at my graduation."

"That you did, sweetheart," Ross said, embracing Cain next.

"Let me get to work so we can celebrate later." Cain left them to find Lou and Muriel in the kitchen.

"Where are we meeting everyone?" Lou asked.

"According to Shaun, Santino's here but alone. So let's go see Jasper's new compound." She put on a suede jacket and sat in the back with Muriel. "Nunzio didn't learn anything last time, so this might get his attention, and once he pops his head out of whatever hole he's hiding in, I'm going to blow it off."

"I put my guys over at the Hilton like you asked, Cain, and it got them to move," Jasper Luke said once they'd driven through his newly built security entrance at the end of his private street. Jasper and his family had been friends for years, and no matter how successful he became, he'd never had the desire to move out of the lower ninth ward.

Twenty-five feet of water had destroyed the old place he had and shared with his Aunt Maude, but Jasper had wasted no time rebuilding. The main house was almost finished, and the rest were in various stages of construction. Cain laughed when the first place he'd shown off was the kitchen he'd built for Maude, who'd raised him from the time he was three.

"That's what we needed so I could see who was with him. From what your guys and mine have said, Nunzio is so far a no-show." Cain glanced at Remi and her brother Mano. "I had other plans for Nunzio, but I think the time has come to eliminate the threat. What I need from you and you, Vinny," she said to Vincent's son, "is for you to be ready to pick up the slack. Hector's got problems, from where I'm not sure, but we can't let him move in on this action."

"You say when and where and we're there," Vinny said.

"Wait," Remi said, holding her hand up. "What was your original plan?"

"I wanted to be sure of all his holdings and dealings so Jasper and Vinny wouldn't have to go looking. That would've been easier, but now he's sending people to Hector to say I stole from him and that you must be a part of it because the stuff was found in your building. I think between all of us, we're smart enough to figure it out."

"I can be patient if you want to do that." Remi seemed relaxed, but Cain knew how deep her hatred for Nunzio went. "Like I told you before, as long as he ends up dead, I'm not interested in how long it takes if it helps us."

"We can't kill what we can't find, and he's not here or in New York. I'm guessing Santino has become his mentor since Junior's death." She thought of the old man she'd met in her early twenties with her father. "Junior and Nunzio didn't learn much from him, but they should've paid attention. Santino is no dummy, so that's where we'll start, and the rest should take care of itself."

"When?" Remi said, smiling like she'd just been given the winning lottery numbers.

"As soon as we hear from Shaun that he's headed out, we'll be waiting. I need him in a secluded-enough spot that we can take him without too many witnesses." As if conjuring him up by mentioning his name, Lou's phone rang. It was Shaun.

"He's leaving now, Boss."

Cain smiled. "See, and my mother-in-law thinks God doesn't love me."

❖

"Are you sure?" Nicolette asked, skeptical of the information Freddie had given her. "Why would someone call you with that?"

"When I worked with Emray we picked up a few of the shipments, and it was my job to be there to meet them with girls. For some reason, those guys loved hookers from Airline Highway, and I'd pick up a few so they could party while I unloaded. Then they'd turn around and head back."

"Don't you think that's a big mistake on the part of whoever's in charge?"

"Look, if they're running again, this is how they started. Eventually the shipments came directly to the bar once they figured out the guys at customs only ever looked at the boxes. Once in a while, they'd open a few, and since all the stamps and shit were there, it was like brushing your teeth every month after that," Freddie said in a flat tone. "You said you wanted in. If that's true, tonight's the night."

"What do I need?"

"The way it worked before, four guys were on the boat, and me and Mitch would come and unload. We did that for like six months, and then all we did was go pick up the finished product from this guy on the west bank that knew how to turn it back."

"There was no more security than that?"

"The place they come into is deep in the woods south of here. You don't need security if no one's around for miles."

"So how much in each shipment?" Nicolette started plotting as Freddie answered each question.

"Each shipment was the same since it was all they could fit on the boat. It's enough to get you started, if that's what you're interested in." He crossed his arms over his chest and stared at her. "I'll go and show you, but you have to keep me on. If Nunzio and his grandfather find me, I'm a dead man."

"You have no idea who it's coming for?"

"The guy just said they'd be here around eleven tonight. He didn't say who the delivery was for because he guesses I'm going to be there to pick it up."

"Get dressed and be ready to go in an hour. I'll get enough people to wipe out whoever's there and take the shipment. If what you're telling me is for real, then I'll set you up here to deal with this from now on."

"That's what Nunzio Luca told me, and then he fucked me."

She winked at him and stood, her hand gliding from the side of her breast to her hip. "As you can see, I'm not Nunzio Luca, so you're going to have to trust me. Either take my offer, or after tonight, you can go back to him and beg for scraps. If you live long enough, I doubt you'll be your own man ever again."

"An hour then, and make sure you bring enough people to get us both out of there alive."

"Don't worry. You can hide behind me," she said and laughed.

CHAPTER THIRTY-FOUR

The sedan that picked up Santino at the hotel started driving southwest out of town and turned off eventually where a string of small fishing towns was located. All of them were sparsely populated, and the people who did live there were always suspicious of outsiders. A line of cars like the ones Cain's group was in would be as obvious as a drunken guy masturbating in the middle of a Sunday mass.

"Doesn't Emile keep his boat around here?" Cain said as they drove down the ramp off the highway. They'd let one of their people follow so they in turn could lose their own shadows. With Vinny and Jasper's help that had been easier than usual.

"About fifteen miles in," Remi said as they both watched the three cars with Santino. "How about I call him and ask him to get some of his friends to give us a buffer?"

"Tell him to drop Dallas at the house and come down and meet us. We might need him later since he's familiar with the area," Cain said of Dallas's bodyguard.

It didn't take long for a few pickup trucks to pull out in front of them and stay between them and the three sedans they were following. After another twenty miles, the sedans turned left on a dirt road and disappeared into what looked like a swamp. The pickup closest to them pulled over, and the guy got out and started walking toward them, waving them off the narrow road.

"You the guys with Emile?" the man said with a thick Cajun accent.

"That's us," Lou said, shaking the man's hand. "What's in there besides the makings of a good horror movie?"

"You don't get out the city none, do you, cowboy?" the man said with a laugh. "There's an old pier about a mile in, but that there's the only road in or out since there's water on either side. Rumor is the drug guys use it to bring that shit in from the Gulf. Pretty cars like that make me believe it."

"Are you familiar enough with the place to go in without turning your lights on?" Cain asked.

"My truck's not bulletproof, no."

"Lou up there will go with you and a few others in the bed of the truck, in case there's trouble, and we'll be right behind you." She thought of going it alone since this guy was a potential witness and was about to tell him that.

"I do that favor for you, friend, and you do one for me?"

"What's the favor?" she asked, wondering if she'd be boat shopping after this.

"My little girls had to go live by their mama's place because the judge man wouldn't listen to me. My old lady can live with that bastard all her life if she want, but that man went to prison for touching kids. I want my girls out of there with me."

"You drive me in there, and I'll take care of it. I'm persuasive when I want to be."

Cain and Remi got in the front and watched as Lou and a few others got in with their new friend. Right before they took off, a car came speeding up the road and stopped right next to her. It was Katlin and Shaun.

"Let me drive," Katlin said, so Cain and Remi moved to the backseat. "We hung back to make sure Nunzio wasn't with them, but the old man's on his own on this one."

The shooting started right when they turned off the highway, but their guide kept going in as if he did indeed have a bulletproof truck. He stopped as soon as the narrow road that appeared to hover over the swamp opened into a clearing large enough for a house to have once been there. Apparently, someone else had been waiting for Santino and had shot up the first of his vehicles, which was now almost standing up in the water after having gone off the side. The two cars following it had no choice but to stay and fight since Cain's group had them hemmed in.

"Katlin, who are those people?" Cain said, crawling into the back of the SUV and retrieving a weapon. "Open up the back."

"Let's ask later," Katlin said, turning to the right to use Santino's remaining cars as a shield. "Shoot anything that moves," she yelled as the night lit up with gunfire. They concentrated their fire on the four SUVs close to the water, while Lou and their guide kept Santino's party under control.

Cain stepped out of the SUV and aimed her machine gun at the flashes coming from the direction of the water. Lou had brought enough clips to wage a war so she didn't let up. When Remi joined her, the people shooting back immediately went down in number until the night went silent.

"Stop shooting," a man yelled and came out with his hands up.

The guy in the truck aimed a spotlight at him. He seemed like the only survivor, but Cain wasn't taking a chance. A few more shots rang out, but she guessed it was Lou shooting at Santino's people when they tried to clear the road so they could get away.

"I'd take a stroll to see who the hell all these people are, but it's darker than the inside of my ass out here," she said, and Remi laughed.

"You alone?" Lou asked. "If you're not, you'd better drop and roll. The order spurred another round of shooting, and Katlin, Shaun and Lou took the opportunity to advance to where Santino's cars were and found only two people alive.

"I'm shocked the cops aren't all over this place," Cain said as she tried to make out anything in the darkness.

"You in the middle of nowhere here, my friend," the guy from the truck said. "Ain't no law or anyone else coming, but if you wait here, I'll go see who's left." He took his white rubber boots off and got in the water. It took what seemed like a second for him to disappear.

"You couldn't pay me to do that," Cain said. "What do you think Santino was doing way out here?"

"All clear, friend," their guide called out, and the man who'd stepped out to give himself up to Lou got up with his hands way over his head.

Lou jogged to keep up when Cain headed to the ring of cars along the water's edge. None of the dead guys seemed familiar until she got to the third one and saw the blond hair. Nicolette was still alive but had gunshot wounds to the shoulder and right abdomen, the blood marring her suit.

"You bitch," Nicolette said when she squatted next to her. "How did you know?"

"This is what you've come to?" she asked, shaking her head at the fact that Michel would allow his daughter to lead him in this direction. "You never did know your limitations did you, Nic?"

"Help me," she said, holding her hands to her abdomen. "I can tell you what Hector has planned for you and that little family of yours."

"That you would know seals your fate. Remember how you got here and who was responsible," she said as Katlin stood behind her with her gun at the ready.

"How I got here?" Nicolette laughed weakly. "I got here because of you. Always you, who couldn't learn to just accept that I love you and you belonged to me. Kill me, or I swear I'll kill you the minute I'm able to hold a gun."

Cain started to walk away.

"Cain, wait," Nicolette screamed again. "Don't leave—"

Katlin's shot silenced whatever else Nicolette was going to say. Cain stopped and glanced back. No more loose ends, she'd vowed, but for once she wished Nicolette had gone home and back to the grapes she loved so much. Instead, she'd died in this mysterious place and would have no headstone or coffin in the French countryside of which she always spoke so fondly.

"Found these two hiding in the trees," Lou said as Santino and some other guy glared up at her from their knees. "The rest of them are dead."

"How'd you know about this?" Santino asked.

"The woman trying to kill you asked me the same thing, but I only wanted you. I'm not sure about the rest of it."

"Look, they're coming," the only man alive with Nicolette, standing there with his arms up, said loudly as a power-sounding engine seemed to be getting closer.

"You know them?" she asked, and the guy frantically nodded. "Do they know you?"

"Yeah."

"Good. Make the transaction and don't get cute. If I even think you've made a wrong move, I'll make you sorry." Cain glanced around her and waved everyone back. "Take cover. I don't want to fire another shot tonight."

Lou knocked Santino and the other man out and dragged him into the trees. They all watched as a cigar boat pulled up to the rickety dock.

The man Cain had let live pointed to the cars Nicolette's people had come in and seemed to be telling them a story. "Just help me get them on land and I'll call for help," he told the guy who didn't appear to speak very much English.

"Freddie, you owe me," the man said thirty minutes later before he shoved off.

"Freddie, what's in the boxes?" she asked, and was surprised at his answer. "Mano, can you escort Freddie back to town and introduce him to Vinny and Jasper, please?"

"What about all that stuff?" Mano asked.

"Should fit in two of the Suburbans if we pack them up right," Remi said, waving for Simon to pull their vehicle closer. "If not, leave the rest here and we'll bring them with us after we take care of things here. Call Vinny and tell him you need a safe place to unload, and have this guy Freddie walk you through it."

"And after he does?"

"Leave that to Vinny and Jasper. But if there's even an inkling of a problem, cut him loose," Cain said while Remi answered the phone.

"Feel like an airboat ride?"

They loaded Santino in the back and drove the few miles to where Emile kept his boat. The trip to his camp was always interesting at night, but she needed a secluded spot to talk to Santino about his plans for his very limited future. Emile hoisted Santino over his shoulder, and they followed him up the shaky stairs before he went back for the other guy.

Emile dumped the second guy on the floor, and then they waited for the two to come around.

"Do you think he knew Nunzio hired that guy to shoot me?" Remi asked.

"I can't imagine Junior not telling him. Santino always comes across as the kindly grandfather, but he raised Junior and made it so the man didn't feel comfortable making a move without consulting him first."

"I wasn't much different than Dalton in that regard," Santino said softly.

"My father's gone, old man, and I'm not the one laying on the floor bleeding, so I'm confident in that he taught me to stand on my feet without a prop."

Emile picked up the other guy and set him on the empty chair at the table. The man groaned and blinked rapidly as his eyes opened. The lights were run off the generator outside so they weren't extremely bright, but the blow to the head had likely left him with a splitting headache.

Cain pulled out a chair across from him and sat. "What's your name?"

"Mike." He glanced between the two of them, then reached to his side as if his gun would still be there.

"Mike, you work for Nunzio and Santino here, don't you?" It wasn't really a question she was waiting for him to answer.

He didn't answer, his eyes following Remi as she took out her cigar clipper and cut the end off the Cohiba she'd taken out of her pocket. Cain noticed it wasn't the gold one she usually used at home.

"You want to tell me where Nunzio is?" Cain did expect an answer this time.

"You keep your fucking mouth shut," Santino said.

"Let me tell you a little story. The last time I was here, the guy sitting where you are got his fingers taken off one joint at a time." She turned sideways in the chair and casually crossed her legs as if they had all night. "My friend here took them off with that neat little gadget."

Mike blinked again when Remi blew some smoke in his face.

"Look, I don't know. I work for Mr. Santino. I haven't seen Nunzio for a while now."

"Okay, let's try something easier. Who's the blonde that bears a striking resemblance to the late Kim Stegal?"

"Where'd you see her?" Mike said, then clicked his mouth shut as if he'd said too much.

"A name, Mike," she said, but he shook his head. "Okay, how about your plans for the future? How'd you get mixed up with Nicolette Blanc?"

"I'm a flunky. No one tells me anything," he said, curling his fingers into his palms.

"That's three questions you don't know." She shook her head.

Emile stepped behind him and pressed a large knife to his throat. "Open your hand." He pressed the knife tighter against Mike's throat, making him come up in the seat. "Put it on the table or I'm going to cut once and be done with it."

Mike put his hand down, sweat beading on his forehead, and waited.

"You sure you owe this bastard this kind of loyalty?" Cain asked. She gave him a few long seconds to decide, the room quiet except for Mike's panicked breathing and the repeated snick of metal sliding against metal as Remi worked her blade a few times.

"Nunzio's in the hospital in Lafayette. He got sick in—"

"Shut up, you asshole," Santino screamed. Emile kicked him in the head, silencing him.

"You were saying?" Remi prodded him with another few snicks.

"He got sick in Mexico where he went to see some guy named Roth Pombo in a jail down there. Santino and I stayed at the hotel, but Nunzio said he wanted to restart some pipeline of drugs this Pombo guy used to do."

"The bottles of liquid coke, you mean?" Cain asked. The thought of Hector getting his hands on that idea made her take a breath.

"Yeah. Nunzio came back from seeing Pombo, but before he could tell us what the score was he got really sick, so Santino returned to town to wait for tonight." Mike put his hands under his armpits, his eyes darting from Cain to Remi. "I really don't know who that woman Nicolette is. If she was there tonight, she was with whoever started shooting the second we got there."

"And the woman who looks like Kim Stegal?"

"It's her sister, Tracy Stegal. She was with Nunzio at first, and they were really together for a while, but she left and he hasn't been able to find her. He looked though."

"Did Santino tell you who you were meeting at that dock tonight?"

"No. He doesn't like to share too much." He smiled and then started laughing. "Now you have to decide if I'm lying or not. The only way to know for sure is to let me go, and I'll tell you as soon as you do."

"What do you think, Remi?" she asked and moved back a little.

"I think it's enough of the truth," Remi said, and then Emile buried his big hunting knife in the guy's chest. When he pulled the knife out, Mike slumped forward, his head hit the table with a muffled thump, and he gurgled his last breath.

Cain made a call to Ramon on the satellite phone Emile kept at the camp and told him where to find Nunzio. If they were able to get to Lafayette in time, they could maybe finish this tonight. But Cain would let her friend make that decision, and she'd do her best to back Remi up if she needed it.

Remi worked her cutter a few times as though she felt cheated of the chance to use it. She spoke without looking at the man on the floor. "I know you're awake, Santino. So have the balls to open your eyes." She kicked a chair over to him, and Emile grabbed him by the collar to haul Santino up and seat him in it.

Santino stared at Remi with an almost blank expression.

"Do you know what it's like to get shot in the chest?" Remi asked, but he didn't answer. "What, no smart comeback?"

"If you can't understand it was only business, then there's nothing else to say," he finally said. "You, your father, or Cain would've done the same thing."

"Business to you is killing someone's child, a lover, a sister because they won't buy something you're selling?" Remi hit him before he could answer. "Junior's dead because that's what he thought. Your grandson will be dead before the sun comes up, and it'll all be on your head."

"The death of my family will haunt you for years to come. You can kill me, but that'll be a huge mistake." Santino lifted his hand as if to point his finger at her, but it dropped quickly when Remi shot him through the heart. It was a poetic thing considering what the Lucases had planned for her.

"Emile, are you sure about the guy who drove us down that road?" Cain was ready to go back and spend the rest of the night with Emma.

"I had him take the dead out to the Gulf. You won't have to worry about him because his pockets are full of cash now. But mostly because he knows me and what'll happen to him if he double-crosses us."

"Then we're almost done."

CHAPTER THIRTY-FIVE

Emma was waiting up for her when she got home and let her hold the baby to put him back to sleep. "Will this take long?" Emma asked as she watched Cain dress completely in black.

"I'm hoping to be home late tonight, if it goes like I think it will. It's Thanksgiving in a few days, and you know how much I love turkey."

The trip to California would be completely off the grid so she'd turned down the offer of Remi's plane, and, instead, Jasper had arranged what she understood was a plane that transported ghosts. No one on board existed. Colin and Judice were next to her, but she wasn't interested in conversation so she closed her eyes and went to sleep. Her brain needed a break from all the thinking she'd been doing since Nicolette had taken a bullet in that swamp.

Before she went to sleep she wondered if Shelby had accepted her invitation. Salvatore was her true target, but there wasn't any reason to not do a favor for someone in a black hole. Three hours later she woke up and smiled at the sleeping duo sitting close together holding hands. Maybe Colin was starting to wear Judice down. Now all she had to worry about was whether Carlos Luis had come through for her.

Colin jerked awake when the wheels hit the tarmac in what looked like an airstrip in the middle of nowhere. The guys waiting outside hopefully were Colin's people, because she'd left Katlin and Lou behind to give the illusion she was still home.

"We're not dying yet, cousin," Colin said as he stretched. "They're mine, so let's go." When she left the plane, she noticed some people who still sat in their cars, so she walked in that direction, surprised to see the late Rodolfo's son, Carlos Luis.

"Good to see you again," she said and shook his hand. "Have you been well?"

She waited for the translator, but Carlos nodded, answering himself. "I do well, and get good business again."

"It's good to meet you," the young woman at Carlos's side said. "I'm Carlos's wife, Paloma, and he's hoping the next time you meet his English will be better. But for now he understands what you're asking for, and we're ready to go."

"Tell him I'll owe him a favor, and I don't say that often," Cain said. Paloma immediately repeated it in Spanish, and Carlos responded.

"It was because of you that he was able to avenge his father's death. He owes you more for that than doing this for you. If you like, you can ride with us." She pointed to the large black Suburban. It felt almost like a test.

"Sure." Cain waved to Colin. He nodded and got into his car, to follow. "Are we ready to go?" she asked as they pulled out to head for LA.

"Carlos called our contacts in the gangs here, and they're waiting for our phone call. They know Salvatore Maggio because they're doing a lot of business with him. It's an easy contract since they buy from us, then turn around and sell to Salvatore for more. The setup has dropped exposure to the watchful eyes of the police so the gang has grown."

"Please let Carlos know the arrangement will continue, but with only Colin Meade. Salvatore intends to cut Colin out. If that happens you're going to be dealing with someone who'll eventually bring war to get what he wants. That easy money isn't going to last."

Paloma had a small conversation with Carlos, and he gave short answers to whatever she was saying. "He trusts you, so all you have to say is you're ready to go, and he'll call his friends."

"We're ready to go." She gazed out the window at the large expanse of the city passing below them, quiet until they reached the spot she'd requested. The place, well off the main highway, appeared as if it'd been abandoned for years. She walked through the house to enjoy the view behind it, trying to imagine why someone would've let this place go like this.

The pool was dry, its bottom littered with dead vegetation, but the chairs nearby appeared clean and fairly new. All they had left to do now was to wait. She planned to hit Salvatore hard and fast, but not leave any of her family's fingerprints anywhere on the action. When the shit settled, the police would think it was simply another skirmish between the local criminals over drugs.

Carlos came to sit with her, holding out a picture of his wedding day.

Cain smiled at him. "Beautiful," she said. "Your father would be proud."

"I find happiness, and you help me. I work like my papi, and I thank you for Gracelia. Today you owe me nada."

"Thank you, Carlos, and I think you're doing a good thing." He waved Paloma over. It seemed important that he know what she said. Cain repeated what she'd said, then waited for Paloma to translate before adding the most important part. "Today he'll make more than one friend."

They sat and talked for five hours about nothing else of importance, and as the day grew overcast, a man came out and reported something that made Carlos nod.

"It's done," Paloma said. "Salvatore as well as everyone of importance to him is gone."

"Thank you, and the other thing I asked for?" Cain asked.

Carlos held up two fingers, and his men carried two guys out of the house and into the empty pool. Their hands and feet were then tied and their heads covered by hoods. They'd die on their knees.

"If you want, go ahead and take off," Cain said. "I need to do the next part alone."

"What they did for Gracelia, they did without the sanction of their leaders," Paloma said.

"I have a feeling they did it for the money and for someone else we're both looking for. Anthony Curtis, the tainted FBI agent, is still out there, and he'll survive only if both of us are dead."

"Carlos hasn't stopped looking, so keep in touch. Whatever your plans, delivering these men won't put you in debt to anyone involved today."

She accepted Carlos's embrace and watched them leave. Her next visitor arrived forty-five minutes later. Shelby appeared in the doorway of the house, her Glock extended with both hands and sweeping the area in a wide arc, as if she expected an ambush. She relaxed when she saw Cain.

"I didn't think you went anywhere alone," Shelby said.

"I'm not really here. I'm a figment of your imagination," Cain said and wiggled her fingers. "Did you bring the paper I gave you?"

"Yes." Shelby lowered her gun and walked toward Cain, but her eyes stayed on the hooded men kneeling in the pool.

"Read the names," Cain said, watching as the men's heads turned toward their voices when Shelby called them out. "Holster your weapon, Shelby." Cain handed over one of the guns Carlos's men had left wrapped in the bandana of their gang colors. "There's no more real irony in this world than getting shot with your own gun."

"It's really them?" Shelby said, taking the gun and sliding her finger onto the trigger.

"From what the guys who found them told me, they killed your parents on direct orders from Gracelia Luis and her business partner Anthony Curtis. The guys working for Gracelia had no idea he was an agent, but they wouldn't give up anything else about him." She pointed to the two guys. "These two, though, were responsible for the actual killing. So Shelby, the next step is your choice. I've led you to your orchard, but to pick the fruit isn't something I can force on you."

"And if I don't, what happens?"

"They killed two people on the order of an FBI agent, one of them a retired cop. The FBI and employers of the two men in the pool won't take kindly to that, so they're here to give you the chance you said you wanted."

"You'll stay and watch so you can use it against me, I guess," she said, bouncing the gun nervously against the side of her leg.

"Actually, I'm leaving. My ride should be here in a few minutes, so you have an hour to decide, I'm told. You can see these two aren't going anywhere. If you choose to do nothing and leave, the cleanup crew will finish the job. They'll be dead no matter what, and whether it's by your hand or theirs, I'll never know."

"Did pulling the trigger help you?"

"No life can be free of regret, Shelby, but I sleep well at night no matter what you think of me."

Shelby laughed and shook her head. "You never really answer anything, do you?"

Cain rose at the sound of a car pulling up in front of the house. "My answer is clear enough, so good luck." She put her hand on Shelby's shoulder and squeezed. When Shelby kissed her cheek, Cain returned the gesture, then started toward the house.

"Can you do one favor for me before you go?"

Cain stopped and nodded.

"Can you remove the hoods? I hate them so much I can't really get that close to them, and I want to avoid—"

"No need to elaborate," she said and walked down the pool's stairs. "Remember one thing," she said as she uncovered their heads and pointed to the teardrops tattooed on their faces. "They carry different reminders of your parents than you do. These little mementos are earned only with bullets and killing."

"Thanks again," Shelby said when Cain left the pool and, again, headed to leave.

On the ride back to the airfield, Cain reviewed her actions to ensure she'd left nothing of herself behind. Whatever Shelby decided would be on Shelby alone. Her debt was paid.

❖

"You've watched that video about a million times already," Abigail said from the sofa where she was reading a book while Finley worked. "I'd think you'd have memorized it by now."

"There's got to be something I'm missing." Finley had hacked the police department in St. Charles Parish's files on the warehouse case. The explosives didn't have any kind of special ingredient, and they were still reeling from this happening in their quiet town.

"Maybe you need a fresh set of eyes," Abigail said, getting up and putting her arms around Finley's neck to kiss the top of her head. "Play it from the beginning in real time."

Finley pressed the mouse, and they watched the two people walk around the office before going to the back, supposedly to set a bomb. Something made Abigail want to run. "Play it again please," she said, leaning down to get closer to the screen. "It's impossible." She hadn't noticed it before when she'd only briefly looked at the footage.

"What?" Finley asked, turning so Abigail could sit on her lap.

"Play it again, but slow it down when that one starts to go through the drawers of the desk."

On the video, the door opened and two people entered, glancing around the room. The taller of the two walked to the first desk with a pronounced limp, and Finley slowed the action like Abigail had asked. The person paused with a hand on the drawer, then yanked it open as if expecting something to jump out. When nothing did, the person ripped the rest of the drawers out of the desk, but all were empty.

"Did I miss something?" Finley asked.

"Watch," she said as the person flexed their hands from a fist to a completely open palm. "One, two, three, four, and five," she counted along as the person repeated the action.

"How'd you know that?" Finley asked, replaying that part again.

"It was an old injury," Abigail said, "something about landing on broken glass on the playground when she was seven. The cut was deep, and though it healed, it left residual pain that got worse with age. The only thing that helped was physical therapy, and that's where she learned to stretch it to ease the ache."

"Who are you talking about?"

"Nicola, that's her," Abigail said, fighting the sudden urge to throw up. "That's her. She did that all the time."

"Nicola died in a plane crash."

"Finley, that's her. I lived with the woman for years and watched her do that move about a thousand times a day." She repeated it in the cadence Nicola had used as Finley played the video again. It was the same. "It's her."

"Where's she been then?"

"I don't know, but it explains what happened in New York. No court would give her back the kids, so she had to kill me. Maybe she really was in a plane crash, and it's taken this much time for her to rehab her injuries. She didn't have that limp before."

"Are you sure?"

"No, but why would someone copy her on purpose? An accident might have changed her distinctive stride, but that move with her hand…" Abigail restarted the video and they watched it again. The person repeated the hand movement when the pair stepped into the security closet. "That's Nicola. I'd swear to it in court."

"I noticed it before, but I attributed it to the gloves. Not everyone is used to wearing them, but I believe you. If it's her, though, we've got a problem."

"It's a huge problem," Abigail said, biting her lip. "No way did her parents come down here without her knowledge, so, if she's alive, she's going to follow the breadcrumbs back to us. What are we going to do?" Abigail held onto Finley. She felt like she'd fall from a great height if she let go. "She's going to kill us and take the kids."

"She doesn't know we've figured it out, so we'll look through David or Yury's stuff until we find the clue that will lead us to her first."

"Do you think Cain will help? I can't lose my children, Finley. I can't."

"She's already offered us protection, so I can't see this changing her mind. Do you feel comfortable with that, or do you want me to put you someplace safe until we find her?"

"You want me to go?" She put her hand on Finley's cheek and kissed her. It was like finally finding the needle in a haystack the size of Manhattan, then being asked to let it go. She was tired of putting off her happiness because of the Eatons.

"I want you and the kids to live here with me. Cain's already offered to add on to this house so you'll feel comfortable and more like it's ours. Some people might think what we've been through builds false feelings, but I love you, Abigail. I love you and I want a life with you and the children—a life we can make our own."

"I love you, and I'm glad you showed up that day. I have faith that you'll keep us safe, but even if I didn't, I'd go through hell to stay with you because I love you."

"It'll change how we live until we find her."

"Do you think we can talk to Cain? I don't want to run anywhere. Not for Nicola, her family, or any other reason." She kissed Finley again, loving the way Finley held her. "If she wants me that bad, she's going to have to come and get me."

❖

"Where is she?" Marisol asked the woman in Nicolette Blanc's apartment. She'd seen the woman before and vaguely remembered she was Nicolette's secretary or something. "She's not answering her phone, and everyone else with her is gone."

"I really don't know," the woman said for the fifth time. "She left last night and hasn't returned."

"Was she with someone?"

The woman hesitated, so Marisol grabbed her by the collar. "Where is she?"

"She's got another apartment not far from here. She was going there."

Marisol got her people moving and waited outside the small rental while Julio picked the lock. Inside was minimal furniture and a bag of stale pastries, the kind Nicolette always ate. The clothes on the bed, though, belonged to a man, and Marisol tore the shirt in half in a fit of anger. The bitch had been playing her.

"Stay behind and see if you find anything else," she said to one of the guys with her. "Julio, let's go." They drove back to the house, but when she stepped into the office, the only one there was Tracy. "Where's my father?"

"He's upstairs talking to Mrs. Delarosa." Tracy stood and handed her a file. "I put together the numbers for this month. Mr. Delarosa wants you to look at them and then try to find some new places to move his stuff through. He wants to find some that are better defended and limit who knows about them."

"He didn't want you to do it?"

Tracy's face, as always, was hard to read. "Mr. Delarosa was specific in that he wanted you to do it."

"Have you heard from Nicolette?" Admitting to Tracy that she'd lost track of Nicolette made a pain blossom over Marisol's right eye.

"She cancelled an appointment with your father last night at the last minute. She said something about having to do something for her father. I haven't heard from her since." Tracy flipped through her appointment book and put her finger on a phone number written in it. "Hang on and let's ask, if you're worried."

Tracy had a brief conversation with someone after punching in more numbers than a normal call, then thanked whoever was on the other end.

"Who was that?" Marisol asked.

"Her father says he talked to her last night and hasn't found her since, and he's tried all day today. He sounds worried and confessed that she'd gotten a call from someone in Nunzio's organization."

"Someone from Nunzio's people called who?" Hector said, coming in with a leather bag.

"Nicolette. And now she's missing," Marisol said. She stiffened when Hector came close to her.

"The guy I put with you says you've gotten close to this woman. You ran to her after this," he said, putting his fingers on her still-healing lips. "Did you cry to her about what an animal I am?" He pressed harder to keep her quiet. "The time for you to grow up and start thinking is now, Mari."

"I kept her close only because she seemed like she was up to something. I did it for you. I would never go against you."

"Remember that, and forget about the Blancs. If they're trying to play both us and the Lucas, they can drown in their French wines."

"Are you sure? They wanted to move more than anyone else who buys from us," she said. Her head snapped back when he slapped her.

"When I'm dead you can do whatever you like, but for now, forget about her. Your other choice is to walk out and keep going. I'll give you enough of a head start to make it sporting because I'm tired of being questioned."

"Yes, Papa," she said. She had not cried out and resisted the urge to touch her throbbing cheek. "Whatever you say."

For now, she'd play along, but she had another option. She could kill him for putting his hands on her again. She'd discovered that she missed Nicolette's company, and, no matter what, she'd find what had happened to her. Even if it meant going to war with her only family.

CHAPTER THIRTY-SIX

Today isn't a religious holiday, but it's a perfect day to welcome William Cain Casey into the church," Father Andrew said as the Casey family and friends stood at the back of the cathedral for Billy's baptism. Even Finley's parents had come from Florida for this, and to meet Abigail and her family. "Today is a day to give thanks for what we have, those we love, and all God has given us. For Cain and Emma, it's the day to celebrate the addition to their family and the joy this little one will bring."

He went through the ritual of the church, and Lou, Remi, and Dallas took turns holding the baby as Andy anointed his head with oil and poured water over his hair, waking him up. Billy would have a godfather and two godmothers this time around, but it was important to Emma to include Remi and Dallas in this special occasion.

Cain noticed Shelby standing in the shadows of the sanctuary. For once, her eyes weren't focused on Muriel, who was holding Kristen's hand while they watched the proceedings. "Turkey for everyone back at the house, then football," Cain said when Father Andy finished the ceremony with a booming amen.

Dallas took Billy and posed while Carmen took plenty of pictures, so Cain walked over to talk to Shelby. When she was close enough, Shelby handed her back the paper she'd given her right before the wedding. "Thank you for everything, but I won't need that any more."

"I'll tell you that, in this case, confession is not good for the soul, so I hope you'll find some peace now. Your parents can rest easy, and no matter if this looks like there's no place for you," she pointed back to her family, "you can always knock on my door if you need anything."

"For now, let's go back to the relationship we know," Shelby said but hugged her. "And thanks. I do sleep better now, so watch yourself."

Cain laughed, then waved when Emma called her over for a family picture. "One more, and then we eat," she said, and Hayden pumped his fist in the air. She took the baby and handed him to Emma so she could pick Hannah up. Everyone smiled as Dallas took the next few photos.

Cain couldn't help but notice the apprehension in Abigail's expression. Finley had filled her in earlier and told her what Abigail wanted to do, so she let the others go out with Andrew and waited behind with Abigail and Finley.

"Will you help us?" Abigail said, holding her hands.

"Not so long ago, my wife and I had a talk like the one we're going to have, and I told her one thing." She looked from Abigail to Finley and wished she could snap her fingers to make things perfect for them. "You are my family, and in our family we have a saying. 'You're mine but only for a time.' It holds meaning for our children." She heard her family outside laughing, and smiled. "It means that one day we must let them go, but not until they are ready to fly without the fear they will fall."

"And when it comes to us?" Abigail asked.

"You're my family, and I'll let no one hurt what's mine. You aren't alone in this, Abigail, and when we find the people trying to hurt you, they'll wish they'd stayed dead. You have my word on that."

Abigail's eyes filled with tears as she hugged Cain while Finley nodded and mouthed "thank you" over Abigail's head.

Cain nodded and gestured to the door. "Let's go join the others," she said, leading them outdoors.

She wasn't surprised to see Fiona hanging around close by, so she walked over to her and waited for her to speak.

"Are you okay after everything?" Fiona asked, rocking on her feet as if she were nervous.

"My wife says forgiveness is good for the soul, so I'll be okay. You wasting your vacation on me?"

"I have a few days off, but I thought I'd go see my mother when I had more than a few."

"You might have dinner later than you planned, but she's waiting on you." Cain reached in her pocket and took out a plane ticket. "If you hurry, you'll make your flight."

"I can't take this," Fiona said, but held onto the ticket anyway.

"I didn't buy it, your mother did, and sent it to me since she figured I'd see you soon enough and perhaps convince you to go. Use it or don't, but try not to waste the chance. One day your mother is here, and one day she's not. Try not to regret passing up the chance to spend time with her."

"Is that a threat?" Fiona's question didn't carry its usual menace.

"Enjoy your mother's cooking, Fiona, and bulk up on the fiber. It might let you pass that uptight stick you have wedged in your ass. It's not a threat. It's advice from someone who still misses her mum. The Lord only gives us one mother, so go see her and make her happy. Happy Thanksgiving."

"Same to you." She held up the ticket. "And thanks." She hurried away, but not before glancing back a few times.

"You're getting soft, Casey," she whispered to herself.

"Everything okay?" Emma asked as Cain joined her and took the baby so she could hold him up over her head to let the long baptism gown he wore hang down.

"Today, everything is perfect, and I'm going to do what has to be done so that tomorrow will be just as good."

"What about Abigail and everything else?" Emma tugged on the baby's gown so Cain lowered him and kissed her wife.

"I'll spend today giving thanks for what I have and my love for you. Tomorrow, I'll call up hell's fury, if that's what it'll take to keep us whole. But we'll worry about that tomorrow. Today is for us, a new baby, and a family we'll grow old with. I have no other prayer than that."

"And the FBI thinks you're a devil with no soul." Emma scratched her abdomen through her shirt and laughed.

"Even the devil prays sometimes, lass, and when that doesn't work I'll back it up with whatever it takes to keep my clan safe. On that, you have my word. Like I said on my wedding day, I'm yours, for eternity. Our days will be long, and maybe not perfect, but there'll be more laughter than tears, and more love than anything else."

"I could listen to you forever."

"It's a good thing, my love, because I've got so many more tales to tell."